BODY

MEDICI PROTECTORATE BOOK THREE

ARMOR

LIFE. BALANCE. **TRANSFORMATION.**

BODY

MEDICI PROTECTORATE BOOK THREE

ARMOR

LIFE. BALANCE. **TRANSFORMATION.**

STACI TROILO

LAGAN

OGHMA CREATIVE MEDIA

www.oghmacreative.com

Library of Congress Control Number: 2018944174

ISBN: 978-1-63373-328-2

Interior Design by Casey W. Cowan
Editing by Gordon Bonnet

Lagan Press
Oghma Creative Media
Bentonville, Arkansas
www.oghmacreative.com

ACKNOWLEDGEMENTS

TO MY EDITOR Gordon Bonnet… thank you for being a stellar editor and a patient man. Your efforts are greatly appreciated.

To the entire Naccarato family… thank you for the rich heritage, the love, and yes, the delicious recipes.

To Mom and Dad… if I thanked you for everything you've given me, I'd need a hundred more pages. I hope you accept these few words as all-encompassing gratitude. I love you.

To Seth and Sammi, my favorite son and favorite daughter… you, more than anyone, witness the craziness that is this writer's life. Thank you for putting up with me. I love you both for that. And for so many more reasons, too numerous to list.

And to Corey, my husband, my rock… thank you for all the support, patience, and love. I couldn't do this without you. I love you.

For my mother, Carmella Smith

For supporting me always, in so many ways.
For teaching me the importance of family and heritage.
For showing me unconditional and unwavering love.
'Thanks' is too weak a word.

In the twilight hours, starshine glows
as merely tiny embers in the black
Its magnificence to only grow brighter
while the midnight hour forces daylight back

And though the starlight twinkles on in ink
Its purpose not to shine but just to guide
The branches of the tree will bloom new buds
Growing evermore o're the divide

As long as just one leaf in bud or bloom
On the boughs continues not to fade
Starlight will shine in watch over the branch
And guard the new green, always at its aid

The light divines the stones to always shield
And not until the end their duty yield.

1

NICO SWIPED AT the sweat on his brow and snuck a glance at his watch—2:12. He'd made good time. The heart rate monitor registered ninety-two beats per minute. A lot higher than his resting rate of sixty, but perfectly acceptable considering the climb he'd just made. And the stress of the task at hand.

Crickets chirruped a melody over the distant burble of one of the many streams that fed the Aron River. An occasional bat screech interrupted the song, and a couple of times a wolf howl—hopefully far away—sent shivers skittering up Nico's spine. He took a deep breath to calm himself, notes of citrus mingled harmoniously with the moldering undergrowth of the giant beeches he stood beneath. The night was clear, and the nearly-full moon bathed the landscaped grounds in a silvery wash of light. Too bright out there for his clandestine mission. Nico crouched for cover in the shadows of a large yew in the forest bordering the property while he surveilled the facility.

It had taken him several months and every bit of his hacking skills—plus a few new tricks he'd picked up—to determine where Mary Notaro was being kept. Well, he was about ninety-five percent sure she was there. The last two times he'd been one hundred percent certain he'd found her, and he'd been wrong both times—a new and embarrassing record for him. The facilities he'd tracked her to had been a bust. She either had been moved before he got there or had never been there at all. This time, he gave himself a margin of error of five percent.

But after a little recon, he'd be sure. And if he was right? Then he'd devise an extraction plan. Maybe involve his brothers then.

Maybe.

2:17. Pulse rate kicked to ninety-five. Time to get a move on.

To a casual onlooker, the building would just be another hidden gem in the lower crags of the Apennine Mountains. Not too big to attract attention, not so small that people would wonder who had wasted the resources to construct something on such a steep hillside. Classic Mediterranean architectural style, nothing too flashy. If anyone noticed the building from the road below, they'd maybe snap a photo and then move on. No one would bother climbing the steep terrain for something so nondescript, particularly when there were famous ruins to explore mere miles away.

But Nico recognized it for what is was, and he studied the structure. He crept close enough to see the myriad security cameras, the state-of-the-art fingerprint ID pads, the armed guard who patrolled the grounds. It wouldn't surprise him if there were alarms on the windows, retinal scanners inside, and a larger security force.

No way could he break in now. Not without knowing what he'd face inside.

He opened his pack and brought out a few trail cams. Clocked the guard's patrol pattern—thirteen minutes before he was in sight again, then Nico would have to stop work so as not to be noticed.

It had been years since he climbed a tree, and the beeches offered few low limbs to use as leverage. He scrambled up to the lowest branch and secured one of the cameras. When he jumped to the ground, he grazed a juniper. The noise crackled through the night, seemed to echo off the mountain and bounce back to him. Then the night air silenced—not a sound could be heard, other than his panting breath and his pulse pounding in his ears. He stood perfectly still and waited, but no one came to check on the disturbance.

Nico laughed at himself. Animals rustle flora all the time. The noise he created couldn't have made more of a ruckus than a chamois goat foraging for food. He was just paranoid.

The second camera went up without incident. He grew complacent and neglected to track the time. While he worked on the third, the guard came back into view. Nico should have been more careful. Now he was stuck up a tree, dangling from a branch, his grip precarious.

He stopped working and froze so he didn't attract any attention. The soundscape of nocturnal animals hadn't resumed, and Nico was all the more aware of the noises he made—the quiet panting, the subtle scraping of his clothes on the bark of the tree. The camera started slipping out of his bag, and he had to scramble to catch it before it fell. A muscle spasm shot through his arm and he flinched. One of the small twigs he held to the side snapped free of his grasp, flung forward, and stung his face. The leaves tickled his nose, and his eyes watered. He had to sneeze.

God, no.

But the pressure mounted, and he desperately tried to wiggle the tingly sensation out of his nose—to no avail. He couldn't hold it in. Prayed one of those goats would crash into the clearing away from where he hid.

Neither happened. The sneeze overpowered him. He tried to smother the noise—and failed miserably.

The loud burst combined with the rustling in the tree caught the guard's attention. He spun toward Nico, took a few steps in his direction, and shone his flashlight about three feet under Nico's dangling form.

He held his breath, grasped the limb tighter, and remained still. The branches swayed in the wind, formed a scant web beneath him, shielding him from easy detection.

The swath of light from the guard's torch continued to dance beneath Nico as the man approached. Nico had worn black face paint and a black knit cap to hide his blond hair, but even with all his camouflage efforts and the limbs beneath him, there simply weren't enough leaves to hide him if the guard looked up. No avoiding it—he'd be caught. His only chance was to bide his time and pray the guard didn't look up. If he did, Nico would have to jump and subdue him. By any means necessary. He thought about his dagger, sheathed at his back.

Please, God, don't let it come to that. If only something—

A loud rustling in the branches sounded about fifty feet west. Nico glanced in that direction. The guard turned, too, pointed his light toward the noise, and stood still, scanning the woods.

Was someone else out there? Friend or foe? Nico's muscles tensed, his arms trembled. Sweat trickled down his back.

He turned his head as far as he could to get a better look at the situation. The guard was bent low, staring into the woods where the noise had come from. His flashlight beam illuminated his features, and Nico thought he looked familiar. He didn't have time to dwell on it, though. The guard's eyes widened, his spine snapped straight. Nico looked where the guard was looking even as the guy turned and ran.

Something crashed through the brush and darted out of the woods. Nico almost lost his grip and fell.

Three wolves charged through the forest into the clearing, following the guard to the facility.

No damn wonder the woods had grown so quiet. It wasn't the noise he'd made. It was the predators stalking him in the dark. Only by dumb luck and the grace of God did he avoid a bloody end.

He couldn't waste time securing the third camera. Instead, he dropped to the ground, tweaking his ankle on the landing. But there was no way he was letting that slow him down. He darted back the way he came, constantly on guard for either security patrols or the wolf pack.

His progress only slowed once, when he had to scramble over a fallen branch and in so doing, wrenched his knee. he pushed on, ignoring the pain, knowing any delay could cost him his life. Where the fuck had that limb come from? Damn thing hadn't been there on the way in. Must have fallen and caused the noise that initially distracted the guard's attention.

Could the wolves have somehow broken the branch out of a tree? It was awfully high up. It would take one hell of a leap…

No time to dwell on that, though. Nico continued hobbling through the trees, hurrying to safety. He paused once when a loud thrashing echoed from behind him and considered hiding in one of the caves. Scrapped that idea almost as fast as he had it—who knew what he'd find in there, not to mention darting inside could end up trapping him.

When the noise in the brush settled, he continued his quick trek back to the car. He started to relax when typical nocturnal sounds started to resume. Only then did he slow his pace, just a little, to ease the discomfort he felt in his entire fucking leg. But he remained hyper-alert to his surroundings until he reached his vehicle.

The second the door was closed, he leaned his head back and breathed deeply. His ankle throbbed, his knee screamed, his arms still ached a little from how roughly and tightly he'd clutched the tree branch, and his pulse hammered in his chest. He thought he'd been prepared for any contingency, but clearly he wasn't. He didn't expect armed security patrols, so he hadn't brought a gun. Only had his dagger with him, which may or may not have helped against one or two guards, but would have been far less effective against the wolves.

A pack of fucking wolves. Who would have thought?

Once he'd calmed, he turned the key in the ignition. The engine roared to life, the sound thunderous in the relatively quiet night. Would probably attract the guards and the wolves, so he pealed out and headed home, his thoughts racing as fast as his car.

Two cameras weren't going to be enough. Maybe he'd program a camera-mounted drone to do some fly-bys. He glanced at his watch again. His heart rate had almost returned to normal, but he'd wasted a lot of time. 3:27. It would probably be around six—okay, the way he drove, 5:30—when he reached the compound, and the early risers would already be stirring. That would make sneaking in more difficult. Nothing he couldn't handle, though. Just in case, he swiped at the greasepaint on his face with his sleeve—no one would see a stain on the black fabric—and practiced the tried-and-true "needed some air" excuse. A few memorable but nondescript details should sell that story to even the most suspicious of the group.

As he sped past half-hidden cave mouths, around curves, and over the deserted roads, he considered telling his brothers what he'd found. Waffled back and forth before deciding against it. Again.

He hadn't told them, or their charges, that he'd been searching for Mary. The guys would have said it was a waste of time, given Mike knew where she was. But Mike wasn't talking, and Nico thought he knew why—Mike had lost her. That was the only explanation for why he'd brought the girls all the way to Italy only to refuse them access to their mother once they'd arrived. And despite the girls not voicing their concerns, at least not often, he knew they worried about her.

Even before Nico suspected Mary had gone missing, he had been convinced that bringing her back to their compound was the best way to protect her as well as the most expedient way to get the girls' minds centered. And God knew they needed complete concentration during their training, the intelligence briefings, even when they went out—which wasn't often. Too damn dangerous to be in public, even if they were one hundred percent focused. And with Mary MIA, they weren't even close. Her absence distracted them, which distracted the guys.

And any distraction could be fatal.

That was why he'd spent so many sleepless nights searching for Mary. Why he'd driven to the Apennines when everyone else had gone to bed. Why he wouldn't stop until she was safely returned to her family.

He slowed down to a crawl as he drove up the hill to the Brotherhood's compound. No point in taxing the engine to a dull roar and waking up even the sound sleepers. The massive structure was dark, save for two lights on the ground floor and one in a bedroom or bathroom upstairs. Not too many people up and milling about yet. Sneaking in would be simple.

Nico coasted into the garage in neutral, drifted into his spot, and cut the engine. The loudest part of the whole process was the garage door opening and closing, but the insulation and thick walls would easily muffle those sounds. Almost home-free.

He swiped the black cap off his head and tucked it into his pocket. Then he opened the door to the mudroom, closed it gently, and walked into the hall.

Stopped mid-stride when Donni stepped in front of him. Only just managed not to shout out and wake the whole household.

"Where were you?"

Nico shot a glance at his watch. His heart rate had spiked. No surprise there. On the plus side, it was only 5:22. He'd made great time.

He took a deep breath and launched into his rehearsed lie. "I couldn't sleep. Decided to get some air, so I went for a walk. Ended up at the orphanage's olive grove for a while, and I lost track of time, I guess."

He tried to walk around her, but she stuck her hands on her hips and stood her ground, blocking his path. "Six hours?"

"What?"

"No one loses track of six hours. You left the house just before midnight, right after everyone went to bed. And I know you didn't go to the orphanage because, familiar or not, it's not somewhere you find relaxing."

"Vinnie's really the one with the bad memories there. I'm—"

"You took car keys with you, and I heard the motor when you pulled around front."

"Well, the orphanage is kind of far on foot. I drove down to the valley, then I took a walk."

"Bull crap. The grounds here are massive. If you just wanted air, you would have gone out to the patio or atrium. And if you wanted a midnight stroll, you could have gone to one of the grottos or to the hedge maze. But you didn't. Because you aren't a garden-variety insomniac looking to walk yourself tired. You're up to something. If you really couldn't sleep, you would have stayed in your jammies and walked the grounds."

"I don't sleep in pajamas." He suppressed a smile when her cheeks pinked.

She waved her hand like she could swat his comment away. "Regardless. You didn't put on any random pair of jeans or jogging pants from your closet. You're dressed in all black and sneaking around without telling anyone what you're up to or where you're going. I've been up all night, worried sick about you. No one is supposed to be out on their own, particularly at night. You, Mr. Security Expert, know those rules better than anyone, given you made them."

"I'm not the security expert. That's Coz's job. I'm the IT guy who happens to handle the security cameras and stuff. Besides, technically, the rules are for you girls, not us guys."

"Technically, you're changing the subject, and I'm not letting you get away with it. I want to know where you've been sneaking off to and what you've been doing, or I'm telling Mike. It's been months with you up to the wee hours and—"

"Wee hours?"

"—and I haven't said anything. But now you come home limping after being gone all night, and then you lie to me? I've had enough. I want to know what's going on."

He couldn't let her tell anyone. Especially not Mike. He already kept too close a watch on them. Nico would be grounded if Mike grew suspicious.

"You're imagining things, Donni." He stepped around her and headed for the stairs.

"Am I?"

He wasn't going to give her reason to doubt him or question him further. He had the high ground in this argument. Or at least the illusion of it. So he didn't even turn around. Just answered her over his shoulder as he hobbled up the stairs. "Yeah. You are."

Her answer was so soft, he almost didn't hear it. Made him pause for a moment, though.

"Guess I'm imagining the black greasepaint on your face, too."

ONCE HIS HEART stopped hammering in his chest, the guard took stock of what had just happened. They hadn't had a single incident the whole time they'd been at the facility, and all of a sudden commotion and wolves? Didn't sit right with him.

He made his way around the front of the building, senses on high alert for any other anomalies. Didn't see or hear anything odd, but that didn't mean anything. Instead of checking inside, he made his way down to the guard shack.

Idiot was asleep.

He scowled and banged the butt of his gun on the window. The man jerk-ed, almost fell out of his chair, then quickly righted himself.

"You know what happens to people who sleep on the job here, don't you?"

The man swallowed, his face paled. "You… you aren't going to say any-thing, are you?"

"That depends. How long have you been asleep?"

"Just now. I swear!"

"Good. Then you can tell me what you saw about five minutes ago."

Sweat beading on his forehead, he reached up and stretched his collar. "Saw?"

"So you were asleep then?"

"I… I don't know. I didn't see or hear anything. Nothing ever happens out here at night."

"Well, *something* happened." The guard glanced into the trees. "What do you know about wolves?"

"Wolves?" The gate attendant looked around with wide eyes. "Are there wolves out here?"

"You haven't heard them out there howling all damn night? Just how long were you sleeping?"

"Wolves?" he whispered.

The guard sighed. What a moron. How the hell did he get hired, anyway? "Don't suppose you know if wolves sneeze."

He shook his head. "I don't know. I mean, my dog does, so I suppose wolves do. Wolves! Wow."

"Stay the fuck awake." The guard turned and headed back toward the facil-ity. He thought about calling Sal, then thought better of it. What was he going to say? He'd heard a noise in the woods—definitely rustling, maybe a sneeze—and wolves jumped out of the tree line? Hardly a security breach.

Unless it wasn't just wolves.

No, he wasn't going to bother Sal about that. But he would make note of it in his report. If Sal bothered to check in, he could decide whether it was significant or not.

In the meantime, why draw undue attention? The gate attendant wasn't the only one who enjoyed a nap now and then, and telling Sal there was a problem would assure that stopped.

DONNI KNEW THE slamming pots and banging doors would wake the whole household, but she couldn't stop herself. She had rage to burn off, and making all that noise felt good. She had five pounds of loose ground sausage browning in two skillets and was chopping—whacking?—sweet potatoes when Gianni entered, hand over his mouth to cover a yawn.

He tipped his head toward the cutting board and ran his hand through his tousled brown hair. "What'd they do to deserve such a violent end?"

She put the knife down and took a deep breath before meeting his gaze. "Have you noticed anyone acting… odd lately?"

"You mean other than your homicidal tendencies toward the *patata dolce*?"

She picked up the knife and continued dicing, trying and failing to control her temper.

Gianni crossed the room and put his hand over hers, stopping the carnage. "What's going on?"

"Never mind."

"You know you can talk to me about anything. I know Nico's your primary contact, but as I'm head of this crazy group, I'm responsible for all of you."

She stirred the meat in the skillet.

"Or if not Nico or me, one of the other guys. Any of us is open to talking."

"Yeah. Coz and Vinnie love private one-on-one conversations about feelings."

Gianni chuckled. "Maybe they don't love it, but they have your back. We all do, you know."

Donni put the spoon down and started washing sage leaves.

"Come on, Don. What's bothering you?"

"Don't worry about it. Just me borrowing trouble."

"Talk to me."

"Nothing to say, Gianni." So done with that aspect of the conversation, she changed the subject. "Want to help finish breakfast?"

He was silent for a moment, stared at her hard. When she wouldn't meet his gaze, he shrugged. "Sure, what are we having?"

"I'm making a hash with the sausage and sweet potatoes. Figured I'd oven-poach a couple dozen eggs for over top. Then I want to make pancakes."

"Today isn't a cheat day. Can't have pancakes until the weekend."

"These are made with almond flour and stevia. Perfectly acceptable."

"All right. I'll make the coffee, then you can put me to work."

"Make it strong."

"It's not coffee, otherwise." He busied himself at the counter behind her. "And not to be picky, but when you make the eggs in the oven, they're technically not poached."

"You want to stand at the stove poaching eggs for the next half hour?"

"Hey, who doesn't love an oven-poached egg?"

"That's what I thought." Donni smirked and continued dicing the sweet potatoes. When she was done, she added them to a roasting pan and slid them into a hot oven. Then she got started on the pancake batter while Gianni diced onion and minced garlic and added them to the sausage. They worked in companionable silence until the kitchen crowded with her sisters, Coz, and Vinnie.

Franki walked over to Gianni, slipped her arms around his neck, and kissed him. "Morning, honey."

He nuzzled her neck and muttered, "Morning, *cara.*"

Vinnie plucked a grape off the counter and flicked it at Gianni's head. "No. No more public displays of affection. Knock it off or take that shit to your room. We eat here!"

Franki hugged Gianni and rested her head on his chest. "I've seen you and Jo locking lips."

"Yeah," Jo said, "because you have no boundaries and walk into our room without knocking."

"If you're so worried about it, lock your door."

"Learn some manners."

"Ladies," Coz said. "Can you tone it down? I haven't even had any coffee yet."

Toni poured a cup and handed it to him. He smiled his thanks, chugged a few sips, then came up sputtering.

"Too hot?" she asked.

"Too *strong*. Who the hell made it? You can stand a spoon up in the mug."

"I did," Gianni said. "It's early. I needed the extra jolt."

"Why the hell are we up so early, anyway?" Vinnie asked. "It's barely dawn."

"I'm up because Gianni was down here banging every pot and pan we have," Coz said. "Who could sleep through that racket?"

"Wasn't me." Gianni nodded toward Donni.

"Don, did something happen?" Toni placed a cup of coffee in front of her twin and tried to meet her gaze.

Donni refused to look up. Instead, she continued whipping egg whites by hand, the action of beating the liquid into a soft foam somewhat cathartic.

"I can't believe Nico's sleeping through all the noise down here," Coz said. "Think I should go check on him?"

Donni whipped the whisk so hard and fast, she feared she break her wrist. Her muscles burned, but not as hot as her rage at being lied to. Hearing Nico's name just made her anger flare.

"Nah," Gianni said. "We still have probably half an hour before breakfast is ready. Might as well give him another twenty minutes or so. No use waking him early. If he's in such a dead sleep, he must need the rest."

Oh, yeah, he needed the rest. He had to be exhausted. But that's what happened when people were awake all night, up to God knew what. Again. She fervently hoped he felt too guilty to sleep, but just in case he was sleeping, she got out the blender, threw fruit, nuts, chia seeds, and coconut water in, and blended it on high. When it wasn't loud enough, she put in a cup of ice and listened to the motor roar and the blades chunk the contents into a liquefied emulsion.

She was so focused on what she was doing, she tuned out the rest of the room. When she turned the blender off and spun around to get glasses for everyone, she noticed the kitchen had emptied. Everyone was gone but Gianni, who had pulled the sweet potatoes out of the oven and was preparing the eggs to go in.

"You want to cook the pancakes or make another batch of smoothies?" She reached into the cabinet for glasses.

He leaned against the counter and crossed his arms over his chest. "What'd Nico do to you?"

She opened the refrigerator and let the cool air envelop her. It took the heat out of her cheeks but not out of her heart. She barely managed a reply through clenched teeth. "Get the griddle out. You can do the pancakes. I'll do more smoothies. Do you think I should stick to the same flavor, or should we give them a choice? We have kiwi and pineapple—"

Gianni gripped her shoulders and spun her around. "We're only as strong as our most compromised member. Whatever's going on, your head isn't in the game. Talk to me."

She shoved an armful of fruit into his chest. "You finish breakfast. I'm not hungry, anyway." And she stormed out of the kitchen, listening to the soft thuds of kiwifruit bouncing on the floor.

2

NICO SAT ON the edge of his bed, a towel wrapped around his waist. He had thought he might get at least an hour of sleep, but the racket from the kitchen had kept that from happening. The cold shower did little to wake him. Now, damp and exhausted, he dreaded facing the day and hadn't quite mustered the energy to get up and deal with it.

He glanced around the spacious room. The tan walls and olive-colored fabrics were soothing, but they did nothing for his mood. What he needed was dark walls. Maybe some black-out blinds.

Someone banged on his door.

Wouldn't hurt to have noise-cancelling headphones, either.

He started to get up to answer it, but his knee gave out and he dropped back onto the bed. Then he realized the door wasn't locked, which would save him the pain and the explanation. So he adjusted the towel to cover the swollen joint and called out, "Come in."

The door had begun swinging in before he finished speaking. Gianni stormed in and slammed the door behind him.

Nico winced at the noise, rubbed his temples. Not only was he exhausted, he had another burgeoning headache.

"You hungover?" Gianni asked.

"What? No. Why?"

"You're holding your head. And you haven't come down yet."

"The sun's barely up."

"Lots of noise in the house today. No one else slept through it."

"I didn't, either. I just got out of the shower."

"Why'd you shower before a training session?"

Great. He'd forgotten training was on the agenda for the morning instead of the afternoon. Just what he needed at the moment. How the hell was he going to do anything with his head exploding and his knee swollen and incapable of holding his weight? At least his ankle felt a little better, small comfort that was.

"I asked you a question."

"Relax, would you? I'm still trying to wake up. It's early."

"What'd you do to Donni?"

The pressure in his head ramped up to vice-grip pain, and he kneaded the knots in his neck. "I don't know what you're talking about."

"She was slamming shit around the kitchen, so she's clearly in a bad mood. And when I pressed her for information, she wouldn't say anything."

"Maybe she has PMS or something."

His brother snorted. "Yeah, you try saying that to her or one of her sisters and see how far that gets you."

"I'm just getting up, Gianni. The shower hasn't even washed away my brain fog. What could I possibly have done to her?" Okay, more a lie of omission than an outright untruth, but he could live with that.

"Because when I mentioned you, she stormed off."

"So obviously I did something to her."

Gianni crossed his arms over his chest and raised an eyebrow.

"Don't know what to tell you. I haven't seen her all day."

"Well, something's bothering her! She never loses her temper like that. Left me alone in the kitchen with fruit all over the floor."

"So, no breakfast?"

"That's your take on all this? Donni's pissed at something you did, and you're worried about eating?"

"Not really. I'm getting a migraine, so I was going to skip breakfast. I'd probably just throw up any food I ate, anyway."

"Screw you, Nico. I'm worried about Donni, and you're up here acting like a royal dick. I know you did something to her."

Nico rolled his body down onto the mattress and looked up. Sunlight streamed through the window and cut a bright stripe across his ceiling. "Thanks for the vote of confidence. You can see yourself out."

"Intel briefing on the patio. Thirty minutes. Wear gym gear. We'll have training right after."

"Migraine. Need to sleep it off."

"Sucks to be you. You're running the briefing, so don't be late." Gianni left and slammed the door behind him.

Nico winced through the pain and squinted at the sunlight on the ceiling. The day had barely begun and it already sucked.

DONNI CHOSE A chaise lounge at the far corner of the patio. She slouched in it, wide-brimmed hat low on her head, sunglasses covering the little portion of her eyes that would otherwise be visible.

People didn't need to see the dark circles brought on by lack of sleep. Or the daggers her gaze shot toward Nico. Damn liar.

She needed to know what was going on. More to the point, she needed to know he was safe. The last thing she wanted to deal with was another serious injury to someone in the group. They'd seen too many tragedies already. Bad enough she didn't know when Mike would let them see their mother again, or even if he ever would. Didn't even want to think about her being in a coma and maybe never waking from it. The longer it lasted, the less likely they'd get her back.

And stupid Nico was up to something shady, probably going to get himself injured, too. Or worse.

An image of Chuck flashed through her mind. When Jo had received the video of their most reliable foreman, they'd all been heartsick over it. He'd been captured keeping Jo safe, and he'd been tortured mercilessly. No one would say the words, but Donni had a feeling Chuck was dead.

Just thinking about death brought up painful memories of Papa's murder, and her stomach lurched.

Papa, Chuck, Mama. Nico, the damn fool, would be next if he wasn't careful.

Maybe she should tell someone what he was up to.

But what would she say? Other than knowing he'd been keeping late hours and had left the compound, she didn't know what was going on. Gianni would be angry at Nico, but he'd be frustrated with her for assuming something without proof. And if Nico convinced his brothers that nothing was going on? They'd all be angry at her for wasting their time.

No, she needed hard evidence of what was going on before she told on him.

What she really needed was for him to stop, but that wasn't going to happen.

The next best thing was for her to spy on him and figure out what he was doing. Then she'd know what to do. She sighed. More sleepless nights in her future. Wonderful.

Her twin was the first one to come out to the patio. And as was typical for Toni, she didn't respect Donni's need for space—not that Donni minded. Usually. Her sister grabbed a chair and dragged it over to the corner, dropping it right beside the chaise.

"You're blocking my sun."

"It's not even noon yet, Don. You can't tan in morning sun."

"It's summer. The sun is strong enough."

"I know the damn sun is strong. It's already so humid. You'd think this close to fall the weather would be cooling down. Why the hell are we even out here?" She sipped on a blood orange San Pellegrino and looked out over the property. "I mean, I get holding weapons training out here, especially when the guys practice with their powers. But we should be inside in the air conditioning until then."

"You and your American constitution." Coz stepped outside, grabbed a chair, and brought it over to the girls.

So much for Donni hiding alone in the corner.

"I take umbrage to that." Toni shoved her bottle in his face. "Look. I've only been out here a minute and already the glass is covered in condensation. It's too hot to sit here and talk."

He pushed it aside. "If you're too hot to have a discussion, how do you think you'll fare in a battle?"

"Battle?" Toni's face paled.

"What do you think all the training's been for?"

Donni tried to ignore them. She didn't want to think about battles and injuries. Those things already occupied too much of her headspace.

Franki and Gianni walked out together. Given the glow each of them sported, Donni had a feeling they'd already worked off their breakfasts in a pleasurable way.

Sometimes she hated everyone and everything around her.

Okay, that was just exhaustion rearing its ugly head. She was happy for her sister. But no one could blame her for wishing they weren't so obvious about the benefits to being in love.

Or for wishing she might reap some of those benefits herself sometime soon.

Jo and Vinnie followed them out. She had a strained expression on her face, and his jaw was clenched. Didn't look like they'd burned off their breakfasts in bed. Might have done it arguing, though.

Franki and Gianni dragged a chaise over toward the group and snuggled together on it.

Didn't those fools realize it was too hot for all that… canoodling?

Jo and Vinnie just plopped down on the tile, Vinnie's back against the house and Jo's back against him. He didn't wrap his arms around her, and she kept her hands on her lap. Looked like they were trying to hide their tensions from the rest of the house, but Donni didn't think they were doing a good job of it.

Then Nico stepped out on the patio, capturing Donni's attention. She discreetly peered at him through the safety of her dark glasses. He wore gray gym shorts and a black Led Zeppelin t-shirt. He'd never know her gaze traveled over every chiseled muscle his clothes didn't cover, over the high cheekbones of his handsome face, over the ticking jaw that proclaimed his irritation, over his gorgeous hazel eyes and thick, dark blond hair.

Damn him for looking so good when she was already wishing she had a man in her life.

Not that she'd ever consider Nico in that way. He was a liar. Couldn't be trusted. And she needed dependability. Well, she could count on him. She just couldn't believe him. Which was almost as bad.

Besides, he was her assigned warrior. After her two older sisters fell for their protectors, it would just be cliché if she fell for hers. And she was nothing if not original.

She snapped out of her reverie when she realized Nico was staring at her like he could tell where she looked and what she thought. Her cheeks warmed—burned was more like it—and she pretended to feign interest in her nails. Not that she'd had a manicure in weeks, but her hands were the only place she could look that didn't require her to turn her head. Hopefully he'd buy it.

When he raised his eyebrow, she knew he didn't.

Nothing to do but deflect attention.

"So, are we going to get on with this meeting, or what?" she asked. "We have a long day ahead of us."

Nico sat on the chair closest to the door.

"What are you doing all the way over there?" Coz asked.

"Why are all of you clustered in the corner?"

"Come over here so we don't have to yell back and forth," Gianni said.

"Yell? I'm what? Twenty feet away?"

"Get your ass over here and drop the attitude," Vinnie said.

And Donni thought Nico had been clenching his jaw before.

He grabbed a chair and practically threw it toward them. Before anyone could complain, he limped over and dropped into it. "So, I got an email from Mike."

"Are you limping?" Jo asked.

"No."

"Yes, you are. What happened?"

He sighed. "Just tweaked my knee. Working out. Last night."

"You worked out last night?" Vinnie asked. "You should know better than to have a strenuous workout before a day of rigorous training."

"Well, I forgot we were working on powers today. And I couldn't sleep, so I went for a run."

"Did you try to heal it?" Gianni asked.

He paused for just an instant too long. "It's not bone or cartilage, G. Just some swelling."

Sounded like another lie to Donni. And for what? Lying about it would only make him suffer more.

Jerk deserved to suffer more.

"Want me to fix it?" Gianni asked.

"Later. Let's just—"

The swelling in his knee reduced until the joint returned to normal. The bruising faded until the skin showed no discoloration.

"Show off," Nico said. "I told you later was fine."

"Didn't see the point in letting you suffer."

"Instead we're wasting all this time talking about it."

"By all means, then, stop your bitching and start the meeting."

Nico leaned his head back and closed his eyes. "As I was saying, I got an email from Mike."

"Can't you sit up and address us properly?" Gianni asked.

"What are you, my mother?" Nico and Gianni glared at each other.

"It's common courtesy."

Nico stood up and walked into the house, a slight limp visible in his gait.

"Well, that was a productive meeting," Vinnie said.

Gianni started to stand.

"Don't," Coz said. "I'll go."

Gianni sat back again. "Not like you to volunteer for heartfelt discussions."

"Who said we're going to talk? Seems to me he needs a swift kick in the ass. And seeing he's still limping, it won't take much out of me."

Donni bit her lip when Coz walked inside. She hoped he was joking. Given the state Nico was in last night, he'd already been through enough.

Then again, maybe he needed the crap kicked out of him.

NICO SAT ON the edge of his bed, marble dagger pressed against his knee. He closed his eyes and concentrated on drawing healing powers out of the green stone weapon and into his body.

When he felt the pain subside, he knew it had worked. Didn't know why he hadn't thought to try that last night or even this morning. Swelling might have subsided on its own and the others never would have known he was hurt.

Well, most of the others. Donni had caught him red-handed. Or swollen-kneed, as it were. Cool of her not to have ratted him out. Not that she had any proof of what he'd really been doing. Other than the face paint, anyway.

His door burst open before he had a chance to put his dagger away.

"Thought you already checked to see if your power could heal your knee." Coz stood in the doorway, arms crossed over his chest.

"So I lied." He tucked the weapon back in its scabbard. "What's it to you?"

"Of all of us, you're the one that *never* lies. Not even little white ones. And now you're stringing fib after fib together—about stupid shit, too. What gives?"

"I don't know what you're talking about."

"I'm talking about you saying you tried to heal your knee when clearly you hadn't. So either you tried to earlier and your power didn't work—which you're now lying about—or you never thought to try, which means you were mentally compromised by something and are lying about that. So which is it?"

"Neither."

"Another lie."

Nico rolled his head on his shoulders to try and alleviate the pain in his neck. Didn't work, but it kept him from meeting his brother's gaze.

"Look." Coz ran his hand through his hair and shifted his weight. "You never lie, man. You always keep your cool. You find answers when the rest of us are stuck."

"Your point?"

"This isn't like you—the lies, the outbursts. The lack of logic when it comes to your health. Or anything else. I'm worried. We all are."

"You're making too much out of this. I couldn't sleep last night. I have a migraine today. That's why I'm short-tempered and not thinking clearly. It's no big deal."

Coz closed the door and crossed the room. He dropped into a chair, rested his elbows on his knees, and leaned toward Nico. "I know you're lying. I heard you leave last night. Heard you come in early this morning, too. Not the first time, either. What's going on?"

Nico cycled through a string of curses in his head. Why did everyone analyze his every freaking move? That's what sucked about everyone living in the same place. Sure, it was convenient for protecting the girls, but it afforded him zero privacy.

"We've all been under the same roof for months now. We've got a lot on our plates. I'm just a little stir-crazy. It's nothing."

"I thought we were best friends. Thought we didn't keep secrets."

Nico was taken aback. Coz wasn't the type to have a touchy-feely conversation. That he would even venture toward a declaration of emotion was a testament to how concerned he was. But as much as that mattered to Nico, it mattered more to him to keep his brother safe. He wasn't ready to involve the group when he didn't know what dangers they faced. Not when they already had so much to contend with. So he evaded the issue, averted his gaze by taking out his dagger and pretending to examine it. "We are. Since we were kids at the orphanage. Nothing will ever change that."

"Another lie. All you do is keep secrets these days. Didn't think you'd ever pull that shit on me."

"Coz—"

"Don't." He stood up, walked to the door, then flung it open. Didn't give Nico the courtesy of a face-to-face conversation, just stood there facing the hallway. "You better get your story straight. I told the guys I was going to get answers. Which clearly I didn't. And if I couldn't, I'd kick your ass until you stopped being a dick. So when you come back down, act like I did."

"Got answers or kicked my ass?"

"Either. Or both. Doesn't matter. You've become so accustomed to lying, neither should be hard for you." And he strode out.

Nico sighed and tested the mobility in his knee. Didn't hurt in the slightest.

No, this time the pain was in his heart. And none of them had the power to heal that.

DONNI WAITED UNTIL Coz walked down the hall. Nico's door had been closed, so she didn't hear what was discussed, but given the scowl on Coz's face, she had to assume the talk didn't go well.

Despite her anger at being lied to, she sensed what Nico really needed was someone to talk to. And she never ignored a person who suffered—she always offered to listen, or help, or just give them a hug and a smile. With charity in mind, she crept to his door.

The last thing she expected to see was Nico clutching his dagger against his head and rocking back and forth.

"Oh, my God. Are you all right?" She barged into his room without knocking and knelt in front of him.

He lowered his hands and looked up at her, the pain evident in his eyes. "It just—hurts."

She climbed onto the bed behind him and placed her fingers on his temples. Her thumbs ran through his soft, thick hair as she rubbed circles on his head.

He moaned under her ministrations and leaned back a bit.

Donni stroked her fingers along the ridge of his brow, down alongside his nose. Nico whimpered, tipped his head forward so she'd rub harder.

She massaged his head from the bridge of his nose, along his eyebrows, to his temples. Then she dropped her hands to his neck and shoulders. The muscles were tight, knotted. His shirt got in her way, so she reached for the hem and tugged it up.

He resisted, but she persisted. Finally he raised his arms and allowed her to lift the tee over his head. It tangled briefly with the dagger in his hand, but she yanked and freed him, the blade tearing the material just a bit in the process.

Neither of them seemed to care.

She flung the soft cotton aside and again reached for his neck. This time, her fingers felt the heat of his skin and the hardness of his body as she tried to knead the tension from his tense frame.

When he groaned, a powerful sensation shot through her body and settled in her core. Her eyes widened, and she bit her lip. What the hell was she doing?

But she couldn't stop herself. She wanted to help him, but more, she wanted to keep touching him. Needing to get closer, she guided him until he lay face down on the bed, then she climbed on top of him and straddled him. His skin was hot beneath her, and she felt her own body flame. She trailed her fingers up his sides, felt him tremble as she traced his ribs and moved on to his shoulder blades. Again she massaged his neck, but the muscles seemed even more taut.

She inched back until she sat on his thighs. He started to rear up, but she pushed him back onto the mattress and lightly danced her fingers down his spine until she reached his waistband. This time, when he jolted up, she let him. He rolled and ended up on his back under her. He had a death grip on his dagger, and she smiled knowing she'd panicked him. Then she leaned forward, took the weapon from him, and set it aside. As she moved, she felt his reaction to her ministrations throbbing beneath her, and this time she freaked and scrambled to her feet.

Nico sat up, grabbed his shirt, and held it in his lap. He panted for air and stared at her.

God, she wished he'd say anything to break the tension in the room.

"What the hell was that all about?"

Okay, she wished he'd say anything but that. She had no good answer, no reason for her behavior. What on earth had come over her? "I… You… Your head. You were in pain, and I was trying to help."

"By stripping me and climbing on top of me?"

Humiliation usually silenced her, but in extreme cases, it sparked an enraged outburst instead to camouflage her embarrassment. "Don't flatter yourself, Nico. Besides, I may have been the one who initiated the contact, but you were the one who… rose to the occasion."

He'd already had a tinge of red to his cheeks, but her barb caused him to flush a deeper shade of crimson. With his fair coloring, his embarrassment was easy to see. And she used it to her advantage.

Before he could reply, she stalked out of the room and slammed the door behind her.

Donni ran into her room and entered the *en suite* bath. There she ran cool water and splashed her face, trying to get her own coloring under control. It worked, until she thought about Nico's body under hers. Then she blushed all over again.

She had to get back downstairs, so she pushed the image of his hard body out of her mind. Instead, she pondered where he'd been sneaking off to and how she could find out when he wasn't telling anyone.

A smile crossed her face as a plan formed, and she headed back to the patio.

3

NICO COMPOSED HIMSELF and then walked downstairs. His headache raged on, but that was the least of his problems. He'd managed to piss off his brother—well, probably all of his brothers—and somehow got involved in an intimate moment with Donni. Still couldn't figure out how that happened. Or how he felt about it.

Was she purposely making an advance or was it really all innocent? Why did he react the way he did? He'd had plenty of massages before and that had never happened.

It was no damn wonder his head hurt so much.

He tried to ignore all those thoughts as he walked back onto the patio. He also tried to determine his best course of action. Everyone was owed an apology, but it might be better if he just ignored everything that happened earlier and jumped right into the briefing.

"You done acting like a royal dick?" Vinnie said.

So much for acting like nothing had happened.

Jo smacked Vinnie in the arm and whispered something to him.

He scowled and shrugged. "Anyway, I guess you have a briefing to lead."

"Better late than never, I guess," Gianni said.

Fine. Apology first, briefing second. He scanned all the faces on the patio, lingering slightly too long on Donni's. When his cheeks burned, he looked away, sat down with his laptop on his lap, and pretended to be busy opening files. Like he couldn't do that in his sleep. "Sorry about earlier. My head is killing me, and I'm exhausted. Not that that's an excuse. But it won't happen again."

"Whatever," Coz said.

Everyone else accepted his apology or mumbled something he chose to take as their forgiveness. He noticed Donni didn't make a sound, but he refused to dwell on it. Instead, he chose to move on to the briefing.

"So, I've been monitoring the news as well as chatter on the dark web. Also got an update from Mike. He wants me to fill you guys in on everything."

"The dark web?" Toni said. "How'd you get on that?"

"Where do you think I've been getting my intel? Fox News?"

"You don't have to be snippy," Donni said. "She was just curious."

Nico sighed and squeezed the bridge of his nose in a futile effort to relieve some of the pressure in his head. "Look, I'm sorry I'm so short-tempered. Really. And if you want a lesson some time on how I do what I do, I'll be happy to show you. But right now, it's not the how that's important. It's the what."

Toni shrugged and nodded. When she spoke, her voice was soft, and she didn't make eye contact. "You're right. So what'd you learn?"

Would he always be an ass or was it just a temporary condition?

Too bad there wasn't a cure—short of finding Mary and getting everyone focused again. He'd just have to make a stronger effort to be patient.

"Okay. So, first of all, Scalzotto."

"Who?" Franki asked.

"Are you kidding me?" Nico stared at her. "All this time, everything going on, and you don't know who Scalzotto is?"

"I know I should have been paying better attention these last months, but with the abduction, my mom, Vinnie…" She swallowed, a look of guilt crossing her face. She wouldn't meet Vinnie's gaze. Or Jo's. Both of whom glared at her.

"Don't put this on me." Vinnie's voice was hard, controlled. His face darkened, and he glowered at her.

"I don't remember, either." Jo grabbed Vinnie's hand and stroked his arm, but he yanked away from her. She took a deep breath before she continued. "Not because of Vinnie, or Mom, or anything. There's just been a lot to take in. Remind us."

Nico couldn't remember who knew what anymore. Maybe he was the only one even watching the news. He was definitely the only one scouring the web. "Okay. A quick current events lesson to catch everyone up."

Franki offered a weak smile of thanks.

"You know there have been riots in Italy. The government is falling, the police are making things worse in some of the cities, but they've been helping the people in others. The government shut down all Internet access to try and keep protestors from organizing."

"But we all have Internet," Donni said.

"I hacked into the government's network so we wouldn't be cut off."

"Oh. I didn't realize you could do that."

Nico shrugged. It had taken him all of two minutes, but that was unimportant. "Anyway, rioters have been chanting 'Medici, Medici, Medici' in their protests, demanding a change in government."

"They're chanting for us?" Toni asked.

God, they'd already been through this. This was all a total waste of time, because they obviously weren't taking any of it seriously enough to commit it to memory. But Nico took a deep breath and powered on. He didn't want to waste more time with an argument.

But, come on, really? Not one of them remembered anything or recognized how crucial it all was? It was at least as important as self-defense training, if not more so.

"They're not really chanting for *you*, specifically. Remember, no one even knows you exist. They just want a revolution. A better government."

"Because the Medici were so great," Gianni said.

"Some were. But this isn't the time for another history lesson." Nico rubbed the tense muscles of his neck. Flushed when he thought about Donni doing the same. "The protestors have a short memory. They want better economics, better education. They're remembering the Medici who governed well. And as such, they've chosen the face of their revolution. Carmen Remo Scalzotto."

"But we're the only Medici descendants, right?" Jo asked. "Is he a long lost relative, or something?"

"No. Again, remember, no one knows the Medici line isn't extinct. Scalzotto is just an amazing man. He has a doctorate in political science as well as a law degree. He's lectured in universities in three continents and toured much of the world with a missionary group when he graduated. He even met Pope John Paul II, and rumor has it they enjoyed a lively discussion about the consecration of Russia and the secrets of Fatima. He is an articulate, highly-educated, well-traveled man. I can't believe none of you has heard of him. You really need to watch the news more."

"*Capo* says he will change the world," Mike said.

Nico jumped, as did most of the rest of them. "Would you please stop teleporting in? A little warning would go a long way."

Mike ignored him. He sat beside Nico and looked at his laptop screen. "I had expected this briefing to be completed by now."

"I'm filling in some backstory. Not everyone has kept up with current events."

"You must be ever vigilant!" Mike pounded his fist into his palm. "This pertains to all of you. It is all interconnected."

"Let me pull up one of his interviews," Nico said. "It will give everyone a better idea of who this guy is."

"Do that. You must hear from him. You must learn from him, learn where he comes from, where this is all leading."

Nico typed "*Carmen Remo Scalzotto*" in the search box. Even though he'd been keeping up with current events, he was surprised by how much had appeared on the man in such a short amount of time. "Holy Mother of—"

"Dominico."

"I just didn't realize… A lot more has emerged about him since the riots started. Give me a minute." Nico's fingers flew over the keys until he found the interview he was looking for.

"I thought you were keeping abreast of things." Mike scowled at him.

Nico didn't acknowledge the barb. "Here it is. There's no point in everyone gathering around this screen to watch it, but I'll play it so you can all hear it. It's Scalzotto and an American interviewer. He speaks pretty good English."

"He is fluent in five languages, I believe," Mike said.

"Listen." Nico raised the volume.

News: Mr. Scalzotto, what do you say to the government who is denouncing the revolutionaries as crazy, saying that the Medicis were tyrants who were only interested in money and power?

Scalzotto: Well, I'd tell them it would depend on which Medici they were talking about. The Medici were like any ruling family. There were good ones and there were bad ones. If the government is focusing on the bad ones—the Alessandros and the Catherines—then I would have to agree. But that isn't what I believe the young men in the crowd meant. I'm certain they were referring to the Cosimos and the Lorenzos of the Medici line. The benevolent rulers. The benefactors. And that's all the people are asking the government for now. Some compassion. Some assistance. Fair laws.

News: What did Cosimo and Lorenzo do that made them so benevolent?

Scalzotto: Cosimo was a very popular ruler and managed the country's finances quite well. Lorenzo was an amazing patron of the arts. Both were, in their own ways, diplomats. That's what the people want from the government today. Strong fiscal management. A focus on education—the arts and sciences—to prepare our youth for the workforce. Strong relations with other countries. Italians want a nation they can be proud of again.

News: How were you chosen to be the face of the people?

Scalzotto: Me? I wasn't chosen. I'm not the face of the people. You asked me to do this interview because I'm a professor at the university.

News: *No, Mr. Scalzotto. We asked you to do this interview because you are the leader of the revolt.*

Scalzotto: *(Long pause. Then quietly.) I wasn't aware anyone felt that way. I'm honored anyone would think so highly of me to ask me to lead such a worthwhile effort. But no one has approached me regarding leading anything. Could you tell me where you got that information?*

News: *If you'd just answer the question, Mr. Scalzotto.*

Scalzotto: *Thank you for your time.*

Nico closed his laptop. "He left the stage then and the reporter blathers on about the revolt. Scalzotto seemed genuinely stunned. At that point in time, I don't think he had any idea he had become the poster boy for the revolution."

"And *Capo* says he's going to change things?" Gianni asked.

"Indeed," Mike said.

"So he's a pawn in this game, too. Just like the girls. Just like us."

"He has free will, Giovanni. You all do. You are not chess pieces on a board."

"Sure doesn't feel that way," Gianni said.

Mike shot him a hard stare. "Your destinies are prophesied, not preordained. As Josephina and Vincenzo have recently proven, the future is not set in marble. It is malleable."

"That still doesn't mean he's not a pawn," Gianni said.

"Everyone has a role in this, Giovanni. What his role is does not affect you, nor does your role affect him. He will be told what he needs to be told, when he needs to be told, as will you. *Capo* has been around a bit longer than you have. I believe he knows what he is doing."

Nico rolled his eyes away from Mike's view. *Capo* had been around for centuries. Someone that powerful should have been able to avoid all of this. All he'd done is dump the problems on the Brotherhood's doorstep.

"So, Scalzotto," Donni said. "Where is he? What's the next step?"

"Dominico?" Mike looked at Nico and nodded for him to continue.

"Scalzotto's in hiding. The people are protecting him. He shows up at protests, offers words of encouragement, and disappears again before the government can get to him."

"Words of encouragement. Sounds life-changing."

"Donnatella, revolutions take time. This one has been centuries in the making. It is why you are here."

"I thought we were here because our lives are in danger from people who know our secret. Seems to me if the revolt happens, Scalzotto can take control and we're off the hook."

"I am afraid none of you will be free of your burdens until your enemies have been vanquished."

"Vanquished?" Vinnie said. "What the hell does that even mean? We aren't soldiers in some medieval war."

"You of all people, son, should recognize this situation is life-or-death. It *is* war."

Vinnie bristled. Nico didn't know if it was use of the term "son" or the reminder that Vinnie had been the first of them to take a life for the cause. Probably didn't matter what his brother took exception to, though. He'd been volatile since he'd killed Pasquale to save Jo's life. Any little thing set him off these days.

Nico was shocked when Vinnie didn't burst into argument. Instead, he climbed out from behind Jo and stormed inside.

Mike called after him. "Do not go far. You have weapons training."

A slamming door was Vinnie's only reply.

"There is much more to discuss regarding Legatus and Scalzotto, but—"

"Are you telling me Scalzotto is part of Legatus?" Gianni said. "Carla mentioned them in the letter she left me, but I don't think Nico's made much headway there."

Nico flung his hands in the air. "Always 'Nico-this' and 'Nico-that' from you guys. Has it occurred to you that someone else is capable of doing a little research? No. Of course not. It's always me."

"You are head of IT," Gianni said. "Isn't research kind of your thing?"

"And you are supposed head of this whole damn group." Nico stood. "But as usual, it's all on me. Screw you, Gianni." He headed for the house.

"Dominico," Mike said. "You have weapons training. Retrieve your brother and report to the clearing in five minutes."

Rage roiled through him, but he went inside to find Vinnie. No point in arguing with Mike. He had a way of getting whatever he wanted, and after all, he was both their boss and adoptive father. And no one said no to dear old Dad.

Besides, it might feel good to beat the shit out of something.

DONNI SAT IN the sun and watched Mike direct Coz and Gianni in setting up targets at the far end of the clearing. She really enjoyed watching the guys train—a lot more than she liked her own training sessions.

Jo was the only one who thrived on the workouts. Donni and Franki tolerated them as necessary evils. Toni griped about them constantly, but she worked like a beast when they trained. If Donni was honest, Toni was doing great. She could probably easily beat her twin and her oldest sister. Only Jo would give her a run for her money now.

No, Donni didn't love the training like Jo or loathe it like Toni. She just accepted that she had to exercise every day, so she might as well be sparring and grappling than jogging or something else tedious and dull.

Today, though, exhausted as Donni was, she was glad to just sit there and watch the guys train.

"Do not fret, Donnatella. You will also have a training session today."

Did Mike read minds now, too? Fabulous. "Great. Thanks."

"You do not sound pleased."

"I'm kind of tired. I was just thinking it was going to be nice to skip a workout today and watch the guys. Vinnie and Gianni especially have gotten really good with their powers."

"Yes, they have. Both have full control now. It is only a matter of time until Dominico and Roberto also master their gifts."

Donni smiled at Mike's use of Nico's and Coz's proper names. She found his formality endearing, but she knew Coz—more than any of them—hated it. She spoke quietly so the guys wouldn't hear. "Between you and me, neither Nico nor Coz seems to have made much progress with the powers-part of their daggers."

Mike's gaze seemed to pierce her soul.

She squirmed under the intensity of his attention. Felt even more self-conscious when he smiled.

"I have been monitoring their progress. More than you or they know." He patted her shoulder. "Do not worry, Donnatella. I think you will find Dominico makes great strides today." And he walked away.

Now what the hell did that even mean?

The yard was set up. Franki and Toni joined her in chairs near the patio. Gianni and Coz stood in the center of the clearing, talking as they warmed up. Mike stood by the targets, staring at the house. He nodded just before Vinnie, Jo, and Nico stepped outside. Jo joined her sisters, and the guys walked over to their brothers.

"How's Vinnie?" Franki asked.

Jo sighed and slumped in her chair. "Not good. He's unraveling. Pasquale was his friend."

"No," Toni said. "He only thought Pasquale was his friend."

"Potato, patato." Jo waved her hand in a dismissive gesture. "Does it really matter? Vinnie killed him. Because of me."

"He would have done that to save any of us." Franki patted Jo's arm.

"But none of you went off alone. Against the rules. I put him in that position. And I don't know if we're ever going to move past it."

"I thought you guys were okay," Toni said. "After you woke from the coma, you two were in such a good place."

"As good as a relationship can be when one person was in a coma." Jo grabbed her water bottle and took a long drink. "He was elated I survived. Of course we were in a good place. But that relief has worn off, and now he has to live with what he's done. I made him a murderer."

"Oh, honey, no," Franki said. "This is war. He was defending you."

"That's why we didn't report it to the police. Because it was a justified kill."

"There was nothing to report," Toni said. "The body was gone."

"Doesn't change the fact that Vinnie killed him."

"We don't know that for sure, though. Not really." Franki took a drink from her own bottle. "I mean, look at Chuck. We thought he was dead, then we got that video of him."

"Yeah, of him being tortured," Jo said. "Also because of me. And we have no idea what's happened to him since, either."

Donni stayed silent. She had a damn good idea of what had happened to Chuck, and discussing her theory wasn't going to help anyone, least of all Jo.

"Are you and Vinnie going to be okay?" Franki asked.

"Yeah. I mean, I guess. I think so." She swiped at the tears welling in her eyes. "I don't know. I mean, when he manages to put it out of his mind, we're so good together. But then he remembers, and he's haunted by it. He has to blame me, right? Is that something we can recover from? God, it hurts so much to think I might lose him."

"I hate to rain on your pity parade, but you're way off base."

Jo turned and stared at Donni. "I'm sorry? What?"

"The problem between you and Vinnie isn't that he blames you."

"How could he not?"

Donni shook her head. "He loves you, Jo. He'd do anything for you. He's a mess right now because it was his job to protect you, and he almost failed."

"Because of my reckless behavior."

"No. He knew about that. He was prepared for that. As much as one can be, anyway. What's really bothering him is that he let Pasquale into our lives to begin with."

"In our lives? We never even met him! He was an employee of Vinnie's. That's all."

"Yeah, but because Vinnie hired him, he became the perfect spy for our enemies. Vinnie blames himself for that."

"He's still a murderer. Because of me."

"And that will stick with him. I'm sure it's another reason he's such a wreck.

But I have a feeling we're all going to be stepping over some pretty nasty lines before all is said and done. We're all going to have crosses to bear."

All three of her sisters stared at her. She didn't acknowledge the shock on their faces, though. Instead, she stared straight ahead. "Looks like the show's about to start."

NICO STRETCHED, BUT his tight muscles refused to relax. Performing under Mike's critical eye always stressed him out. Doing so when he was already exhausted and in a bad mood was a recipe for disaster.

With an almost imperceptible nod of his head, Mike bade them to begin. At least Nico was cognizant enough to recognize that.

They all took out their daggers and formed a circle—clockwise Gianni, Vinnie, Nico, and Coz. Nico gained a small measure of strength with his best friend left of him, but Vinnie on his right side negated it. And then some.

He was too weak and distracted for this. But he had no choice. With Mike watching, there would be no storming off and stalling until later. Or skipping it all together.

Probably why the bastard was there. He was likely aware that Nico had been letting things slide. Did Mike know how he'd been spending his nights, too?

Gianni began with a salute. Nico snapped back to attention but was a fraction of a second late raising his dagger, and Mike pierced him with a burning glare. Then muscle memory took over, and the flurry began.

No time to think, no time to plan or prepare. It wasn't action or reaction. It just was. His mind disconnected, and his body moved to music no one heard. Kick, strike. Parry, thrust. Swing, swipe. He and his brothers danced a vicious choreography of precise and deadly martial arts moves, so fast and so furious that even the smallest error could be lethal.

His body was a cyclone of movement, but all was calm inside him. Tranquil. Serene. He grew hyperaware of his surroundings—smelled the heady aroma of freshly mowed grass, the cloying perfume of the potted roses, the pungent odor of freshly-turned earth. It was as though he floated out of his body and became one with the nature around him, grew strength from the earth itself. It was the first sense of peace he'd felt in weeks.

Why had he put off these workouts for so long?

When the routine ended, Nico came back to full awareness. He was beyond winded. His clothes stuck to him from a sheen of sweat, and he ripped his t-shirt off. As he tossed it aside, he caught a glimpse of Donni. Her expression was of awe, wonder.

It probably was quite the sight to see, four large men moving with such grace and speed. His heart swelled a bit with pride.

What the hell did he care what she thought, anyway?

He shook his head and turned his attention back toward his brothers. They had also stripped their shirts off, and they'd already finished their water break and were returning to the circle. He hadn't even opened his bottle yet.

"Nico, come on," Coz called.

He took a quick swig of water, the liquid cool and refreshing on his tongue. But it did nothing to bank the heat of his anger and frustration. Of his confusion.

Mike cleared his throat, and Nico hurried back to the circle.

"To the targets," Mike said. "I want you working on attacks."

Nico followed his brothers to the edge of the clearing where four targets had been set up. He chose the leftmost one, farthest from Mike.

Didn't make a difference, though. Mike crossed the clearing and stood right beside Nico's target.

"You might not want to stand there."

"You should be able to direct your attacks precisely by now. I should not be in any danger."

"We're a little out of practice. I haven't done this drill in a while."

"Why not? Were you not told to hone your gifts rather than squander them?"

Nico glanced to his right. His brothers were already sending bursts of energy from their daggers toward the targets. As he expected, Gianni was flawless. Vinnie, when he hit the target, was deadly accurate. He seemed to have trouble concentrating, though, and missed a few times. Still was better than anything

Nico could throw out at the moment. He was wiped, and his concentration was shot. Which totally sucked, because energy bursts were usually a strength.

To his chagrin, even Coz was fairly successful.

"You know, I have been a little busy. Finding and vetting the mentors—"

"I told you where they were."

"Arranging and managing our exodus here."

"Which was done a while ago."

"Helping with rebuilding the orphanage."

"Josephina has that well in hand."

"Research, which no one else seems to care to do."

"True, but is that not part of your job?"

"Regardless. It all takes time. And while everyone else has the free time to practice or do God knows what else, I'm trying to keep everyone safe."

"Ah, but that is not all you have been doing, is it, Dominico?"

So he did know about his nighttime excursions. But how much did he really know? "What are you implying?"

Mike crossed his arms and leaned against the target. "What do you infer?"

Hell with it. He'd never get an answer from Mike, but he'd be damned if he'd give up any info, either. Nico stepped into a riding horse stance, pointed at the target, and fired a bolt of energy. The instant the power left his dagger, he realized he had aimed at Mike and not the bullseye. But before he could call a warning, Mike disappeared. The bolt of energy seared past the side of the target and hit a cypress tree behind it, shattering it into splinters. Had Mike not dematerialized, the force would have hit him right in the chest.

"What the *fuck*, man?" Coz said. He and his brothers stood rooted to their spots, mouths open in awe. "Did you hit him?"

Nico shook his head. "N—no. He's fine. He ghosted out be—before it reached him."

"Did you fucking take aim at my father?" Vinnie's voice started low, but it became a bellow by the end.

"No. No! I—"

Vinnie lunged for him, but Gianni and Coz grabbed him and held him back.

"Get out of here, Nico." Coz's voice strained under his struggle. "Go!"

Nico dropped his dagger in the grass and dashed to the house. The last thing he saw before reaching the door was Donni's face, pale and wide-eyed.

Dear God, had he really tried to kill Mike?

Inside, he headed down to the gym instead of up to his room. He strode straight over to the practice dummy and let loose all his turmoil. He battered the bag with rapid-fire kicks and a flurry of punches until he could barely stand and his knuckles were bloody. Winded, he stepped back, his energy depleted, his mind still whirling with accusations and admonitions.

"Nico?" Donni's voice was soft from the doorway.

He hadn't heard her come in, and he was startled by her presence. Her face was pale, her eyes wide. And before he could answer her, the room spun and went dark.

4

NICO CAME TO on a gym mat, a cold compress on his forehead. Donni sat beside him and watched him carefully. Coz stood silently in the doorway, a sentinel on high alert.

He moaned and sat up. "What happened?"

"What do you remember?" she asked.

What did he remember? There was the facility, the guards, the wolves. But that was last night. What had happened today? He had a vague recollection of a security briefing. Mike was there, and—

Mike!

He groaned. "Mike's okay, right?"

"He never came back after you... after. Vinnie called him to make sure he was okay. And he is. He's fine."

"And Vinnie?"

"Pretty pissed off still, but calming down. He came to check on you, though. They all did. Everyone was worried."

Coz mumbled something and walked away.

Looked like Vinnie wasn't the only brother he'd pissed off.

"How long have I been out?"

"That's kind of hard to say. I mean, it's been a couple of hours, but I'm pretty sure you went from collapsed and unconscious to merely sleeping after only a few minutes."

"How can you tell?" He rubbed his head where a huge bump had formed.

"You started snoring."

Perfect.

"Look, Nico—"

"I know. I owe everyone an apology. Especially Mike and Vinnie. I'll do it as soon as my head stops spinning. I'm not sure I can even stand up right now."

"That's not what I was going to say."

He looked at her and raised his eyebrow. Even that hurt.

"Coz and I were talking. We both know you've been up crazy late every night for weeks now. Sneaking out sometimes. Based on what Coz overheard between you and Mike, he knows it, too. We're all worried about you."

"You don't have to worry." Of course he'd been up. He had work to do. Powers to learn. Her mother to find. When the fuck was he supposed to sleep? "I'm fine."

"Clearly you aren't. You've always got a headache. You're tired all the time. Work is slipping. Practice is falling by the wayside. You nearly ki—" She swallowed, paused. When she spoke again, her voice was quieter, her words measured. "Your focus is off. You shot at Mike today."

He tossed aside the compress and stretched. The rest had done him some good. When he noticed Donni staring at him, he looked down. Now apparently they were both acutely aware that he was shirtless.

"I, uh… I brought your dagger back." She handed it to him, her fingers brushing his and sending a tingling charge up his arm and through his body.

They stayed connected through his dagger, their fingers intertwining. "What else did you bring me?"

"Your shirt." Her voice was barely above a whisper. She handed him the soft cotton, which he took with his free hand and tossed aside. Her gaze never broke contact with his. Now her eyes were hooded, darkened.

Intense.

He didn't know what had come over them, what game he was playing. All he knew was he desperately wanted to win. "Anything else?"

She leaned closer to him, and her gaze dropped from his eyes to his mouth. She licked her lips and inhaled deeply.

Nico bent toward her, their mouths nearly touching. He felt the heat of her breath on his face, noticed the flush bloom on her cheeks and chest. Instead of kissing her, he nuzzled her ear, noted the faint lemony scent of her shampoo. Then he spoke into her neck, letting his lips lightly graze her silken skin. "Anything at all. All you have to do is ask."

She tipped her head back and sighed.

God, she was tempting. He traced her collar bone with the tip of his tongue, moved on to her jaw line, then he pressed his lips beneath her ear. She trembled under him, and he smiled against her skin.

"Yo."

Coz's voice startled him, and he pulled back. The dagger tumbled from their hands to the mat, making a dull thud in the otherwise quiet room.

"Training with the girls down here. Ten minutes. Get... put together before anyone else comes down." He turned and left.

Donni's eyes were wide. Her glance darted back and forth between the empty doorway and the dagger on the floor. "I—I don't know what came over me. I'm sorry." And she ran.

Again Nico had a physical reaction to her that he had to conceal until he'd calmed down. He didn't know what had come over either of them. Coz's appearance had saved him from doing something he'd never recover from.

He glanced down at the dagger. They'd been out of control when they were touching it, only hitting the brakes once they'd dropped it. Same thing had happened in his room earlier. He didn't know what that meant, but he knew one thing.

There was no way he would hold the dagger when Donni was around.

Fuck. He was so screwed. She was his training partner.

DONNI STOOD OUTSIDE the gym, her legs trembling so badly they barely kept her upright. She'd tried everything to get out of the training session. She was going to clean up from breakfast, but someone had beat her to it. She told Franki she had wicked cramps, but her sister told her the exercise would make her feel better. She suggested to Gianni that switching partners might be a good idea—for variety. He considered it but ruled against it, probably because he didn't want one of his brothers working with Franki.

Finally, she swallowed her pride and approached Coz. She told him after what had happened, she didn't think it was a good idea for her to work so closely with Nico. At least not at the moment or for the foreseeable future. But he had no sympathy for her plight. In fact, he seemed pretty angry with her. He scowled and said she should have thought about that before they were lip-locked in the gym.

He didn't stick around for her righteous indignation. True, she and Nico hadn't actually kissed, but Coz didn't know that, and from his perspective, the atmosphere probably crackled with a sexual charge.

Hell, it did from her perspective, too. That was why she didn't want to partner with Nico any longer. How would she maintain a professional distance with his hands all over her? With him holding her tightly against his hard body? With them rolling around together on the mat—the mat they'd just almost kissed on.

Donni closed her eyes, took a deep breath, and willed her legs not to give out on her. Then she entered the gym.

She was the last one there. Franki and Gianni were shamelessly flirting—which was an incredibly chaste word for what was going on—over by the weight rack. Jo and Vinnie were in the corner. By the hard set of his jaw and the tears welling in Jo's eyes, they were arguing again. Toni was with Coz by the kicking dummies, watching with awe as he executed what the guys called a seven-twenty kick. She didn't know the real name of it, but it required two full turns in the air before landing the blow. All of the guys could do that skill, and she doubted she or any of her sisters would ever learn it. Jo maybe, if she could get her head back into training. Why Coz was trying to teach it to Toni, she had no idea.

And that left Nico. He sat on the mat nearest the door, nearly in the same spot they'd been in just moments before. His legs were spread wide and he arched his arm over his head, stretching toward his toe. The muscles in his legs and arms rippled until he relaxed into the stretch. Thank God he'd at least put his shirt back on.

He sat up straight then copied the movement to the other side. Donni's mouth went dry as she stood there, staring at him. How the hell was she supposed to work with him for the next couple of hours?

"You just going to stand there staring at my brother all day?" Coz said. "Or can we move on to why the rest of us are here?"

Busted. The whole room turned at looked at her. Even Franki and Gianni put the PDA on hold to see what was going on. Donni's face flamed. Shit, not just her face. Her whole body felt like it was on fire. So she did the only thing she could think of—she squared her shoulders, lifted her chin, and joined Nico on the mat.

Hushed conversations broke out in the other three couples, but Donni and Nico didn't say a word. She sat facing him, her toes inches from his, and mirrored his movements, never tearing her gaze away from him. Sure, she might be humiliated—especially after Coz called her out to the whole group—but Nico had more to be embarrassed about than she did.

Nico kept the wide straddle but leaned down between his legs and touched his chin to the mat. Donni did the same. She was close enough to see the shadows under his eyes, the strain in his features.

"Why are you here?" he whispered.

"Because I was summoned to training." She glanced around the room, no easy feat with her head on the floor. No one was listening. "Why didn't you come up with a reason not to be here?"

"I'm one of the trainers. Why didn't you?"

She thought about lying, but didn't see the point. "I did try. No one bought any of my excuses."

"Maybe you should have tried harder."

"And maybe *you* shouldn't be lying to everyone and acting like a royal ass."

She sat up, pulled her legs together, and rose. "Apparently I still have more to learn, so let's get this over with."

Nico climbed to his feet, his movements nimble and quick. Looked like his nap did him some good, after all.

"Everyone warmed up?" Gianni asked. He didn't wait for any answers, though. "Good. We've burned enough daylight, so we're going to skip the drills and move right on to grappling."

Wonderful. So much for having twenty minutes to get used to being so close to Nico before having to touch him.

"Why don't we start with sparring first?" Jo asked. Her eyes were red but dry. It was obvious she wanted to burn off steam before being wrapped in Vinnie's arms. "We're going to fight someone before we get tackled to the ground."

"Because we haven't spent enough time on grappling."

Donni knew better. Gianni would take their training seriously, but he just wanted to have Franki in his arms. That was fine for them, but there were two couples in the room who would just as soon walk out the door.

"Everyone break into your training areas," Gianni said. "Leave plenty of room between you and the pair next to you."

Nico stepped a few feet closer to the wall and stared at her. While Franki and Gianni and Toni and Coz chose their spots, Jo and Vinnie lingered a bit, staring at each other.

Donni saw her opportunity and seized it. She darted over to Jo. "Switch me."

"What? No. Why?"

Jo liked to be tough, liked to be in control. She wouldn't want people to think Donni was rescuing her. But Donni saw the hope in her eyes, the flicker of relief on her face. So she pushed the issue. "I feel like I'm starting to anticipate Nico's moves. I want to try against someone I'm not used to."

Gianni looked over toward them. "What's going on? Get with your partner."

"Just a sec," Donni said. "We're switching partners."

"No. Not today. We're going to teach you some new moves in a little while. I need you with your regular partner so the lesson goes faster."

"When we get to the new stuff, we can switch back."

He looked back and forth between Jo and Donni, then between Nico and Vinnie. Finally, he shrugged. "Fine. For now. But you're switching back later."

Jo didn't even look at Vinnie. She darted over to Nico and they immediately started working on the straight arm-bar. Coz and Gianni chose the same skill for their partners.

"Looks like it's me and you, then," Vinnie said. "Arm-bar?"

"Are you angry that I pulled Jo away?"

He sighed and ran his hand through his hair. "No. It's probably for the best. You're right. Switching up is going to give us a fresh perspective."

"Are you talking about training? Or your relationship?"

"Come on, you guys," Gianni said. "Or you're switching back."

"Let's get in the guard position," Vinnie said.

Donni complied, lying on her back and wrapping her legs around his waist. He leaned forward and held her neck.

"Did Nico ever teach you this position?"

She spun to the side, her ear by his knee. Then she lifted her belly off the ground, wrapped her leg around his neck, and applied pressure until he tapped out. She rolled back to the floor. "You're avoiding my question. Are you and Jo okay?"

"Let's do it to the other side. Then we'll switch, and you can practice from the top." Donni choked him harder that time, and he glowered at her after tapping out.

"Would you please answer me?"

"We're supposed to be training, not talking."

"And you swore you'd never hurt my sister. I need to know if you're going to honor that vow."

"I'm her sworn protector, Don. I'm not going to let anyone hurt her."

"What about you?"

He sat back on his haunches and sighed. "What do you want from me?"

"I want to know that your love is enough to overcome your challenges. I know what you're going through."

"You can't know what I'm going through. No one does."

"Vin—"

But he'd already jumped to his feet and stormed out of the gym.

"Now what?" Gianni said. Franki flipped him to the mat, and he groaned. "I wasn't paying attention."

"And that's how you die," she said.

"Donni, where'd V go?" Gianni asked, still on his back but contorting his head so he could look at her.

"I don't know. I'll go find him."

"No," Jo said. "I'll go."

Donni watched her dart out of the room. She'd wanted to make things better for her sister, but it seemed she'd only made it worse.

"Don, go pair off with Nico," Gianni said. "We might as well start with the new skills."

She looked over at Nico. His teeth were clenched and his jaw ticked a staccato beat. Clearly he was as happy about this as she was.

JO HAD BEEN the perfect partner. She was agile, strong, and best of all, he felt nothing with her in his arms.

He wished he could say the same about Donni, but memories from earlier in the gym said otherwise. Then again, it could just be the dagger…

Donni approached him slowly, dread apparent on her face. He knew just how she felt.

They stared at each other, neither speaking. Her breasts heaved with her rapid breathing, and he had to force himself to look away. He called across the room, "All right, Gianni. What are we teaching?"

"Heel hooks."

"Are you crazy?" Coz said. "Those are too dangerous."

"That's why they need to learn how to get out of them."

"When would they ever be in a position to be in a heel hook?" Nico asked.

"What's the problem with heel hooks?" Franki asked.

"They're designed to incapacitate people," Coz said.

"Aren't all these holds?" Toni asked.

"Yeah. But this one has a reputation for hurting people in practice as well as in combat." Nico sat down. "It's illegal in most competitions. Too dangerous."

"And completely unnecessary," Coz said.

"I want to learn it," Franki said. "I want to learn everything and anything that might protect me in the field."

"In the field?" Nico said. "This isn't a war maneuver or a secret op."

"Isn't it war? It feels like it." Toni sat beside Coz. "Mama and Franki were kidnapped. Jo almost died. Twice. Who knows what's happened to Chuck. The orphanage was bombed." She sighed. "Vinnie killed someone, for God's sake. We're all in danger every day. That's why we're living together, why we left America, why we have you as our personal bodyguards. The last thing I want to think about is being attacked and not knowing the one release that could save me."

"You won't be attacked," Coz said. "Like you said, that's what we're for."

"Then why are we training at all?" Franki asked. "You guys do a hell of a job protecting us, but you aren't foolproof. Sal and Dante have already proven that they can get to us."

"But a heel hook?" Nico said. "Come on, Gianni. What's the likelihood of them being attacked and having that move put on them?"

"What was the likelihood of Pasquale being a traitor and almost killing Jo? Or of Sal killing Papa?" Franki lowered her voice. "What are the chances of all of us getting through this unscathed?"

Nico looked at Donni. She'd been uncharacteristically silent through the whole exchange. Her eyes were wide, her face pale—an expression he felt like she'd worn too often lately.

But she lifted her chin. "Show me."

So much could go wrong. He couldn't bear to see her hurt. "Okay, but listen. This isn't like those other holds where you can go as long as you can hold your breath or try to tolerate the pain. When this one hurts, you're about to tear ligaments in your leg. You have to tap out. No trying to last a little longer. Got it?"

"Yeah."

"I mean it, Donni. This is serious."

"I got it. Don't wait to tap out."

He looked around the room. Her sisters looked as determined as she was. Gianni was already instructing Franki. He and Coz shared a grim look before he turned his attention back to Donni.

"Okay. Let's start." He dropped to the mat. "Sit on the floor and face me, legs out in front of you."

She did as she was told.

Nico scooted forward so their legs tangled together, hers sandwiching his left leg, his sandwiching her left. He lifted her foot, pausing a fraction of a second at the silkiness of her skin. She seemed so fragile.

Shaking off that revelation, he tucked her foot between his ribs and his bicep, resting her heel in the crook of his arm. He reached his left arm across his body and locked his hands together, pinning her leg. "This is the beginning position. Your mobility is already severely compromised."

She wiggled underneath him, but she didn't go far. "Didn't expect that."

He loosened his hold. "Am I hurting you?"

"Nico, please. I'm fine. Teach me."

He put her in position again. "Remember, you have to tap out when the pain starts."

She sighed. "What's next?"

"Okay. This is a rotational leg-lock. There will be very little time between feeling pain and damaging your knee's ligaments. So I won't do the move fully."

"Then how will I learn?"

"This move is never done fully in practice. It's a very gentle motion to protect the student. Remember, this lock isn't even legal in tournaments."

"Fine. Be gentle."

"Okay. Next, the attacker—me—would twist, rolling onto my stomach and clasping my hands together. The pressure is intended to destroy your knee."

"What do I do?"

"Tap out."

"Yeah, that'll work in the real world."

He glared at her. "Let's start to do it, and tap out when the pain starts. I need to see your threshold."

They practiced the move a few times. He went so slowly, so gently, he doubted she was learning anything.

"Okay. Now you need to learn how to counteract this."

"What do I do?"

"You need to roll the other way, flipping me, to get out of the hold."

"Seems simple enough."

"Not really. You probably won't be able to move, and even if you do, all I have to do is roll with the momentum and apply a knee bar on the other side."

"So there's no way out?"

"You have to roll out, but not let me counter."

"That's highly unlikely. You're a lot bigger than I am."

"That's why Coz and I think this is stupid. It's too big a risk in practice, and you're not likely going to get out of it in the real world, but more to the point, you'll probably never even encounter this in real life."

"Show me the roll again."

They worked on it a few more times, then switched legs and did it all again to the other side. Nico thought she picked it up rather quickly, but he knew he could easily counter her defense.

"Okay, enough. You've got it. Let's move on to something else."

"One more time. I don't want to roll out this time, though."

"Then what's the point?"

"I want to see how far my leg flexes."

"It doesn't. End of discussion."

"Nico, come on. I need to know what my leg can take, because chances are I'm not getting out of this hold."

"You're never going to be in this hold, so it doesn't matter."

She entwined her legs with his. "One more."

He shook his head. "No."

"Okay, guys," Gianni said. "Now move on to reverse heel hooks."

"Fuck," Nico said under his breath.

"What's the problem?"

"They're less forgiving. I can hurt you faster."

"You're a great teacher, Nico. You won't hurt me."

He glanced across the room at Coz, who looked as sickened as Nico felt. But he helped Toni get in position, so Nico did the same with Donni.

"We start in the same position as before. But this time, I'm going to pop my hips up, which will straighten your leg." He demonstrated, and her leg easily lifted above him. "Now I'm going to push it to my other side. When I roll now, your leg will go out instead of in, so the pain and damage will happen faster."

"Okay."

He proceeded to instruct her in the finer points of the lock and was gratified that she listened so intently. After a few more practices, he thought she was ready to roll out. "Want to try the release now?"

She nodded.

"Remember, if you can't get out of it, tap out."

"I know, Nico. Geez."

"Okay. Here we go." He started to apply pressure, but she didn't even attempt to roll. He was about to pull up when he heard a snap. Then she screamed.

DONNI'S HEAD SWAM, and she thought she was going to be sick. The pain was sharp, explosive. Began in her knee and roiled over her body in agonizing waves.

What the hell had she been thinking? He told her to tap out, but she didn't listen. Curiosity—no, stubbornness—had won out. And look what she got for it.

She turned her head to retch, but her whole being was focused on her knee. There was no energy left for the nauseating flops in her stomach.

Donni heard Nico swearing as if she were separated from him through a long tunnel. She could vaguely make out indistinct chatter from her sisters and his brothers, too.

But none of that mattered. All that mattered was her knee. Her knee and the blooming torment radiating from it.

Someone grabbed her hand, but the contact, meant to comfort, barely registered. My God, had she crippled herself? Would she ever walk again? Didn't feel like it.

It took every ounce of energy she had left to try and focus. She knew on the cellular level, without looking or listening, that her twin held her hand. Donni concentrated on that touch, on that one act of kindness and compassion.

The pain didn't lessen, but soon other sounds grew clearer. The guys shouting instructions, more like shouting at each other. Franki grabbed her free hand and crooned nonsense in her ear to try and soothe her.

The pain didn't recede, but her focus sharpened. The room came into focus, the voices intelligible and clear.

She took a deep breath. "I've got it under control now. Can someone help me out of here? Bring a car out front. I need a hospital."

Everyone stopped talking. The silence grew almost deafening. Then something... unexpected happened. The pain began to ebb. She felt fluid sloshing around in her leg, and something mending, reattaching, fusing together. Donni managed to open her eyes and look down at her leg. Purplish bruising faded away even as the swelling reduced to nothing.

The pain was gone, a strange ghost of an ache the only reminder of her injury.

She sat up, bent the joint.

"Be careful!" Toni said.

"It's okay. I'm okay. I'm fine, actually."

Vinnie and Jo rushed into the room.

"Don!" Jo ran over to her.

"What happened?" Vinnie asked.

Coz sighed and walked over to Vinnie, probably filling him in. Nico flopped down to his back on the mat, and Gianni patted Donni's leg then walked over to Franki, who buried her head in his chest and wrapped her arms around him.

"What do you mean he introduced heel locks?" Vinnie yelled and stormed into the room, headed straight for Gianni.

"They'd been doing so well," he said. "I thought they were ready."

"You should have talked to me first."

"I'm in charge here."

"And I have the power of strategy." Vinnie waved his marble dagger in Gianni's face. "I could have told you not to."

"We told him that," Coz said. "We didn't need powers to know it was a bad idea."

"What were you thinking? After the shit Nico pulled earlier? He's not in the right headspace to do something like that."

"I can hear you," Nico said. "Don't talk about me like I'm not here."

"Well, you sure as hell haven't been here mentally lately," Vinnie yelled. "You might as well not be here at all. Probably be better if—"

"Excuse me." Donni's voice was soft in comparison to all the yelling the guys were engaged in, yet it seemed to echo in the room. Everyone stopped and looked at her. "It wasn't Gianni's fault. Or Nico's. It was mine."

"Yours?" Coz said. "You weren't the one bending your leg the wrong way."

"No, I was the one who was told to tap out but refused to. I thought I had more flexibility than that."

Nico didn't sit up, but he turned his head to look at her. "I told you—"

"I know you did. But there was no way I was ever going to roll you out of the lock, so I wanted to know if I could just withstand the pressure."

This time he did sit. And looked a little green in the process. "Donni, there's a reason we were so careful. This... this... I don't even know what to say to you right now."

"I know. I told you, I'm sorry. I should have listened. I just didn't think—"

"No, you didn't think," Vinnie said. "You were damn lucky G and Nico were here. What if one of them had come after me? They wouldn't have been here to heal you. Doctors can't fix that with crutches and a brace. You'd have needed surgery and months of rehab."

"Well, if you weren't always storming off and brooding somewhere, you would have been here to stop Gianni and none of this would have ever happened, anyway."

"Don," Jo whispered.

Vinnie slowly blew out a pent-up breath and strode over to her. "Well, I'm here now, and you don't seem too fucking happy about it."

Jo put her hand on his arm, but he shrugged it off.

"Tell you what." His voice was low, menacing. "Since you don't want me here, I'm going to storm off and brood somewhere. If no one cares what I have to say and you're going to hate what I do regardless, I might as well spend my time however I fucking want." He turned and left, slamming the door behind him.

Donni cringed at the reverberation. "I didn't mean it. I never should have said that. I'll go apologize."

"No," Jo said. "Just give him some space. You okay?"

"Fine. Better than usual, even."

"Good. That's good." But Jo's voice was trailing off, and her attention was directed toward the door. She patted Donni's knee and left the room.

"You sure you're okay?" Toni asked.

"Fine. Just want to sit here for a minute."

Toni stared into her eyes, then she stood. "Come on, guys. Let's go." Everyone but Nico and Donni filed out of the room behind her.

"Are you mad at me?" Donni said.

Nico was again on his back, eyes closed, dagger in his hand at his side. "No. I'm mad at myself."

"It was my fault."

"I should have known better. You were asking all those questions, I should have known you weren't going to tap."

"Yours isn't the power of foresight. That's Vinnie."

"He doesn't have foresight. It's just strategy. And it's a good thing that's not my power, or you really would have been screwed."

"See? It's all good in the end."

He turned to look at her. His face still had a greenish hue. Then he turned his head away again.

"Are you okay? You don't look well."

"Just a little drained. I'll be okay in a bit."

"Still struggling with your powers?"

"Well, as you've already noted, I haven't been sleeping much. And we'd been working out for a while. You can hardly expect me to have one hundred percent healing power when I'm not one hundred percent energy-wise."

"I'm sorry I put you in that position. It won't happen again." She moved over beside him, took his hand, and pushed his hair back from his forehead.

"You scared me." His voice was soft, low.

"You scare me all the time."

His eyelids fluttered open, and he turned to look at her. "What? Why? I'm your protector. It's my job to make you feel safe."

She shook her head. "I can't help it. Lately, I've been off balance around you. I worry when you aren't around, and when you are, I..."

"You what?"

"I can't stop thinking about you."

He stared at her, unblinking, expression unreadable.

She'd already made about a hundred mistakes that day. What was one more? She bent down and pressed her lips to his. Just a feather-light contact, a small gesture of good will to heal the tension between them. It was supposed to be an I'm-sorry kiss. Or maybe an it'll-all-be-okay kiss.

It wasn't supposed to be a life-altering kiss.

Her eyelids popped open, and she stared into the hazel depths of his eyes, lost in the calming greens and tranquil golds that should have cooled her ardor but rather fueled the fire.

Nico shook his head slightly and whispered, "*Merda.*" Then he reached behind her and pulled her down to him. When she gasped, he slipped his tongue inside her mouth, and when she moaned, he deepened his exploration.

Banked fires ignited inside her, threatened to consume her. His fingers tangled in her hair, tingling her scalp. He trailed his hand down her spine, electric charges sparking everywhere he touched. His fingers kneaded her backside, and desire exploded inside her.

She needed more. Much more.

Donnie lifted her head, chilled by the sudden break of contact. Then she flung her leg over to sit astride him, felt his longing as big and hot as hers was. She leaned down to resume the kiss, but a twinge in her knee made her pull up.

Nico's expression changed, hardened. Talk about a chill. He looked positively frigid.

She ran her finger across his lower lip. "What's wrong?"

"Your knee. It's still bothering you."

"It's fine." She again bent down, but he lifted her off him and sat up. "Nico, what—"

"This isn't right." Instead of making eye contact, he stared at the dagger he'd dropped on the floor beside them.

"I thought it was more than right."

He closed his eyes and took a deep breath. "Donni."

"Don't, okay? Just don't. I know when I'm not wanted."

"It's not that."

"Well, it really doesn't matter what it is, does it? Because it's over." She clambered to her feet and headed for the door, crushed that he didn't stop her. When she looked back, he was staring at his weapon instead of staring after her. Something broke inside her.

When she said "it's over," she had meant the kiss. But now she wondered if she meant something more, instead.

5

NICO LAY ON his back and stared at the ceiling. He was still a bit depleted from healing Donni's injury, but more to the point, he just didn't want to face anyone yet. Especially not her.

He was an honest guy, despite Coz catching him in a few lies as of late. As such, it wasn't hard for him to be honest with himself.

He'd been thinking about kissing Donni for a while now.

There, he admitted it, even if he didn't say the words aloud. Though he was alone and silent, he looked around the gym to see if anyone noticed.

And sighed in relief that his secret was safe.

The problem wasn't admitting his feelings. That was easy. Mostly. The problem was knowing whether they were real.

He glared at his dagger. The lustrous green marble made the lethal weapon beautiful. But was it also emotionally deadly?

Every time things with Donni advanced, he'd realize he was holding the dagger. Or if the damn thing wasn't in his hand at those moments, he was wearing it in its scabbard. They weren't supposed to go anywhere without their weapon.

The magical, alchemically-created, power-inducing dagger. The same compulsion that had drawn Gianni and Franki together. And Vinnie and Jo.

And look what was happening to those two.

How was Nico supposed to trust his feelings when it seemed they were being manipulated by supernatural forces beyond his control? Gianni and Vinnie hadn't come into their powers fully until they fell in love. And now Vinnie and Jo were having problems and Vinnie's powers were faltering.

Maybe it was all one big cosmic joke.

He sat up, expecting the room to spin. Instead, it was still, heavy, oppressive.

Nico wanted answers. And he wasn't going to get them by hiding in the training room. He'd do what he did best—research.

He needed to go to the Brotherhood's secret chamber.

NICO RAN UP to his room to shower and change. When he was done, he felt refreshed. His head was still bothering him, though, so he took out his contacts and put on his glasses. Felt better already. Then he slipped out of his room and listened for any activity. The house was quiet. Perfect. He headed for the basement.

He took care that he wasn't followed or heard entering chamber. Unless Mike was supernaturally spying on him, he made it without detection. He turned on the lights and closed the door behind him.

This room was bigger than the chamber in the Pennsylvania house. Bigger than the New York house, too. Which only made sense, as Italy was originally their central base of operations.

He took a second and inhaled deeply. Something about the scent of old books and ancient parchment soothed him, and he stood there, taking it all in and calming his mind.

Despite the room having been updated decades ago with electricity, beeswax candles still stood on iron stands, drip-trails cascading down them, the aroma of honey faint in the air like the walls themselves had absorbed it.

A giant chandelier dangled above a pentagon-shaped wooden table adorned with an inlaid marble star, each point composed of a different color marble—

red for Gianni, white for Vinnie, green for him, black for Coz, and gold for Mike. Well, for the daggers each wielded. Throughout the centuries, different men took their places at the table. Nico imagined in another generation there would be a new set of warriors corresponding to those places.

Leather chairs clustered around small tables near the bookshelves, which stretched floor to ceiling along three walls. On one table in the corner stood a glass-enclosed pedestal. That's what he was interested in, why he had come to chamber to begin with. It held the prophecy Michelangelo had written about the Medici line. Ultimately about the Notaro sisters. He approached the case and read the verses to himself.

In the twilight hours, starshine glows
as merely tiny embers in the black
Its magnificence to only grow brighter
while the midnight hour forces daylight back

And though the starlight twinkles on in ink
Its purpose not to shine but just to guide
The branches of the tree will bloom new buds
Growing evermore o're the divide

As long as just one leaf in bud or bloom
On the boughs continues not to fade
Starlight will shine in watch over the branch
And guard the new green, always at its aid

The light divines the stones to always shield
And not until the end their duty yield.

Damn prophecy, anyway. Mike had all kinds of theories about what it meant. Hell, he'd been so persuasive, Nico had not only bought into it, he'd provided some theories of his own.

Time passes—*the final battle approaches.*

New buds—*four daughters instead of one son.*

Just one bud or bloom—*even one Medici survivor.*

Guard the new green—*warriors to protect the daughters.*

Not until the end—*the Brotherhood and Medici descendants' lives will always intertwine.*

That's what he was searching for. Proof that the Brothers and the Notaros were preordained to be together. What did that mean, though? Did it merely mean that the Brotherhood would protect the girls, or—and this is what concerned him—did it mean they needed to be together romantically for the powers to fully manifest?

Nico looked at the bookshelves and pulled down several old tomes. He was looking for more of Michelangelo's sonnets, trying to see if, like Nostradamus, the verses were all prophecy. If they were, then perhaps he'd be able to tell if the dagger was influencing his emotions.

He bent over the books, pushed his glasses up, and pored over the pages.

"Ah-hem."

Nico jumped. He was so engrossed in his research that he ignored all else in the room, and consequently missed Mike teleport in. Not that he would have had advance warning to prepare, anyway.

"You've got to stop doing that."

"Would you prefer I project outside the door and knock?"

Like that would ever happen. "What do you want, Mike?"

"I think the more appropriate question is, what do you want, Dominico?"

He sighed. "If you're here, you already know what I want."

"You will not find the answers you seek here."

"Then where will I find them?"

Mike walked over to the case holding the prophecy. His finger moved over the glass like he pointed at the words as he read them to himself. "Michelangelo agonized over writing this. He feared providing even a small amount of future foreshadowing might alter the way the descendants or the Brothers reacted to their situations. Or to each other."

"If he was so worried, why'd he write it?"

"Because it was truth."

"Okay. Why'd he share it, then? He didn't have to."

"He wanted his warriors armed with as much information as possible." He walked over to one of the bookshelves and analyzed its contents. "It is difficult to fight a battle partially blind."

"Then maybe he shouldn't have been so cryptic."

Mike turned and stared at Nico. "Do you believe there are alternative interpretations to this prediction?"

Nico ran his hand through his hair. "I don't know what I believe. That's why I'm down here. Researching."

"I thought you preferred to do your research online."

"Kind of hard to find handwritten obscure documents written by secret and not-so-secret alchemists on the web."

Mike took a nondescript book off the shelf and flipped through it. "*Capo* has told you everything you need to know. He has provided you with powerful weapons, armed you with the latest technologies and the oldest wisdom the world has to offer. What more can you search for?"

"I want to meet him. Face to face."

"You know he does not allow anyone but me to—"

"Yeah, yeah. Wielder of the gold dagger. Blah, blah, blah. We've been following him blindly since we were brought into the Protectorate. More carefully since becoming Brothers. If this prophecy is really about us—and I still don't understand how he even has the power to see the future—then he owes it to us to talk to us about it."

"He owes you?" He threw the book on the table. "Has he not seen to you and your brothers' every need since you were a boy? Rescued you from the orphanage? Seen to your placement with me?"

"Are you telling me you would have let your son, your own flesh and blood, rot in the orphanage if Michelangelo hadn't let you take him and the rest of us out of there?"

Mike's face darkened, his expression hardened. "How dare you question my love for my biological son? Or any of my adopted ones? What gives you the right to speculate on my feelings or my intent?"

"The fact that I *am* one of your adopted sons. You just told me you only took us on because Michelangelo told you to. Talk about feeling unwanted and unloved."

"I said no such thing, Dominico. And I will not tolerate this insubordination."

"What are you going to do? Boot me out of the Brotherhood? Not if you believe in this prophecy nonsense. You need me. Seems like the guys and I have the upper hand now. And I want to meet Michelangelo, or I'm not doing this anymore."

"You will walk away from the sisters, who need you now more than ever? If you can do that, you are not the man I raised."

"You didn't raise me. Our mentors did."

"And who do you think was responsible for that?"

"What do you want? A 'Father of the Year' medal? You were hands-off. We were a burden you were saddled with and you passed us on to your underlings to deal with. No wonder Vinnie wants nothing to do with you. You care more about your precious *Capo* and his whims than you do about your own flesh and blood."

Mike opened his mouth, closed it again, and teleported out of the room.

"Damn you!" Nico yelled. He didn't know if Mike was still listening even though he was no longer visible, but it felt good to yell at him regardless.

He dropped into the chair and looked over the pages he'd been studying before Mike ghosted in. Nothing useful. He started gathering them up to put them away, and he saw the book Mike had tossed onto the table. Figured. More of Mike's messes to clean up.

The book's leather cover was scarred and stained with faded paint splatters. What would such a ratty old thing be doing with the priceless collection Michelangelo had saved for centuries?

He opened the cover, the spine protesting with a quiet squeak. In faded but familiar handwriting were the words, *Il Giornale di Michelangelo di Lodovico Buonarroti Simoni.*

Mike had given him Michelangelo's journal.

DONNI SPENT THE afternoon looking at interior design magazines and making notes for the new Protectorate headquarters they were building. Or she tried to. Her efforts were halfhearted at best.

She couldn't get her mind off Nico.

Off the kiss.

Off what more it might have led to.

And then, of course, his rejection of her advances. Certainly couldn't get that off her mind.

Her thoughts drifted back to the first time she'd met Nico, back before she knew anything about her heritage or the prophecy or the Protectorate. Franki and Gianni had started seeing each other, or were thinking about it, anyway. The four brothers came to the house, presumably to discuss NBD building their new headquarters. Franki had only had eyes for Gianni, but Donni was more objective and could see all of them were handsome.

Nico, though, especially caught her eye.

She always had a thing for blonds, even the dark blonds. And his body was the definition of what a warrior should be—hard, huge, chiseled. Drool-worthy. But despite his being a physical specimen the gods would be jealous of, he was a little less rough around the edges than his brothers. Had an air of intelligence about him, not that his brothers weren't smart. But unlike them, he wore it on the outside, too. That was what really attracted her to him.

The first time she saw him in glasses, she nearly swooned.

But all too quickly she learned her heritage—the Notaros were the secret descendants of the Medici line, and some organization was out to control them or destroy them. The Brotherhood had been guarding her family for centuries, and these four men were the latest in a long line of warriors tasked with protecting their legacy. Protecting them. How could she possibly entertain a relationship with a man who was assigned to her? The mere thought of it felt tawdry.

But Franki and Gianni fell in love. And then Jo and Vinnie. Perhaps it was possible, after all.

Except by the time her sisters had paired up with the Brothers, she and Nico were friends. Training partners. Business associates. It would be too hard to blur those relationship lines. And he had never shown her anything other than a friendly interest and a professional concern.

So why did she feel like he had wanted the kiss as much as she had?

And why was it so easy for him to dismiss it afterward?

God, it was all so humiliating.

She didn't want to talk to anyone, but she didn't want to be alone, either. What she wanted was to get drunk and put it all out of her mind.

No, what she wanted was Nico, but that was a no-go. Getting drunk would be her consolation prize.

Donni tossed aside her magazine and headed for the door. When she opened it, Toni stood there, a frosted bottle of limoncello in one hand and two aperitif glasses in the other. Sometimes she really appreciated the twin-bond.

"Thought you might want to take the edge off."

"What edge?" She only had about thirty raw edges at the moment. Who knew which one her twin had picked up on.

"Your knee."

Right. Donni had forgotten all about that.

"Let me in. My hand's freezing."

Donni opened the door farther, and her sister slipped inside.

"So, how's it feel?" She poured them each a glass and plopped down on the bed with a sigh.

"How's what feel?"

Toni's brow furrowed. "I meant your leg, but clearly something else is on your mind."

"No." Donni took a sip, the yellow liquid sweet and cold on her tongue.

"I've got a whole bottle and nothing but time." Toni poured herself a second glass. "Talk to me."

If anyone would understand, it would be her twin. She shrugged and dove in. "Just between the two of us, right? I don't want this getting back to Franki or Jo. Or any of the guys."

"I can't believe you even have to ask me that." Toni refilled Donni's glass and leaned against the headboard.

"Nico and I kissed."

Toni's eyes widened, and she covered her expression by lifting her glass to her lips.

"Say something."

"I need more information."

"Me, too." Donni rose and paced at the foot of her bed. Her knee felt great. Her stomach, not so much.

"What happened?"

"Nico and I were—*are*—just friends. I mean, I've thought he was cute since I met him—"

"He's hot."

Donni scowled at her twin. "But I never entertained us being anything other than friends."

"Why not? These guys are the stuff fantasies were made for."

"Two of the men you're talking about are your sisters' boyfriends."

"I didn't say I was fantasizing about them. I just said they're fantasy material."

Donni sighed and threw herself down on the mattress.

"Was it good?" Toni asked.

"What? My fantasy?"

"So you *did* have a fantasy about Nico."

Her cheeks burned. "What? No! You were just talking about fantasies, so I thought that's what you meant."

"Uh-huh." Toni sipped on her third glass of limoncello. "I was talking about the kiss. Which likely prompted a fantasy or two. But I'll drop the subject for now. What's the problem?"

"Have you not been listening? We kissed!"

"Is it a crime now or something? You should tell Franki and Jo."

Donni sat up and grabbed her drink. The cheery color mocked her foul mood, and she drained the glass. "You don't get it."

"So explain."

"I kissed him."

"You harlot. Better go to confession."

"Toni—"

"Look, I don't see the problem. These days women can make the first move and no one thinks less of them for it."

"I know that. That's not the point."

"Then what is?"

"He rejected me, okay?" She got up and paced again, unable to meet her sister's gaze. "He put the brakes on. Now I'm embarrassed and humiliated and mortified and… well, it's just demoralizing."

"Those all mean the same thing."

"It bore repeating."

"Don, listen."

She managed to look at her sister.

"There are a thousand reasons why Nico slowed things down."

"Stopped them cold."

"Maybe he was still upset about your knee. Vinnie is going to bring the wrath of God down on him for you getting hurt."

"It wasn't his fault."

"Doesn't matter. They're already fighting about something. This will just fuel the fire. He's probably trying to keep you away from the fallout."

"I think it's much more likely that he doesn't feel the same way about me."

"I think your timing is just off. How long have you felt this way, anyhow?"

"I don't know. I mean, I told you, there was an instant attraction when I first saw him. That didn't go away. Even when things became more professional, then more friendly, I still felt that pull."

"You need to talk to him."

"And say what? 'Why don't you like me?' I'd die first."

Toni downed her fourth glass and rose. She wobbled a little.

"You're drunk."

"I'm tipsy. I didn't eat today."

"I made a huge breakfast. There had to be leftovers for lunch."

"I was just going to have a protein shake, but I never got around to it."

"Let's go get something in your stomach to absorb all that liquor."

"I have a better idea."

"Why do I get the feeling it's not better?"

"Come with me." She stumbled toward the door.

Donni shrugged and followed her down the hall.

DONNI CRINGED WHEN Toni flung Franki and Gianni's bedroom door open without knocking first. God only knew what private moment they'd be barging in on. Thank God her sister was alone in the room.

"Don't you knock anymore?" Franki said.

"We never knocked at home," Toni answered.

"I didn't share a room with a guy when we lived at home."

"You should lock your door if you're doing something indecent."

"What we do isn't indecent. And he's not in here now, anyway."

"Then why are you freaking out because I opened your door?"

"Are you drunk?" Franki looked past Toni to Donni. "Is she drunk? She's slurring her words."

"I think she considers herself pleasantly tipsy."

"Sit before you fall down." Franki pointed at her bed, and Toni wobbled over to it. "So, what do you guys want?"

Donni shrugged. "This was her idea."

"Toni? I've got stuff to do. What do you need?"

"Where's the mirror?"

Franki pointed at her wall and rolled her eyes. "Above the dresser, where it's always been. There's a full-length one in the bathroom, too. But don't you have a mirror in your room?"

"Not a mirror. The mirror."

Donni's stomach flopped like she'd been the one overindulging in liquor.

"Oh." Franki was quiet for a moment, then she turned to her dresser. After rummaging in the top drawer, she retrieved a scarf-wrapped bundle. Handling it gently, she offered it to Toni.

"Huh-uh." She pointed at her twin.

Franki held it out to Donni.

"Nope. Not touching it."

"You want answers, Don," Toni said, "and you won't talk to Nico. That mirror is where you'll find them."

Franki looked at Donni. "What's this about you and Nico?"

"They're having a will-they/won't-they crisis."

Donni sighed and rolled her eyes. So much for Toni's promise to keep things a secret.

"Well, by all means, open that puppy up and let's see your future." She shoved the mirror into Donni's hands.

The occult mirror of Catherine de' Medici. Growing up, Donni hadn't even heard of it. When they met the Brothers, the guys told the tale of the fortune-telling properties it possessed. Her mother and Franki had both had visions from it, and yet Donni had only half-believed in its powers. But when Jo also saw the future, Donni was convinced.

And frightened.

No one should know too much about her future. Franki walked right into the trap her vision foretold. Was that because she'd been guided to it? Did the visions simply result in a self-fulfilling prophecy?

God, she was sick of prophecies.

Jo, though, had been able to change the details of her vision and alter the outcome. So was the future not set? Did one's reaction to the vision determine its validity? Honestly, she really didn't want to find out.

Donni held the mirror gingerly, careful to only touch the smallest portion of it, and only with the scarf as a buffer. She extended her arms back toward Franki and shook her head. "No. You take it."

But Franki backed away. "What answers are you looking for?"

"At the moment, I'd settle for a way out of this room without any more questions or using the mirror."

"Well, I think we both know that's not going to happen."

Donni grasped the mirror more carefully and sat down on the bed. "You know you can't just ask it a question and see your answer. You and Jo didn't ask it anything, and you both got visions."

"But maybe you can guide the vision if you have a specific question in mind before you look into it."

"I really don't want to."

"I really don't care," Franki said.

"Me, either." Toni hiccuped.

"Fine." She snatched the scarf off the mirror. "It's not going to work, so it doesn't matter, anyway."

"Remember." Franki reached over and stopped her from raising the looking glass in front of her face. "You have to think of a question first. Focus on what's troubling you."

Donni would have done a spit take if she'd had anything in her mouth. "On what's troubling me? It would take the better part of the day to get even halfway through that list."

"Just focus." Franki squeezed her hand. "Focus. Focus."

She yanked her hand away. "Stop chanting. You aren't a meditation guru."

Franki and Toni leaned forward and stared at her.

That wasn't unnerving at *all*.

Okay. Focus. On Nico.

She lifted the mirror. Prayed nothing would happen. She looked at her reflection. A little pale, hair a little mussed. But nothing happened. Thank God. After Jo and Franki had scared her about what she'd see, after her mother told her—

The mirror fogged, rippled.

Fuck.

But she couldn't pull out of it, couldn't drop the mirror, couldn't look away. It was dark. Cold. Dank.

An earthy smell, the sounds of rattling chains.

Where was she? A dungeon? Somewhere deep below the earth, no sunlight, no fresh air. Her wrists were restrained by cold, rough metal. Shackles.

A man stood in the shadows, watching her. Laughing. He held a blue marble dagger and pointed it at the person imprisoned in the cell beside hers.

"Please." A woman's weak voice came from the other side of the wall. "Not my daughter."

Mama!

"A life for a life." Then he turned and left, his footsteps echoing throughout the chamber.

Someone approached her mother's door.

"Don't! No!" Donni pleaded.

A key clanged in the lock, then her mother screamed.

Fog rolled in, and Donni was once again sitting on Franki's bed.

"What'd you see?" Toni asked.

"You looked distressed," Franki said. "What happened? Things not work out between the two of you?"

Tears welled in Donni's eyes, and she brushed them away with the back of her hand.

"Oh, sweetie." Toni leaned toward her and reached for her hand. "It'll be okay. We're here for you."

"Nico doesn't know what he's missing," Franki said. "Want me to have Gianni talk to him for you?"

They had no idea what Donni had seen. It was so much worse than unrequited love. What she needed was advice—not from her family who would overreact, not from the Brothers, who would probably lock her in a tower somewhere.

"I—I have something I have to take care of. And no, don't talk to Gianni, or anybody, about this." She jumped to her feet and bolted out of the room.

WHEN DONNI WAS alone in her room, she closed and locked the door. A few slow, deep breaths didn't do much to calm her racing thoughts, but they did slow her racing heart. She plopped on her bed and grabbed her phone.

"Ciao."

"Teresa?" Just hearing Vinnie's mother settled her nerves. "It's Donni. Do you have a moment to talk?"

"Donni. Hello, dear. How are you?"

"Something's happened."

"Vinnie?" The panic in Teresa's voice punched Donni in the gut.

"Sorry, no. No, he's fine. We're all fine. For now. I... I'm... I've..." She couldn't find the words.

"It's okay, honey. Take a deep breath and tell me what's wrong."

Donni inhaled deeply and pursed her lips, breathing out a slow and steady stream of air. She closed her eyes and lay on her back on the bed. "I need advice."

"Go ahead."

Just having a mother—even if it wasn't *her* mother—listen made Donni feel safer. Protected. "You know about the mirror and the visions, right?"

"I do."

"I had one."

Teresa was silent for a moment. *"Tell me everything."*

Donni poured her heart out. She revealed every detail of the prophetic daydream, the words pouring from her, fast and turbulent as a waterfall. When she'd finished, she wiped a few tears from her face and waited.

"Oh, sweetie. I wish I was there to wrap you in a hug. Are you all right?"

"I'm terrified. We've already been through an abduction. I can't handle another. And Mama's not recovered from the last one!"

"What can I do?"

"If I tell my sisters, they'll insist I tell the Brotherhood."

"I think you have to."

"But they'll lock us in here like prisoners. Our freedom is severely compromised as it is."

"Doesn't that beat the alternative?"

Donni sighed. "But remember what happened with Jo."

"She nearly died."

"Yeah, but she also changed the vision. Changed her destiny. Either that, or the visions aren't prophetic to begin with."

"So you want to change your destiny?"

"Do you think I can?"

Teresa muttered a few phrases in Italian that Donni didn't understand.

"What was that?"

"Yes, of course I think you can affect the outcome. You have free will. The future isn't set."

"Great."

"But Donni, you need to tell the boys. Tell Vinnie. Give him a chance to plan for this, to work on a strategy to avoid it. He's your best chance at avoiding your fate."

"You're right." Well, she was *probably* right. Maybe. "I just need a day or two to wrap my head around this."

"Don't take too long, Donni. You don't know when that's supposed to happen. Any delay can cost you a chance to change your fate."

"I won't. I promise. But you'll keep my secret, right?"

The silence at the other end of the phone seemed to go on forever. Finally, Teresa said, *"For now. But if you don't tell someone soon, I will."*

"Thanks, Teresa. I'd hug you if you were here. You've been a big help."

"Soon, Donni. I mean it."

"Gotta run, now. Thanks again. Bye." She ended the call before Teresa could continue the lecture.

She didn't have to tell anyone. Not yet, anyway. Jo had changed her fate, there was no reason Donni couldn't change hers.

6

NICO HAD REPLACED all the books on the shelves but the journal. That he had taken up to his room. There he spent hours transcribing the text to English in a word processor app, making notes in the margins where something struck him as important. He figured the girls would want to read the entries, and their Italian wasn't very strong, so the transcription was necessary.

Rewriting *Capo's* thoughts also helped him make sense of his own.

The journal was about an inch thick, and it was filled cover to cover with entries. The first thing Nico noticed was that he hadn't written every day. He would have needed hundreds of journals if he had. More to the point, the entries he bothered to make had to be important or significant in some way if they were the days he chose to record. The second thing that struck him was that the last entry was the day the four of them were initiated into the Brotherhood. And it wasn't written from the perspective of a man who had been told about these events. It was a first-hand account.

That meant Michelangelo wasn't always sequestered. He'd been to the compound. Recently. And secretly.

Scanning through some of the entries near the back of the journal, Nico saw that he'd also been to New York and Pennsylvania.

So was Mike lying all this time about where *Capo* was and who was allowed contact with him? Or maybe Michelangelo was only avoiding the four of them and had actually interacted personally with the warriors who came before. But if so, why?

Nico took off his glasses and rubbed his eyes. Then he rolled his shoulders and stretched the kinks in his neck. Next he cracked his knuckles, flexed his fingers, and shook them out. Nothing relieved the tension in his body.

He'd been at it for hours. Made decent progress, though. After a brief glance through the whole book, he'd begun transcribing at the beginning and was up to the 1700s.

Being immortal certainly gave Michelangelo a unique perspective on life. But so far, Nico hadn't found much to indicate whether the prophecy was true or how it could be interpreted. No, the entries in the journal focused more on the Medici line, what the warriors had to do to guard them—which truth be told, was precious little compared to what he and his brothers were dealing with—and what the socio-economic and political climates were like.

When a guy lived forever, a dip in the economy wouldn't tend to affect him much, would it?

Two sharp raps sounded on his door.

"Who is it?"

Vinnie stepped in and walked over to the window. He lowered himself to lean on the sill and looked at his brother. "We need to talk."

Nico sighed. He wasn't looking forward to it, but there was tension between them that needed resolving. Didn't have to be right that second, though. "By all means, come in."

Vinnie glared at him. "Smartass. I'll let that one go. We have bigger issues than your attitude."

"You're here for a reason. Spill it."

"In the yard today. The tree trunk you hit split in two. I didn't even know you had that much power."

"Well, you and Gianni have come fully into your powers since hooking up with Jo and Franki. That put me at a disadvantage. So I've been practicing."

"When? You're always busy with something at MDH or here. When are you working with your dagger?"

"When I can't sleep."

"I hear that's pretty often these days."

"You come in here to discuss my insomnia? Don't sweat it, man. I'll buy some melatonin."

"That's not why I'm here."

"Well, I know it's not because my powers are growing, either. So get to what you really want to say."

"I'm concerned about your powers. I've tried to see what's going on, but I can't. All the strategies I've considered for helping you and Coz along have failed. I don't understand how your powers have grown. Unless you found a way to boost them. Unify with another energy. Are you and Donni—"

"That's none of your damn business."

"When it comes to the well-being of the Brotherhood or our charges, everything is my business."

Nico stood and stared him down. "Not that."

Vinnie pushed away from the window and stalked over to him, standing nose to nose. "I say it is."

Nico pushed him. "I say it's not."

Vinnie balled up a fist and swung at his jaw.

He saw it coming and bent back to avoid the strike. Then he countered with a palm strike to Vinnie's solar plexus.

Vinnie stumbled back, gasped for breath, then grinned. And he took a running leap at Nico.

They crashed to the floor, kicking and punching at each other through a tangle of arms and legs.

Coz burst through the door, Gianni right on his heels, and they began the arduous task of peeling the two off of each other.

Nico kept swinging and kicking even after Coz shoved him into the corner. Gianni held Vinnie on the opposite side of the room. All four of them panted for breath while continuing to struggle. Finally Nico lifted his hands in surrender and dropped to the floor. Coz plopped down beside him. Then Vinnie settled down, and he and Gianni sat at the foot of the bed.

"What the fuck is going on with you?" Gianni asked.

No one answered.

"Well?"

"Are you talking to me or him?" Nico said.

Gianni puffed his cheeks and released a slow breath. "At the moment, I'm talking to you."

"He started it." Nico nodded at Vinnie, who started to his feet.

Gianni pushed him back down. "Look, there's a lot of testosterone in this room, and that's bound to make for some heated debates. But we're brothers. We grew up together, work together, live together. We've always gotten past our differences. And now more than ever, it's important that we do."

"Has it occurred to you that we're having all this conflict because we don't get a break from each other?"

"Since when the hell did that become a problem? We've all been tight since childhood."

"Ask your strategist." Again Nico nodded at Vinnie. "On top of us always being together, we have the added stress of protecting the girls. That already changed our dynamic, then two of you paired off with your charges. You're looking for harmony like we had as kids, but we aren't kids anymore. And this isn't our childhood. The stakes are higher. A lot higher."

"You want to talk stakes?" Vinnie stood, walked to the window and back. "What about murder?"

"Are you talking you and Pasquale?" Nico said.

"Me and—" He ran his hand through his hair. "*Che cazzo!* Are you kidding me? How oblivious are you? I'm talking about you almost killing *my* father!"

Nico knew they'd have to talk about it, but he didn't want to do it then and he definitely didn't want to do it with an audience. He jumped to his feet, fists balled at his side. "First of all, he's *our* father. Biology or adoption, family is family. And since when do you care about Mike's well-being? You've been shutting him out since you found out he was your biological father. What happened by the targets was an accident. Mike knows it. You know it. Everyone knows it. You expect any of us to believe your reaction is a familial concern about him? That's bullshit. You freaked out because you killed Pasquale, and now you've got a bug up your ass about death and murder so you're taking it out on me."

Okay, he knew he was crossing a line as the words tumbled from his mouth. But he couldn't stop them. When Vinnie's face darkened and his jaw clenched, Nico braced for impact. When his brother took a swing—hell, if he took him to the ground and pummeled him bloody—he wouldn't react, wouldn't defend himself. He'd take what was coming to him, because what he'd done was lower than low.

But Vinnie didn't strike. Didn't even say a word. He crossed the room, stepped into the hallway, and closed the door quietly behind him.

"Fuck, Nic," Coz said. "That was cold."

"I didn't mean to come down so hard on him. But we all know killing Pasquale messed him up."

"Wwe weren't talking about him," Gianni said. "We were talking about you."

"I'll apologize."

"You're damn right you will. But not now. Give him some space."

"Fine. But someone has to do something about him. He's not in a good place in his head."

"Like I said, Nico. We weren't talking about him. We were talking about you and the fact that you're not in a good place right now, either. So why don't we focus on that?"

"I've got work to do right now."

"Don't we all?"

"Just go. Please. I'll find Vin later and make things right."

"And you?" Gianni said. "What can we do to get things right with you?"

"You can leave me alone."

He stood up, gestured to Coz to join him. "You might think you dodged a bullet here, but this conversation isn't over. If I didn't have to go talk to Jo about Vinnie, we'd get into it."

"Whatever."

Gianni sighed and rolled his eyes. "You're not twelve, Nico. Grow the fuck up."

"Whatever."

He glared at Nico and stormed out of the room.

Coz started after him, then turned back around. "You need to talk?"

"What?" That was the absolute last thing he expected to hear from his brother. Coz was the emotionally-distant one, and between the four of them, that was saying something.

"Look, I know you haven't been sleeping and you've been sneaking out. I told you that already. Between that, you and Vin butting heads, and whatever you have going on here," he nodded toward the journal and Nico's piles of notes, "I thought maybe you needed a sounding board."

"I'm tight, Coz. But thanks."

"You sure?"

"Yeah."

Coz shrugged. "Well, if you change your mind." He headed for the door then turned around before stepping into the hallway. "We're only as strong as our weakest member. Vinnie's already a mess. We can't afford to have you compromised, too."

"I'm good."

"Like you said, whatever." He walked out.

Nico chuckled. "Asshole."

But then he sobered. Coz was right. They couldn't afford to have more than one team member compromised. Hell, they couldn't afford to have even one member compromised.

That only made him all the more determined to get Mary back and get things on course again.

DONNI SPRINKLED SEASONING on the chicken wings she'd just taken out of the hot grease, then she dropped the next batch into the fryer. No one but Western Pennsylvania made seasoned wings—at least, not that she knew of—and they were a hell of a lot better than the kind drowning in sauce. Lower carb count, too. She didn't care to think about the calories, though.

They were over four thousand miles from home, and she wasn't going to get wings unless she made them herself. And she wanted bar food tonight. Needed it. There was something comforting about greasy, spicy wings dunked in blue cheese dressing that soothed the soul and eased emotions.

Until indigestion set in. And guilt.

But she didn't care. Every girl ate junk food when she had boy trouble. It was in the handbook—or would be if a handbook existed. Maybe she should write one and give it to all the men in her life. It might make things easier.

Gianni walked into the kitchen, took a deep breath, and sighed. "Mmm. Wings. They smell great. You need any help?"

"No. I already made the coleslaw. I just need to finish frying these, and we can eat."

"In that case, have you seen V? I want to talk to him before dinner."

"Check the gym. Jo came up from there a while ago looking more than a little irritated, so that's where I'd put my money."

He snatched a wing off the platter and took a bite. "These are better than the ones we got in Pittsburgh."

"Did you doubt my abilities?"

Gianni finished the wing and tossed the bone in the trash. "Never."

"Uh-huh. Go find your brother."

He grabbed a wing to go and left the room.

Donni sighed and put another batch of wings in the fryer. Poor Jo. She had her hands full with Vinnie. Wish there was something she could do to help them.

Jo walked into the kitchen, body drenched in sweat. She headed for the refrigerator, grabbed a water, and guzzled it.

"You look wiped out."

"Just had a long run."

"You're not supposed to go out alone."

"I stayed on the grounds. Ran through the hedge maze and around the grotto five times."

"That is a long run."

Jo shrugged.

"Trying to work something out?"

She shrugged again.

"You know," Donni lowered her voice, "you don't have to stay with him if things aren't working out."

Jo put the cap on her water bottle and tossed it in the recycling bin. "What kind of royal bitch would I be if I left at the first sign of trouble?"

"No one would blame you."

"I love him, Donni. That means taking the good with the bad."

"How much bad are you supposed to take?"

"You do realize that in a matter of days he reconnected with his biological mother, learned who his biological father was, and killed a man. While protecting me, I might add. All things considered, I think dealing with a grumpy temperament every now and then is a non-issue."

"Then why are you always crying?"

"I don't cry."

"Oh? Must just be your allergies, then, huh?"

"Don, I know you're just worried about me. And I appreciate that. But until you fall in love, you're in no position to offer me advice about my relationship."

"He's distracted, Jo. That's impacting his powers. Which could ultimately impact you."

"And me breaking up with him would make things all better."

"Isn't that just fucking wonderful?"

Jo looked up, startled. "Vinnie—"

His face looked chiseled out of rock—hard, impassive. He glared at her from the doorway, his arms crossed over his massive chest moving rapidly up and down as he nearly panted through his rage. "Save it, Jo. If you wanted out, all you had to do was say so." Then he strode through the kitchen and stormed out to the patio, the door slamming behind him.

"Vinnie!" She called after him, but he didn't acknowledge her. "Thanks a lot, Don." Jo chased after him.

"Damn it!" Donni had forgotten to watch the fryer and burned a batch of wings. When she took the basket out, acrid smoke wafted through the room. Perfect.

She set about cleaning up the kitchen as she pondered what happened. It might not be a bad idea to offer each of them an apology. Hopefully they would be at dinner and she could try to make things right.

Then she'd deal with Nico. She had some things to fix there, too. But that situation required a whole different course of action.

FOR THE FIRST time since they'd all been under the same roof, no one sat down to the evening meal.

Franki and Gianni took a picnic basket of some chicken, a container of coleslaw, and a few bottles of Peroni, and they ate their supper down in one of the grottos. Donni figured they were celebrating another of the plethora of anniversaries they marked. Probably the anniversary of the first time they ate wings together. It was kind of nauseating how lovey-dovey they were. But she smiled. Her sister was happy, and that was all that mattered.

Toni and Coz decided to visit the orphanage and check on Teresa and the kids. They said they'd eat when they got back if they didn't eat there. Teresa would never let them visit and not feed them, but the meal wouldn't be low carb, and Coz would make Toni exercise to burn off the extra calories. Then they'd both be hungry, so Donni set food aside for them.

Jo and Vinnie were nowhere to be found, so they didn't join Donni for dinner. Which meant Donni's apology would have to wait. Gosh, she hated having that hang over her head.

With everyone scattered, there was no reason to set the dining room table. She put two plates on the bar and figured she and Nico could have a casual dinner in the kitchen.

She also thought it would be a good chance to press him for details about what he was doing at night.

She grabbed two bottles of Peroni, then thought better of it and put the beer back in the refrigerator. Instead, she took two bottles of San Pellegrino—the blood orange was her favorite, and it wasn't easy to find in the States—and put them by the plates. She set a large platter of wings and the bowl of coleslaw on the bar, and she grabbed extra napkins.

Then she waited. And waited. And waited.

But Nico didn't show up for dinner. Nor did he check in with a reason why.

Donni sent him a text, but he didn't reply. And she saw red.

No way did she spend all evening in that kitchen over a hot fryer to have everyone blow off dinner. Especially him.

Okay, she wasn't going to explore why Nico's absence made her angry when she didn't really care about anyone else attending. The important thing was that she'd gone to a lot of trouble—well, it wasn't difficult at all, but rather therapeutic—and he wasn't there to appreciate it.

So she stormed up to his room and banged on the door.

"What now?" The door muffled his response, but Donni heard the aggravation in his tone.

Well, he wasn't the only one bent out of shape. She flung the door open and stepped inside.

"I didn't say come in," Nico said. "I said—" He turned around from his desk and stopped short when he saw her. "Sorry. I thought you were one of the guys."

"Do you know what time it is?"

He glanced around the room, then down at his bare wrist. "Um, no. Why?"

Donni's attitude softened. He looked exhausted—his hair was mussed, he wore only sweat shorts, and his glasses sat low on his nose. Probably because the black eye he sported hurt when the frames were pushed up into their regular spot on his face. Poor guy had a split lip, too. And on closer look, he had a nasty bruise on his ribs. Maybe it wasn't exhaustion. Maybe it was pain.

"What happened to you?"

"Huh?"

"The bruises. The cut lip."

He touched his mouth with the tip of his finger and winced. "Oh. That."

"Yeah. *That.* What happened?"

"I had a chat with Vinnie. No big deal."

"It is a big deal. Why are you fighting?"

A flush colored his cheeks, and he turned back to his desk. "I'll apologize. It'll be fine."

"Why didn't you find Gianni and have him heal your wounds?"

"Because I deserve them. Besides, Gianni's pissed at me, too."

"What'd you do?"

"Why are you here, Donni?" He still didn't turn around.

"Because it's dinner time."

"I'm not hungry."

"Well, that's too damn bad. I spent the last couple of hours in the kitchen, and you're the only one available for dinner."

"I'm not available."

"I'm not eating alone."

He turned around and met her gaze. "No one's here? Really?"

"It's safe. You won't have to eat crow. Just chicken wings."

"Wings sound good." He stood, stretched, and headed for the door.

"Uh, aren't you forgetting something?"

"What?"

"Your shirt?"

"Oh." He grabbed a t-shirt off the chair and slipped it over his head, pulling it down gently over his bruises.

She bit her lip as she watched him, riveted by the movement of contoured muscle. When she looked up, he raised an eyebrow and grinned at her.

Busted! Her cheeks flamed, and she turned to walk into the hall. She heard him following her, but she didn't turn around.

In the kitchen, she took her seat and began piling wings and coleslaw onto her plate.

Nico did the same. It didn't escape her attention that he was sitting very close to her. She felt the warmth of his skin on her legs and arms despite them not quite touching.

She opened her San Pellegrino and took a few deep pulls on the bottle. The cold, effervescent liquid did little to assuage the heat she felt. She took a bite of the slaw, then chanced a glance at Nico.

He already had a small pile of bones on his plate and was breaking another wing apart.

She hated that she had no effect on him when his mere closeness had her off-kilter. Time to put the pressure back on him.

"So, what were you working on up there?"

He wiped a napkin across his mouth, winced when he swiped the gash on his lip, and then swiveled in his seat to meet her gaze. "You mean at my desk?"

"No. In the attic. Yes, at your desk."

He dropped the napkin and took a drink. "I was doing research. What I wanted wouldn't be available online, so I went down to chamber to see if I could find any ancient books or scrolls."

"What were you looking for?"

Nico looked away, kind of mumbled when he finally answered. "Stuff about the prophecy."

"Well, you're right. You wouldn't find anything about that online. What about it, exactly? Can I help?"

"No!"

She recoiled a little at his outburst. It was unexpected and inexplicable.

"Sorry. I meant, no, I don't need help. I found something that should answer any questions any of us has."

"Yeah? What?"

"A journal. Written in Michelangelo's own hand. If he won't meet with us, then at least I can read his thoughts on things."

"His journal? Can I see it?"

"Sure, but it's in Italian. I've been transcribing it so you and your sisters will be able to read it."

"You find out anything interesting so far?"

"The whole thing is fascinating."

"Find the answers to your questions?"

Again he looked away. "Not exactly. But I'm going to keep investigating."

She put her hand on his arm, and he jumped off the stool. "Sorry. I didn't mean to startle you."

"I'm just tired. Makes me jumpy."

"What are you looking for in the journal?"

He stared at her a second too long. "I'll know it when I see it. Thanks for dinner, Don. It was good."

"You barely ate."

But he'd already dashed out of the room.

She'd had enough of his secrets. Tonight, she'd put her plan into action. She'd get to the bottom of things once and for all.

7

HE STOOD AT attention and met Sal's gaze. Hoped his knees weren't visibly knocking, but man, his legs were shaky.

He didn't expect a spot check that night. Of course, the unplanned nature of them was why they were so effective. And why his job—possibly his very life—was on the line. He'd grown complacent, too, and wasn't ready for inspection.

"You are the one in charge here, yes?"

"Yes, sir."

"Yet you've got the gate attendant sleeping on duty, and you're either unaware or unconcerned."

He was going to throttle that moron at the gate. "When I made my rounds last, he was alert."

"Sure he was."

He swallowed.

"Against my better judgment, I'm not going inside tonight. I'm in a hurry as it is, and I have a feeling I know what I'd find."

Yeah, he did, too, and it wasn't anything good.

"I'm going to give you a week to get this place in shape. The next time I drop in, I might just bring him with me. So you better get your shit together."

Relief and dread swirled together in his stomach, churned it until he almost vomited. It was a stroke of luck that Sal decided not to check inside. The staff in there was even lazier than the gate attendant. Sal would rain holy hell down on him if he saw what was going on in there.

But… him? God help them all if the big boss showed. Sal would be the least of his worries.

Sal walked away, and he headed inside. It was time he whipped them all into shape. Before it was too late.

NICO LEARNED HIS lesson from his previous excursions. He used to leave from the garage, and clearly Donni and Coz had heard him. This time, he wouldn't be caught. Earlier that evening, after Gianni was kind enough to heal his face, he'd made excuses about a headache and slipped away. Then he loaded his SUV with the equipment he'd need and pulled it down the road, hiding it from view. He spent the rest of the night alone in his room, waiting until he was certain everyone was asleep. Then he crept down the stairs and left the compound.

He looked behind him a few times to be sure he wasn't followed, but the villa remained dark and he didn't hear any footsteps on the road behind him. A sigh of relief escaped him when he slipped into his Levante S. It was a little slower than his sports car, but it was also quieter. Another lesson learned—his Gran Turismo was too loud.

"Let's see if I can't beat my time." And he took off.

The ride was uneventful. Winding roads were no match for his driving skills, even on the narrow paths in the darkness. The full moon made the route nearly as bright as daylight, which actually worried him. That meant he'd be more visible to the guards surrounding the home where he suspected Mary was being held.

Nothing he could do about that, though. He had a feeling they were running out of time, so he couldn't delay any longer.

He opened a classical music playlist. If he wasn't so nervous, it might have soothed him to sleep, but he was wired, so it merely calmed his nerves.

He made the rest of the drive in only ten minutes longer than his best time. Not bad for an SUV.

A quick scan of the area, and he headed off-road a bit to hide his vehicle near an entrance to a cave, where a few loose boulders and some extra-large foliage provided excellent coverage.

He got out of the car, walked to the back, and opened the hatch. He'd put his equipment in there but hadn't sorted it yet, and it took him a few minutes to get everything he wanted loaded into his backpack.

A wolf howled in the distance, answered by another. Once again, he wouldn't be the only one stalking through the woods.

He set about programming the drone. He'd fly that from his current position, so if the guards saw it, he'd be able to make a fast getaway.

A soft snick of a closing car door broke the quiet of the night. Adrenaline shot through him like lightning. He grabbed his dagger in one hand, his gun in the other, and jumped to his feet.

"Nico, it's me." Donni stepped into the faint light from the SUV's interior, hands raised.

"What the—I could have killed you! How'd you get here?"

"Wasn't it you who told us to always check our vehicle's interior for threats before getting inside? You should practice what you preach."

"You shouldn't be here."

"And you should put those down before someone gets hurt. Namely me."

He looked at the weapons in his hands, surprised he still pointed them in her direction. He quickly holstered the gun and sheathed the dagger as she lowered her hands. "Damn it, Donni. You shouldn't have stowed away. This is dangerous."

"What is? Where are we? What are we doing here? Why—"

Nico covered her mouth with his hand. "Ssh. You're going to get us both killed. Will you be quiet?"

She nodded behind his hand, eyes wide and bright. When she spoke again, she whispered. "Who's going to kill us?"

He sighed. "Get back in the car. I'll take you home."

"We were in the car for more than two hours. It would be crazy for you to just turn around and leave. I've been training. I can take care of myself. I'm ready for whatever this is." She looked around. "What is it?"

He shook his head. "You're not ready."

"Yes, I—"

"Fine. Then I'm not ready for you to be ready."

"It's not up to you."

"The hell it isn't. Get in the car."

She stomped her foot, crossed her arms over her chest, and held her chin high. "No."

"Donni." The word barely escaped his clenched teeth.

"Tell me what's going on, or I'm not going anywhere."

A wolf howled again, this time closer. Two howls answered, closer still.

"Well, for starters, there are the wolves."

"Wolves? Are you sure? Maybe they're just harmless coyotes."

"We don't have coyotes in Italy. They're wolves. And they're not harmless."

She gulped. "No?"

Okay, it was pretty shitty of him to try and scare her. "Well, usually the packs here only hunt chamois or deer. Sheep if they get close enough to a shepherd's unprotected livestock. Wolf packs are smaller here than in the States, so they don't usually go after bigger prey, like humans, unless they're provoked or for some reason form a larger pack."

"So we're safe?" She released a long, slow breath, and her body relaxed.

"I didn't say that. There are at least three around, based on the howls and what I saw last time. They're getting closer. And that doesn't even take the security guards into account."

"Guards? For wolves?"

"No, not for wolves. There's a facility I'm here to check out."

"Why? What's in there?"

"You're a pain in the ass sometimes. You know that?"

"What's in the facility, Dominico?"

She'd never called him that before. Guess he was in the dog house. "I don't know yet. That's why I'm looking into it."

"There are probably thousands of buildings in Italy that you don't know anything about. What makes this one so special?"

Should he tell her? He'd probably lose an hour arguing with her and end up telling her in the end, anyway. One more chance to dissuade her. "Tell you what. Let me send up the drone, see what I can find out, and if it's what I think it is, we'll discuss it."

She pursed her lips and studied him. "Fine. For now. Send it up."

He made a few last modifications on the drone, then he sent it toward the facility. Keeping it low to the trees helped him both camouflage it and search for wolves at the same time. Five, by his count. More than last time. And more than he wanted to deal with. But they seemed to have caught the scent of something appealing. They were moving away from his and Donni's location.

When the drone reached the tree line he had spied from before, he zoomed in on the windows and doors. One guard, one keypad at the door. The windows were all dark, so he couldn't see inside without getting up close to the building, which would give him away.

He guided the drone in a wide circle around the building. The front of the building was opposite of the area Nico approached from. There was a large parking lot there with a few cars in it. A guard manned the shack by the gate, probably did double duty as the gate monitor and security for the front door. Nico was just about to pull the drone back when the door opened. A man stepped out, his features undetectable in the shadows. He strode toward the guard shack, but his back was to the drone. After a brief and seemingly heated exchange, the man turned around and headed toward a car in the parking lot.

"Son of a—"

"What?" Donni stood on her toes and leaned over Nico to get a better view of the computer monitor.

"That's Sal. I'm sure of it."

"Sal, my dad's killer?"

"None other."

"Is this their headquarters?"

"No. It's too exposed and not guarded well enough." He pulled the drone back and directed it toward Sal's vehicle. If he could follow him and not be noticed, he could maybe put an end to their troubles once and for all.

"What are you doing? What's going on?"

"Give me a second."

"You promised you'd tell me."

He peered at her in the darkness, her face green in the glow of the computer screen. She was frightened, but she didn't back down. He had to give her props for that.

"Nico?"

"It's where I think they're keeping your mother."

"My *moth*— No. Mike has her."

"I don't think so. That's what I've been working on for the last month."

"Mike said he had her."

"That's right. He *had* her. Don't you think it's kind of weird that you've been in Italy all this time yet he still hasn't taken you to see her?" The drone captured Sal's vehicle turning onto the main road. He'd be driving right past them in ten minutes.

"He said he's worried about us being followed and putting her in danger."

"Yeah, we deal with the potential of being followed all the time. That's not it. They got to her. That's why Mike hasn't been around much. He's been looking for her, too."

"How do you know?"

"Get in the car."

"Nico, I want answers."

"And you'll get them. But right now, Sal is driving this way. We have to hide."

She pursed her lips, hesitated, then threw up her hands. She walked around to the front passenger door and climbed in.

Nico tossed all his equipment back in the car and followed her. He tapped on her window.

Donni opened the door. "What? Let's go!"

"You have to drive."

"I don't even know where I am!"

"Unless you can steer the drone, you have to drive."

"Damn it, Nico."

"Hurry up. He's either going to spot us, or we're going to miss him."

She climbed across the center console and settled into the driver's seat. He took the seat she just vacated.

"Where to?"

"Just head down the hill. We'll look for some kind of rock outcropping or makeshift clearing to hide in, then we can pull out after him and follow him."

Donni headed down the hill while Nico kept one eye on the road and the other on the computer monitor. The trees were beginning to thin. Pretty soon, they'd lose all cover. Another cave entrance would be perfect, but there didn't seem to be anything remotely like it this far down the slope. If they didn't find shelter soon, they'd have to abort or be caught.

He took his focus off the screen, desperate to find any place to hide. Fifty yards ahead of them, wolves darted out of the foliage and dashed across their path. Donni slammed on the brakes, and the car vibrated, fishtailed on loose rubble and cinders, and slid dangerously close to a drop off on the other side of the road.

She fought for control and managed to skid to a stop at the berm, mere feet from plummeting to their deaths.

"Did we blow a tire?" Her voice trembled.

Nico's eyes widened and he pointed out the windshield. "No. Look!"

A boulder and a few smaller stones rolled onto the road right where the wolves had been. The giant rock smashed into a tree and stayed where it landed.

"Earthquake?" she asked.

"No. I don't think so. Just a rockslide."

"Just. Right. We were lucky. We barely missed it."

"We're very lucky. We can hide behind that boulder."

"Won't the ground there be compromised? Or drop off like it does here?"

"No. Where the slide started, the ground will be weak, but not there where the boulder ended up. And the ground is wider there, so we shouldn't have to worry about going over the edge."

Donni sat there, a white-knuckled grip on the steering wheel.

"Don, we've got to hide the car."

"Where's Sal?"

"I don't know. The drone crashed when we were skidding on the road. He could be anywhere. More importantly, he could have seen it crash and now he might be looking for the people spying on him. So for the love of God, *go!*"

She hit the gas a little too forcibly and the tires spun on the dirt and pebbles left behind from the slide. When she gained traction, she steered the car behind the boulder on the side of the road, put the SUV in park, cut the engine, and panted for breath.

Sal's car rounded the bend not twenty seconds later. He drove slowly through the remains of the rockslide, but finally his car was out of sight.

They hadn't been spotted.

Donni let out a long sigh.

Nico noticed he'd been holding his breath, too, and he let out the air in a slow huff. "He's far enough in front of us. Let's follow him."

"I don't want to follow him. I don't want anything to do with him. I just want to go home."

He knew it was dangerous to follow Sal with her in the car, but he was so close! Still, his job as her protector mandated that he put her safety above all else. "Switch me sides. I'll drive us home."

"No, I don't mean back to the villa. I mean home. Can't we just go get my mother and return to Pennsylvania? We'll contact Sal, tell him we want no parts of ruling Italy. We can sign a release or something. Then they can leave us alone, and we can get back to our lives."

Nico frowned. He'd forgotten how hard this must be for her. For all the girls. He got out of the car and walked around to the driver's side. Before he could open her door, a thrashing in the bushes behind the tree and boulder caught his attention. He took his dagger out and stepped toward the noise. Stillness and silence greeted him. Not even a cricket chirrup or a rustling leaf disturbed the quiet of the night. He began to walk around the tree to investigate the noise, but Donni opened her door.

She tumbled out of the vehicle and into his arms. He stayed alert while he held her, and she cried in his embrace, her head nestled under his chin.

Her hair was so soft. He inhaled deeply. She smelled like lemons, fresh and clean, a stark contrast to the earthy, moldering scent of their surroundings. His whispered, "Ssh. It's okay," became a mantra as he waited for her to calm.

The sobs turned to hiccups, then the occasional sniffle. Finally she let out a long sigh and stepped back. He didn't release her, but she was able to look up at him. "I'm sorry."

"You have nothing to be sorry for."

"If I hadn't stowed away, you would have been able to follow Sal."

"If you hadn't stowed away, I wouldn't have been able to operate the drone and drive at the same time."

"But you crashed the drone when I lost control of the car, so it's my fault."

"Are we really going to fight about this now, too?"

Her gaze drifted to his mouth. "Is there something else you'd rather be doing?" Her voice was low, husky.

It shot straight through him, lightning in his veins.

She tilted her head up to meet him as he bent down to her, her lips soft and yielding. He breathed in her small sigh and turned his head, deepening the kiss.

He could so easily get lost in her. He ran his hands up her back, fully intending to thread his fingers through her silken tresses when he noticed he still held his dagger.

Damn it. Again he wasn't sure if what he felt was real or was just the dagger yearning for a female counterpart before it bestowed on him its full complement of powers. Well, he wouldn't be manipulated that way. He stepped back from her, held her at arms' length, and stared at her. "Are you okay?"

Her brow crinkled. "Y—yes. Yes, I think so. Are you?"

"I'm fine." He released her and looked around. The night was still too quiet for his comfort.

"Now what?" she asked.

Nico glanced at his watch. The moonlight glinted off his dagger as he turned his wrist, and he scowled and tucked the weapon back in its scabbard. "Let's head back."

"But what about Mama?"

"We still don't know for sure that she's there. I'll come back tomorrow night."

"But if Sal is onto us, they might move her, and we'll never find her."

He sighed. What a clusterfuck. He had his charge out in the wilderness, surrounded by wolves, rockslides, and a militia of their enemies, and all she wanted to do was retrieve her mother—not that he knew how to get to her or even if she was definitely there—and go back to Pennsylvania. Two wishes he simply couldn't grant her.

"Don, it's almost three-thirty. As it is, we'll probably get busted coming in."

"Then we might as well have a good reason. Like retrieving Mama."

"But I don't know if she's even there. It's better if I come back."

"We don't have time for that. And I'm not getting in that car until you swear we're going to get her."

A little deception never hurt anyone. Not when it was for her own good. "Fine. Get in the car."

"If you don't turn around and head back the way we came, I'll jump out and walk there. I'll go right up to a guard or knock on the damn door."

"Why do you have to be so stubborn?"

"Why do you?" She glared at him.

"You're incorrigible."

"And you're wasting time."

He growled. When she recoiled, he softened his voice. A little. "Get in the damn car, Donni."

"Are we going to get Mama?"

"I'll see what I can do. Get in the fucking car."

She gave him a sweet smile and walked around the hood of the SUV.

They were so screwed.

He got in and started the engine. "You sure about this? It'll be dangerous. Next to impossible."

"I'm sure."

Nico shook his head and pulled onto the road. As he drove around the boulder, he noticed five sets of bright eyes staring at them from a thick outcropping of overgrowth.

Wolves.

A chill skittered up his spine, but he didn't tell Donni what he'd seen. Offering a silent prayer of gratitude for their safety, he headed back up the mountain toward the guarded facility. This time, he cut the lights early and pulled as close to the building as he could without being detected.

Everything he could think of had to go exactly right—plus probably a few things he hadn't considered, too—or they were dead.

NICO GRABBED HIS pack and made sure Donni was quiet when they left the relative safety of the car. A couple of times he had to tell her not to smile. The face paint hid her features in the dark, but her teeth were quite noticeable in the moonlight.

Didn't know why the hell she was smiling, anyway. Nothing to smile about out here.

Oh, right. Because he was a total idiot and let her have her way. He might smile, too, if he ever got what the fuck he wanted.

Time to clear his thoughts. They were getting close, and he needed to focus. He led her through the trees to the area where he'd watched the guard the last time he was there.

"So," Donni whispered, "what made you so sure Mike had lost Mama? And what led you here?"

"You know how he can spy on us at will without us knowing? Astral projecting in, but not becoming visible?"

"Yeah. It's annoying."

"Well, I decided to do a little spying on my own."

"On Mike?"

"Yeah." He rummaged through his pack, then he looked through night vision binoculars toward the facility he suspected Mary was in. The guard he could see left his post and walked the perimeter of the building. He rounded the corner, and about thirteen minutes later, Nico expected him to reappear at the opposite side of the building and head toward the door.

Thirteen minutes wasn't long enough.

"And?"

"I used his phone to keep tabs on him. Where he went, how long he was there. When his patterns changed, I investigated."

"How did his patterns change?"

"Come with me. I need to check the trail cams." He started making his way through the trees to where he'd installed the first device, and he whispered over his shoulder as he picked his way through the overgrowth. "Mike had been making daily visits to a place in Florence. I looked into it. It was an isolated villa. There was no reason for him to be there unless he was visiting the occupants. But Mike's not really the social type. As it turns out, he wasn't visiting friends. There was a small medical staff there, however, and all of them were murdered and left to rot. They were nearly unrecognizable when the authorities found them."

"Did Mike kill them? Oof!" She bumped into the back of him when he stopped. "Sorry. It's hard to see with the trees blocking the moonlight."

"Just try to be quiet." He climbed up the tree and reviewed the footage on the camera. As he suspected, there was round-the-clock surveillance. The thirteen-minute window seemed like the best he'd get. He jumped down from the tree and landed soundlessly beside her.

"So? Mike? Did he kill them?"

"Of course not. I think they were caring for your mom, and Sal's group found them, killed them, and took her."

"Are you sure she wasn't one of the ones…"

"No. There were just three of them. A doctor, an anesthesiologist, and a nurse. There were signs of a patient having been there—empty bed, monitors, different medicines—but no other body was found. The operating theory is the patient woke, panicked, attacked and killed the three professionals, and ran. Police are searching for a sick or injured fugitive."

"You think Mama did that?"

"No." He grabbed her hand and led her toward the other trail cam. "The detectives think that. I think Sal's group abducted your mother and killed the staff caring for her. Mike stopped going there on the day the staff was killed. Since then, he's spent less and less time with us and more and more time sequestered or popping up in the oddest places. He's searching for her."

"Let's say that's what happened. Why? Why would they abduct Mama instead of killing her?"

"Leverage."

"But they haven't ransomed her yet. Or whatever they plan on doing."

"Remember when they took Chuck? They didn't contact us right away about him, either. They're biding their time, and they'll use her when it's most advantageous to them." The guard returned. Thirteen minutes. And unless he missed his guess, fifteen minutes later he'd make his rounds again. He and Donni were about fifty yards from the building. He wasn't optimistic about their chances. They might make it to the door, assuming no one was watching the feeds from the security cameras, but he doubted he could bypass the code before the guard returned.

"For what?"

"Hmm? Oh. For if or when we get the upper hand. She's a bargaining chip."

"But they already have Chuck."

The Brotherhood was going to have to have a frank and painful discussion with the girls regarding Chuck. It was likely their friend and loyal foreman was dead, and they'd all take it hard. Particularly Jo, who was closest with him— and was the reason for his abduction in the first place. That Sal's organization took Mary was just another indicator Chuck was no longer in play.

Nico scaled the tree, checked the footage, and confirmed his suspicions. He jumped back down. "Look, if we're really going to do this, you need to listen to everything I say and do exactly what I tell you, when I tell you, with no questions asked. Can you do that?"

She nodded.

"Say it. I need your word."

"You have my word."

"Fine." He checked his watch. One more minute, and the guard would make his rounds again. "Get ready to run."

8

DONNI WAS NEARLY yanked off her feet. Nico grabbed her hand and pulled her in a mad dash across the grounds to the door the security guard had just vacated.

They stood in the shadow provided by the overhang, and she panted for breath. His legs were a hell of a lot longer than hers. She nearly face-planted three times as he dragged her to the door.

Nico held his finger to his lips to shush her. He pointed two fingers at his eyes, then at her, then back and forth at the grounds.

Guess that meant she was supposed to be quiet and keep a look out while he worked on the keypad. So she scanned the property and the woods beyond. Fear skittered up her back like thousands of insect legs, making her skin crawl and tingling her scalp. Those were eyes—five sets of glowing eyes in the thicket of trees. Lower to the ground than the shining eyes of deer in headlights she was used to in Pennsylvania. And more… predatory. She gulped and turned to tell Nico about it, then thought better of interrupting him. He had some device attached with wires to the keypad and was trying to detect the code before the guard returned.

She turned her attention back to the trees. The eyes were gone. All five sets.

Was that better or worse? Donni wasn't sure, but before she needed to decide, the guard rounded the corner. Damn it!

She turned to tell Nico just as she heard a soft click and the swoosh of a door swinging open. Nico stuffed the device in his bag and held the door open for her.

"Hurry," she whispered. "The guard is coming."

They scurried inside and Nico held the door so it didn't bang when it closed. Donni saw the guard at the door just as Nico pulled her around the corner. God, she hoped they hadn't been seen.

Nico stopped and looked back, a scowl on his face.

"What's wrong?" she whispered.

"He looks familiar."

"So?"

He shrugged. "You're right. Doesn't matter right now."

They crept down the hallway, staying tight against the wall to try and avoid the cameras. There were so many, though, she couldn't imagine their presence hadn't been noticed yet. Nico was right ahead of her, peeking through every doorway they passed before urging them forward.

At the fifth doorway, he stopped short. Donni tugged on his sleeve, and he held his finger to his lips and gestured for her to look inside.

They'd found the security office. A dozen monitors along the wall cycled through images of the entire property. A single guard sat in front of them. He reclined in his chair, his head tipped back and eyes closed, an occasional soft snore escaping his lips.

Donni met Nico's gaze and smiled.

He took a deep breath and nodded toward the hallway, where they continued to a staircase. Nico took a look around then guided her up. The door at the top also had a keypad.

She bit her lip and looked around while he used that gizmo again. At one point, she heard voices on the floor below them, but they got softer as the men walked away from the stairs. Even so, she was too nervous to even breathe a sigh of relief. She continued holding her breath while Nico worked.

After what seemed like hours—days, even—she heard the click and swoosh of the lock disengaging and the door opening. Nico popped his head through and scanned the hallway. Then he grabbed her hand and pulled her inside.

She wasn't sure what she expected. Something akin to a hospital, she supposed. But the upstairs of this facility looked remarkably similar to the Brotherhood's villa, only smaller. The hallway began just past a common area by a large window where a few comfy chairs and two full bookshelves waited for visitors. In the hallway itself, a few doors stood open leading to unoccupied bedrooms beyond. She followed Nico down the hall, tiptoeing on the tile floor to make as little noise as possible. He poked his head in each room, but he never lingered long and never let her take the time to peek inside herself.

There was nothing left in the hallway except for another staircase and a closed door with a window in it—odd, given the rest of the hallway just looked like a regular second story. As they approached the door, she noticed another infernal keypad lock. Donni looked through the glass while Nico rooted in his bag.

Mama!

The room inside was an exact replica of a hospital room, complete with privacy curtain, monitors, and hospital bed. The curtain was only partially closed, and behind it lay Donni's mother in the bed, IV needles and tubes attached to her arm. The machine beside her fluttered and beeped in time with her pulse. It seemed strong enough to Donni, but what the hell did she know? Mama's coloring wasn't great, and she'd lost weight. She looked frail and sickly, not at all like the strong woman who'd been taken from them. Tears welled in her eyes and she pressed her hand to the window.

She again heard voices—the men from below must be climbing the stairs. Nico, sweat beading on his forehead, frantically tapped at the device he'd attached to the keypad. The door down the hall opened, and shadows stretched across the floor.

Click. Swish.

Nico pushed her inside her mother's room and shut the door behind them. She headed for her mom's bedside, but he grabbed her hand and dragged her into an adjoining bathroom. He left the door ajar, and Donni strained to hear what was going on in the room and hallway beyond.

It was difficult to make out what the men said, but the volume of their voices made it seem like they were right outside the door. Then a woman's sounded, and there was a rumbling of laughter. Donni looked at Nico, but his attention was trained at the door.

Click, swish. Donni held her breath and peered into her mother's room through the slender opening between the door and doorframe. A woman slid the curtain aside, walked over to Mama's bed, looked at the monitors, and then at the IV bag. She prepared a needle and injected it into the tube running into Mama's hand.

She spoke with a thick accent. "Well, Mary, another day done. I'm going off duty now. In another hour or two, Adalena will come to you. She'll get you up, walk you around, get you some food. Maybe I'll leave a note for her to help you shower, no? You could use some freshening, I think. But you must promise to be quiet this time, or we'll cut back to every other day again. *Capisce?*"

She patted Mama's hand, made a note in the file, and left the room.

Donni started to open the door, but Nico shook his head and held her back. She stared at her mother through the small opening for a full five minutes before Nico let her out.

She rushed to her mother's bedside, held her hand and kissed her face, tears dripping onto her mother's pale and sunken cheeks. What had they done to her?

"Don," Nico whispered, "we don't have time for this. Help me unhook her, and we'll go."

"But what about the medicine? What if she needs it? What if—"

"That's propofol. She doesn't need it. It's what's keeping her under."

"Are you sure?"

Nico walked around her and turned the monitor off. Then he started unhooking the machine and IVs. "Yes. I've been researching."

Of course he had.

"We have to hurry. I don't know if turning off the monitors will alert anyone." He scooped Mary into his arms, hefted her onto his shoulder in a fireman's carry, and headed for the door.

Donni pulled the curtain around the bed to camouflage her mother's absence then followed close behind him. He hurried down the hall but stopped short near the sitting area. Male voices and thundering footsteps came from below. They'd been discovered. She grabbed his arm and pulled him back in the direction they'd come.

She dashed down the hall, Nico right on her heels, and burst through the doorway leading to the other staircase. Halfway down, when she rounded the landing, she came face-to-face with the nurse who had just vacated the room. Both of them stopped short. The nurse's eyes widened.

Donni heard the soft *shash* of Nico unsheathing his marble dagger, but he was in no position to fight with her mother on his shoulder. The nurse's gaze hardened, and Donni feared she'd come to a similar conclusion.

Then she had an a-ha moment, and she smiled. She'd been trained for this. And she had the high ground.

Gripping the railing with both hands and using it like a pommel horse, Donni swung her body into the air. When the heels of her feet connected with the woman's face, she thrust her legs out. The momentum of her vault combined with the force of her kick knocked the nurse backward, and she tumbled down the stairs.

Donni landed several stairs down from where she started and used the railing to stabilize her balance. She glanced back at Nico, whose eyes had widened, but he hadn't frozen—he already followed her down. She released the railing and ran to the bottom where the nurse lay in an awkward position, moaning. No time to worry about her, though. Donni cracked the door open and looked left and right. "Which way?"

Nico nodded toward the left, and she slipped into the hallway. They again stayed against the wall to try and avoid the cameras, but she felt like that was a waste of time.

Footsteps pounded nearby. It was only a matter of time before they were caught. She took a step toward another hallway, but Nico pulled her back and tried to hide them in a doorway. Three men with guns burst from the direction she'd been about to enter and turned down another passageway. She released a slow breath through pursed lips.

She let Nico lead, and she followed him down yet another hall. She was totally lost but trusted he knew what he was doing. A glass door loomed at the end of the passageway, and three armed guards ran past it. What luck! They never even glanced inside.

Nico reached the door and opened it quietly. He was breathing heavily, and she knew he was growing tired of carrying her mother's dead weight. They had to get to cover.

The coast was clear, and they dashed across the property. The tree line seemed so far—too far—away. Just as they neared a copse of birch trees, a shot rang through the air. Nico ducked, fell. Rolled with her mother. Yelled for Donni to watch out while he scrambled back to his feet and hefted her mother to his shoulder again.

The bullet had whizzed past her. It was so close, she felt the momentum disturbing the air around her face when it passed. A fraction of an inch to the right, and she'd have been dead.

They ducked and dashed into the woods, but they couldn't slow down. They were being chased by a very determined security staff. Another shot sounded, but this one hit well to the right of her. Hopefully the guards wouldn't find them.

Nico slowed his pace, then stopped altogether. She heard thrashing in the foliage well to their right, but they weren't so far away that they were safe yet. Instead of him starting again, though, he muscled her mother to his opposite side.

"Don." He turned his back toward her and whispered over his shoulder. "Open my backpack. Get out the night vision goggles."

Great idea. She'd been all but blind as they dashed through the trees. She dug through his bag until she found what he'd asked for, then pulled the goggles out and started to put them on.

"No." He held out his hand. "Give them to me."

There wasn't time to debate. She could lead them faster than he could with her mother on his back, but honestly, she didn't know where she was in relation to the car they'd stashed. Also, her pace didn't matter. She had to move at whatever pace Nico set. So she passed the gear over, grabbed onto his belt, and let him lead the way.

How the hell he moved so fast while carrying a body was anyone's guess, but she struggled to keep up with him.

It seemed like they walked for hours, but it couldn't have been more than fifteen minutes. The commotion the guards made grew fainter and fainter until, at last, she couldn't hear them at all. She and Nico might actually get away with it. She mustered a sigh past the stitch in her side and kept running.

In a few moments, the terrain looked familiar. Then they came upon the hidden SUV. She peered through the trees toward the facility. They must have come out on the complete opposite side of the building and circled around.

Donni helped Nico get Mama situated in the back seat, then she rounded the car to the other side. Nico tossed his equipment in the back and climbed into the driver's seat. She opened the back passenger seat and started to climb in beside her mother when a shot rang out.

A searing pain bloomed across her back, then all went black.

MADONNA MIA!

Nico turned when the shot rang out just in time to see Donni collapse. He rushed around to her side of the car, found her crumpled near the tire, a red splotch blooming through her shirt in the middle of her back.

Bile rose in his throat, but he swallowed it, prayed to St. Raphael for his intercession, and hefted Donni as gently as he could into the car. He tried to lay her across Mary's lap so he could keep an eye on her condition, but what if she fell off?

Fear flooded his body in an icy torrent. Executive decision—he strapped her in and prayed again that he didn't damage her spine. Then he slammed the door shut. A bullet shattered his side mirror as he turned to round the bumper. How had it missed him?

He ran to the driver's side, prayed something—anything—would slow the shooters down. A series of howls echoed through the night. Five wolves jumped out of the trees and onto the road right behind them, charging toward the guards.

Nico hoped the wolves got to their prey before the bullets got to them, but he didn't have time to wait and see what happened. He took off down the hill, the vehicle fishtailing on the road.

As soon as he had control, he glanced in the rear view mirror. Donni hadn't moved. The blood spot had grown, though. He stabbed the hands-free phone button and called Gianni.

The phone was one ring from going to voicemail when his brother mumbled into the phone. *"What?"*

"Grab your dagger. Need healing. Now!"

"Where are you?" Gianni's voice was immediately sharp, alert. *"What did you hurt?"*

"I'm in the Apennine Mountains. Not me. Donni's been shot."

"What the fuck are you doing—"

"Gian, shut up and heal her! She's losing a lot of blood. And…"

"And what?" His voice sounded strained.

Nico looked in the back seat, at her legs hanging uselessly off the bench seat. "It's her spine, man. She's going to need more than blood. She'll need to have her nerves repaired."

His brother swore a blue streak. He could hear Franki asking questions in the background and prayed he didn't stop to answer her. "Hurry!"

The SUV speedometer topped out at 164. The needle was already at 157, and he continued to push it. The only thing on his mind was getting Donni the help she needed.

And he prayed he wasn't too late.

HIS HANDS SHOOK as he dialed Sal's number.

"What?"

Nothing like pleasantries to start the call off right. Wincing, he plunged into the deep-end without a flotation device. "Sal? There's been a… complication here. With Mary Notaro."

"I was just fucking there."

"I know, sir."

"Your next words had better be a reassurance that you took care of it."

He waited a beat, unsure what to say.

Sal sighed. *"Tell me. Don't leave anything out."*

"I left my post for a while. Went inside to start getting the place in shape. You know, like you said. But Fabio said the gate guard had left his post, so I went back out before I even got to the security office. While I was away from the building, there was another breach. Nico Micelli and some girl took out a few of our people. Managed to take Mary with them when they left. I shot the girl, but Micelli managed to get her and Mary into his car, and they took off. We couldn't catch him."

It was Sal's turn to remain quiet for a moment. When he finally spoke, his voice was quiet. Too quiet. *"Did you say 'another' regarding a breach?"*

His mouth went dry, and he struggled to get the words out. "Th-that might not be the r-right word. There was a… disturbance the other night. Think it was just wolves, though. It's in my report."

"But you didn't call it in? Or bother telling me about it when I was there?"

"Tell you about wolves? No."

"Are you sure it was only wolves?"

He cringed and whispered, "No."

Sal unloaded a string of obscenities on him.

"Look, Sal, I—"

"Shut up. Shame on me for trusting something this important to you. I should make you report this to him yourself. In person."

A chill skittered up his spine. He'd never had to talk to… him. Not directly. No one wanted to have to do that.

"Stay by your fucking phone. I might conference you into my call to him."

Sal ended the call, still swearing under his breath.

The guard checked his gun and put it back in its holster. If things went south, he'd eat a bullet before suffering the alternatives.

When his phone rang, he cringed. And answered it before the first ring ended.

NICO SPLIT HIS focus between the road, his brother, and Donni. She still hadn't moved, hadn't made a sound. Bile rose in his throat, and he swallowed it as he whipped around a bend.

Franki had stopped talking, or he couldn't hear her over the roar of the engine. He barely made out Gianni's voice. Even though his brother had come fully into his powers, what Nico asked of him was a lot, and it required him to meditate and chant while he worked.

Another glance behind him showed the blood spot had stopped growing. Donni didn't exhibit any signs of moving, or even waking. Probably for the best, as she'd be frightened and in agony until Gianni was done.

"How is she?" Gianni asked.

"I think the blood stopped. I can't see through her shirt."

"Blood's not the problem. I stopped that. Even replenished what she's lost."

Nico sighed and whipped the car onto a bigger, straighter road. "What's the issue, then?"

"The nerves."

"Are you telling me you can't fix her spine?" He whispered, hardly able to form the words.

"No. That's not it. I can do it."

"You need me closer? I'm probably less than an hour away."

"How the fuck did you get so close so fast? Slow down before you wreck and I have to save your sorry ass, too."

"Don't worry about my speed. I'm in control. Why can't you fix her back?"

"The bone is stopping me from splicing the nerves. You need to heal her spine before I can finish."

"*Che cazzo*, Gianni. I'm fucking *driving*. I can't stop and work on her bones."

"And I can't heal the nerves until you do."

Shit. Shit, shit, *shit*.

"Get Vin. Find out if I'm better off stopping or just hauling ass."

"Can't you drive and heal her at the same time?"

Nico thought about it, and his vision swam. He crossed the center line and swerved back into his lane, a truck—the only other vehicle on the road at that hour—blaring its horn at him.

"Nico!"

"I just tried. I can't. I nearly wrecked the damn car. Go get Vinnie."

"Already in the hall."

Nico heard pounding on the door and a gruff, muffled reply followed by a vicious, "What the fuck is he doing?"

He'd take all Vin's attitude and then some. He just needed to know what to do.

"Nic," Gianni said. "V says to get back. Pronto."

"I can probably make it in twenty." He pressed harder on the already floored gas pedal.

"You're no good to us dead. Slow down. You need me to stay on the line?"

"No. I'll call back if I need you. Just get ready for us."

"When this is over, we're going to—"

Nico ended the call. He knew they were going to have a knock-down, drag-out. It didn't need to be discussed before he actually suffered through it.

He spent the rest of the drive talking to Donni. Just saying nonsense. Silly things to pass the time, anything to take her mind off her injury.

Problem was, she wasn't awake. So he was really talking to himself. And no matter how many times he told her—told himself—she was going to be fine, the words never sounded sincere.

Her recovery depended on his ability. And ability was one thing he was in short supply of.

NICO WHIPPED THE SUV into the garage. Wasn't surprised to find the whole house waiting for him.

Coz and Vin had the medical gurney out, and they wheeled it over to the back driver's side door.

"Other side," Nico yelled.

They ran to the other side and flung open the door.

"Are you kidding me?" Vinnie said.

"What?" Toni asked.

"You want to explain this?" he said.

"Later. Let's get them inside."

"Them?" Toni asked. "Them, who?"

Franki opened the other back door. "Mama?"

"What?" Jo and Toni said together.

"She okay to move, Nic?" Gianni asked.

"Yeah."

"Fine. I'll carry her. You guys get Donni."

Vinnie and Coz managed to get Donni out of the car despite Nico hovering over them and micromanaging their efforts. Gianni hefted Mary into his arms and grunted.

"What's wrong with her?" Franki asked.

"Long story," Nico said. "Donni's the one we need to work on now."

The girls murmured between them as everyone hurried inside. Gianni took Mary into one room near the gym while Coz and Vinnie wheeled the gurney into another. Nico followed Donni, as did Toni. Franki and Jo went with Gianni.

In the makeshift medical room, the three men moved her off the gurney and onto a table, lying her on her stomach and resting her head in a padded circle. Toni cut the shirt away to expose her back. There was dried blood where the wound was, but the skin was pristine. Gianni had done a solid job healing her so far.

If only he could do his part. Her spine looked… lumpy where the bullet had entered. Bone fragments. And it was all on him.

"So what's the plan?" Coz said.

"Gianni said he can't heal the nerves until I heal the bone."

"So do it," Toni said.

Nico avoided her gaze and looked at Vinnie. "Vin?"

"Oh, now you want to consult me?"

"Be angry as you want at me, but don't take it out on her. Help me heal her."

Vinnie cursed under his breath. "I can't see what's blocking you. Your emotions are a mess."

"No shit, Vin. I just watched Donni get shot right in front of me after breaking into Fort-fucking-Knox to rescue her mother. I dodged crazy guards and a pack of wolves and nearly broke the damn sound barrier getting back here. Wonder why my nerves are frayed?"

"None of which would have been an issue if you had told us what you were doing and let us form a fucking plan!"

"What's going on?" Franki ran into the room, Jo and Gianni on her heels.

"Just trying to figure out what to do next," Nico said.

"What to do next?" Jo's eyebrows disappeared beneath her bangs. "Heal my sister. Problem solved."

"It's a little more complicated than that," Vinnie said.

"Why?"

"He's stuck. And I can't see why."

"What?" Franki looked at Nico. "What's wrong?"

"I'm just a little… off."

"No," Vinnie said. "You're a fucking mess."

Nico clenched his jaw and his fists and rounded on his brother.

Coz pulled him back, turned him toward the table. "Come on. You got this. Draw some energy from me."

Coz's power was death. That was the last source of power he wanted to tap. Although, dominion over death didn't mean end of life. It meant he could also put a stop to death, right? Kind of made him and his brother two sides of the same coin.

Nico grabbed his dagger and lay it over the area where Donni's wound was. Coz put a hand on his shoulder. Toni laced her fingers with him and placed her free hand on Nico's other shoulder.

He tried to still his mind. He closed his eyes, concentrated on his gift, on drawing healing energy from the marrow of the earth, through the tile he stood on, and into his body. He pulled from his brother and Donni's sister, and when his body felt full to bursting, he released the potential power in a kinetic burst.

He knew before he opened his eyes that he'd done his part. And when he looked at Donni's back, it was smooth and straight once more.

Then he closed his eyes again and slumped to the floor.

9

AN IRRITATING BUZZING sound interrupted Donni's nap. She'd been in a deep slumber, too. The first good sleep she'd gotten in a while. She tried to tune out the noise, but it just kept getting louder. What was making all the racket?

Unable to go back to her dreams, she tried to focus on the sound. Took her a while until she realized it was voices. Her sisters and the guys. Okay, why the hell were they in her bedroom? And what in God's name were they fighting about this time?

Who had the time or energy for all the contention? Seemed like people were always arguing these days. She'd just ignore them and try harder to go back to sleep.

Well, she thought that for about ten seconds. Then curiosity got the best of her, and she tried to make out what they said.

"You sure you're okay?" Coz said.

"I'm fine." Nico's voice sounded strained.

"You collapsed."

"I was just a little wiped out. The chase, the driving, the healing. It took a toll. But I'm fine now."

"You sure?"

"Yes. I'm sure. Can we move on now?"

"Why were you keeping it a secret? We could have helped," Gianni said.

"You should never have done that without talking to me." Something thunked. "Power of strategy, remember?"

"Vinnie, you push, shove, hit, or otherwise touch me again, I don't care how tired I am. I'll drive your ass into the ground."

"You and what army? You can barely stand!"

"Enough," Franki said. "I want to know what's wrong with Mama."

"And I want to know when Donni's going to wake up," Toni said.

"She should have been awake in the car," Gianni said. "Nico called me as soon as it happened, and he said the healing I sent worked right away. Even with a shattered bone, she should have been lucid fairly quickly. Now that Nico's done, there's no reason for her to be out."

"I'm sure she'll wake soon," Franki said.

"Well, I want to know why the hell people are always getting shot," Jo said. "And how to stop it from happening again."

Who got shot? Wait... she got shot!

Footsteps crossed the room and a door slammed.

"Vinnie," Jo said. "Damn it."

"I'll go," Coz said.

Guess Jo struck a nerve with her guy again.

But Donni had more pressing issues to deal with. She struggled to regain full consciousness, but the battle was hard. Her eyes didn't want to open, her body didn't want to move. The buzzing of voices continued around her, but she ignored them as she fought her way to a lucid state.

She finally managed to open her eyes, and she was staring at tile. Expensive, beautiful tile, but tile nonetheless. What the...

Her face felt smooshed, and she realized she lay on her stomach, her head supported by one of those pouffy donut-shaped things she'd used for massages and now apparently surgery. Or the Brotherhood's version thereof, which in their case consisted of blood and bone healing through the powers of their daggers. And that begged the question, if they'd healed her before she got back to the villa, why was she on her stomach? She moved her hands under her shoulders and began the arduous process of pushing herself up and rolling over. That's when she started to pay attention to the talking all around her again.

Thank God.

"She's stirring," Toni said.

"Donni?" Jo said.

"Wait!" Franki pushed her back down. "Let us help."

"I can do it myself. Or I can when you're not holding me down."

Toni whispered in her ear. "You just flashed the whole room. You don't have a top on."

Donni put her head back in the donut and prayed the gorgeous tile would split apart and swallow her whole. Of course, it didn't. No. Instead, her sisters managed to flip her and cover her with a sheet, so now everyone in the room could stare at her had-to-be red face.

Which wouldn't be so bad, but Nico's eyes were a bit lower.

And she was pretty sure her face just turned another shade or two darker.

"How are you feeling?" Toni asked.

She turned to look at her twin and felt a twinge of guilt. Toni's face was drawn, her eyes shadowed. "I'm okay."

"You were shot. That's hardly okay."

"I don't really remember any of it. I felt a pain in my back, and I woke up here. Tired. Maybe a little weak. But okay."

Toni threw her arms around her and squeezed. "You scared me."

Donni patted her back and whispered, "I'm sorry."

"You scared us, too." Franki pointed at Jo, and they both hugged her.

"But I'm fine, right? I don't hurt, so Gianni must have healed me."

Her sisters glanced at each other, refused to meet her gaze.

"What?"

Nico sighed. "The problem is me. Gianni healed you while we were still in the car, but you had bone damage. I couldn't concentrate enough to heal you until we got back here. Then Gianni finished up by fixing your nerves."

"How's Mama?"

Her sisters shared a look.

"What's wrong? Where is she?" She started to swing her legs over the edge of the table, and the sheet over her slipped dangerously low. Her sisters pushed her back onto the bed, and she clutched the material higher on her chest.

"We'll take you to her after you're dressed."

"Where's my shirt?" Nothing like sitting half-naked in a room full of Brotherhood warriors. Well, two of them, anyway. One who she was particularly cognizant of.

"The top you were wearing was ruined. I'll go grab you another one." Toni hurried out of the room.

"What aren't you telling me? What's wrong with Mama?"

"You heard the nurse at that facility," Nico said. "They'd been getting your mom up once a day."

"Yeah. And?"

"The propofol should have worn off by now."

"But it hasn't?"

"No." He ran his hand through his hair. "Maybe. I don't know."

A chill washed over her. "So, she's not awake?"

Nico shook his head.

Tears welled in her eyes, and she swiped them away. "You said she was safe to move. You said she didn't need that medicine."

"I know. I'm sorry." He looked away, muttered more to himself than her. "God, if you only knew how sorry."

Toni returned with a shirt and handed it to her without comment.

Donni put it on and then yanked the sheet out from underneath her top. Hope no one minded her braless.

Her face colored again, and she avoided looking at Nico. "Where's Mama? I want to go see her."

"Wait." Toni handed her a damp washcloth.

"What?"

"You don't want to see Mama with black paint on your face. You'll frighten her when she wakes."

Donni could only imagine how she looked, but she wouldn't take the mirror her sister offered. Just in case. No, instead, she scrubbed blindly until her face felt raw. "Now can we go?"

"She's resting," Nico said. "Mike summoned his medical team. They wanted us to bring her to them, but he insisted our compound is the most secure place for her. They're making a list of the equipment they need, and we're going to get it here."

"Screw that. I don't want to wait for them. Did you guys try to revive her?"

"Once the propofol wore off, she should have come to. An hour, tops. It's been close to four, and she's still out."

"I don't mean medically. I mean you and Gianni. Your dagger power."

Nico and Gianni exchanged looks. Finally, Gianni answered her. "We need to wait for the equipment and the results of the tests. Then we'll know more."

"Maybe Vinnie's strategy power can tell you what you want to know."

Jo cleared her throat and left the room.

"She going after him? What's up with them this time?"

Toni shrugged. "It doesn't matter now. You want some water?"

"I want some answers. Why aren't you guys healing Mama?"

"We tried, all right?" Nico walked to the door and back. "Apparently I'm the problem. Vinnie says he can't see past my emotions to know what's wrong with her. Gianni did all he could to heal her tissue problems. So, I guess Vin's right. The problem has to be me. And I can't figure out how to fix her."

"Can you guys leave us alone for a moment?" She looked around the room at her sisters and Gianni. They all filed out, leaving her alone with Nico. He apparently hadn't used a mirror when he washed, either, because he had faint black streaks all over his handsome but troubled face.

"Come here." She held her hand out to him. He approached, but he didn't take her hand.

She patted the edge of her bed, and he sat beside her. "What's going on with you? I thought you were just being weird because you weren't sleeping. Then I noticed you were sneaking out. Now I know why, and we got Mama back. You did what you set out to do, and I'm grateful. So what's the problem?"

"Who said there was a problem?"

"I may have been out for a while, but I'm not blind. The tension in here was thicker than your head. You and Vinnie both say your emotions are preventing you from using your powers properly. So what's the problem?"

He scowled at her.

"Nico, I'm not angry with you."

"You should be."

"You saved me."

"You shouldn't have been in danger to begin with."

She ignored him. "You saved my mother. You knew to look for her and where to find her when no one else was even aware she was in danger."

"And if I had included my brothers, we'd have rescued her sooner. And maybe healed her by now. I was stupid to keep it from them."

"Why did you?"

"Because everyone already has enough to deal with, I didn't want them doubting Mike, too. Or being mad at me because I doubted him."

"There's your answer."

He furrowed his brow and glanced at her out of the side of his eye.

"Look, if anyone is at fault, it's Mike. He's the one who lost her and didn't say anything. The burden shouldn't have been on you to begin with."

He shrugged and looked toward the door.

"I'm not angry with you. Really. And I think I have an idea about my mother." That wasn't a lie to get him talking. She did have an idea. But she had to break through his walls first.

"Oh?"

"We'll get to it in a minute. Right now, I want you to talk to me." She took his hand. "What's going on with you?"

"Oh, I don't know. I can't wake your mother up. I got you shot. My brothers are pissed at me. So are your sisters. Mike's furious. We're still no closer to learning where Sal's group is or what their next step will be. The government here is crumbling, which puts you in more danger than ever. Anything else you want to know?"

Donni rubbed her thumb over his knuckles. "Well, let's deal with these one at a time, okay? Mike and the guys might be angry, but that's only because they were scared. My sisters, too. They'll all get over it. Not knowing what's going on with Sal is no different than it was months ago, and probably won't change in the foreseeable future. You might as well cross that off your list, too, as well as the impending revolution. Nothing you can do about that, either. And I suppose I was shot, but you didn't shoot me. Besides, you saved me. So there's no reason to be upset about that."

"Of course there is." He pulled his hand away from hers. "You could have died, *tesoro*. Because of me."

Tesoro. Treasure. Sweetheart. He'd never said that to her before. Her heart swelled, but there was no time to dwell on that. "No. Because of the guy who shot me."

"You never should have been there."

"I didn't really give you a choice."

He sighed.

"What do you think is stopping you from helping Mama?"

"I don't know. I have no idea, and Vinnie can't figure it out, either."

"You used your dagger power on her?"

"I tried. Nothing seemed to happen."

"Can I see it?"

"See what?"

"Your dagger?"

He raised his brows but didn't question her. He merely unsheathed it and passed it to her.

It was warm in her hands—whether from being near his body or being full of power, she didn't know. But she expected the dark green marble to feel cold and impersonal, and instead she felt heat and a strong connection to Nico.

"What do you feel when you hold it?" she asked him.

"A weapon. A deadly, and at the moment useless, weapon."

She shook her head. "No. Not useless. I feel it. I feel the power undulating inside it."

He raised an eyebrow.

"I don't know how to explain it. It's almost like it's alive, but not. Like it wants something, but doesn't know how to ask for it."

"It's a hunk of rock, Donni. Sculpted into something elegant, but nothing more than a rock."

"You know that's not true."

He glanced around the room.

She tried to meet his gaze, but he wouldn't look at her. So she tapped his hand with the tip of the dagger.

That got his attention.

"Want to try something?"

"What?"

"I was thinking. Gianni couldn't control his power until Franki helped him. Vinnie couldn't either, until Jo was a part of it. What if—"

"No!"

She recoiled, just a little, but enough that he must have noticed, because when he replied, his voice was quieter, calmer. Still held an edge, though. "I mean, no."

"Why not? I don't mind helping."

"I'm not going to use you to boost my power."

"That's not what I'm suggesting."

"Sounds like it."

She shook her head. "No. Just listen. Remember when we were all working on Coz after he was shot? You guys were drawing power from all of us. I think it was the combination of the Brotherhood and the Notaro family that really amped up your powers. So let's try it on a smaller scale. Just me and you. To help Mama."

"Oh." He studied the floor. "That's not what I thought you meant."

"What did you think I was talking about?"

He shrugged and played with the edge of the sheet she'd tossed aside. It made her very aware of the fact that she wasn't wearing a bra, which made her think about Nico staring at her when she'd first gotten up and the sheet had slipped.

Her body began to react, and she had to cross her arms so Nico wouldn't notice. She still held the dagger, and it felt hot where it touched her skin.

Seemed she was too late. Once again, his attention was riveted on her chest. This wasn't exactly her intention when she planned on getting through to him, but she could definitely work with it.

She might even prefer to approach the situation from this angle. It could certainly be mutually beneficial. She lowered her arms, leaned over, and reached across the bed with her free hand to take his again.

He clutched her fingers and stared into her eyes. His hazel irises had darkened, like wind-churned seas and stormy skies. "You're playing a dangerous game, Donni."

"I like my chances."

"It's a fool's bet." His voice was a husky whisper, his gaze lowered to her lips.

"I'm all in." She leaned toward him and pressed her mouth to his. The kiss sparked fires everywhere his body touched hers—his knee at her hip, his fingers around her hand, his lips on hers. She deepened this kiss and scooted closer to him, lost in the mind-melting sensations and her longing for more.

He reached for the hem of her shirt, lifted it slightly, then he grasped her waist and pulled her closer still. His fingers were molten on her skin, but she craved the burn, leaned into him seeking more. He slid his fingers up her back, traced slow, sensuous circles up her spine.

She tipped her head back and moaned. He ran his tongue along her collarbone, up her throat, and along her jawline, then he nibbled at her ear. She trembled under his touch. When his hands slipped around her rib cage and along the underside of her breasts, she thought she'd combust. She stretched and put her hands around his neck, threaded her fingers in his hair. The dagger had long been forgotten, and she dropped it.

Nico pulled back when it clattered to the floor.

She smiled and clasped her hands together to keep him close to her, but he pried her fingers loose, stood, and stepped away from the bed.

A chill rippled through her. "It was just a little noise, Nico. You really don't have to stop."

"You're wrong."

She looked at him, prayed the betrayal she felt didn't show on her face.

"You didn't know what you were doing." He ran his hand through his hair. "I'm sorry."

"Bullshit." She jumped off the bed and grabbed the dagger off the floor. When she offered it to him, he was careful not to touch her when he took it. "What is with you? Hot one minute, cold the next. I don't get you."

"All the more reason why you should keep your distance." And he stormed out of the room.

Well, crap on a cracker. All she wanted was to hint to him that she could be helpful, that he could draw on her ancestry to increase his power. She hadn't meant to upset him, and she definitely hadn't planned on kissing him. Again. Although when the opportunity presented itself she seized it rather than running from it.

What the hell was she doing? She wasn't even sure she wanted to get involved with him—with someone who lied so easily—but she'd forgiven him even without him seeking absolution. Everything he'd done, he'd done with good intentions, and all his secrets had been revealed. It should be an easy decision for her. For both of them.

So why did he keep putting the brakes on things when they got closer? It wasn't that she didn't appeal to him. Couldn't be. She'd caught him staring—ogling, yearning—more than once. If desire wasn't an issue, then, what was?

Maybe she hadn't discovered every secret he harbored. Yet.

NICO JUMPED WHEN Coz burst into the office. "Let's go."

"Nice of you to knock."

"Since when is the office a private space?"

"Since I'm in here doing private things."

"What? Sulking? You can do that anywhere. Hardly need privacy for that."

"What do you want, Coz?"

"I want you to come with me."

"Where?"

"Mary's room."

"No."

"Excuse me? I don't believe I asked your opinion. Let's go."

"No."

The expression on Coz's face softened. So did his tone. "You know I'm not a heart-to-heart conversation kind of guy, but if you need to talk, I'll listen."

"For not being a heart-to-heart kind of guy, you've done more than your share of psychoanalyzing me lately."

Coz raised his eyebrows.

Nico sighed. "I don't need to talk. I don't need training. I don't need anything. From anyone. Just get the hell out and leave me alone."

His brother walked over to the chair Nico sat on, put his hands on the armrests, and leaned down so his face was an inch from his brother's. "I'm tired of this shit. You're going to tell me what the fuck is going on with you, or I'm going to beat it out of you. Now."

Nico shoved him out of his face and stood. "Why does everyone think my business is theirs? When Gianni walked around flaying himself or everyone else, no one asked him why."

"His power is based on emotion. Heart. It could have been anything setting him off. He just needed to learn control."

"Yeah, it could have been anything. But it wasn't. It turned out to have been Sal."

"Not all of the time. Sometimes it was just him dealing with life."

"So why can't I have some time to deal with my life?"

"Because your power isn't rooted in emotion!"

"Who's the emotional one now?"

Coz took a deep breath. "Look, Gianni was always... passionate. Temperamental. He manipulates blood, for God's sake. That's why he's the heart of this group. Vin was always calculating. Probably why he got the strategy power. He's our mind. But you? You're our eyes and ears. Hell, even your power is based on healing. You're like the body of this bunch. You give us substance, reach. And I'm sorry, but right now we need that reach. Whatever's bothering you, you need to get over it or talk to someone, because it's slowing you down. Which is slowing us down."

"What makes you so sure? You and me... we barely know anything about our powers, because we haven't mastered the damn things yet." Nico turned from his brother to look at the monitors again. Gianni and Vinnie stood in the corner of Mary's room, deep in conversation. The girls all crowded around their mother's bedside. Like hell he was going down there.

"We'll get there," Coz said. "It just takes time. Then we'll have total control."

"Like Vinnie? His power is rooted in logic, which should be the easiest thing in the world to control. Especially for a brilliant legal mind like his. But he's spiraling, and no one's busting his balls for acting like a dick all the time."

"*Cazzo*, Nic. He just killed someone. Someone he knew and trusted. Do you even get the ramifications of that? He took a life. That's going to fuck with anyone's head."

"So Gianni supernaturally flays everyone for weeks and Vinnie is spiraling out of control, and we make excuses for them and move on. Why don't I get the same courtesy? Fuck you, Coz."

His brother grabbed his shoulder, spun him around, and punched him in the face. His head snapped back, and he balled his fist. But he reined himself in before he swung. He licked his lip and tasted blood. It was getting to be a habit with his brothers always swinging for his face. "What the fuck was that for? And give me one good reason why I shouldn't kick your ass right here and now."

"That was because you've had it coming for a while now, always shutting us out and having an attitude. And as for why you shouldn't kick my ass—I don't deserve it, and you couldn't if you tried." And Coz walked out.

Curses caromed through Nico's mind like balls in a lottery machine. Why the hell wouldn't everyone leave him alone in his misery? Now the one person who he always told everything to—the one person who hated anything having to do with sharing private thoughts and feelings but was always there for him anyway—had just punched him in the face and walked out.

Nico was racking up enemies faster than the fucking Taliban.

He plopped down in his chair and looked at the monitors again. The girls looked haggard. Worse than they had when they didn't know where their mother was or what her condition entailed. He'd wanted to help, but every time he tried, he made things worse.

The medical team ushered them all out of the room again. Time for more tests, apparently.

All because his powers didn't work.

He set a box of paper up in the corner and took aim at it with his dagger, shooting small bursts of energy in its direction. Usually he'd nail it dead center. At the moment, he couldn't manage more than a tiny ripple of current. The box didn't move a millimeter.

Damn it. He sighed and shoved the weapon back in its scabbard. The only thing it was good for lately was cranking up his libido around Donni. And wasn't that the epitome of useless?

DONNI LOOKED AROUND the hallway at her sisters and the guys. Despite the recent tensions, there was a lot of love there. Sister for sister, brother for brother, friend for friend, lover for lover.

And yet there was one face missing.

One face that could make all the difference.

She walked over to Coz and pulled him aside. "We need to talk."

"I'd ask what about, but I already know."

"He's not himself lately. He was the sweetest of all of you—"

"Gee, thanks."

"—but lately he's been so hard on himself. So isolated. So miserable."

Coz sighed. "I know. I've tried to talk to him, but he's not ready to share."

"It's not healthy. For him or for any of us."

He took two candy bars out of his pocket and offered one to her. "Don't tell Gianni. It's not a cheat day."

"I won't tell if you won't." She took the bar, unwrapped it, and took a bite. Then her stomach growled and she blushed. It had been a while since she'd eaten, and she was hungry.

"I'm hungry, too." Coz smiled and took a bite of his own candy bar.

"So, what are we going to do about your brother?"

"I'm out of ideas, Donni. I don't know what else to do."

"You know him better than anyone. Has he ever been this way before?"

He leaned against the wall and slid down it until he was seated on the floor. Then he nodded for her to join him.

She was still a little run down from the shooting, so it wasn't a hardship to take a load off.

"I remember him in this mood once. A long time ago. I don't know what brought him out of it. Sure wasn't anything I tried."

"When was this? What caused the problem?"

He rubbed the stubble on his face, the friction sounding like scuffing sandpaper. "It's not really my story to tell."

"I can't help him if I don't understand what's going on." She finished the candy and patted her hips. No pockets.

He held his hand out, took her wrapper, and shoved it and his own into his pocket. "I'll be honest, Donni. I don't know if that'll make a difference."

"I want to try. Tell me what happened."

Coz sighed. "Just between us?"

She crossed an *X* over her heart. "Promise."

"It happened when Mike adopted us and took us to the States. We all reacted a little differently. Gianni missed Teresa, but he adapted quickly. Sal took him under his wing right away. Vinnie stayed removed. He kept Marcus and the rest of us at arm's length for a while until he had a feel for the new dynamic. Never really did let the mentors in. You know all about that, though. As for me, the move was good. I'd fallen in with the wrong crowd at the orphanage and getting away was a bonus."

"I thought you were always tight with your brothers."

"I was. But there were extenuating circumstances."

"What happened?"

"Whose story do you want, mine or Nic's?"

"I'm sorry. I didn't mean to pry. Tell me about Nico."

"What do you know about his early life?"

She thought for a second. "Nothing. He's never mentioned it."

"Look, this is private stuff. It's really not my place—"

"Please, Coz. It might help me help him."

He sighed. "His parents died when he was little. His grandparents assumed custody, but then they died, too. That's when he came to the orphanage. We clicked right away, but it took him a while to come out of his shell around everyone else. He had developed abandonment issues. I think he only trusted me because there was nowhere I could go. Then not long after that, Mike took us to the States."

"And that's when you noticed behavior similar to his now? The sullenness, the irritability, the secretiveness?"

"Yeah. I mean, he was a little quiet when I met him, but nothing like when we moved."

"So what brought him out of it?"

"I told you, I don't know."

"Maybe you didn't know then, but if you think about it now, you'll remember something."

"I was just a kid. I wouldn't know if I was aware of the reason because I wasn't old enough to recognize it. Maybe Enrico would know. He took charge almost immediately when Mike brought us to New York. He could have some insight."

"Because he was so easy to get in touch with in New Jersey."

"Honestly, he was. If he didn't want to talk to us, we never would have set foot inside the hotel, let alone his private office."

"Well, if Nico doesn't snap out of this funk soon, maybe you could call Rico."

"Might mean more coming from you."

"You grew up with him."

"Yeah, but Rico spent most of his life watching you. He has a fondness for you girls."

"What we need is for him to have a fondness for Nico and his well-being."

"In his own way, I'm sure he does."

"Yeah, but is he safe to talk to? We never officially cleared him or Marcus. Hell, we haven't even tracked Paolo down yet to vet him."

"Just another reason why we might need to risk it. We're going to need Nico to work his magic with background checks and digital footprints and all the shit."

"Are you worried about him, or do you think this will blow over?" She met his gaze, searched his face for any signs of deception.

He looked away, and his voice was strained when he answered. "I don't know if it will pass soon or not, but yeah, I'm worried."

Before she could ask anything else, he got up and walked away.

TRY AS HE might, Nico couldn't get that kiss out of his mind. Couldn't get Donni out of his mind.

Couldn't get his monumental failures out of his mind.

He'd done it again. He wasn't thinking when he kissed her, then she dropped the dagger, and reality came rushing back to punch him in the face.

Why the hell was that infernal weapon pushing them together?

Maybe Donni was right. Maybe it wasn't a romance-thing, but rather a Notaro-legacy-thing. That made sense. He didn't have to fall in love with her to tap into her heritage. Just because his brothers did didn't mean he had to.

In fact, his brothers wouldn't even discuss the process of coming fully into their powers. He had assumed it had to do with love, but that didn't mean he was right. He'd been wrong before.

Not often, but once or twice.

He scowled. *Merda!* How stupid was he? That was *his* dagger. He should always be aware of it—should always be in possession of it. Why did he let her hold it? He shouldn't have let her even look at the damn thing. But, no. He not only let her hold it, he forgot he gave it to her. And when they kissed, he thought it was real. He started to lose himself in the moment because it wasn't dagger-inspired.

Until it dropped out of her hand and he realized it was.

What an idiot. And now he was screwing up Vinnie's power of foresight. Which put Mary's life in jeopardy. Again.

So what was the answer? In true cowardly fashion, he hid in the office, staring at the security feed from the room Mary was in. Mike's medical team bustled around, tinkering with settings on the machines. They'd arrived right after the trucks of equipment and had been busy ever since. It shouldn't surprise him that Mike got everything assembled and delivered so quickly, but it still did.

The man was formidable, he'd give him that.

He watched the team run test after test. Watched the girls go in and out of the room. Watched Vin and Gianni try—and fail—to use their powers again.

Deep down, he knew it all rested on him. Life, balance, transformation. The gifts of the green dagger. But he couldn't figure out how to restore Mary's life, how to bring balance to her body, how to transform her from comatose to lucid.

What was he missing?

Donni burst into the office.

"Doesn't anyone knock anymore?"

She looked around the empty room. "Someone else here?"

"What do you want, Donni?"

"Is your lip bleeding?"

"You barged in here to ask about my face?"

"You know, you're a real pain in the ass sometimes."

"So I've been told."

She sighed, hung her head, then squared her shoulders and looked him in the eye. "We've all tried it your way. Now we're going to try mine. Let's go."

He sat there—lip throbbing, head pounding, heart racing. Didn't feel that keyed up when Coz punched him.

"Don't make me drag you out of here."

As poleaxed as he felt, she probably could. His ego couldn't take that. So despite his reservations, he stood and followed her out of the room.

10

NICO LOOKED AROUND the empty hallway and wondered where everyone had gone. His brothers, Donni's sisters, the medical staff—all were MIA.

He stepped through the open door. Mary lay in the room he'd been viewing, once again attached to monitors. Her heart beat steadily, her blood oxygen looked good.

Guilt washed over him. Something had gone wrong on his end. If he'd left her alone, she'd at least be waking once a day.

"I think they were torturing her," Donni said.

He'd almost forgotten she was there. "Why would you say that? She looks fine. Other than not being awake, that is."

"Did you hear what that nurse said? If Mama didn't behave herself, they wouldn't wake her as often."

"That doesn't mean she was tortured."

"If she was acting out, I don't think they gave her a timeout in the corner."

He hadn't thought about it. Getting Mary free, healing Donni's wound, then waking her mother had been his primary concerns. He'd been so consumed with those tasks that he totally forgot what the nurse had said. "Did Mike's medical staff indicate there had been abuse?"

She shook her head and took her mother's hand.

"Then don't dwell on it now. We can ask her when she wakes." If she wakes.

"About that." Donni turned and looked at him.

"What?"

"Can you explain to me how your powers work?"

"No."

"No, you can't? Or no, you won't?"

"Does it matter?"

"I'm just trying to understand what you do. You get a picture of the injury, then you send it a message to heal?"

"It's not an email exchange, Don. It's… well, it's power."

"But what do you do?"

What did he do? It was all innate, really. He held the dagger in his hand and just knew what to do. Knew what bones were broken and how to knit them together. But that wasn't it. Not exactly. If it was, he'd have complete control of his powers by now. It wasn't just cerebral knowledge. There was something more to it. Something not tangible or definable. Something raw. Elemental.

And nothing he wanted to play with when Mary's life was at stake.

"Nico?"

"Sorry. I was thinking about it. I'm not sure how it works exactly."

"Do you think? Do you feel? Does something come to you?"

"Why are you asking me all these questions?"

"Because we're going to heal Mama. Together. And I want to know what my part is."

"You don't have a part, because we aren't doing anything."

"Then try on your own."

"No."

"Chicken."

The dare was a pathetic attempt to goad him into doing what she wanted, but there was no way he was risking any of them. "Donni, I don't know what will happen. If the power doesn't work, then no big deal. But what if it does more damage?"

"How?"

"I don't know. We've been shooting energy pulses at targets. What if I zap her and fry her brain?"

"Vinnie said your powers have grown. Although he doesn't know why. But that means you're stronger now."

"I've been practicing in my free time."

"You don't have free time."

He sighed. "I practice at night. I wanted to be sure I was ready for anything when I found your mom."

"So now, let's heal her. You've been healing bones almost since day one."

"I don't have my full powers yet! Don't you get it? What if I send one of those pulses into her instead of healing her? I don't even know what's wrong with her. There's a good chance I can't heal her at all."

"Well, the tests show that her skull is cracked. Her brain was swelling."

"Then how did the medical people at the facility get her lucid?"

"The doctor said the injury is fresh."

He took that in with a sinking feeling in his gut. When they were being chased through the woods, he fell with Mary in his arms. Her head—her whole body—bounced all around until he got back to his feet and picked her up. And he didn't run gingerly. She jostled and jerked with every step he took. She was unconscious because of him. Because of damage he did.

"Nico, are you listening?"

No. He hadn't been. "It's my fault. From when I fell with her."

"It doesn't matter now."

"Yes, it does! I'm the reason she won't wake up."

Donni tilted her head and looked up at him. "Well, then. What are you going to do about it?"

He blinked a few times, at a loss for words. Finally, one came to him. "Nothing."

"Oh, yes you are, Dominico Micelli. You're *going* to heal the crack in her skull."

"I can't."

"You can."

"No, you don't understand. Even if I was willing to try, even if I succeeded, that could kill her. She probably has swelling on her brain, and the crack in her skull is the only thing alleviating the pressure. I could give her brain damage if I healed her now."

"Gianni was here when the results came in. He already healed her tissue. Swelling's gone. We're all just waiting for you. Mama's waiting for you."

It was a simple bone injury. Something he'd done dozens of time since his powers started to manifest. Something he should easily have picked up on with the medical staff running tests. So why did this one stop him cold? Why did it terrify him so much?

Donni stood and faced him, hugged him around his waist.

He wrapped his arms around her and pressed a kiss to the top of her head. Where did that come from? Before he could process what he'd done and why, she grasped his dagger and pulled it from its sheath.

"Don—"

She grabbed his hand, put it on top of the one she held the dagger in, and touched it to her mother's forehead.

The heat, the strength. The power. The sensations rushed through him. Welled in his core and surged through his body, to his hand then into the dagger. Or did the dagger push the power through him? The current built in his system, and potent energy burst forth. And as quickly as it came on, it receded. His mind and body stilled, his essence calmed.

He looked at Donni.

Her wide eyes blinked slowly. Her breath came in shallow gasps. "That was... that was..."

Yeah. It was.

"My God, look!" She pointed at her mother.

Mary's eyelids fluttered. A soft groan slipped from her lips.

"I'll get the doctor." Nico ran from the room before he was forced to process what had happened. And why.

"MAMA!" DONNI TOOK her mother's hand and stared at her face, willing her to open her eyes, sit up, and start talking.

Wishes sometimes do come true. Her mother blinked a few times, then she turned her head and looked at Donni. She croaked out one weak word. "Sweetie."

Donni both thrilled at the sound and cringed at the hoarseness. "Ssh. Don't talk yet. The doctors are coming, and I'll get you ice chips to soothe your throat."

Mama tried to scoot up in the bed and moaned. Then she squeezed Donni's hand. "Don't go."

Donni blinked back tears. "I'm so glad you're awake."

"Where are we? How did I get here?"

The medical staff bustled into the room, followed by Donni's sisters. The girls all clustered around the foot of the bed, talking over each other in their excitement. The doctor shooed Donni out of the way, bent over his patient, and shone a light in her eyes.

"Mrs. Notaro. I'm Doctor Russo. How are you feeling?"

Her voice rasped. "A little tired. Disoriented. My throat is dry."

The nurse put a pitcher and glass on the table beside her, then she handed her a cup with ice chips in it.

Mary spooned one into her mouth and sighed. She quickly took another.

"That's all to be expected," Doctor Russo said. "Does your head hurt? Are you dizzy?"

"No. Actually, I'm already starting to feel better. Stronger."

"Well, I don't want you out of bed yet. Can you tell me what you remember?"

Mary's brow wrinkled.

Gianni, Vinnie, and Coz rushed in.

"She's up?" Gianni said.

"How is she, Doc?" Coz asked.

"I can answer for myself, thank you." Mary set her cup down and looked around the room. She frowned when she looked at her daughters, all of whom had tears in their eyes. "It seems I gave you all quite a scare. I'm sorry."

"Oh, Mama. No." Franki scooted past the nurse and took her mother's free hand. "Don't be sorry. It wasn't your fault. It was mine."

"Yours?"

"Don't you remember?" Franki asked.

"It wasn't your fault or hers." Gianni's face darkened, his voice deepened. "Blame Sal."

"Sal? Salvatore Trunzo? Your father's friend?" She looked at Franki. "What's he have to do with this?"

Donni turned to the doctor. "Is amnesia common in this situation?"

"Amnesia! I don't have amnesia."

Doctor Russo patted her foot. "Let's give her a moment for her memories to catch up with her, shall we?"

Mama looked around the room. Her gaze settled on Gianni. "You were there."

"Yes, ma'am."

She furrowed her brow. "There was a fire."

"It's coming back to her," Franki said.

"Sal took me from my room. He held us captive in the woods. Gianni, you got me and Franki out."

"Well, sort of," Franki said.

Mama's eyes widened and she touched her neck. "My throat. He—sliced my throat."

Tears fell onto Donni's shirt. Her heart ached as she watched her mother relive the attack. "Don't, Mama. You're fine now. Don't think about it."

"But… but how?"

Coz's face was red and he picked at non-existent lint on his shirt.

"You know how Gianni used his special gifts to save us?" Franki said. "The fire, the tissue-healing?"

Mama nodded.

"All the guys have powers. Coz has dominion over death."

She looked away from Franki and stared at Coz, whose face got even redder. "You control death?"

He shook his head, puffed his cheeks out, and blew out a long, slow breath. "Not exactly. I don't know, really. My powers haven't fully manifested yet."

"But you saved me?"

"I was able to stop your death. Or reverse it. Or something. I don't know. But when Mike took you, you were in a coma. I couldn't revive you fully."

She stared at him for a long while, then whispered, "I owe you my life. Thank you."

He shrugged. "I wish I could have done more."

"Mama," Jo said, "do you remember anything after that?"

She bit her lip and rolled her eyes toward the ceiling. Then she looked at her daughter. "Hazy images. People moving my legs, helping me walk around. Droning on and on about my muscles atrophying."

"Do you know who they were?" Toni asked. "How you got there?"

She shook her head. "No. It's like I'm looking through a fog."

"The drugs will do that," Doctor Russo said. "Those images might be all you recover."

"How'd I get here?"

Donni squeezed her foot. "Nico and I found you and broke you out."

"Broke me out? You? The danger—what were you thinking?"

"Probably not a good time to mention that she got shot, huh?" Toni said.

Donni glared at her. She and Toni almost always had each other's backs, but when they were at odds, her twin fought dirty. And apparently Toni was furious that she'd put herself in danger. Still, she didn't have to throw Donni under the bus.

"You got shot! Are you all right?"

"Yes, Mama. Of course. You see me standing here, perfectly fine."

She made the sign of the cross. "*Nel nome del Padre, del Figlio, e dello Spirito Santo. Amen.* Donnatella, what was Nico thinking, taking you on a mission like that?"

"I stowed away. He didn't know until it was too late."

"And where is he now?"

Donni wished she knew.

And she was determined to find out.

NICO RAN A circuit through the hedge maze and grottos, but the jog didn't settle him. When he stopped in one of the out-of-the-way corners of the property—his favorite one for getting away to think—he was more keyed up than when he started. So he stripped down and jumped into the fountain's pool to cool off. He scrubbed at his body, head to toe, until he felt cleansed—on the outside, anyway. The quick dip cleaned the sweat off his body but did nothing to settle him down. He climbed out, slipped his shorts back on, and sat with his back against the stone wall. It was rough and cold against his bare skin.

He grabbed his dagger and shot some energy bursts at random rocks scattered throughout the grotto. Hit every single one without effort. Why the hell didn't his powers come that easily to him when it mattered?

Bored, he resheathed his dagger and tossed it back on his pile of clothes. Then he sat there for a long time, just staring at the pool. Watching the water spurt from the fountain and listening to the burbling often calmed his thoughts. He took a deep breath and closed his eyes, connected with the world around him on a deeper level. Birds sang and insects chirruped, composing melodic strains in the warm air. The breeze caressed and cooled his damp skin. Another deep breath and he began to relax, began to become one with his world. Felt like the water, the air, or the very earth itself vibrated around him. Scents of fresh cut grass, random florals, and lemons wafted to him when the gentle wind blew.

The bright citrus aroma reminded him of Donni.

Not that he needed a reminder.

He'd kissed the top of her head. A tender gesture, not unlike something a relative would do. But also not unlike a lover. He hadn't been holding the dagger at the time. Had it on him, though. And she was reaching for it.

So was the act that of a lover or a friend?

And was it inspired by the dagger or not?

He sighed again, and his thoughts drifted away from the woman and to what they'd done.

Despite his fears, Donni had coerced him into using his powers. Maybe it was more accurate to say she'd channeled his powers and used them herself.

Hell, he had no idea what happened. All he knew was Mary woke. That, and he'd never felt anything so potent, so visceral, in his life.

Nico glanced at his shirt, laying in a heap with everything else he'd stripped off. He'd had to change his clothes after healing Donni. He had her blood all over him.

His stomach flopped just thinking about it, and he had to focus on something else.

He shoved aside his socks and shoes, pulled his discarded shirt toward him, and grabbed the dagger from on top of it. He unsheathed it from its scabbard and stared at it, willed it to answer his questions. Nothing but silence greeted him. If only he knew whether the weapon was behind his feelings. Did it cause the desire that had been building inside him? Was the pull toward her truly pure and natural? Or did the magic itself crave her, draw him toward her?

"I've been looking for you," Donni said.

He looked up at her. She was a silhouette, the sun behind her head creating a halo effect, like she'd been sent from God Himself. Had his dagger beckoned her? He tossed the damn thing aside, determined it wouldn't sway his emotions.

She stepped closer and lowered herself to sit beside him. Instead of leaning against the stone wall, she rested her head on his shoulder. Her hair was soft on his skin, the tresses dancing in the slight breeze and tickling him.

"Who planted that lemon tree?" She kicked off her shoes and wiggled her toes.

He couldn't tear his gaze from her feet. They were small, tan, and the nails were painted a soft pink. She had a small tattoo above her left ankle of a yin. Or maybe it was a yang. He never knew which was which. But he knew the ink was sexy.

"What?"

Donni nudged him and pointed across the grotto to a lemon tree on its border. "The lemon tree?"

The fruit was plump, ripe, and unblemished. Must have been where the citrus scent came from. He furrowed his brow. He went to that grotto all the time. How could he not have noticed it before?

"That tree," she said. "It's new."

"How do you know?"

"This is one of my favorite spots to come and get away. I'm here all the time. And I don't remember it being here."

That was a weird coincidence. How had they never bumped into each other there before? Rather than asking her about it, he answered her question. A first for him. "Maybe Mike asked the groundskeeper to plant it."

She inhaled a deep breath. "It smells wonderful."

"Is that why you've been looking for me? To tell me how the grotto smells?"

"No." She sat up and looked at him. "I thought you'd want to see Mama, since you were the one responsible for finding her. And waking her. But you didn't come back with your brothers."

"I'm sure she needs recovery time. I'll check in on her later."

"She wanted to thank you."

He scoffed. "She should be reading me the riot act. I took you into the belly of the beast."

Her cheeks pinked, and she looked away.

"I guess that fact didn't escape her notice, either."

"Well, after she's done freaking over the danger, she'll want to thank you."

Nico gently banged his head on the wall once, twice. A third time. Didn't help, though.

"Why didn't you come back?"

There was a million-dollar question. "I just needed some time."

"To recover? Did healing her weaken you? I know it can take a lot out of you."

"No. Not that. I was fine after. Maybe even charged up."

She smiled. "I know what you mean. Me, too. I found it rather exhilarating."

Her skin glowed, her eyes shone. A beatific smile crossed her face.

"I'm glad your mom's better. And I'm glad you didn't get hurt in the process. But you shouldn't have done that. Who knows what could have happened?"

"I knew."

He shook his head.

"Nico, please. You've been healing bone injuries for a while now. I don't know why this one freaked you out so much, but—"

"Because of you, all right?" The outburst startled him, but he couldn't rein it in. "It was because of how important it was to you. And because I can't control my powers around you."

"What do you mean?"

He turned away from her and studied the pool, watched the bubbles froth near the fountain, ripple across the surface, and dissipate near the edge. He felt as fragile as that water—volatile in his core but drifting into nothingness at the extremities. Despite the turmoil inside him, he felt frayed, numb. Like he was about to shatter and drift away. He lowered his voice, spoke barely above a whisper. "The more it mattered to you, the more it frightened me. I didn't want to fail you. And I'd already failed you once. In the car, when you were shot. Gianni sent his power across hundreds of miles, but I couldn't heal you when you were right there with me. I needed my brothers around me just to repair your spine."

"My spine?"

"You were shot in the back, Donni." By all rights, she shouldn't be walking. Shouldn't be alive! They'd been lucky. Again. It certainly didn't have anything to do with his skill. At least Gianni was on his game. "Without my brother, you wouldn't even be alive."

"But I'm fine." She lifted her chin, but her face was pale.

"Donni, I don't know what I'm doing." Thinking about what could have happened chilled him to the core. "You could have been... permanently disabled. Or worse."

She was quiet for a moment. "I'm assuming you were worried about paralysis. Well, don't be. Because I'm obviously fine. Besides, technically, that's on Gianni, being his power is blood and tissue. Nerves. You're bone. That has nothing to do with my mobility. Or lack thereof."

"It does when your splintered bones are severing your spinal column. He had no trouble with his powers. It was all on me. And I almost couldn't do it. In fact, I couldn't do it. Not until I had help."

"So what? You figured it out. And you saved Mama, too."

"Also with help. Your help. What if it had gone wrong?"

"It didn't."

"It could have. And it was so important to you."

"Nico, I love my mother, of course, but I also love all of you. Your ability to heal any of the guys is just as important to me as if you were healing my sisters or my mother. We're all family now. One of us shouldn't mean more than the other."

Ah. But one did. Whether he could say it aloud or not. Then she went and said it. *Love.* The L-word. More turbulence inside him, more fraying of his edges. What did that even mean? And was he included in that? Did he want to be? Did he deserve to be?

She placed her hand on his cheek and turned his face toward her. "Why does that frighten you?"

"I'm not scared." Even he didn't believe himself.

"Well, if that doesn't scare you, then this shouldn't, either." She leaned in and placed a kiss on his Adam's apple.

Her breath was warm on his skin, her lips soft. She trailed her tongue along his jawline and nipped his earlobe, and he squirmed, the rough stone scraping against his head and back.

The pain only added to the heady sensation.

Nico wrapped his arms around her. He shifted so he lay on his back and pulled her on top of him to protect her from the rough ground. It was uncomfortably hard and gritty beneath him, yet she was so soft and pliant against his chest. The contrasting sensations fascinated him.

She fascinated him more.

"*Tesoro.*" He ran his fingers through her hair, grasped the silken locks and used them to tilt her head and pull her mouth down to his. She tasted like chocolate, rich and decadent, and he indulged his appetites.

The clothing between them was too great a barrier. He needed to feel the warmth of her skin as he held her body against his. He grabbed the hem of the shirt and pulled it over her head. Warmth? It was heat—molten, combustible. But for the grace of God, he'd have exploded from it.

Her body molded to his, the friction of her lace bra against his chest a rough reminder that there was something desirable beneath it. He wondered briefly when she'd even donned it, only to immediately wonder what she'd feel like when he took it off her.

He trailed his fingers up her sides, let them dance over her ribcage before moving them to her spine. Her precious spine. His hands stilled, and she groaned into his mouth.

She wanted more from him, and he had to oblige. He might not deserve it, but he'd be damned if he'd deny her.

She squirmed under his touch, and with one hand he flicked open the clasp while the other lowered a shoulder strap. Donni reared up, ripped the thing off, and tossed it aside. His eyes feasted on her appearance until she lowered herself back to him. He breathed her in, lost himself in her kisses. She was everything he'd been afraid to hope for. And more. Didn't matter how close they were, how she felt pressed against him. He had to touch her, as much for his pleasure as hers.

Nico sat up and pulled her onto his lap. She straddled him—wrapped her legs around his waist and tangled her hands in his hair. Could she possibly want him as much as he needed her? He doubted it. No one could be consumed with the kind of desire he felt.

He fondled her breasts, and she tipped her head back and moaned. Her throaty whimpers harmonized with the fountain burbles and animal song and became a melody he'd hear in his dreams. He wanted to hear her groan, hear her scream his name. So he reached between them, hissed when he accidentally grazed himself before finding her.

She giggled into his mouth and groped him.

Her hand was in his way, and he pushed it aside. Then he found her again, touched her, stroked her. She jerked, trembled, all traces of amusement gone. Her movements against him nearly sent him over the edge, and he picked her up and lay her beside him.

Thank God for stretchy yoga pants.

He slid his hand under the material. She writhed beneath his touch, was slick with desire. He stroked her—his fingers moving faster, her hips bucking harder—until she cried his name, her voice mingling with the chorus of birdsong and rhythmic burble of fountain streams.

And he let her ride the wave to oblivion, carried through the air on nature's sweetest anthem.

DONNI SMILED AND opened her eyes. Things were going better than she could have dreamed.

"I'm sorry. I shouldn't have put you on the ground like that. Are you okay?"

Okay? That was laughable. She felt fantastic. Yet she wanted so much more. She trailed her fingers over the broad plains of Nico's chest, down to the sculpted muscles of his abdomen, and under the waistband of his shorts.

He grabbed her wrist and pulled her hand back to his belly.

She wrinkled her forehead and looked down at him. "What are you doing?"

"What are you doing?"

"I was taking the next step."

Nico rearranged them so she was no longer splayed on the ground beneath him. Instead, he held her in his lap, her back against his chest, and cradled her in his arms, resting his chin on the top of her head. "Your back okay? No scrapes or anything? How do you feel?"

"I feel phenomenal. Now it's your turn." She turned her head, looked up at him, and smiled. Reached for his waistband. "Or we can share the next turn."

"Donni, stop." He interlaced his fingers with hers and brought her hand to his lips.

She squirmed out of his grasp. How utterly humiliating. Bra to this side, shirt to that side, she began gathering her things and hurrying into them.

"Where are you rushing to?"

"Anywhere but here."

He swore under his breath. "So I somehow made you angry. Again."

She stopped dressing with her shirt barely pulled over her bra. The breeze was warm on her stomach, but she didn't bother adjusting the hem. "You're joking, right?"

"I don't see why you're so upset. I just got you—"

"Say the word 'off' and I'll break every one of your nimble fingers."

Nico cleared his throat. "To relax. I was going to say, 'I just got you to relax.' Which you very much needed."

At least he had the good sense not to smile at the 'nimble fingers' compliment she let slip. "Oh, did I? I can't imagine why you'd think I needed to relax. I wasn't the one out here fretting."

"Men don't fret."

"Yeah? Men don't shy away from their problems, either. Call it what you want. I was inside facing my drama. You ran from yours." She yanked her shirt down the rest of the way and slipped her shoes on.

"I'm not hiding from anything."

"Bullshit. You didn't want to deal with me and the dagger. You fled the room when Mama woke up. And now that we got carried away out here, you're resisting that, too."

"You realize I had you half naked in what is essentially the backyard, right? Anyone could have come out here and seen us."

Her cheeks burned. She never even considered where they were. Only how right it felt. But was that just a convenient excuse for him? "So you stopped to protect my virtue?"

"Sure. If you want to put it that way, yeah."

"What way do you want to put it?"

"Shit, Don, I didn't want to strip you naked and fu—" He sighed. "And have my way with you on the filthy ground."

"Okay. So you want to go inside and finish what you started? Plenty of doors in there to close and lock."

"Why are you pushing this?"

"Because you just—" She ran her hands through her hair. "Never mind. This was my mistake, not yours."

"Donni."

He looked broken, but she felt shattered. "Don't. Just don't. Like I said, my mistake. This is one thing you don't need to torture yourself over. I'll see you when I see you."

Before he could answer, she ran toward the house. She was the one running from a problem this time. But for the life of her, she couldn't think of a better response.

11

NICO DRESSED AND stared at the fountain, its song not nearly as beautiful as it had been earlier. He couldn't blame the dagger for his feelings. Not now that he'd been carried away with Donni and the dagger had been cast aside. He had to own his lust.

Should be castigated for it. Yet another of his many sins.

He had no business coming on to his charge. Maybe he should ask Coz to switch him. Then Donni could *really* say he ran from his problems.

Che cazzo. He was always the one in control. Why was he falling apart now? Especially when everyone needed him to have his shit together.

Maybe if he did get things under control, he'd deserve a woman like Donni—smart, funny, beautiful, kind. Determined as all hell.

What he couldn't figure out was why she would be interested in him. And she was. Even as dense as he was, he recognized her signs. They were about as subtle as gunfire.

Hadn't he seen and heard too much of that in the last few months? Maybe he should try to ignore what she was putting out there.

Like he had a chance in hell of that. He couldn't even look at her toes, how was he going to look her in the eye and not tremble with need?

Maybe he should have let her finish what he'd started. No, he didn't deserve any kind of happy ending, physical or otherwise. Not until he could solve some of the Brotherhood's problems and assure Donni's safety.

Didn't make his shorts any less tight where it counted, though.

Well, if he wanted a shot with Donni, he had some serious work to do. He turned his back on the grotto and headed toward the house.

AFTER HIS SHOWER, Nico popped into the office and checked the security feeds. Donni was nowhere to be found, so she was probably in her room. Her sisters were in the kitchen. Toni and Jo were making trays of something and doing their best to keep Franki from interfering. She was lucky to have hooked up with the one Brother who loved to cook, because she was a disaster in the kitchen.

Guess they were the perfect couple, even if they didn't understand the concepts of PDA and TMI. He supposed he could suffer through their unending anniversaries and constant snuggling, though. Because Gianni was happy. Because they both were happy. And given the danger the Notaros faced, small moments of happiness were all anyone could hope for.

Vinnie and Coz were in the gym. Good thing Coz was there to spot Vin, because he was benching a ridiculous amount of weight. Clearly he hadn't worked through whatever set him off earlier.

That left Gianni. Took a while, but Nico finally found him in Mary's recovery room in the basement. Why would he be alone with her?

Well, Nico needed his own one-on-one time with her, so he made his way down there. Maybe Gianni would be done by the time he arrived, and he'd have a chance to deal with one of his problems.

His brother was just leaving the room when Nico got to the door. "Oh, hey."

"Hey, Gianni. What's the goofy grin for?"

"Can't a guy just be happy?"

"Sure. But you don't usually look like that unless Franki's draped all over you."

His brother chuckled. "I'll give you that one."

"Well, I'm glad you're so happy."

Gianni looked around, then he leaned and whispered in Nico's ear. "Can you keep a secret?"

"You know I can. What's up."

The goofy grin turned into a Cheshire smile. "I'm going to propose to Franki. I just talked to Mary."

"Going the traditional route and asking for parental permission. Classy. Nice touch."

Gianni nodded his head, still grinning. "Yeah. I thought John would have wanted me to."

"Congratulations, man." Nico gave him the awkward one-armed man hug. "I'm happy for you."

"She didn't say 'yes' yet."

Nico scoffed. "I don't think you have to worry about that."

Gianni's smile somehow grew bigger, and he darted down the hall.

At least someone was happy. That made one of them. Nico turned toward Mary's door, squared his shoulders, and knocked.

"Come in," she called.

He poked his head inside and, as was his habit, surveyed the room before entering. Mary lay in the bed, still looking frail and tiny. Her coloring had improved, though. Nico offered a weak smile and stepped across the threshold.

His gaze was drawn to her bedside table, which held an assortment of flower arrangements. No one had left the compound, so that meant anyone who brought her a bouquet had gone to the gardens and hand-picked their selections. Wasn't he the biggest ass ever to drop by empty-handed? Probably didn't matter, though. She was just going to tell him off and send him on his way.

"How are you feeling?"

She studied him for a moment.

He couldn't read her expression, but he wilted under her gaze like a student who didn't finish his homework. His throat tightened, and he cleared it. "I should have brought flowers. Sorry."

Tears welled in her eyes and flowed down her cheeks.

But still she said nothing.

Nico lapsed into panic-mode. He was useless with crying women. Didn't know how to make them feel better, didn't know how to react when they wouldn't stop. He lunged for a tissue box on the table and managed to knock a vase onto the floor. Blue pottery shattered into jagged shards interspersed between tall stems of sunflowers. He tossed the tissue box onto the bed and bent down to clean the mess. "I'm really sorry. I'll replace them for you."

She sniffled. "It was top-heavy. Only a matter of time before it toppled. Don't worry about it."

He tossed the big pottery pieces and the larger stems of flowers in the trash-can and dabbed at the floor with wadded up paper towels. The more time he spent on the floor, the longer he could put off the inevitable.

She dabbed at her eyes with a tissue. "Leave it, Nico. Come sit with me."

So much for a reprieve. He looked at her, and she stretched her hand toward him. Not only was he in for it, he'd have a close-up view of her anger.

Merda.

He took her hand, sat on the edge of her bed, and met her gaze. "Before you begin, I just wanted to tell you how sorry I am."

"Sorry?"

"You're right. That word is pathetically weak. But I don't have a stronger one. I'm so sorry I had Donni with me. I'm sworn to protect her, and instead I put her in danger. It's unforgivable."

She searched his face, squeezed his hand, and smiled. "Dominico, it's not unforgivable. In fact, I don't think there's anything to forgive. I had a long talk with Donni. She told me she hid in your car and forced you to take her with you. I have no doubt she would have marched right up to the door if you hadn't adapted your plan to include her. You aren't to blame for what happened. In fact, I'd like to thank you."

"Thank me? For putting Donni in harm's way?"

Mary shook her head and chuckled. "No. For saving me."

"You were out of the coma, and I put you back into one."

"I was out of Mike's care and under someone else's control. You rescued me."

"Your head... I—"

"Nico. Stop. I was in a bad place with bad people who did bad things. Nothing you did—even accidentally—was as bad as what I endured."

He thought back to the nurse's comment. Dread settled like a rock in the pit of his stomach. "Again, I'm sorry. What hap... I mean, do you want to talk about it?" Please, God, don't let her want to discuss it.

Again tears welled in her eyes. This time, she managed to blink them away. When she spoke, her voice was strong, unwavering. "No, thank you. Not right now. I just wanted to be sure you knew how grateful I was."

Nico wasn't really a demonstrative person, certainly not as much as Gianni had become. But he felt a connection to Mary at that moment. And on some level, he knew she needed more than a smile and a handshake. He leaned over and hugged her. Despite her small size and weak stature, her return embrace was strong, and he held her a while, taking as much comfort as he gave. When he pulled away, he could have sworn some of the shadows under her eyes had cleared.

He stood and walked to the door. Just before he stepped out, she said, "Nico, wait."

Nico turned, looked at her, and raised his eyebrow.

"One more thing. Before you go."

He stepped back inside. "Anything."

"What can you tell me about Donni's vision? What's your take on it?"

His mind totally blanked. He'd been so worried about all the secrets he'd been keeping, it completely slipped his notice that Donni was keeping some, too. "You mean, from Catherine's mirror?"

Mary nodded.

He scowled.

"Uh-oh. I guess she didn't mention it to you."

"No, Mary. She didn't."

"Talk with her, Nico. She needs you."

In the compromised mental and emotional condition he was in, he seriously doubted he'd be of use to anyone. But Mary needed comfort. And Donni needed a severe dressing down. "I'll find her now."

"No, I mean, she needs you. And I think you need her."

He shook his head. "I don't know what she'd told you, but—"

"She didn't tell me anything. I've been reading that girl since she was in my womb. I know her. Now, I'm getting to know you. And I'm not blind. I see the way you react when her name is mentioned. It's on your face, in your eyes. There's something there."

"It's the training, the constant close proximity. She's my charge."

"It's more than that."

"It's guilt over the danger I put her in, when it's my job to protect her."

"It's more than that, too."

"It's—"

"Nico, we can do this all night. Call it whatever you like. Just don't hurt my little girl."

"I'm her protector. I'll never hurt her." Guilt washed over him when he thought of the danger he'd put her in, of the look on her face when he'd refused her in the grotto. Seemed all he did was hurt her, regardless of his intentions.

"That's all I had to say. I think I'll rest now. Would you mind getting the light on your way out?"

So that was that. He'd been dismissed. As he left the dark room and closed the door behind him, he thought about what Mary had said. Too many options drifted through his baffled brain.

Easiest to focus on the one thing he wasn't at fault over. He went looking for Donni. They needed to discuss her vision.

And the hypocrisy of her secret-keeping.

FRESH OUT OF the shower, Donni sat at her vanity, towel wrapped around her damp body, hair dripping down her back. She intended to comb out the tangles and apply moisturizer before dressing. Instead, she simply peered into the mirror. Not Catherine's cursed mirror. If she had a choice, she'd never look into that damn thing again.

No, she stared at her reflection. Barely recognized the woman gazing back.

She and her family had been with the Brotherhood since shortly after Papa died. She'd witnessed atrocities that she once thought only happened in guerrilla warfare and fictional stories. Papa's grisly murder. Franki's and Mama's abduction. Gianni's uncontrolled supernatural flaying. Coz and Gianni both getting shot. Jo's throat getting slashed. Chuck—and whatever his tragic fate might be. Jo's capture. Vinnie killing a man he thought was a trusted friend.

All this in the name of that damned prophecy. Why hadn't Papa told them they descended from the Medici? They couldn't have changed their destiny, but at least they could have prepared.

Who was she kidding? There was no preparation for what was happening.

The woman staring back at her had shadowed bags under haunted brown eyes that were open a little too wide, that blinked a little too often. Her skin seemed pale beneath her tan, like she was a battered victim hiding inside a healthy but transparent shell.

She turned in her seat and looked at the reflection of her back in the mirror. Quite the opposite image there. Not so much as a discolored dot marred the surface of her skin.

Yet she'd been shot. Given what Nico had said by the fountain, she'd been paralyzed. Possibly close to death.

And like everything else, she was healed and the problem was put behind them, not to be discussed. Sure, her sisters had yelled at her for her recklessness. But the injury itself? The potential ramifications? All taboo topics.

Jo had to be dying to talk about her near-death experience. And about Chuck. Maybe the guys were too cool to talk about their issues, but she saw the cracks in Vinnie. He was one incident away from losing it.

She could have been that incident.

When would it all end?

Mike had hired discreet, experienced medical staff to care for Mama. Maybe he could bring in a psychologist, too.

Better make that a psychiatrist. More likely than not, one or more of them needed medication to get over all the traumas. Hell, she wouldn't say no to a tranq at the moment.

She'd settle for a hug.

A soft *rap, rap, rap* sounded at the door. Probably more yelling. Or more topic-avoidance. She sighed, too tired for either, and ignored the knock.

"Donni, you in there?" Nico spoke softly through the closed door.

She thought about not answering, but she couldn't deny him, even knowing he would probably lie and evade any question she asked. "Come in."

He stepped inside, all alpha-male body and guardian-concerned expression on his face. The dichotomy of his vulnerable look and powerful physique was a punch to her gut, and all logic and reason evaporated, leaving her with only raw lust and unquenched desire.

Nico closed the door behind him. "How are you feeling?"

The low timbre of his voice vibrated through her like an electrical current. How could four little words make so large an impact?

"Better. Now."

"We need to talk."

Exactly what she didn't expect. She was usually trying to drag information out of him, not the other way around. But she didn't feel like talking, so she rose and turned to him. "Or we could talk later."

Nico swallowed. His voice cracked when he started to speak, and he cleared his throat and tried again. This time his words were deep, husky. "Maybe I should step outside. Until you're dressed."

Donni reached for the loose knot securing her towel and slowly released it—a sensual, one-item striptease. The towel pooled on the floor at her feet. "Maybe you should get undressed and join me."

He demonstrated more willpower than she thought he would. Didn't close the distance between them, didn't even let his gaze wander over her naked body. He maintained eye contact when answered, although his voice was strained. "You just got shot. You need your rest."

She crossed the room and stood directly in front of him. Brazen was never a word she'd have used to describe herself, but at the moment, it fit her perfectly. Standing before him—completely exposed while he was fully clothed—should have been humiliating. But it wasn't. It was empowering. Stimulating. "That's right. I got shot. But I don't need to rest. I need something to reaffirm life."

He looked up at the ceiling, closed his eyes, and took a deep breath.

"I need you, Nico."

"Don't ask me to do this. I don't want to take advantage of you. Again."

"You didn't before and you won't be now. How is it taking advantage of me when I'm asking?"

"Because if you weren't reacting to a near-death experience, you wouldn't want this. You're not thinking rationally. You're emotionally compromised. It's no different than if you were drunk."

She wrapped her arms around his neck. "I'm not drunk. And I'm not emotional. What I want—what I need—is for you to finish what you started at the fountain."

"You were compromised then, too."

Donni was undeterred that he didn't return her embrace. His hands balled into fists at his side, and she knew he struggled to resist her. So she stood on her toes and pressed her lips to his. "Maybe you're right. I don't know. But if I am struggling to process what happened, you can take my mind off it for a while. Take me, Nico. Make me forget everything. Everything but you."

He took a deep breath and muttered something under his breath. That's when she knew she'd won.

"God, forgive me." Nico wrapped his arms around her, carried her across the room, and lay her on the bed. He stared at her, and a predatory smile crossed his face. Then he stretched out beside her and claimed her mouth with his.

His lips were soft, warm. She sighed, and he deepened the kiss. This was what she wanted. Her mind reeled until not a single coherent thought remained. Just sensations—heat of contact, thunder of heartbeats, thrill of more to come. She needed to feel his skin against hers, and she tugged at his shirt.

Instead of him helping her, he grabbed her wrist and lifted her hand above her head.

"Nico—"

He silenced her by kissing her again, even as he grabbed her other wrist and lifted it, too. He pinned her hands together, the long fingers of his left hand easily controlling both of hers, leaving her helpless to his whims.

Her breathing quickened as she succumbed to his will, her breasts rising and falling quickly, her sensitive nipples brushing off the soft cotton of his shirt and tightening almost painfully at the contact. Her skin broke out in gooseflesh even as her insides flamed.

With his free hand, he explored her body. The rough pad of his finger stroked her lower lip, traced her jawline, and trailed along her collarbone. He continued the journey down her breastbone, then he cupped her breast and rolled her nipple between his fingers.

She hissed at the touch. Her breath came in short gasps, and she writhed under his ministrations. The pleasure was nearly unbearable, yet she wanted so much more. She strained to release her hands from his grasp, yearned to touch him. But he only held her wrists tighter.

"You wanted this, *tesoro*," he whispered in her ear. "You wanted to forget. So forget. Relax. Just breathe."

Breathe. That was the one thing she seemed unable to do. She always found him sexy, but with him taking charge, holding her captive, her body his plaything to use as he desired—it thrilled her to her core, left her breathless and mindless and out of control.

His breath was hot against her flesh, yet it sent shivers down her spine. He nipped at her ear, then he nuzzled her neck. The scratch of stubble combined with the tender touch of his lips on her skin made her tremble.

His tongue took the same path his finger had—collarbone to breastbone to breast. She squirmed, sighed. He scraped his teeth against her sensitive flesh, and she moaned. Then he sucked on her nipple while reaching between her legs.

When he found his target, she nearly bucked him off the bed.

His finger moved in tiny circles—sometimes slow, sometimes fast. Sometimes gently, sometimes stronger. She writhed under his ministrations, and when his tongue traced the same pattern on her nipple, she thrashed beneath him.

"Please." She barely managed that one word. Wasn't even sure she said it aloud, but then he slid his finger inside her. A sound she didn't recognize slipped past her lips, and the visceral need continued to build in her core and flare out to her extremities. He stroked her harder, faster. Drove her higher and higher.

And then he carried her over the edge as she screamed his name.

DONNI LAY THERE, panting, hands still pinned above her head. The position thrust her chest up and forward. Nico continued to stroke her until she calmed down, then he turned his attention toward the breast he'd neglected, teasing her nipple with gentle flicks of his finger.

She was lost in the moment—every touch, every caress. Her desire and need should have banked, but instead, she needed him more.

Again she tried to get him to release his grip on her hands, and again he didn't let her. "Nico. Please."

He continued teasing her. "Please, what?"

"Please let my hands go. I need to touch you."

"No." He bent and pressed his lips to her throat.

"I asked you to finish what you started outside."

"Aren't you satisfied?"

How to answer that? Yes, and he stopped touching her. No, and she hurt his feelings—and then he stopped touching her.

"Well?" He kissed her in a sensitive spot behind her ear, his hot breath sending tingles racing through her.

It was difficult to speak when her thoughts splintered and her body thrummed with aching need. "I... feel wonderful. But..." What was she trying to say? "More."

"Mmm." He spoke with his lips on her neck, the vibration sending shockwaves through her system.

"Please." She barely recognized her voice. "I need you."

He kissed her softly on the lips. This time it was she who tilted her head and took the kiss deeper. She must have taken him by surprise, because he relaxed his grip on her wrists, and she took that opportunity to free her hands and wrap her arms around him. The muscles in his back rippled as he shifted his weight away from her, but she tightened her grasp and held him against her.

"Donni. Stop."

She looked up at him and saw the internal struggle plainly on his face. Even though she knew he was conflicted, knew he was in pain, she felt like the injured party. "Why do you keep rejecting me?"

"Rejecting you? I'm in your bed."

"No, you're on my bed." She wiggled out from under him and sat up. Unable to pull the covers around her, she held the pillow in front of her.

"Same thing."

"Not even close."

He got up and paced.

She set the pillow aside, stood, and wrapped herself with her discarded towel. "Twice now, I've offered myself to you. Hell, I begged you. And twice you turned me down."

"So you didn't like what we just did? Or what we did outside?"

"I don't know how to answer that. Of course I like it. Loved it. But the best part of being with someone is knowing you make them feel as good as they make you feel. And you won't even let me touch you. It makes me feel cheap. Like a *puttana*."

"You can't think that way. Besides, sluts are paid to give pleasure to others. They don't receive it for free. If anything, I—" He stopped short and turned away.

"By all means, Nico. Tell me how I'm using you for sex. That'll make me feel much better."

"I didn't say that."

"Might as well have."

"That wasn't what I meant."

"All I wanted was something to matter. Something to help me feel normal again. To help me feel again, instead of the numbness and the cold. I guess I should thank you for taking one—no, two—for the team."

"It's not like that. It wasn't a hardship for me to be with you."

"But you weren't with me. You clearly have no desire to ever be with me."

He stormed across the room, took her in his arms, and pulled her body against him. The hot bulge pressed against her stomach through his jeans, then he ground his hips against her, emphasizing his point. "Still think I don't want you?"

She looked up at him, but he wouldn't meet her gaze.

His cheeks flushed, and he released her and turned away. "I'm sorry. That was—There's no excuse for that."

Donni put her hand on his shoulder and turned him around. She was about to tell him apologies weren't necessary, but then she decided actions spoke louder than words. She grabbed his waistband and pulled him close. Before he could stop her, she reached down and stroked him.

He hissed and tried to back away, but she still held tight to his jeans.

"I guess we both want this, then." She squeezed him again.

Nico gasped, swallowed. Again tried to step away. "Donni, I don't have my wallet with me."

Not the response she expected. At all. She loosened her grip, and turned away. "Are we back to talking about payment again? I can't believe you think—"

He spun her around and pressed his lips to hers, stopping her mid-tirade. She stayed rigid in his arms for a moment, but then relaxed into the kiss.

After she'd calmed, he released her. "I wasn't talking about money, Don. What kind of man do you take me for?"

She shook her head. "Then what—what are you talking about?"

He took a deep breath. "I don't have a condom with me."

Donni's face flamed, and she smiled. Then chuckled. Then dissolved into a full-out belly laugh. The whole time, Nico stood there, staring at her. Almost glaring at her. Not a trace of mirth on his face. She sobered pretty quickly, then asked, "That's what's been stopping you?"

"It's one reason."

She was certain he had a plethora of others, but at the moment, she didn't care what they were. This was one problem she could solve—happily and easily. So she again approached him and took him in her hand.

Nico grabbed her shoulders to push her away, but she tightened her grip on him. Not hard, but just enough. She stood on her toes and whispered in his ear. "I'm on the pill. And I don't sleep around. I'm clean. You?"

He moaned and dropped his arms to his side. Managed one word that came out in a groan. "Clean."

She smiled and guided him across the room. It only took her seconds to strip his clothes off him, then they lay on the bed, limbs tangled and bodies pressed together.

He was hot and hard, and she was more than ready, but she let him set the pace. Kisses, strokes… both of them exploring, savoring. Indulging.

Then Nico pinned her under him and looked down at her. He positioned himself at her entrance and took a deep breath. His voice was a guttural growl when he spoke. "I don't think I can be gentle."

"Who asked you to be?" God, not her. She didn't want the man, she wanted the beast. And he unleashed it.

"Oh, *tesoro*." In one quick move, he was deep inside her. She'd never felt so full, so hot. He set a frenetic pace, one she matched stroke for stroke, thrust for thrust. The world fractured—became only bursts of color, bars of melody, bolts of electricity. The pressure built, the sensations swelled and morphed into something beyond description, and he took her over the edge of sanity as this time he called her name.

12

WHAT IN GOD'S name had he done?

Nico lay in Donni's bed, staring at the ceiling to avoid looking at the beautiful woman in his arms. She'd fallen asleep, and he didn't want to wake her. After being shot—supernaturally healed or not—she needed her rest.

Consequently, he tried not to move so he didn't disturb her.

Night had fallen, and the room was cast in shadows. A sliver of moonlight shone through the open window blinds, landing right on the abandoned pile of his clothes on the floor. He also tried not to look at his belongings—particularly his dagger at the top of the pile, mocking him, lustrous in the darkness.

And back to his original question—what the hell had he done?

He'd promised himself not to let his dagger influence him. When he and Donni were together in the grotto, he'd tossed it aside and hoped that distance was proof it wasn't motivating his desires. At the time, he thought it had been enough, though a kernel of doubt had niggled around in the back of his brain.

But after what had just happened, he had all kinds of questions. Again. He may not have been touching the dagger, but he feared it still influenced him. Both of them, actually. Donni had been single-minded in her pursuit of him. And try as he might, he'd been unable to deny her.

Everything just got a whole lot more complicated. When his brothers and her sisters found out what happened, there would be hell to pay. And they would find out. The sisters didn't keep secrets from each other, and Franki and Jo didn't keep secrets from Gianni and Vinnie.

It was only a matter of time before Nico had to answer for his actions.

He and Donni had missed dinner. Now that he thought about it, he didn't think either of them had eaten all day. Even if neither of them talked about what had transpired, their absence from every meal would be a neon sign that something was going on.

His stomach growled. Kind of cramped. Funny how just thinking about food made the hunger stronger.

Nico looked at Donni. Looked like she was out cold. Maybe he could just pop down to the kitchen for a snack.

He managed to scoot out from under her without disturbing her. She sighed and rolled over, and he knew he was in the clear. It only took a few seconds for him to slip his jeans on. Then he grabbed his dagger and the rest of his things and left the room, closing the door as softly as he could.

The villa was quiet. He thought about taking a trip outside and working on his powers like he often did on nights he didn't search for Mary, but it was later than usual and he wanted to get some sleep.

Nico didn't know what time it was, but he hoped everyone had gone to bed for the night. He'd grab something from the kitchen, make a tray for Donni, and go to bed. In his own room. Maybe no one would ever know what he'd done, and if he never did it again, it wouldn't be a problem.

DESPITE HIS HUNGER, guilt kept Nico from feasting in the kitchen. After just a couple of bites from an antipasto tray, his stomach churned and he pushed the food away. If Donni woke before morning, though, she'd be ravenous. So he put some fruit, cheese, crackers, and olives on a tray for her, and he grabbed a couple bottles of water.

After collecting the rest of his things, he headed upstairs.

Strange how everything could change in such a short time.

He'd gone to her room earlier that night to chastise her for not telling him about her vision. And instead of an argument, instead of learning what she'd seen, he used her for his own satisfaction. Well, they were both satisfied. At least, he thought so. But still, it was wrong.

Not only did he let his dagger influence his behavior, he neglected his duties as a guardian. And after he promised Mary he'd get to the bottom of things.

He was a first-class jerk.

When he tiptoed down the hall, he caught a whiff of one of the many fresh floral arrangements scattered throughout the house. Donni, the interior designer of the group, appreciated them more than anyone else. She never failed to stop and smell the roses. Literally.

On a whim, he stopped at one of the large vases and pulled a bloom out of the bouquet. In the dark, he had no idea what it was. Probably wouldn't if it was broad daylight, either. But it smelled nice, and she'd like it. And it was all he had to offer.

He let himself back into her room. Thankfully, she still slept, so he left the tray on her nightstand. Only then did he realize she might be hurt to wake and find him gone.

He really was a first-class jerk.

The room was dark, but he looked around for a piece of paper and a pen. No luck. He couldn't see a damn thing, and he didn't want to make noise and wake her while looking for a way to leave a note. He'd just have to talk to her later, apologize in person. She deserved that.

Hell, she deserved a lot more, but he couldn't give her anything but grief.

He was sick of carrying his shirt and shoes and shit all over the house, but there was no need to put them on just to go down the hall. So he picked it all up again and let himself out. Once he made it to his bedroom door, he breathed a sigh of relief that no one had spotted him. If he could just talk to Donni in the morning before she saw her sisters, maybe he could convince her not to say anything and he could avoid a lecture he didn't need.

Nico turned the knob carefully and opened the door slowly so as not to make any noise. He slipped into his room, closed the door, and leaned against it. Home free. He let out the breath he was holding and tossed his things toward the chair in the corner.

"Oomph."

He jumped, and the light turned on, blinding him. Muscle memory had him in a fighting stance before his vision adjusted to the brightness of the room. After he blinked and could see again, he kind of wished he couldn't.

All three of his brothers were in there, just waiting for him. Coz had been in his chair and apparently took a boot in the face. He tossed Nico's things to the floor and rubbed his eye.

Nico dropped his hands and leaned back against the door, waiting for his heart to stop racing.

So much for getting away with anything.

"That hurt," Coz said.

"You shouldn't have been hiding in the dark."

"Wasn't hiding. Waiting."

"You wasted your time."

"You missed dinner."

"I was busy."

"Long night?" Gianni asked.

"Like I said, I had things to do."

"Things? Or people?" Vinnie said. "Or should I say one person in particular?"

Nico bristled. His dagger might be influencing his actions, but Donni didn't deserve to be discussed like that. "Watch your mouth."

"Have you thought all this through, Nico?" Coz asked.

He was glad to have a reason to turn away from Vinnie. "Thought what through, exactly?"

"Come on, man. You're standing there barefoot, jeans unbuttoned, no shirt. You've been alone with Donni for hours. We can connect the dots. Question is, can you? We can't afford a mistake here."

"It's none of your damn business."

"I think it *is* our business." Vinnie tapped his temple. "Strategy, remember? Mike might see all that's going on, but I see all the contingencies."

Nico strode to his dresser and opened a drawer, but there was nothing he needed. As soon as his brothers left, he was stripping down and going to bed. So he slammed the drawer shut and turned to face them. "Think what you want. I can't stop you. But think it somewhere else. I'm exhausted, and I want to go to sleep."

"We're not done," Gianni said.

"*I'm* done."

"There are still some things you should know."

"Gianni, I'm beat." He walked to his bed and dropped down onto it. "And there's nothing any of you can say that I haven't already thought myself. I'm going to talk to her in the morning. End it before it gets out of control. Hopefully I haven't already screwed things up, but if she's really pissed, Coz and I can switch charges. I can deal with Toni being pissed at me, and Donni won't have to see me except at briefings. I won't even join you for meals. I'll do whatever it takes to make things right. But not now. Donni's getting some much needed sleep, and I'm about to pass out." He rolled down to a prone position, closed his eyes, and wished he had thought to take his jeans off first. He honestly didn't know if he had the energy to get up, take them off, and lie down again.

"That's not what we're here to talk about," Coz said.

Nico didn't get up, but he did crack one eyelid open. "Can it wait until tomorrow, then?"

"Not if you're going to break Donni's heart," Gianni said.

He summoned energy he didn't know he had and sat up. "Neither of us is that serious."

"I wouldn't be too sure about that."

Oh, he didn't have a good feeling about that. "What are you talking about?"

Gianni ran his hand through his hair. "This is going to come out weird, but just listen, okay? When my powers manifested, when I learned to control them, I discovered they were emotionally-based."

"No shit."

"Listen. Vinnie's the brains of this outfit. Strategy. The mind. But I'm feelings. Emotions. The heart."

"What's the point of all this, Gianni? I'm tired, and I want to go to sleep."

"Not if you're going to break things off with Donni in the morning."

He sighed. "Again, my love life is none of your business."

"Yeah, it is," Vinnie said.

Nico glared at him and lay back down. He put his arm over his eyes. "Turn off the light on your way out."

Vinnie grabbed him by the shoulders and yanked him up. "Listen to us, dickhead. I know what I'm talking about." Again he tapped his temple. "And Gianni feels it." He patted his chest. "You and Donni *need* each other. If you aren't together, *bad shit is going to happen.*"

Nico pulled away from him. This was exactly what he feared. It wasn't his feelings affecting him, it was his dagger. And he wouldn't be manipulated— wouldn't let Donni be manipulated—by a hunk of rock and an alchemical ritual. "I'm not going to get into a relationship because your powers say I should. That's not fair to Donni or me."

"It has nothing to do with our powers," Gianni said. "Your feelings are your own. We didn't cause them."

"And the dagger has nothing to do with it?"

"We're not really supposed to talk about the dagger and fully claiming our powers. It could impact your destiny, and we're not allowed to do that."

He took a deep breath and looked each of his brothers in the eye. Only Coz looked uncomfortable, sitting there, squirming and silent. He never was one to enjoy discussing anything personal. Vinnie and Gianni looked determined, set jaws and crossed arms. Unmoving, unyielding. Uncompromising.

He kind of hated them at the moment. "The best I'll give you tonight is I'll think about it."

"You're just saying that so we'll leave you alone," Gianni said.

"I'm fucking tired, Gianni. Can we discuss this more in the morning?"

"Give us your word you won't do anything stupid," Vinnie said.

Nico crossed an *X* over his heart. "My word I won't do anything stupid."

"Anything *we* consider stupid."

"That's a different promise."

"Damn it, Nico." Coz stood and walked to the door. "We're fucking tired, too. We're the idiots who waited up for you all night. The least you can do is promise to think about what we said and not say anything to Donni until we can talk about it when we're not all short-tempered and falling asleep."

"Fine." Nico sighed. "Now leave me alone."

Vinnie and Gianni left without another word. Coz hovered by the door. "You all right?"

"I don't fucking know."

"Need anything before I go?"

"Yeah. Turn out the damn light."

The room went dark. A couple of heavy footfalls, and the door closed with a soft *snick*.

Nico was exhausted—too tired even to take his jeans off.

But despite how weary he felt, his mind reeled with what his brothers had said, preventing him from falling asleep.

DONNI WOKE WITH a smile on her face. She stretched and reached her arm out—

—and found the sheets cold, the bed empty.

Well, *that* smile sure as hell didn't last long.

She sat up, blinked, and looked around the room. Nope, he wasn't there, tucked into a corner trying to stay quiet while he typed on a laptop or checked something-or-other on his phone. If she didn't know better, she would believe it had all been a dream.

Then she saw her nightstand.

The smile returned.

At some point while she slept, he'd gone and gotten her food and water. Even thought to decorate the tray with a sprig of freesia. Did he know it was one of her favorites? She lifted the blossom to her face and inhaled deeply. The sweet aroma would always remind her of the night they'd spent together.

She hadn't eaten the day before, and Lord knew she'd expended quite a few calories. But she wasn't tired. She was refreshed. Maybe it was the healing. Or the good night sleep.

Again she smiled and sniffed the flower.

Maybe it was something else entirely.

Didn't matter. Her back was fine. She'd had a glorious night with a gorgeous man. And she felt fabulous. Good enough to make breakfast for everyone, as soon as she cleaned up. But first—

Donni opened one of the bottles of water, took a few sips, and put the freesia stem in it. It was a green glass bottle and not a fine crystal vase, but she'd never seen anything more beautiful. She gave it a place of honor on her vanity and headed for the bathroom.

She took a quick shower, and after she dressed, she grabbed the tray and headed down to the kitchen. It wasn't like everyone to sleep so late, but they had all earned a good rest. She got the coffee started, then she mixed up batter for a sour cream coffee cake. Carbs be damned. It was her mother's favorite, and they all had cause to let loose a little.

After she got the cakes in the oven, she put two dozen eggs on to boil—they needed some protein, after all—then she began cutting melon. Looked like she could get a little more protein into their breakfast, after all. She tossed the cantaloupe with white balsamic vinegar, freshly ground pink pepper, and finely diced mint. Then she wrapped the fruit in prosciutto and put it on a tray. Eggs, fruit, and cake. It wasn't going to be a glamorous meal, but it would be delicious.

She poured some coffee into a portable carafe, cut a large slice of the warm-from-the-oven cake, and put them plus two eggs and six pieces of fruit onto a tray. It bothered her not to make groupings of odd numbers—even numbers weren't as visually pleasing—but she knew how much her mother would eat. Still no one had come downstairs, so she put a plate, a napkin, and flatware on the tray and took it to her mother.

The door was open, and Donni peeked inside. Even Mama was still asleep. She didn't want to wake her, so she slipped inside to leave the tray. Her mother opened her eyes and smiled.

"Morning, Mama. How'd you sleep?"

"I should have slept well, but I kept waking up. It was like my body feared being put under again, so it didn't want to waste any lucid time it had."

Tears welled in her eyes, and she hugged her mother. "I'm so sorry. I bet the doctor will give you something to help you—"

"No! I mean, no, thank you. But I don't want to be at the mercy of drugs ever again. I'll sleep or stay awake based on what my body needs."

Donni bit her lip, but she didn't argue. She could understand, even if she would worry until Mama got back in a good sleep schedule.

"So, what'd you bring me?"

She slid the tray table over to the bed. "Your favorite coffee cake. And some other things."

"It smells delicious. Join me?"

Donni poured her mom a cup of coffee and passed it to her. "I'll eat upstairs."

"There's too much here, Donnatella. Have some."

Too much? There wasn't much there at all compared to what she used to eat. If Mama had no appetite, they must have been starving her. She made a mental note to talk to the doctors about that while she grabbed a bite of melon to appease her mother.

Only when Donni had begun eating did her mother pick up her fork.

"So, Mama, do you remember anything else?" She was almost afraid to hear the answer.

"Don't you worry about me, young lady. I'm fine. I'd rather talk about you."

"Me? What about me?"

"You and Nico. What happened last night?"

Madonna mia! How did *Mama* know? Did everyone know? She choked on a bit of prosciutto and coughed. Her mother handed her the cup of coffee, and she took a big gulp. The hot liquid scalded her tongue and throat, and she almost dropped the rest of the contents on her lap.

"Are you all right?"

Donni put the cup on the tray, jumped to her feet, and kissed her mother on the cheek. "Yeah. I just need some water. I'm going to go up to the kitchen. I'll check on you later. Try to eat."

"Okay…"

She dashed out of the room before she had to answer any questions. If Mama knew about her and Nico, and she was down in the basement, did that mean everyone upstairs knew, too? She wasn't embarrassed about what they'd done, but it was still private. Her business. Their business. And she still didn't know what Nico's feelings were about them. Honestly, she didn't know what her own feelings were. The last thing she needed was a public referendum on the subject.

BACK IN THE kitchen, Donni saw that the household had come alive. Everyone milled around, picking at melon and peeling hard boiled eggs, drinking coffee and munching on cake.

Everyone, that is, except Nico.

A momentary flood of doubt and insecurity washed over her, and she nearly ran out of the room. But then she realized his absence wasn't a reflection of what had transpired between them. It didn't even seem like anyone else knew. Why had she let her mother freak her out like that?

She made pleasantries with everyone and sipped on her coffee. A few moments later, Coz told an off-color joke relying on the wordplay between "liquor" and "licker" which had everyone laughing.

Then Nico stepped into the room, and she thought she went deaf. The room grew so silent, she could have heard a feather hit the floor.

"Morning, everyone," he said.

Her face flamed, and she refused to look up. She didn't want to see the expressions on any of their faces. Their silences said all she needed to know.

His brothers mumbled greetings, her sisters remained quiet. Why had she gone to the kitchen after leaving Mama? She should have gone straight to her room and stayed under the covers. Preferably until their war was over and she could return home.

"Donni?" Nico said. "If you're free after breakfast, we need to talk."

"No, you don't," Gianni said.

"Yes, we do."

"Nic." Coz shook his head and glanced at Donni.

"You gave your word," Vinnie said.

"And I don't plan on going back on it."

Toni walked up to Vinnie and shoved him, not that he budged. "Are you bribing your brother to sleep with my sister?"

"Excuse me?" What was her twin doing? If Donni wasn't blushing before, she certainly had to be now.

"Jo," Vinnie glanced at Toni, "do something with her."

"Oh, I know you didn't just tell my sister to deal with me like you can't be bothered to answer my question." Toni shoved him again, and this time he moved. About an inch.

Jo stepped between them. "Knock it off, you two. He didn't mean that the way it sounded—"

"Yes, I did."

"—and you need to calm down."

"I will *not* calm down. This is Donni we're talking about, Jo. Whose side are you going to take?"

"Ah, if I might interrupt a moment." Everyone stopped and looked at Donni. She swore her cheeks burned hotter still, if that were even possible, but she held her head high and continued. "I'm not sure what you're all discussing or what you think you know, but this is my life. I don't need my twin sister to defend me against another sister's boyfriend, and I certainly don't need everyone talking about me like they know what's best. If Nico wants to talk with me, that's my call to make, no one else's. *Capite?*"

Murmurs of "*capisco*" and "I understand" filled the kitchen.

"Nico, let's go out to the patio and talk." She didn't wait for him to answer. She stepped around Vinnie, whose nostrils flared, and patted Toni on the shoulder, turning her away from him as she made her way to the door.

Outside, she took a deep breath and waited for Nico to join her.

He came out a few seconds later.

"I'd ask you what you wanted to talk about, but I think I'd rather know what your brothers didn't want you to say."

"I don't give a flying f—*fig* about what my brothers do or don't want. But I do need to talk to you."

A loud spate of fake coughs sounded from inside, and Nico held out his hand. "Want to take a walk?"

She took his hand and let him lead her through the large grassy clearing down to one of the many grottos. It wasn't "their" spot, but it was a lovely area, with lion-head fountain spouts in the wall spurting streams of water into a small pool, flagstone paths winding through manicured boxwood hedges, and bordered by tall, thin cypress trees that cast shadows over marble statuary. He walked over to a bench and pulled her down beside him.

"I'm sorry about all that."

"Want to explain what that was?"

"No." He bent down, grabbed a handful of pebbles, and started tossing them into the pool one at a time. Just when one ripple would dissipate, he'd throw the next stone and disrupt the smooth surface all over again.

She watched him repeat the process about a dozen times without speaking. Finally, she grabbed his hand and stopped him from tossing another rock. "Are you trying to find the words to tell me last night shouldn't have happened?"

He threw one more pebble, then he turned to look at her. "Do you think it shouldn't have happened?"

"I asked you first."

"This isn't why I wanted to talk to you."

"Well, the question's out there now, so you might as well answer it."

"Maybe we'll circle back to that later. I did want to apologize to you, though."

"For what?" Here it comes… the taking her for granted speech.

"For not being there when you woke up."

"Oh." *Not* what she expected to hear.

"I didn't want you to think I just wanted to… well, you know. And then bail on you. I'm not like that."

"Nico, I've known you for months. I know you aren't the 'wham, bam, thank you ma'am, love 'em and leave 'em' type."

"Well, I didn't want people to get the wrong idea if they saw me leaving your room this morning."

Now, that hurt. Why would the idea be wrong? What would people think that he didn't want them to? That he cared for her? That he might find her attractive on some level?

"I wanted to leave you a note, but I couldn't find paper in the dark."

She held her chin high and powered through the pain. "You left me food and a flower. Message received. Now, are we done here?"

He furrowed his brow, but he didn't explain his confusion. "No. I told you we needed to talk."

"I thought that's what this was." Please, end this misery. She wanted to run screaming from there and hide forever.

"No. We got off track because you wanted to know what my brothers wanted."

"Thanks for reminding me."

"But that's for later. I owed you an apology—"

"You're forgiven." She stood.

He reached up, grabbed her hand, then pulled her back down. "But now you owe *me* something."

She blinked a few times, completely at a loss. She'd given him the most personal, private parts of herself. What more could he want? "I owe you something? What?"

"You had a vision. You shared it with your mother and sisters, but not me. Didn't you learn anything from Jo keeping secrets? You know it's important to tell your protector everything. How am I supposed to keep you safe if I don't know what's coming?"

"I'm not worried about it."

"Well, I am. Tell me the vision."

"There's no point. The vision—if that's what it even was—didn't take place here. And you won't let me off the property, so it's not going to happen."

"That's not true."

"Not true that it won't happen?"

"Not true that I don't let you off the property. We take you to church every week."

"Under armed guard. And we come straight back."

"You were just in the Apennines when we rescued your mother."

"You didn't let me go with you. I stowed away."

"Semantics. You left the property. And if I had known about the vision, I never would have stayed once I found you."

"I didn't give you a choice."

He threw the handful of stones he still held into the pool. "Damn it, Donni. I would have forced you back if I had known about the vision."

"Well, we both know how you like to be in control."

His face darkened. "That was low, Don."

She should have felt bad about that—and maybe she did on some level—but she couldn't backtrack. "You want to be in control in the bedroom? Fine. I can enjoy that once in a while. You want to be in charge of my training and my safety? Okay. I can deal with that because my sisters voted to let the Brotherhood manage the situation. But you don't get control over me, Nico. You get that? My thoughts, my feelings, my visions… they're mine. What's inside me is all I have left, and I won't turn my whole self over without getting something in return."

He took a deep breath and let it out slowly. "I wasn't trying to control you in bed, Donni."

"Could have fooled me." She crossed her arms over her chest and studied the path through the grotto.

"I was trying to control myself."

That admission kind of deflated her, and she turned to look at him.

"I didn't think we could sleep together. For various reasons. And with you touching me, I was never going to hold out as long as I needed to."

"What various reasons? I know of one. And it was a non-issue."

"And then we slept together, all other reasons be damned."

"What other reasons?"

"Like you said, thoughts and feelings are our own to share when and if we want. I don't want to talk about it now."

She turned away from him again. Despite the heat of the summer day, she felt chilled.

"Right now, I don't want to talk about us. Whatever we have or don't have, I need time to process everything. And you do, too. Regardless of how good it was, our timing was terrible. So keep your thoughts until you've worked through them, and I will, too. But the vision isn't a private thought, Donni. That's directly related to your Medici bloodline, and therefore directly related to Brotherhood business. I need to know what you saw."

Donni mulled that over for a while. She could choose to dwell on him being bossy and shutting down the dreaded relationship conversation, but there was an upside. Two, actually. One, if she were honest, she wasn't ready to define what they had or didn't have any more than he was. And two, he said it was good. She might have said mindblowingly phenomenal, but she'd take the compliment the way he gave it.

"Don? The vision."

She thought about what she'd seen. About the shackles, the stone prison. Her mother screaming and the man's ultimatum—a life for a life. She saw it in her head like it was right in front of her eyes. It was too real, and she shuddered. If she had to relive it, she was getting something out of it. "Fine. But I want field trips."

"What?"

"You want to know what I saw, and you're claiming Brotherhood priority. I'll accept that. But I can't be housebound anymore. I want to take trips to town. Get out and shop or sightsee or just walk somewhere that isn't on these grounds."

"That depends on how dangerous the vision is."

"My terms are non-negotiable."

He scowled. "Fine. Tell me everything. Don't leave a single detail out."

She forced back another shiver and launched into a resigned description of what she'd seen.

13

NICO EXPECTED HIS brothers to be waiting for him inside. And he fully intended to ignore their lectures and demands for information in favor of discussing Donni's vision and the current state of affairs in Italy. Their briefings had been put on hold for way too long, and refocusing everyone's attention on the big picture would take the heat off him for a while.

He prepared for diverting their attention.

He *didn't* prepare for what he found.

Donni proceeded him into the kitchen. Everyone else was still gathered there, but Mike had joined them. So had Marcus and Enrico.

"Dominico," Mike said. "You are supposed to be monitoring the property. You had no idea we had arrived."

"I was outside. I can't sit in front of the computer twenty-four, seven."

"It is too dangerous not to have constant surveillance."

Nico fished in his pocket for his phone and saw a notification that the perimeter had been breached. He showed the display to Mike. "I am constantly monitoring the grounds. And I was notified. Considering it was you, there was no reason to sound an alarm."

"And yet you looked surprised to see us when you came in."

Bastard saw too much. Maybe Mike was right that he hadn't been watching the feeds closely, but for Pete's sake, his brothers were all on the property with their charges, and all were armed. It was unreasonable to expect him to camp out at the computer. Besides, his priority had to be watching Donni, not watching a computer screen.

"For the record, I'm the tech guy. Coz is actually the head of security."

"And Roberto is here, aware of my arrival."

Nico glanced at Coz, who smirked and shrugged. He looked back at Mike. "Like I said, I was notified of the perimeter breach. What I wasn't notified of is the reason for your visit."

"As you can see, I have brought Marcus and Enrico with me."

"Good to see you again, Nico." Marcus shook his hand. "Donni." He gave her a hug.

Rico smiled and nodded.

Nico smiled at them both. Maybe it was more of a grimace, but it was the best he could muster. "So, what's going on?"

"You are in need of assistance. They are here to help."

"Help with what?"

"Whatever you need." Marcus grabbed a piece of prosciutto-wrapped melon and popped it in his mouth.

"If we could please retreat to chamber," Mike said. "We have a few things to discuss. Gentlemen, if you could entertain the ladies until our return." It wasn't a request.

Rico nodded. Jo and Franki started to object, but Marcus shook his head, and surprisingly, that silenced them. Wonder why the current Brotherhood didn't have the same ability to keep them quiet?

It was futile to argue with Mike, so Nico and his brothers filed out of the kitchen and headed for the secret room that housed the prophecy, the sacred table, and myriad ancient texts that could help them in their duties. Once inside, the door was closed and the Brothers took their assigned places. There was no point in trying to skip the formalities. Mike would insist on them.

The table was a wooden pentagon with an inlaid, multicolored, marble star.

Gianni stood at the red point. To his right, Vinnie took his place at the white point. Beside him, Nico stood at the green star point. Coz took his place next at the black point.

Mike headed the table at the gold point. He pointed his gold marble dagger at each of them, then said, "Brotherhood of the Stone, how say you?"

Gianni held his red dagger to his chest then placed it in the groove on the table. It was a perfect fit. "Brother of the Red Marble. Here do I serve. Passion. Blood. Vengeance."

Mike replied, "Welcome, Brother of the Red Marble. Here you will serve. Passion. Blood. Vengeance."

Vinnie copied Gianni's movements. "Brother of the White Marble. Here do I serve. Purity, Clarity, Beginnings."

Mike's response followed the same pattern. "Welcome, Brother of the White Marble. Here you will serve. Purity, Clarity, Beginnings."

Nico sighed before continuing. He, like his brothers, hated the ritual. They all felt it was a huge waste of time. But complaining or refusing was futile. So he held his green marble dagger to his chest then placed it in its slot on the table. "Brother of the Green Marble. Here do I serve. Life. Balance. Transformation."

"Welcome, Brother of the Green Marble. Here you will serve. Life. Balance. Transformation."

Coz mimicked the actions of the Brothers. When his black dagger was fitted into its spot on the table, he said, "Brother of the Black Marble. Here do I serve. Resilience. Protection. Potential."

"Welcome, Brother of the Black Marble. Here you will serve. Resilience. Protection. Potential." Then Mike put his own dagger on the table. "Protector and Benefactor."

They replied in unison. "Welcome, Protector and Benefactor of the Order."

"Concentration. Honesty. Defense," Mike stated.

The Brothers all repeated his words.

"As they need," Mike said.

"So we will serve," came their unified reply.

Mike sat and gestured for them to sit join him.

"Why are we in chamber instead of meeting with the girls?" Nico asked.

"It is not prudent to discuss Brotherhood business in front of Marcus and Enrico until we are certain they are not double agents."

Nico ran his hand through his hair. "If you're not sure they're on our side, why'd you bring them here? And why are you leaving them alone with the girls now?"

"At least for the time being, the Notaro family is under no danger under this roof. As to why your mentors are here, the political climate is getting more dire. You would know this if you were following the news."

"I am following the news."

"Then why have your brothers and your charges not been briefed?"

"I actually planned on doing that when Donni and I came back inside. But your appearance put that on hold."

"I see." Mike steepled his fingers and looked over his hands at Nico. "And just what were you and the lovely Miss Notaro doing away from the rest of the group?"

Why did everyone butt into his personal life? "I was convincing her to share her vision with me. She didn't want to because she thought it would make us be even more careful about letting her and her sisters leave the villa. But I convinced her that, for everyone's safety, we needed to know what she saw."

"And what did she see?"

He glanced around the table. Everyone looked at him, waiting for his answer. He always intended to share what he learned, but with Mike there, it felt like he was on trial. "She and her mother are shackled to a stone wall, held captive somewhere she doesn't recognize. A male voice she doesn't know taunts her. Says 'a life for a life' and laughs. That's all she saw. Doesn't know who he is, where they are, or how it happened."

"That's precious little to go on," Gianni said.

"I know. But that's hardly a surprise. None of the visions the girls have had so far have been full of detail. And given that Jo was able to change the details of her vision, we don't even know how reliable this information is."

"Good point," Vinnie said.

"So why are we here now, Mike?" Coz asked. "What aren't you telling us?"

"I am not the one keeping secrets, Roberto." Mike stared pointedly at Nico. Nico scoffed but refused to meet Mike's gaze.

"I brought two of your mentors here because you will need the extra security, and while you have not yet fully vetted them, I believe they can, for the moment, be relied on to help. The rest of the Protectorate is busy in America keeping watch over Carmina and researching the former Brotherhood members."

"Marcus and Rico are former members." Nico felt like Mike blamed him for lack of information, so he launched into his defense. "We already tracked them down and looked into their recent activity."

"And even after visiting two of them, you are not able to say with certainty they are loyal to us and not working for the opposition. As I said, they have not yet been fully vetted."

"So you brought them here without knowing their allegiances?"

"As I said, you will need the manpower. And what better way to surveil someone than by having them under the same roof?"

"What do we need help with?" Vinnie asked.

"Mary is here now, and—"

"Speaking of Mary," Nico said, "why didn't you tell us you lost her?"

"I had been searching for her. Like you, Dominico, I cannot be everywhere at all times. She was abducted when I was assisting you with Coz's surgery."

"That was a hell of a long time ago. They could have killed her while you neglected to tell us she was gone."

"And what purpose would it have served? You were not in Italy then. You could not have joined in my search. When you finally did come home, you had other problems to deal with."

"Well, I still think you should have told us. We could have helped."

"None of that matters now."

"Funny how when you screw up, it doesn't matter. But if you even think we messed up, you're up our asses about it."

"Lay off, man." Vinnie glared it him. "It's all working out."

"You defending him because you agree, or because he's your dad and you want to suck up to him?"

Vinnie jumped to his feet, and Nico rose and squared off against him. Gianni held Vinnie back while Coz grabbed Nico. Each of them struggled to get free, but both were muscled into their seats by their brothers.

"I believe you owe your brother an apology," Mike said.

"Not happening. I stand by what I said. Since he found out about you, things have been weird. I'm not wrong to question his motivations."

Mike looked at Vinnie, and an expression Nico couldn't define crossed his face. When he turned his attention away from his biological son and back to Nico, his features were again mask-like and unreadable. "Vincenzo and I have much to work through. But none of that impacts my relationship with the rest of you, nor does it relate to the work we have to do. Now, Dominico, apologize to your brother."

That was the most fatherly Mike had sounded since he adopted Nico, Coz, and Gianni. Nico was tired of fighting with everyone, so he gave in. "Sorry."

Vinnie shrugged and grunted something unintelligible.

"Well, that was not the bonding moment I had hoped for, but for now, it will have to do. We have preparations to make."

"Preparations for what?" Coz asked.

"For Carmen Scalzotto. I am bringing him here for you to protect."

NICO HAD ARGUED against Scalzotto coming to the compound, but he was voted down almost immediately. True, they could probably protect him better than his security detail could, but the Brotherhood already had enough on their hands. They didn't need additional responsibilities.

Particularly ones Nico was responsible for. Like surveillance.

As usual, though—like it was even a question—Mike got his way. He said he'd be bringing Scalzotto the following day, and they should make the necessary preparations.

Other than having the housekeeping staff prepare one of the bedrooms, Nico didn't know what they were supposed to do. He already had the villa completely monitored, and Coz kept track of everything that happened at the compound.

Coz pulled him aside when the meeting was over. "Hey. What do you say to a little break tonight? A chance to blow off some steam before shit gets tough."

"You don't think things are tough yet?"

"You know what I mean."

"I don't know." Nico had planned on practicing with his powers again that night. With two of the mentors in the house, Scalzotto coming, and Donni's vision haunting them, he wanted to be as prepared as possible.

"Look, Marcus and Rico are here, so they can watch Mary for us."

"And if one of them is working against us?"

Coz shrugged. "Then we'll have learned it before the girls get hurt."

"If Mary gets hurt, the girls will be hurt. Remember Donni's vision."

"We aren't leaving the country. Just relaxing a little. On property. I know I could use the break. I'm sure Vin could. And you."

"What about the girls?" Nico asked.

"I heard Toni talking about a girls' night. That's what gave me the idea."

"That's even worse! They can't leave here unwatched."

"They aren't going anywhere. Pretty sure their plans include alcohol and movies in the media room."

Nico sighed. "Fine. As long as we don't leave the compound. The most I'll agree to is splitting up onsite. Mike would have my head if something happened to the girls and we weren't around."

"I agree, that would lead to a royal dressing down. For both of us. But like I said, we'll all stay on property. We'll just split off tonight. Guys' night and girls' night."

"If you can get Gianni and Franki separated, I'm in."

"They could use the time apart. So could Vinnie and Jo."

"Set up whatever you want, then tell me when and where. I need to blow off some steam. I'm going to the gym."

"Need a spotter?"

"Nah. Just kickboxing the dummy."

"All right. Catch you later."

Nico changed and headed to the gym. He had more nervous energy than he cared to admit, and he needed to burn some off.

DONNI SLIPPED INTO Mama's room and closed the door, tiptoed over to the bed so as not to disturb her if she was resting. She slept so soundly, Donni had to put her hand in front of her face just to see if she was breathing.

Satisfied she was fine, Donni adjusted the covers then went back into the hall. There, she took the phone from her pocket, leaned against the wall, and slid down to the floor. After a brief prayer thanking God for Mama's safe return, she dialed the familiar number.

"Hello?"

"Nonna? It's Donni."

"Don't say your name! You shouldn't even be calling here."

"It's okay. Nico took care of it. The line is secure."

"Are you certain?"

"Yes, Nonna. It's fine. We can speak freely."

"Oh, cara, honey. How are you? And your sisters? Are you eating enough? Are the boys keeping you safe?"

Donni laughed. "We're all fine. In fact, that's why I'm calling."

"What?"

"Mama's here. And she's fine."

"Che? Mary's with you? No coma? She's awake? Oh, honey. I'm so relieved. Let me talk to her."

"Sorry. She's sleeping right now. But she's under our roof and no longer in a coma. She's going to be just fine."

Nonna's soft sobs filtered through the phone. *"Thank you, Donni. Thank you. I've prayed so hard…"*

"Us, too. I wasn't sure anyone had called you, so I thought I'd let you know."

Nonna was quiet for a moment. When she spoke again, she was composed, her voice once again strong. *"What's wrong, cara?"*

"Nothing."

"I can hear it in your voice. Very little joy for something that should have you over the moon."

"I'm thrilled, Nonna. Really."

"Oh, I'm sure you are, getting your mother back. But there's something else."

Maybe this was why she really called. Nonna always did have a kind of second-sense about matters of the heart. "It's not that important."

"If it's troubling you, it is important."

Donni sighed. "In the grand scheme of things, when we have kidnappers and murderers after us, my love life kind of pales in comparison."

"Something happen with Nico?"

Her chin dropped. "How'd you know it was Nico?"

"I'm not blind, Donnatella. Anyone with working eyes can see how you two look at each other."

"Okay, one, you can't see me at all. I'm in a totally different country. And two, nothing happened with us until after we left the States, so what is it exactly you think you saw when we were there?"

"Maybe nothing happened before Italy, but your eyes said it would."

"What?"

"Eyes are expressive. They reveal feelings, sometimes before you put them to words. And my darling Donni, you do not have a poker face."

"I don't suppose you read Nico's eyes before we left?" It was more question than comment, and she dreaded the answer.

"The very first time I met him, cara."

"And what'd you see?" She bit her lip and looked away, picking at some non-existent lint on her shirt.

"It doesn't matter what I saw in his face. What matters is what was in yours. You have unrequited feelings. You need to express them."

Oh, she'd done a lot of expressing lately. Didn't get her any closer to an answer, though. Only led to more questions.

"Nonna, I can't possibly open up to him more than I already have. And I still don't know what he's thinking."

"Keep the naughty bits to yourself, please."

She cheeks burned. "That's not what I meant."

"And you're not denying it, either."

"Nonna, I—"

"I know how young people are. I'm not going to lecture you about the milk or the cow. That's not what this is about, anyway."

Her cheeks had to be seven shades darker than crimson at the moment.

"You want a guarantee. You want to know if you let yourself love him, he'll love you in return."

"Is it so wrong to protect my pride?"

Nonna chuckled. *"No, cara, I suppose not. But it's not your pride you're trying to protect. It's your heart."*

"Well, given the choice, I think I'd protect my heart over my pride, seven days a week."

"Love doesn't work that way."

"Who said anything about love?"

This time she laughed outright. *"You wouldn't be worried about your pride or your heart if it wasn't about love."* Then she grew serious. *"You'll never get what you want without risking it all."*

"I'm scared, Nonna. If I read this wrong, I can mess up more than our relationship. I can make things hard on all of us."

"Don't worry about everyone else. People are resilient. You'll all muddle through if things go badly. But just think how wonderful things could be if they go well."

"I just wish I knew for sure what to think. I can't read him."

"It's in the eyes, cara. You can see everything you need to know in the eyes."

"What did you see in his eyes?"

Nonna sighed. *"Will you have your mother call me when she's feeling up to it? I'd love to hear her voice."*

Guess that conversation was over. "Sure. I have to go now. I love you."

"Y ti amo, *Donni*. Ciao."

God, how she missed her grandmother. Funny how Nonna could make anyone feel better, even if she didn't give the answers people wanted. Donni wanted assurances and got nothing but more questions.

But hearing Nonna's voice was like being wrapped in a warm hug. It was the next best thing to actually seeing her in person.

In the meantime, she'd pay closer attention to Nico's eyes. His beautiful, hypnotic, hazel eyes.

Maybe she shouldn't look too closely. That was what got her into trouble in the first place.

DONNI LOOKED AT her fingertips, the buff nail polish her sister had applied—after a complete nail reshaping and half-arm paraffin wax treatment— transformed her neglected appendages into female hands again.

She sighed. How long had it been since she'd even looked at her manicure set or a bottle of lacquer? No clue. Yet she'd recently had black paint on her face.

What had her life become?

Her sisters chatted while she blew on her fingers. She had nothing to say. They'd made a pact in advance of the night beginning to avoid boy-talk. Didn't leave them with much else, in her opinion. Franki waxed poetic about her designs for the orphanage. Jo prattled on about the construction work and the crew. Toni answered every wood or plaster comment with a shrub or flower reply. The three of them had been leaving the compound every day to work onsite—architect, builder, landscaper. Only she, the interior designer, wasn't granted the freedom to go.

They weren't far enough on the project to need her.

The orphanage didn't have need for extravagant things.

The church was holding fundraisers and asking for donations, so it was likely she wouldn't have to shop for them at all.

If Nico told her those things one more time, she might punch him in the face. He left the villa all the time. So did his brothers, and now her sisters did, too. Being grounded wasn't fair.

And it made her stir-crazy.

She needed to change the topic of conversation before she slapped someone silly and ruined her manicure.

Franki beat her to it. "Think we should go get Mama? She'd enjoy this."

"I checked on her right before I came in here," Donni said. "She was asleep. I didn't want to wake her."

"No. Of course not. I'll check on her later. Maybe she'll want to join us for a movie or something."

"Rom com?" Toni asked.

"Action," Jo said.

And the typical argument ensued.

Donni tuned them out. It was going to be an evening of silly bickering and shop talk, and she didn't know which was worse. She'd rather hear Franki gush about some stupid anniversary she and Gianni celebrated last night.

Well, maybe not that.

She looked around the room. Even the biggest bathroom hadn't been big enough, so they'd set up in the kitchen. Foot baths, paraffin wax tubs, and an assortment of nail, hair, and facial products had been hauled downstairs. They wore jammies and robes while they sat around the large kitchen table, snacks and drinks intermingled with bottles and tubes of beauty products.

It was supposed to be a happy affair, but Donni was irritated with all of them. She took a sip of wine and scowled into her glass.

"So, sis." Toni ran a brush through Donni's hair. "Want to talk more about that vision?"

"No, I do not." She winced when her twin yanked a little too hard through a tangle. "And don't even think about handing me that mirror again."

"We really should talk about it," Franki said.

"We really shouldn't. Not tonight. We're supposed to be relaxing, remember?" Donni's head snapped back with another tug from the brush. She swatted her sister's hand away.

Toni tossed the brush aside and began weaving an intricate braid in Donni's hair. "If we had answers, we could relax better."

"You're hurting me."

"'The pain passes. The beauty remains.' And you're changing the subject."

"I agreed to the no-boy-talk terms of the night. I think you guys should agree to my no-shop-talk request. Brotherhood or otherwise."

"Otherwise?" Franki asked.

"Yeah. Otherwise. NBD business. The three of you keep going on and on about the construction site, the blueprints and designs, the landscaping needs. But I'm in the dark because I'm not allowed down there. Have to just sit up here and stew, all by myself, housebound. No better than a common criminal. So no more business talk, either."

"I'd hardly call this compound a prison," Franki said.

Donni scowled at her. "Says the woman who's paroled every day."

"Fine," Toni said. "No shop-talk. What are we supposed to talk about, then?"

"How about food?" Donni popped an olive in her mouth, and her head again jerked back. The hardest tug yet. She rubbed her scalp where the hair pulled too taut.

"Why'd you bring up food with me? Because of everyone, I'm the one who'd be interested, right? Always safe to talk to the fat girl about food."

"You aren't fat. And that's not at all what I meant." Donni better than anyone knew food was a sore spot for her sister. Toni had always had body issues because she was bigger than Donni. Bigger than Franki and Jo, too. Not that she could be called "big" by any stretch of the imagination. But it had caused numerous image-issues for her over the years. Had also caused Donni to get interested in cooking so she could make healthy yet delicious meals for her twin. She wanted to take that comment back, but didn't know how to make things right.

"She likes cooking, Toni." Franki admired her manicure. "And there's this excellent spread right in front of us. The comment wasn't personal."

Toni stopped the braiding when the plait was only half-completed. She walked around to the other side of the table, grabbed a bottle of water, and started peeling at the label.

"Come on, Toni. Chill." Franki put her hand over Toni's and stilled her movements. "This is supposed to be relaxing, remember?"

"Yeah. Whatever."

They were all silent for a while. So much for resting and recharging. Donni's neck hurt from the tension building there, and she tried rubbing the muscles. Didn't work, so she gave up. Then she ran her fingers through her hair to release the unfinished braid. After her hair hung free, she lowered her hands.

"Damn it."

"What now?" Franki asked.

"I forgot my nails were wet. I messed them up in my hair."

She slid the remover across the table. "Take the polish off. I'll redo them for you."

Donni worked on her fingers, the room still thick with silence. She was pondering the wisdom of reapplying the color—going natural was much easier—when Jo spoke up.

"Can I call a moratorium on the no-boy-talk rule?" Her voice was soft, distant. She rarely shared her feelings. Something must really be troubling her if she wanted to talk.

"Of course, honey," Franki said. "What's wrong?"

A few fat tears ran down Jo's face, and she swiped at them with the back of her hand. "I don't know what to do. Vinnie is destroyed. He killed a man. A friend. Because of me. He's devastated, and it's all my fault."

Franki hugged her sister and held her while she cried. Toni wrapped her arms around the two of them, and Donni around them all.

When Jo calmed, everyone broke apart. Franki held her sister at arm's length and stared at her until she met her gaze. "You listen to me, Jo. Pasquale was not a friend of Vinnie's. Or of any of the guys. He was a traitor and a betrayer and it's good he's gone."

Jo shook her head. "It was my fault. Because I was headstrong and had to do it my way."

"You didn't make Pasquale join Sal and Dante. You didn't make him capture you and set the explosives. You didn't blow the bomb. That's all on him."

"If I hadn't been there, Vinnie wouldn't have been there. He became a murderer because of me. I broke his soul." She broke into sobs again, and Franki held her.

"He's not a murderer, Jo." Toni grabbed her hand and squeezed. "War isn't murder. Self-defense isn't. Neither is defense of another. Vinnie saved your life. He's a hero."

"He's a mess. And it's my fault."

"Is it?" Donni took a deep breath, faced a fact she'd been avoiding. "You saw it in the mirror long before it happened. It was destined. Just like Franki's vision was preordained to come true. Just like the prophecy. You aren't to be blamed for your actions any more than Vinnie is for his, or any of us is for anything. The story's already written. We're just acting out the play."

"You don't really believe that, do you?" Toni asked.

"We have proof. What else can I think?"

"God, Donni. We were raised Catholic. Free will. Nothing's predetermined."

"And yet we believe God knows everything we'll ever do. Like we've already done it, or are destined to."

"He's outside of human time. The rules don't apply to Him."

"Are the two of you really going to have a philosophical or metaphysical debate right now?" Franki asked.

"Nothing to debate. It's inevitable. We've seen it." Donni got up and paced. "And my stupid vision is next."

"No." Jo turned and looked at her. "You're forgetting. I changed the details of my vision. Foresight gives us a chance to impact our destiny, change our future."

"Do you really believe that?" Donni asked.

"I do. We've seen it. I've done it."

"Then you of all people should know Vin isn't broken because of you. He's hurting right now because of the choices he made. Him. Not you."

"Still doesn't change the fact that he is hurting. And my decisions put him in the position it did."

"Any decision any of us makes impacts the future. Michelangelo forming the Protectorate. Papa hiding our identities. Mike bringing us to Italy. Vinnie leaving you alone when you were a flight risk. It's kind of like the butterfly effect. Step on a butterfly and kill Hitler. Leave the compound and get abducted by a crazy man. Predestined or not, every little thing we do ripples through time. You aren't responsible for what Vinnie's going through. No one is. He just needs time to come to terms with things."

"You think so? You think time will make a difference?"

She wanted nothing more than to buoy Jo's spirits. So she said the best thing that came to mind. "They say time heals all wounds."

Jo smiled.

Donni grabbed her glass of wine and stepped outside for some air. She didn't know if time would make a difference in how Vinnie felt about Pasquale's death. Nor did it matter.

She had a date with destiny—and more pain was headed their way.

14

DONNI SAT ON the patio and stared across the grounds. During the day, the beauty of the property was clear in the manicured foliage, the ancient statuary, the grand scope, and the breathtaking view.

Nighttime provided a different impression. Or maybe it was her mood.

Someone had turned off the landscape lighting, plunging the property into an ominous black. The plants and stone cast long, amorphous shadows, transforming the vista into an inky, nebulous landscape that could be hiding all sorts of mysterious—potentially deadly—threats. Clouds rolled in, obscuring the moon and stars and cloaking the entire compound in stygian darkness. The valley disappeared behind a misty brume, effectively isolating them from the rest of the world and the protection society offered.

Nighttime at the villa made Dracula's castle look like a luxury resort.

She sipped her merlot and shivered despite the balmy temperature.

"Need a blanket?"

Donni jumped and nearly spilled her drink. Would have if she wasn't almost done with it. "Vinnie! You scared the crap out of me!"

"Sorry. I just needed some air."

She sat back and drained her glass. "Yeah, I know the feeling."

"I'll leave you to it, then." He turned to go.

"Why? You breathe enough in the last thirty seconds?"

He glared at her. At least, she thought he did. It was too dark to make out his features clearly. "I assumed you wanted to be alone."

"More I wanted to get away from my sisters for a moment. You're welcome to stay. Unless you want to be alone?"

He didn't answer, but he took a seat beside her.

"You okay?"

"I'm not really up for a deep discussion, Donni."

"Maybe that's just what you need."

This time when he looked at her, she could make out some details in the shadows. His face looked pinched, tense. His eyes were hooded, troubled.

"I told you I needed to get away from my sisters. I didn't tell you why."

"I'll bite. Why?"

"We were talking about you."

He started to stand, but she grabbed his arm. "Please. Listen a minute."

Vinnie sat again, but stayed perched on the edge of his seat.

"Jo is beside herself because of you."

"What? Jo and I are in a great place in our relationship."

"Really? You honestly believe that?"

"She's more outgoing now. She's growing out her hair, wearing better-fitting clothes. She's not hiding from the world anymore. I think she's made great strides."

"I'm not talking about that. Although I'll be eternally grateful to you for breaking through her shell."

"Then what? I've never been happier. I thought she was happy, too."

"She is happy with you, Vinnie. She loves you. More than you probably even know."

"Okay. So what's the problem with us?"

"I'm not talking about you as a couple. I'm talking about you. She blames herself for your guilt over Pasquale."

"What?" His voice was barely above a whisper, but the pain was evident in it nonetheless. "I killed him. Me. She had nothing to do with it. Why does—? Why would she—?" He stood, ran his hand through his hair, paced. "Why?"

"Because you wouldn't have been in that position if she'd included you in the plan. Or if she didn't go at all."

"I'm her protector. She was in danger. If he didn't target her at the orphanage, he would have found her somewhere else. It was only a matter of time and opportunity. But how I reacted to the threat? That's on me. Will always be on me."

"Look, I'm no psychiatrist or anything, but I can tell you're messed up over this. You have soldier's guilt. PTSD. Moral injury. Or some combination of those. I don't know the clinical terms, but I know you're struggling with what happened, which is taking a toll on all of us who love you. And what happened is not your fault."

"So you can all notice a difference in me? I thought she was the only one who noticed."

"We all see it. And it's eating at all of us. But especially Jo."

"I didn't want this to touch her. To touch any of you."

"I don't know how to tell you to get past this, or even if you ever will. I imagine taking a life, even when it's justified, changes you. Stays with you. But what I do know is it's impacting everyone, especially you and Jo, which worries me. And my sisters. Add to that reuniting with your mother and finding out Mike is your father, and no one could blame you for needing time to adjust."

He made a sound like a wounded animal. It broke Donni's heart.

"None of this your fault. It's all going to take time. Worse still, I don't think our problems are over. Things are going to get worse before they get better."

Vinnie sat again. "I know. I've seen some of our paths out of this. They're all bloody."

"Then you understand. This is war. Our retaliation is justified."

"Yeah. But it doesn't make it hurt less."

"No. I'm sure nothing does. But we've got to see this through to the end. You're going to be able to do that, right?"

Floodlights illuminated the lawn, and the patio door opened. Gianni, Coz, and Nico stepped out.

"Wondered what happened to you," Gianni said. "We're going to play *bocce*. You're in, right?"

Vinnie gave Donni a tight smile. "Yeah."

She heard the double meaning in his answer. He wasn't happy about their path, but he was on it for the duration of the journey. And maybe their talk would help him deal with the pain a little.

Nico half-nodded to her and loped out to the yard, offering neither a smile nor a greeting.

Man, she wished she had something to help dull her pain.

BOCCE HAD TWO types of throws. Pointing, where a player rolled the ball with finesse toward the *pallino* and tried to score a point, and spocking, where a player rolled the ball with force toward his opponent's balls and tried to knock them out of the way.

Nico invented a third type. The I'm-mad-at-the-world-and-need-to-vent-my-temper throw. He hurled his *bocce* ball across the lawn, scattering Gianni's balls and launching the *pallino* several feet back, out of the range of the floodlights.

"I know we don't have a court," Coz said, "but do you think you could at least try to keep the balls on our property?"

"Sorry," he muttered. "Guess I don't know my own strength."

"Maybe if you didn't treat the opposition's balls like targets," Vinnie said. "Or your ball like a missile."

"Are we going to stand here analyzing my technique, or are we going to play?"

"Kind of hard to play when you lost the *pallino* and half the balls are off the court," Gianni said.

"We don't have a fucking court. We're playing in the dark on the damn lawn. How am I supposed to keep the balls in play when there are no boards or boundaries?"

"Pretty sure if you hit a ball far enough that it goes past the floodlights and into the shadows, you're out of play." Coz walked the periphery of the lights, peering at the ground in the darkness.

"I'll keep that in mind the next time I shoot."

"Don't think that'll be tonight." Coz took out his phone, activated the flashlight, and scanned the ground. "Can't find the *pallino*."

"Whatever. I didn't want to play, anyway."

Vinnie scooped up a few of the balls and juggled them, their heavy weight not posing the slightest issue. "It was a nice distraction. While it lasted."

"Yeah, Nic, lighten up." Coz turned away from the shadows. "This night was more for you than any of us. You've been burning the candle in the middle and at both ends, and tomorrow things get harder."

Nico stepped out of the light and into the darkness. He used the flashlight on his own phone to scan for the *pallino*. Damn little ball wasn't painted like the others, and the natural color of the wood helped it blend into the grass and mulch on the property. He walked further into the shadows. Coz had only looked about a few feet out, so he searched a little further. The beam of his phone light landed on a foot, and he whipped the light higher to see who had infiltrated the compound.

Mike stood there. He held the *pallino* out to Nico. "Now you may continue your game."

"What the fuck, man? You scared me half to death."

"You said you were always aware of who came and went on the property."

His brothers ran to him, their daggers brandished in front of them.

"Oh," Vinnie said. "Thought you were in trouble."

Nico seethed, but instead of lashing out at Mike, he shrugged and answered his brothers. "Just a little caught off guard."

Gianni sheathed his weapon and took the *pallino* from Mike.

"Gentlemen," Mike said.

"What are you doing here?" Vinnie asked.

"I often walk the grounds at night. I find you can never have too many people watching over precious things."

Nico knew Mike came to the property once in a while. He didn't know it was frequently, though. It irked him that Mike didn't trust him to do his job. Irritated him further that he probably kept tabs on Nico's nighttime practices, effectively eliminating any private time or space he had.

Pissed him off more still that Mike might be right about protecting the girls. "I trusted Marcus and Rico to look after things. Coz has the place locked down tight. Other than someone teleporting in, we're secure."

Mike merely blinked and stared at him.

"We're supposed to be recharging before Scalzotto comes tomorrow."

"Ah. I see. So this is… socialization time?"

"Sure. If you want to call it that."

The pregnant pause in conversation was unbearable. But Nico didn't have anything more to say. He just wished Mike would go away and he could go in the house. He was more than ready for the night to be over so he could just crawl into bed, get some sleep, and put the day behind him.

No such luck.

"Why don't you join us?" Gianni said.

Nico shot him a dirty look. Noticed he wasn't the only one to do so. Vinnie didn't look thrilled, either.

"You cannot play *bocce* with five men."

"Take my place," Nico said. "I'm kind of tired and don't feel like playing. Besides, apparently I'm doing it wrong."

"I didn't say it was wrong, Nic," Coz said. "All I said was without boards defining the court, you had to be more careful in how you shot."

"You guys play. I'll watch." Nico headed back into the lighted part of the lawn. After standing in the shadows for so long, the light seemed bright. He crossed over to the other light/shadow boundary, stepped into the darkness, and sat on the grass. Maybe he'd get lucky and they'd be quiet enough that he could fall asleep.

It wasn't long before play resumed. He and Coz had been partners, which meant they stood on opposite sides of the court from each other, as did Vinnie and Gianni. With Mike taking his place, it meant Mike and Vinnie were on the same side of the lawn. Nico watched with fascination as the two of them struggled to make polite conversation. Eventually they decided on an uncomfortable silence.

Mike was much shorter than Vinnie, but they had similar builds. They handled the balls with similar techniques, too. And while Mike was far more formal than Vinnie ever was, they both shared a quick and explosive temperament. For the first time, Nico could see the family resemblance between the two. Couldn't believe he'd never noticed before.

The game ended quickly—his brothers were all gifted athletes, but Mike was some kind of *bocce* wizard. Gianni and Vinnie never scored a point.

"Thank you for the game. I had not played in… well, I am not sure how long it has been. It feels like centuries."

Phewfft. Guy played like he'd been playing for centuries. How'd someone that busy get that good at a recreational game? Did he even have friends to practice with? Nico knew next to nothing about Mike's private life, but he wished he had the time his boss apparently had for such frivolity.

"Best of three?" Vinnie asked.

"All right. Yes. It would be a pleasure."

Mike's smile might have thawed the icy chill between him and Vinnie about two degrees. But it was enough to take Vin from frosty silence to generic—albeit nervous—chatting.

"Remember when we used to play *bocce* at the orphanage?" he called across the lawn.

"I remember you used to be in trouble all the time and didn't get to join us very often," Gianni said.

"That wasn't my fault. Sister Catherine hated me."

"That's Mother Superior now. Show some respect."

"Bite me, G."

Mike chuckled and threw his ball. He knocked Vinnie's out of scoring range. Vinnie scowled.

"Fredo used to fill in for Vinnie when he was—" Coz cleared his throat "—otherwise occupied."

"I forgot about that," Nico said.

"I remember. I used to try and watch out the window."

"I remember, too," Coz said. "All too well."

"All too well?" Mike threw his last ball and ended up with three more points. Vinnie and Gianni had yet to score one. "Who was this Fredo?"

"You must remember him." Coz threw the *pallino* and then tossed one of his balls after it. "Fredo. Alfredo Baroni. He was a groundskeeper for the orphanage and the church. He… he was nice."

"Sal said he was one of his spies," Gianni said.

"No way," Coz said. "Sal just said that to rattle you. Fredo was kind. He introduced me around when I first showed up. Tried to steer me toward you morons."

"Better than the alternative," Gianni said.

"He was the one who was murdered, no?" Mike said.

Coz nodded. "Yeah. After he was gone, one of his crew took over."

"Bruno Dragone," Vinnie said. "Real hard ass. Hated me as much as Mother Superior did."

Gianni smirked.

"Bruno Dragone." Nico sat up. Something about him scratched at a memory he couldn't quite pull to the surface.

"Yeah," Gianni said. "Remember him? He was always trying to split you away from us to hang with Dante and his crew. When we put a stop to that, he set his sights on Coz."

"I never trusted him," Vinnie said. "I don't think anyone did. Teresa told me to keep an eye on you, and it was a good thing I did."

"He was nice to me," Nico said.

"He was bribing you."

"So even the staff didn't trust him?"

"You can see it in the eyes. We shut him down before he got his hooks in you."

"Then he went after Coz," Gianni said.

"He introduced me to Dante and his gang," Coz said. "They're the ones who taught me how to pick locks."

"I'm pretty sure Bruno was behind Fredo's murder," Vinnie said.

"Fredo," Gianni said. "Shame what happened. He was a good guy."

"The best. And Bruno had him viciously executed. Orchestrated it all. Payback for us taking Nico and Coz from them. Had Dante and his boys do the deed."

"That was never proven," Nico said. "Could have been someone else."

"Sal basically took credit for it," Gianni said. "Him and his goons."

"None of that really matters now, does it?" Coz said. "All that matters is a good man is dead. Yet another innocent life in the way of Sal's miserable quest for power."

"Sal's not behind all this," Gianni said.

"You just blamed him," Vinnie said. "Said he admitted it."

"This your loyalty to him talking?" Coz asked.

"No loyalty there anymore. He betrayed us. I just don't think he's the mastermind type. He's the muscle."

"He's a problem we have to address," Vinnie said.

"All right," Gianni said. "Enough of this. We're supposed to be putting work out of mind for the night. Let's stop the shop talk and have a little fun. Maybe make a wager on the game."

"You want to bet on who's going to win?" Coz laughed. "I'll take that bet. You haven't scored a point all night."

"We were just warming up," Vinnie said. "I'm in for a hundred."

Mike grinned. "How about two?"

"So that's how it is, old man?" Vinnie cracked his knuckles. "It's a deal. G and I were hustling you. You're going down."

"Bring it on, boys." Mike stooped and picked up his balls.

Nico marveled as they slipped into casual banter. If not for Mike's perpetually formal tone, it would sound… like a family. Like father and son. He was glad his brother got that time to bond with his biological father. They didn't often have moments to forge relationships with others, and Vinnie deserved some happiness. Especially if it was the beginning of him coming to terms with all the upheaval he'd experienced recently.

A yawn escaped him, and his eyes drooped. He lay back in the cool grass, content to listen to the game without watching it, allowing the nighttime breeze to lull him into a state of relaxation.

He still searched his thoughts for what eluded him about Bruno, but his brain moved slower, his memories grew more distant.

The breeze turned chilly, downright frigid, and he was sucked through a violent vortex.

He opened his mouth to scream, but he was mute. Reached for his dagger, but it was gone. Tried to slow his momentum, but he had nothing to grab.

As suddenly as he plunged through the maelstrom, he stopped. A quick assessment revealed he was uninjured, but he still had no voice, no weapon. He peered through the darkness, focused on a pinprick of light. It flickered in the distance, and he picked his way carefully toward it.

Fire.

The flame raged, its heat almost unbearable, its light stopping just short of illuminating a figure in the shadows. Someone chanted, his voice rising over the crackling blaze. Stone, metals, plants… it happened too fast for Nico to make sense of it. The spitting sparks slowed to a soft burn, and maniacal laughter rose over the sizzling embers.

A blue marble dagger floated above the kindling.

Nico lunged for it, but a hand reached out from the shadows and snatched it away from him.

Where'd the guy go? Where'd the dagger go?

Nico yelled, "No!" This time his voice worked, and the call echoed through the cavern.

Then cold, strong fingers snatched at him, clutched his arm, held him tight. He struck out blindly, needing to find the blue dagger, desperate to break free. But before he could fight for the blade, he was again sucked into the aether.

NICO THRASHED VIOLENTLY against the person restraining him. He screamed and tried to break free, but the hands only gripped him tighter. Desperation had his heart pounding in his chest. Sweat slicked his skin, soaked his clothes. His eyes snapped open.

He looked into the concerned faces of his brothers. Coz had him pinned to the ground.

His muscles ached from constriction, his breaths came in labored gasps. It took deliberate effort on his part to relax his body and slow his breathing.

"You okay?" Coz asked.

Nico nodded, and his brother released him.

"What the hell was that all about?" Gianni asked.

"Just a—" What was it, really? It was a hell of a lot more real than a dream ever felt. But he wasn't about to claim he'd had a vision. That was too bizarre. "Just a nightmare. No big deal."

"No big deal? Right." Gianni sat back and stared at him. "You were screaming so loud, I expected the girls to hear you and come running."

"I half expected Mike to hear you and come back," Coz said.

"He left?"

"Yeah. You fell asleep about two points into the game. After the prick collected his winnings, he left."

Coz smirked.

Vinnie ignored him. "You started screaming about five minutes after he was gone."

"Sorry. But I'm fine. Stop hovering."

Vinnie stared at him, expression serious and focus intense. "I can't tell what this means. What did you dream about?"

His brother was taking his strategy power to the next level, which usually would impress Nico. Instead, he felt violated. He wished everybody would just leave him the hell alone, at least until he could get a grip on things. Instead, even the illusion of privacy was gone. Sharing his... whatever it was would only lead to more scrutiny, something he was desperate to avoid.

But he'd just lectured Donni on the importance of full disclosure. It would be pretty hypocritical of him not to tell them what he'd felt, what he'd seen.

On the other hand, he was Donni's protector, so he needed her to be open with him. Didn't mean it had to work in the other direction. He had no guardian, nor did he need one, so what he revealed was up to his discretion. Right?

Probably not.

"Nico!" Vinnie nudged him with his toe. "What did you dream?"

Damn it. He hated it, but he knew what he had to do. Despite him wanting to keep his private life private—and more importantly, wanting to completely forget about what he'd just experienced—he told them about his nightmare.

"Fuck." Vinnie's eyes were closed, his brow furrowed in concentration, his expression grim. "This isn't good."

15

WHEN ANYONE ENTERED the grounds at night, motion sensors would usually activate discreet landscape lighting along the paths and the occasional spotlight on a particularly lovely plant or sculpture. Donni had turned it off earlier, craving the darkness and anonymity, but the guys had turned the system back on, along with some floodlights, to play *bocce*.

Their game was long since over and they'd all gone upstairs an hour ago, so Donni again turned off the system and stepped outside. She wanted to be alone, and if anyone saw activity on the property, they'd investigate, effectively ending her privacy.

The cloud cover had only grown thicker as the night progressed, and the grounds were completely dark, so she used the light on her phone to illuminate the path as she walked away from the villa toward her favorite grotto.

It wasn't that she didn't love her family… she did. More than anything. And a girls' night, in theory, was fun. Was probably just what she needed to cut loose and relieve some tension.

But the opposite had happened—it stressed her more. She just hadn't been in the mood for the bonding and camaraderie.

Everything was getting to her.

The prophecy.

The traveling and hiding.

The fact that she wasn't allowed off property.

The whole situation with Mama.

The thing with Nico. Whatever the hell it was.

Her thoughts drifted to the night they'd spent together. Every kiss, every caress. Her body began responding to the mere memory of him, and she forced the thoughts out of her head. He clearly had second thoughts, so the likelihood of a repeat performance was slim to none. Why dwell on the improbable? It was too painful.

But what had she done wrong? Why did he want time and space?

Okay, she was out in a maze—alone, in the middle of the night—so apparently she wanted time and space, too. Made her a hypocrite for being angry with him, didn't it? Oh, who knew? But there she was, out there, alone with her thoughts. Miserable as they were.

It only made sense to strike out on her own. In her current mood, she made lousy company. And everyone else was asleep, anyway. Being alone made sense. The distance and the freedom of being outside was just gravy on top.

Did it make sense, though? Given she'd essentially been sequestered for weeks, logically she should want company. But she was tired of everyone. She was even tired of herself. And there would be no reprieve... She was stuck with her current situation.

To at least get a change of scenery, she changed direction and picked her way to the center of the hedge maze. She hadn't been there since they'd first arrived, and she couldn't think of a better way to spend a sleepless night than to try to find her way through a labyrinth in the dark.

There was something seriously wrong with her.

Finally she broke into the clearing. Even in the dark, it took her breath away.

An enormous fountain stood in the center. The water was off at the moment, but the absence of burbling, running water didn't detract from its splendor. Four larger-than-life sculptures surrounded it. Venus, goddess of love, took her place north of the fountain. She gazed longingly over her shoulder toward the west, where her mate, Mars, god of war, stood poised for battle. While Venus looked west, she pointed east, toward their beloved son, Cupid, god of desire. Directly opposite of Venus, on the southern side of the fountain, stood Psyche, goddess of the soul and mate of Cupid.

Donni liked to believe the fountain blocked Venus's view of Psyche on purpose—because she was jealous of Psyche's beauty and enraged that her son loved her.

And they said Greek relationships were messed up. Romans knew a thing or two about complications in love.

Donni sat on a bench and shone the beam of her light over all the statues. "Exquisite" didn't do them justice. There was no public record of these figures even existing, but given their quality—and their owner—she had to assume she was in the presence of original works by Michelangelo himself.

They took her breath away. Donni placed her hand on her chest and tried to take a few deep breaths. She focused the light on Cupid's face, and a tear rolled down her cheek. He was beautiful beyond words.

And he looked remarkably like Nico.

"Hey."

She shrieked at the sound and dropped her phone. The beam of light cut a swath through the darkness and briefly illuminated Nico's face before falling bulb-side down and pitching the clearing into inky blackness. Good thing she already had her hand on her chest, because she needed the palm-to-heart contact to try and calm her racing pulse.

"Sorry. I didn't mean to startle you."

"What the hell did you think was going to happen when you don't let me know you're around?"

"How was I supposed to tell you I was here without telling you I was here?"

Donni took a deep breath and blew it out slowly. "I don't know. How about you make noise when you walk, like a normal person."

"I do walk like a normal person. I just actually pick up my feet."

"Are you telling me I shuffle?"

He sighed. "I'm not trying to pick a fight with you. Besides, if you heard me coming in advance, you'd have been scared longer. So it seems this way was better. Whether I intended it that way or not."

"I don't think scaring me for a long or short period of time is acceptable."

"I didn't try to scare you, Donni. If I did, I'm sorry."

"So you weren't trying to sneak up on me?"

He was silent for a moment. "I was trying to stay quiet. I didn't know it was you, and if you had been an intruder, I wanted the element of surprise."

"You have this whole place monitored. You could have just looked at the security feeds."

"It's too dark to make out features. The lights are off."

"I did that. I wanted privacy."

"I see."

"Why didn't you turn them on?"

"I guess I wanted privacy, too. Then I saw your flashlight, and I was glad for the chance to sneak through the grounds."

It was her turn to be silent for a moment. Then she said, "I thought you went to bed. What are you doing out here?"

"I could ask you the same question."

"I asked first."

Nico picked up her phone, handed it to her, and sat beside her. "Like we both said—privacy."

"And you didn't have it in your room?"

"Didn't you?"

She couldn't argue with his logic, so she changed the subject. "What are you even doing up at this hour? It's after three."

"What are you doing up?"

"I asked first."

"You only get to use that answer once."

She let the beam of light play over his features—concerned eyes, high cheekbones, aquiline nose, chiseled jaw. Didn't dare let the light drop lower. Didn't have to. She'd committed every muscle to memory, and now more than ever she knew he was as beautiful as the Roman gods standing sentinel there.

She turned off the light. No point in being caught ogling him. Or blushing because of it.

"Donni?"

"I couldn't sleep."

"Me, either. I got a glass of wine and took it out to the patio. Figured I'd just enjoy the evening. Didn't plan on a romp through the hedge maze, but then I saw your light."

"Sorry."

"No worries. All things considered, I've had worse nights."

She wondered if he meant the night he spent with her, and another tear rolled down her cheek. Never had she been so grateful for darkness. Why did he have to be there, witnessing her near-meltdown? He sat so close to her, she could feel the heat of his body although they didn't touch. Was that coincidence or by design?

She was driving herself crazy.

The tears flowed freely, and she swiped at them with the back of her hand. Unable to stop herself, she sniffled.

"Donni?"

The helplessness in his voice was her undoing. She burst into gut-wrenching sobs and tried to run away.

Somehow, despite the darkness, he grabbed her hand before she could escape and pulled her down to his lap. He held her while she cried, rocked her and soothed her, allowed her to let it all out.

She totally soaked his t-shirt, and she loved him all the more for not caring.

Wait. What? The L-word? Where'd that come from?

Startled, she stopped crying and jumped off him.

"*Tesoro*," he said. "What's wrong?"

But her defenses were up and on high alert. "You don't ask what's wrong while I'm crying, but you ask when I stop?"

"I—I don't know what to say to that."

"Of course you don't. When it comes to giving orders, you speak volumes. But when it comes time to—God forbid—share a feeling or two, *nothing*. You clam right up."

"Share feelings? What are you talking about? Neither of us was talking."

"And you don't want to. You said so yourself up at the house. Said you wanted to take some time, figure things out. So I give you space. And what do you do? You come out here at night by all these love statues—"

"Love statues?"

"—and you pull me onto your lap. Hold me close and whisper endearments in my ear. What am I supposed to do with that?"

"You were upset. I was trying to comfort you."

"You made me upset, you moron. I wouldn't have needed comfort if it wasn't for you."

"Me? What did I do?"

She squared her shoulders and lifted her chin, knowing he couldn't see the gestures but needing them for strength. "You did nothing. Absolutely nothing. And I imagine it's going to stay that way."

"What are you..."

But she'd already turned her light back on and returned through the maze, leaving him sitting there alone. Too late she wondered what she would have seen in his eyes if she'd have paid attention.

NICO THOUGHT ABOUT chasing after Donni, but he decided against it. He glanced at the security feeds on his phone and knew the area was secure. As long as she didn't get lost in the maze or a stray wolf didn't wander onto the property and cross her path, she'd be fine.

Besides, he wasn't sure what to say to her if he did follow her.

He didn't know what had led her out there to begin with, and he certainly didn't know what had made her cry.

He'd also grown pretty good at lying to himself.

Fine. She was crying because of him. Because he came off as the biggest jerk on the planet.

How would he feel if someone he was close to took advantage of him one night and then said she needed space the next? Used. Mortified. Insecure. Unwanted. And that's exactly what he'd done to her.

His brothers told him to get more serious with her, a far cry from the consensus when Gianni started to fall for Franki or Vinnie for Jo. This time, he had everybody's blessing—he had everyone's encouragement—but he resisted.

Was he hesitant because he had legitimate concerns? Or was it simply to be contrary to what everyone else wanted?

How the fuck was he even supposed to know anymore?

His feelings were all over the place. He could hardly be honest with Donni when he couldn't be honest with himself. Or, if he was being truthful, he could only say he was attracted and confused.

Not much of a ringing endorsement.

If he only knew for sure their feelings weren't being manipulated, then he'd act on them in a heartbeat. Or faster.

He kept an eye on the security feeds until he saw Donni emerge from the hedge maze and cross the lawn. Only after she walked inside did he rise and head toward the house.

Dodged a bullet there. He wouldn't have to see her on his way to bed.

Yet ten minutes later, he stood in the hallway outside her door, hand poised to knock.

And he stood like that for countless minutes, still as the "love statues" she'd referenced outside. It wasn't fair of him to knock on her door if he couldn't promise her anything more than physical closeness.

But, God help him, he couldn't get her out of his mind. He worried about her emotional state. Worse, even as he knew he was poison to her, he yearned for her.

When the door flung open, he still stood with his hand raised in a fist.

"You've been there a while now, but you didn't knock."

He lowered his hand. "I wasn't sure you wanted to hear from me."

"Then what'd you come to my room for?"

How could he say it and not sound like a total jerk? "How'd you know I was out here?"

She scowled. "What do you want, Nico?"

He fought a small war inside himself. Wasn't sure what side he was rooting for, but he knew what side would win before the battle was over. "You. I'm here because of you. God help me—God help us both—but I need you."

She smiled, grabbed his tear-dampened t-shirt, and yanked him inside.

DONNI WOKE TO sunlight streaming through the window and birdsong in the air. A glorious morning, to be sure.

And then she noticed—once again—there was no Nico, no note. Not even a tray of food this time.

And the glory of the morning melted into the gloom of shame. She'd gone and done it again. She'd used him for bodily pleasure, physical release. Emotional connection. And he'd stepped up, at least for the physical stuff. And then he stepped out when the emotions came into play.

You'd think she'd learn, but no.

She took a long, scalding shower, like she could scrub the embarrassment and stupidity away.

Didn't work.

With nothing left to do but face the day—and the man who ruined it—she left her room and headed downstairs.

The villa bustled with activity. Gianni had already made breakfast. Platters of food stretched from one end of the vast sideboard to the other. The table was crowded. Not only were all three of her sisters and all of the Brothers there, but Marcus and Enrico had joined them, as had Mike, a few men she'd never seen before, and one other familiar face.

Carmen Remo Scalzotto.

She'd seen pictures and video, heard the stories. But all of that paled in comparison to the real thing. It was instantly apparent why the people rallied around him. He was attractive, intelligent, charismatic. At once gracious and welcoming, even when he was the guest.

A born leader.

He was in the middle of saying something when she entered the room, and he didn't single her out, yet he effortlessly included her in the discussion. And she felt his presence as palpably as she would have if he had risen and embraced her.

Nico sat beside him, fully concentrating on their conversation, showing him something on one of his ever-present laptops. Everyone else seemed equally oblivious to anything but Scalzotto.

It surprised her when Mike joined her in the doorway.

"He is the future."

Funny, but Donni wasn't sure if Mike meant Nico or Scalzotto. She turned to look at him, but he'd already walked away. And rather than stay and face Nico, she took Mike's lead and left the room, too.

NICO FINISHED SHOWING Scalzotto their security measures and then made his excuses and left the room. He needed to find Donni.

As he walked down the hall, he poked his head in a few rooms, even knowing she wouldn't be there. It was like he could sense her presence, and he followed that feeling to the kitchen.

Okay, maybe he put more stock into his feelings than was warranted. After all, where else would she be? She hadn't made a plate in the dining room, so she'd probably want breakfast. At least a cup of coffee.

And that's exactly where he found her. Serendipity? Fate?

Logic.

Didn't matter. He'd found her. "Good morning."

She put the carafe down and added a splash of cream to her mug. "Morning."

"I'm sorry. But I can explain."

"Explain what?"

"I didn't plan on leaving you this morning. I fully expected to be there when you woke up."

"You don't owe me anything, Nico. Not your presence in my bed. Not an apology. Not even an explanation. You're under no obligations to me."

Women were so damn confusing. First she wanted the moon. Then when he apologized for not giving it to her, she said she didn't want it.

Or was it just that she didn't want it from him?

"I don't understand. I don't know what you want from me."

"You asked for time and space, Nico, and I tried to give it to you. I'd thank you to give me the same courtesy." And she walked out of the room.

He stared after her, completely at a loss. How was he supposed to make things right with her when he didn't know what was wrong?

"Looks like you fucked that up. Royally."

Nico turned around to see Coz in the doorway, a smirk on his face.

"Who asked you? And aren't you supposed to be going over our security protocols with Scalzotto's staff?"

"We're done. Now I'm in here to offer my brother moral support before we all gather for a briefing."

"Isn't that what we just had?"

"That was introductions and security info. Now Mike wants to go over strategy." He glanced at his watch. "And now you're out of time for moral support."

Nico shoved him as he brushed past. "I don't fucking need moral support."

Coz laughed and followed him toward the den. "You need something."

Nico flipped him off without looking back.

16

DONNI LOOKED AT everyone in the room, then her gaze went back to the man of the hour. Carmen Scalzotto impressed her. He exuded an aura of strength, determination, and compassion. Being near him was to be in the presence of greatness.

It was visceral. And a little disconcerting. He wasn't a god. He was, however, Italy's best chance. Better than any of the four Medici descendants Italy chanted about.

They all sat around the dining table because the den didn't have enough surface area for everyone who wanted to use a laptop or notebook. The brothers were the most boisterous of the group. Her sisters made small talk when there was a lull in the conversation. Marcus and Enrico sat near Carmen's security detail, and none of them said a word.

Mike, as usual when he was there, moderated the meeting.

"Two days ago, another series of riots broke out across the country. The situation was most dire in Venice, where Carmen happened to be at the time. The city sustained heavy casualties. His supporters, now thought to be in the hundreds of thousands and growing, used their own bodies as shields to get him away from the gas, batons, and bean bags and to shelter. Now that he is safely away from the government retaliation, he wants to release a statement via the Internet."

"I need to tell the people not to despair. I need them to know that we'll fight for them."

"Well," Nico said, "I can post any statement you want to write, but I don't know what good it will do. The rest of the world will see it, but the government shut down the Internet. Most of Italy's citizens won't have access to it."

"But you have access," Carmen said. "I assumed the Internet had been reestablished nationwide."

"No. The country's still dark."

"Then how to you…?"

"If you want to be a ruler someday, you might not want to know the particulars about what I'm doing here. Plausible deniability, and all that."

Mike scowled at him. "The government has shut off public access, but they did not disable their own ability to access the Internet. Dominico has tapped into their secure servers and is using their access for his own needs."

"You hacked a government?" Carmen said.

Nico shrugged.

"I see. I don't need more details."

"Didn't think so."

"Are you able to turn the rest of the country back on?" Carmen asked.

"That would be trickier. It might take a while, but I think I could."

"Perhaps you should do that before I release my statement."

Nico rubbed the knotted muscles in the back of his neck. "Thing is, if I do turn it back on, the government will know. And they might be able to trace the hack back to us. They'll definitely shore up their system so it will be harder to get back in. And it's doubtful enough people will see your message before we're shut out."

Carmen sighed. "So it's pointless for me to even release a statement, then?"

"I don't think so. What if you recorded a statement rather than writing your response?"

"Excuse me," Jo said. "I don't understand."

"Can you be more specific, please, Josephina?"

"Mr. Scalzotto—"

"Carmen, please," Scalzotto said.

"Carmen is the face of the revolution. And I'm all for that. The sooner we're off the hot seat, the better. But why is Sal and his organization after us and not him?"

"It is my belief you both are in danger," Mike said. "That is why I brought him here."

"But the people shout 'Medici' even as they look to Mr. Scal—Carmen to lead them. Which is it? Us, or him?"

"If I may," Carmen said to Mike.

Mike nodded and held out his hand.

Carmen turned to Jo. "I have become the face of this movement because our countrymen don't know any Medici exist. They want just rule rather than corruption, and they're chanting for not a Medici descendant, but someone who will rule benevolently, as some of the Medici did. When we come forward and introduce you to the world, I will cease to be the face of the revolution. I've only agreed to this point because Mike convinced me it helps protect the four of you."

Jo shook her head. "No."

"Yes, Josephina, it does."

"No. That's not what I mean." She ran her hand through her hair. "Don't you see? This is our out. We don't have to tell the world we exist."

"I think it will be beneficial if you do," Carmen said. "When all the pieces are in place and your safety is secure, that is."

"How does revealing our identity help anyone?" Franki asked.

"If the world knows about you, you'll be safer. The organization can't attack you without an investigation. It would be like—no, not *like*—an assassination of a world leader or leaders. They would be hunted and killed on sight."

"Then why not go public now?" Donni said. "For our safety."

"We need more of the country to embrace the Medici concept, first," Mike said. "And we need to make sure we can prove your lineage."

Donni shook her head. "But we don't want this. Let's just let Carmen lead, and we can go back home."

Several people spoke at once, and Donni couldn't make out anything other than the occasional name.

Finally, Mike raised his hands and silenced them all. "We shall table this discussion until another time. Right now, we need Mr. Scalzotto to get a message to the masses. Dominico, what is your suggestion?"

Donni zoned out for a while, content to watch Nico, Mike, and Carmen discuss their options. Carmen was truly charismatic. She could easily see the whole nation following him.

But Nico? When he was in his element, his mind went into overdrive. He talked fast, gestured faster, and used a language all his own. His passion for his work was evident on his face, in his voice… in those long, competent fingers that flew over the keyboard.

She'd seen him like this before. When he got excited about work, he always behaved that way.

But when he got excited in bed, the ardor was even more pronounced. And she knew precisely what those fingers were capable of. What that mouth was able to do. What that voice sounded like in the throes of passion.

Carmen might be the man to ignite the revolution in Italy, but only one man could ignite her.

Too bad he was only interested in banking those fires instead of fanning them.

Donni needed to keep her distance. She'd train with him, work with him, share meals and a house with him, but she was done sharing her body. Because when the fire burned out, the cold was too difficult to bear.

NICO MADE FINAL adjustments while fielding about a thousand questions. When he couldn't take it any longer, he slammed his laptop shut.

Everyone quieted and looked at him.

"I know you don't understand exactly what's going to happen here. That's okay. I'm the tech guy, so I'm the only one who has to know the mechanics behind this. What I need you all to do is calm down, keep your questions to yourselves, and watch what happens. If, when this is all over, you want a lesson in the upload and loop, I'll walk you through it. But right now, time's wasting. Let's get this thing shot so I can edit it."

He had to content himself with a few muttered obscenities from his brothers and general murmurs of agreement from everyone else.

"Carmen, do you need cue cards, or do you know what you want to say?"

"I think I'd rather not read the statement. Speaking from the heart will sound more natural, don't you think?"

"You're an expert public speaker. I think you'd do fine either way. But whatever you're most comfortable with is fine with me. We'll shoot the speech, and then we'll see if you need additional takes."

"Very well. Thank you."

"Dominico, are you certain a network video broadcast is not the wiser choice? Carmen is very charismatic. I believe if the nation can see him, they will be more inclined to respond favorably."

"No." Vinnie had a distant look for a moment, then his eyes cleared. "If Nic hacks into the networks, he'll get shut down too fast. He'll be able to send the signal through ham radio for much longer."

"I can broadcast video through ham TV frequencies, but most people won't view it. Besides, the range is too low. Best we could get is fifty or sixty miles. The audio-only is the best bet. It'll reach the most people this way."

"Aren't you required to have a license or register your name or something with ham radio?" Carmen asked.

Nico raised his eyebrow. "Do you *really* want to discuss legalities right now?"

"No. No, this is fine. I put myself fully in your capable hands."

"All right. Everyone quiet." Nico shushed the room. When everyone was silent, he looked at Carmen. "You ready?"

"As I'll ever be."

Nico raised five fingers, lowering them as he counted down. "And five, four, three...." The last two he was silent for, but continued with his fingers.

He pointed at Carmen to begin.

While he'd been speaking in English so the girls could understand, he spoke in Italian for the recording. Despite the language barrier, the girls seemed riveted by his speech.

"Brothers and sisters. This is Carmen Scalzotto, broadcasting to you from a secure location. If you're hearing this message, please tell your family, friends, and neighbors how to access this recording. It will be played on a loop until the government manages to shut it down.

"The riots of two days ago weigh heavily on my heart.

"It pains me that so many good citizens lost their lives in their efforts to merely make their voices heard. They should never have been put in that position. I never asked that of them. Who am I that they would lay down their lives for me?

"I never wanted the burden of leadership or the responsibility for so many, but I will gladly bear all these difficulties and more in their memories so they might once again have a voice in our great nation.

"Italy was once the greatest empire on the planet. We aren't seeking global domination again, but merely a just government. Italy was once at the forefront of the Renaissance, bringing enlightenment to the world. We aren't seeking to dictate how religion and education should be pursued, but we deserve the right to pursue our interests freely.

"We are a proud country of merchants, artisans, businessmen, inventors… people of all trades from all walks of life who want the chance to make an honest wage at an honest job. We want to send our children to good schools and not worry about losing our houses and our land in the process. We want to go back to the days when art and education were celebrated and good business made good sense, when our banks were full and so were our bellies. We want fair governance again. No, we demand it.

"No more tyranny! It is time we reclaim this nation for its citizens. I stand with the people, for the people, now and always.

"Thank you for your time. God bless you all, and God bless Italy!" He gestured for Nico to stop the recording and switched effortlessly to English again. "How was that? Should I speak off cards the next time?"

"Next time?" Nico shook his head. "You don't need next time. You nailed it."

"Are you certain?"

"It was perfect," Mike said. "I think you will be pleased with it when you hear the playback."

Nico played the recording for him.

"I feel like I could do better."

"You'll never do better than this," Nico said. "Doesn't need anything in editing. It's good to go as-is."

"If you're sure." Carmen looked around the room. No one disagreed. "Okay, then. Broadcast it."

Nico worked his magic at the keyboard, and Carmen looked away. Nico didn't blame him. If he did rule someday in place of or alongside of the Notaros, the less he knew about the illegalities of what the Brotherhood did, the better. He finished typing with a flourish of his fingers. "And you're live."

"And now we wait," Mike said.

"Wait?" Carmen said. "For what?"

"For the government's response."

"Or for Sal's group to make a move," Gianni said.

"I'll keep monitoring things," Vinnie said. "When I sense something, I'll let you know."

"And I'll keep an eye on things through the computer," Nico said. "We'll know if anyone's making a move."

"Come on," Coz said. "We'll show you the rest of the villa."

"You should end the tour in the gymnasium. I want you to have another training session today."

"Sure thing." Coz led Carmen and his men out of the room.

Nico was the last to leave. He had been so proud of pulling off the recording upload, but hearing about the workout just deflated his mood.

He'd be working with Donni again. And she'd be in his arms. In a room full of people.

And just what the hell was he going to do about that?

DONNI WAS DOUBLY surprised—one, that Mike would call a practice session with strangers in the villa and two, he'd actually invited them to *watch* it.

She sat on the mat and stretched, trying to prepare for the session. Honestly, she thought it was more difficult to prepare for the emotional toll of the workout than the physical one. Her body was used to being pushed to its limits. Her emotions weren't used to any romance at all, let alone the kind of relationship—if you could call it that—between her and Nico.

Merda, it was going to be hard to be in his arms. Especially in front of people. She felt him behind her before he spoke, his breath a warm tingle on her neck.

"This time, tap out if you need to."

Didn't have to tell her twice. Still, it was annoying that he thought he had to. Even as it was toe-curling having him stand so near.

She rose and faced him, nose-to-nose. Well, he towered over her, so it was more like she tipped her head up to stare him down, and her chin jutted toward his chest.

His broad, firm, muscular chest.

How the hell was she going to get through their first challenge? The second he put a hand on her, she'd combust. Or melt. Or just throw herself at him.

The room dimmed and lurched a little. Note to self—breathe.

She went from not breathing to shallow, rapid breaths. Okay, panting. She was actually panting after that irritating, infuriating, handsome man. In front of her family, his, and their guests.

Maybe if she kept hyperventilating, she'd pass out and not have to face any of them.

Mike stepped into the room and looked around. "I am sorry. I should have been clearer. I want the Brotherhood to work on their powers. Ladies, you may have this time off. Stay or leave, the choice is yours. But you will not be part of this practice session."

Donni took her first easy breath since Nico walked in the room. She could leave, get some distance, some perspective and clarity.

"Might as well stay," Vinnie said. "You might learn something by watching. And if we get done early enough, we'll do a session with you."

Fabulous. Just what she needed—to sit in a room full of people and watch Nico get all sweaty.

NICO GRABBED A towel and a bottle of water. He did everything he could to avoid looking in Donni's direction. She was a distraction. One he couldn't afford at the moment.

After stretching, he loosened up at the bag. A fast flurry of roundhouse kicks with each leg and he was warm and limber—and vibrating with pent-up energy. He did a five-forty kick off each foot, easily clearing the top of the bag both times.

It was completely illegal in competition and not very practical in combat—easier kicks would be much more effective—but he knew few people who could execute that many spins with that much power and height. Because of the level of difficulty, they were fun to do. And they looked impressive. He tried not to, but pride and curiosity had him sneaking a peek at Donni's reaction to the skill.

Mission accomplished.

Her eyes were wide, her jaw slack. And didn't he puff up just a little bit more when she pulled rapidly on her shirt to cool off?

He hid his grin by bringing the bottle to his face and chugging some water. Didn't do anything to cool him off, but at least she didn't know he was showing off for her. And why the hell was he trying to impress her, anyway? They weren't together. And shouldn't be. He lowered the bottle and scowled.

"If you're done trying to dazzle your lady," Coz said to him, "come line up."

Jackass.

"I'm not trying to dazzle anyone," he mumbled as he got in line. "And she's *not* my lady."

"Sure she's not."

Being called out like that was embarrassing, but there was no time to continue the verbal sparring. They'd be doing the physical kind soon enough. But first, Mike called out instructions, and they responded by executing the skills he requested.

Front kicks, side kicks, roundhouse kicks—to both sides and to three different heights. Axe kicks, scissor kicks, back kicks. Hook and crescent kicks. Nico worked up quite the sweat, and they hadn't even done jump kicks yet.

When they stopped fifteen minutes later, he peeled his dobak top off. It and his pants were drenched. Mike gave them a five minute break and expected them outside to work on their powers.

They'd all learned their lesson about power work inside when Gianni manifested the power of fire. Now that Vinnie manifested control over water, it wasn't quite as risky. But there was no point in taking chances.

He walked into the adjoining bathroom to strip out of his pants and into a pair of gym shorts. His brothers had already changed and were walking out as he walked in. Coz lingered while Gianni and Vinnie joined the girls in the hallway.

Nico eavesdropped on their conversations as they walked out of earshot. A lot of compliments, a lot of banter. But nothing from Donni.

"You okay to do this?" Coz asked.

"What?" He stepped out of the sweat-soaked pants, ran a towel under a stream of cold water, and wiped himself down head-to-toe. He wanted to cool off and clean up before going back out.

"You know what. Your powers have been fritzing for a while now. Somedays they're stronger than they should be. Other times you can't do things you learned months ago. We've got guests watching us now. People who depend on us. You can't go out there if you're going to crash and burn. I'll make an excuse for you."

Nico huffed out a slow, steady breath and stepped into his shorts. "Why is everyone always on my case? You don't have your full powers yet, either."

"No, but I'm consistent. You're all over the place. Vinnie can't even predict what you're going to do because he never knows which version of you to expect."

He still had guilt over not being able to heal Donni or Mary. He didn't need his best friend busting his chops about it. "I'm tight, Coz. Don't worry about it. Powers work is going to look like we scripted it. Even Mike will be proud."

Coz raised his eyebrows but didn't say anything. He just walked out of the room and headed out back.

Nico followed, not nearly as confident as he'd led Coz to believe.

NICO JOINED HIS brothers in the clearing. He faced Coz, Vin faced Gianni. They each held a dagger in front of them. A few deep breaths to center themselves, and they began.

Despite the vigorous warmup and martial arts session beforehand, Nico felt ill-prepared for the form they performed. His thoughts swirled in a messy vortex of concern—what did Mike think, what did Scalzotto and his men think, what did Donni think?

Donni. Why couldn't he come to grips with what they meant to each other? He pulled away when she advanced. She retreated when he stepped up. The hell with the dagger influencing them. Fate seemed to be intervening enough on its own.

And what did he feel about that?

Nico tried to focus on executing the form, but he struggled. His motions were jerky, robotic, and just a fraction of a second behind that of the group. The tempo increased, as did his troubles. Near the end, he missed a series completely, waited a beat, and joined his brothers for the finishing pose.

"What the fuck, Nic?" Coz glared at him. "We're supposed to be making a good impression."

"Get your head in the game," Vinnie said. "You look like a rank amateur."

No point in arguing. He felt like one, too. Didn't mean they didn't piss him off, though. He knew he sucked. Didn't need the scouting report.

"Come on. Let's go to the targets." Gianni grabbed his arm as they walked together. "Remember what happened last time. You need to focus. If someone gets hurt—"

"I got it, Gianni. God, maybe if you all fucking let up a little, I could concentrate better."

No one answered him, which was probably for the best. He glanced at Mike, whose face had darkened with disappointment or anger. Or both. It didn't escape his notice that when he approached the target on the far left, his adoptive father walked across the yard to stand at the far right.

Nico sighed. If he was going to get them to trust him, he'd have to earn it.

Coz took the target next to him. Nico appreciated the buffer between him and the rest of the Brotherhood. Gianni and Vinnie had their full powers, which made Nico feel even more inadequate than he appeared. And Mike's patented blend of superiority, anger, and mock fear would only distract him and make his performance worse. He nodded a discreet thanks to his brother and faced the targets.

They started this session by throwing the daggers. Each one hit closer and closer to the bullseye, and as he increased his distance, he only got better. Competition marked the longest throwing distance at sixteen feet. He and his brothers stood somewhere between twenty and twenty-five if he had to guess. The guys were doing as well as he was, maybe better. He'd redeemed himself but wasn't satisfied. Yet. Before he could throw another dagger, Mike suggested they move on to power bursts.

Nico grinned. He had been so excited to learn how to throw energy blasts from his dagger. He not only practiced that with the Brotherhood, he spent sleepless nights working on the skill. It was now second nature to him, and without Mike nearby goading him, he would excel. As they shot at the targets, Nico was deadly accurate. He fired off several bursts in rapid succession until the target fell over, smoldering.

"Where'd you learn to do that?" Vinnie asked.

Coz and Gianni turned to look at him, eyes wide.

Vinnie strode down to him. "Doesn't make sense. You can't even finish the form, but you can out-shoot me and G? I can't figure out what's going on with you. How am I supposed to prepare battle strategies if I don't know which Nico we're going to war with?"

"I don't know what to tell you, Vin."

He wasn't going to get into his late night practice sessions. Nobody's business but his. If he could come into his full powers without using Donni, then he'd know his feelings for her were genuine.

"Come on," Gianni whispered. "They're watching. Let's scrap targets and work on the final session."

They took their same positions in the circle, but this time they all sat, legs crossed. The blades of grass were cool to the touch and tickled the soles of his feet. But Nico ignored all that and focused on their drills. He was determined not to be the weak link, and his brow furrowed in concentration.

A small flame ignited in the center of the circle, branched out until it formed a five-pointed star like that of the table in chamber. Mist vaporized above it, then a gentle rain fell and put the fire out. Where the water hit the lawn, plants sprouted and buds formed on the stalks. Before they could bloom, they withered and died. The brown, brittle brush burned and turned to ash, and another shower doused the blaze. A warm breeze carried the damp embers into the tree line. The ground shook violently beneath them, and they all scrambled back.

A boulder sprang forth from the center of the circle. Cracked. Exploded. Chunks of rubble rained down on them, and they all ducked their heads and ran for cover.

When the ruckus calmed and the debris settled, everyone—even Mike and their guests—approached the rock.

It had formed a near-perfect replica of the table in chamber. The five-pointed star in the center had indentations for the daggers, just no marble inlays.

Nico placed his weapon in one of the grooves. It was a perfect fit.

"What the fuck?" Enrico said under his breath.

That's just what Nico wanted to know.

17

DONNI SAT ON her bed, ignoring her books of paint samples and cloth swatches. She couldn't get the afternoon out of her head. The thoughts swirled in her mind, a cyclonic vortex she couldn't escape.

Nico had been all over the place—screwing up his form, improving on the targets, in his element in the power circle. At least he was in his element—but he claimed he didn't bring the boulder forth.

Of course, everyone else claimed the same thing.

Mike asked the Brothers to reform their circle and remove the boulder-table, and they tried to. But nothing happened. It was like all the mojo was gone. Everyone's. Not a flame flickered. Not a raindrop fell. Not a flower bloomed nor plant withered and drifted away on a breeze.

The group broke up almost immediately after the failed attempt to dispose of the rock. Donni was glad to have the time to herself. Watching a half-dressed Nico as he worked out had her libido on overdrive. Watching a perfectly sculpted table emerge from the ground had her nerves frayed.

She was glad to retreat to her room and ponder what had happened. Spent the rest of the day there, not even going down for dinner. And no one came to get her, so she assumed everyone was as freaked out and distracted as she was.

Hell, she was one of the two people who usually cooked. Maybe no one even made dinner.

By midnight, she'd thought herself into a dull headache and her stomach had begun to growl. Time to set her materials aside—she hadn't made a single decision, anyway—and venture downstairs for a snack.

In the kitchen, she rooted through a cabinet until she found a bottle of ibuprofen. She popped the top, tossed a couple into her palm, and spied a bottle of merlot on the counter. After pouring a generous glass that emptied the bottle, she downed the medicine with the wine. It was herbal, fruity, and mellow. The perfect pre-bed beverage. Would go great with a bite of cheese. Her stomach growled, and she decided to look for some asiago or fontina.

She'd just opened the refrigerator when the floor creaked. Whipping around, she came face to face with Nico. He wore shorts. And nothing else. Her mouth went dry, and she clutched her chest. "You... scared me. Again."

"Sorry," he said. "I couldn't sleep."

"Me, either."

He looked her over, head to toe and back. His irises darkened and his breathing quickened.

She looked down at herself. Given the late hour, she hadn't expected to see anyone, so she hadn't worn a robe. She was in shorts and a tank top, and based on Nico's reaction, he'd noticed. And liked it.

She was rather fond of his state of dress, too. Her cheeks flamed, and she tried to hide behind the refrigerator door. "Want something?"

"Yes." His voice was deep, husky.

It caressed her body, blanketing her in heat and desire.

She fanned some of the cold air toward her, but it did nothing to cool her off. She needed to redirect their conversation before she was straddling him on the table. "Did you come down for something particular? A drink? A snack?"

She peeked around the refrigerator door, but he didn't meet her gaze. He was looking at her bare thighs. Or maybe a few inches higher.

Nico cleared his throat and turned around. He took a few steps away from her. "Actually, I was headed out for some air."

"Want some company?" Why the hell had she said that? Two seconds ago she was trying to hide from his gaze. Now she wanted to what? Walk hand-in-hand in the moonlight while they were both half naked?

She was a moron.

"Yeah, I'd like that." He held his hand out to her.

Maybe dreams do come true. Or, at least silly wishes. She closed the refrigerator door, interlaced her fingers with his, and followed him outside.

NICO REVELED IN the feel of Donni's hand in his. Something about the skin-on-skin contact while walking under the stars and listening to nature's melody of crickets and tree frogs just made all his problems melt away.

Until he considered why. He once again had his dagger with him—he always had his dagger with him—and a small part of him worried that was why he felt that way.

They stopped by the new rock table. He ran his hand over the surface. It was smooth—so smooth it felt polished. Cool to the touch, but heated quickly under his palm.

"It's incredible, isn't it?" she asked.

"I've never seen anything like it."

"How do you think it happened?"

"I have no idea."

"Hmm," she said. "You know, I'd think Michelangelo himself carved it if I hadn't seen it erupt from the ground right in front of me."

It was *that* beautiful. A work of art, really. He had to agree—if he hadn't seen it spring forth right in front of him, he'd also believe a master sculptor had created it.

She placed her hand on the slab right beside his, trailed her fingers lightly over the surface, and sighed.

God, she looked beautiful in the moonlight. Hair pulled up so he could see the delicate curvature of her neck, but tendrils fallen loose, framing her face. Long, tan limbs fairly luminous in the moonlight. The smile on her face peaceful, serene.

She was the work of art.

He let go of her hand, placed both of his on her waist, and lifted her. Her hands went to his shoulders for balance, and they heated his skin. He sat her on the stone table then lay her back.

She looked like a pagan offering to the gods.

He climbed up beside her and let his gaze roam her body. She sighed as though he caressed her and reached up to pull his head down to hers.

The kiss was soft at first, hesitant, then heated into something more wanton and passionate. Nico's head spun. She tasted of wine—rich and sweet. He ran his hand along her thigh, over her hip, and onto her stomach. He tugged the material of her tank up and let his fingers dance over her ribcage.

Donni's breath quickened, and she tipped her head back.

Seeing an opening, he dipped his head and pressed his lips to her throat, her collarbone, her shoulder. He breathed deep and smelled faint traces of lemon on her skin. A smile crossed his face, and he nuzzled her neck, reveling in the sweet essence that was uniquely her.

She ran her fingers through his hair, her touch sending shivers up his spine.

An owl hooted, and she jumped under him.

He opened his eyes and looked at her. She bit her lip, and her gaze darted around the yard.

Merda. He'd done it again. He'd started to have his way with her out in the open, where any prying eyes could see. Shamed, he sat up and turned his back to her.

She scooted to the edge of the rock and sat beside him. When she spoke, resignation tinged her voice. "What'd I do wrong this time?"

He turned to look at her. "Wrong? I was the one who was wrong."

"For being with me?"

"God, no. We can't keep having this argument. Or these moments. We're in the middle of the back yard. Anyone could walk up on us at any moment."

"It's the middle of the night. I don't think anyone's coming out here now."

"Well, they could look out the window, then."

"Is that really what's bothering you?"

"Of course. What else?"

"I thought maybe it was me."

"You should know by now what I think of you. How much I want you." That much was true. Question was, why? Because of the dagger, or because of her?

She gave him the weakest attempt at a smile he'd ever seen. But he didn't know what to do about it, so he decided not to say anything at all.

After a lengthy and awkward pause, she turned and looked at the surface of the rock table. "You know, this is perfectly honed, but it still looks natural. Organic. Why do you think Mike was so determined to get rid of it?"

"It looks too much like the table in chamber. He probably feels like it violates our secret code or something."

"Do you think somehow Michelangelo had something to do with it? It's fine quality. Looks like his work."

He stared at the surface for a moment. "No. He's not here. Doesn't have a dagger, either."

"Mike does."

"Mike is his liaison. Doesn't mean he has his abilities. Besides, he wasn't with us in the circle."

"He's strong enough to do this, though. Right? I mean, he had full powers before any of you."

"Yeah, but his power is all ethereal. He doesn't call forth rock from the earth."

"Gianni and Vinnie have full powers now."

He thought about that for a second. "They do, but this is out of their element. Fire and water. Not rock."

"Wait." She clutched his arm. "What did you say?"

"Fire and water. Not rock."

Donni shook her head. "No. Before that. Out of their element."

"So?"

She jumped off the rock and paced. "I was thinking about this earlier. I said something similar. But I wasn't using the right meaning of the word."

"I'm sorry. You lost me."

"I thought you were in your element today. I meant playing to your strengths. Operating in your wheelhouse."

"Okay. That's what I meant, too. What of it?"

"What if it's more precise than that? What if it's literally elemental?"

He tried to connect the dots, but he couldn't follow her thought process.

She threw her arms in the air. "The *elements*, Nico. *Alchemical* elements."

"Like oxygen, hydrogen?"

"God, you're dense. That's chemistry. I'm talking alchemy. Earth, wind, fire, water, aether."

He blinked a few times, stared at her while he again tried to connect the dots. This time, a picture was starting to form.

"Your brothers didn't just manifest powerful abilities. They're part of something cosmically greater. Elements. Gianni is fire. Vinnie's water. For that matter, Mike represents aether. Don't you *get* it?"

Nico finally had a clear picture. And he didn't like it. Not one bit.

"*You* manifested this rock. *Earth* is your element."

He shook his head.

"Yes, you did. You brought it here. What's your part of the ritual? About your specific dagger? Life, transportation—"

"Life, balance, and transformation."

"*Life*, Nico. Earth—the rock. Transformation—changing it into a carved table. You did this."

He knew she spoke the truth even as he tried to deny it.

She grabbed his arm. "Do you know how much power you had to draw to do that?"

"No. I—I'm not strong enough."

"There's one way to know for sure."

Don't say it. Please, don't say it.

"Let's try to send it back."

She said it. He tried to take a deep breath, but it was like his lungs didn't work or the air was too thin. Something.

Donni grabbed his hands and pulled him to his feet. "Come on. What could it hurt? If I'm right, we get rid of the table. Which Mike wants us to do, anyway. And if I'm wrong, then nothing changes. What have you got to lose?"

Confidence. Pride. Sanity. "I don't think you're right, Don."

"So let's try and see. No one's here. If you're worried about embarrassing yourself because it doesn't work, you don't have to. I won't tell anyone. Besides, I think it is going to work."

He wasn't sure what he was more afraid of—failing or succeeding.

"Come on, Nico."

Why couldn't he tell her no?

"Fine. Let's give it a try."

DONNI COULDN'T WIPE the smile off her face. She didn't wear "giddy" well, but too bad. If looking like a fool was the price she'd pay, she'd pony up. She got to help with the dagger power again—with his agreement this time—and not in a life-or-death situation, but in purely innocuous circumstances where nothing was on the line. Just the exploration of power.

A heady rush flooded her, and she giggled.

Nico shot her a look.

She quit laughing but grinned.

He sighed. "Before we start, I need to warm up."

"What do I do?"

"For now, watch. Concentrate. Meditate. Try to draw energies from the earth and store them in every cell of your body. If you expect me to do anything with this—" he gestured to the stone "—mammoth hunk of rock, I'll need to draw on your strength. If you have some power in reserve, that can only help."

"I know you can do it." She bounced a little on her toes.

"I appreciate your confidence. But don't get your hopes up. Nothing happened today, and all my brothers tried."

"Something happened today. You brought the table forth."

"We don't know it was me."

"Nico, you have to think positively, or it won't work."

"I think you're optimistic enough for both of us."

She cocked her head to the side and put her hands on her hips.

"Fine, I'll be more positive. Now, concentrate."

Donni stopped arguing with him and tried to center herself. She kept one eye trained on Nico, though, and immediately lost herself in his movements.

He performed the form they'd begun with in the practice. Only this time, he wasn't mechanical and off-tempo. He was the definition of fluidity and grace—his muscles rippling, his body nearly glowing as the moon shone off the sheen of sweat on his skin. She got lost in every strike, every thrust.

He was music personified. And it was beautiful. Magical.

Elemental.

She shivered, forced the lust down. Focused on the power and beauty of his routine.

Too soon he'd completed the pattern. Even he looked startled at how effortless his movements were.

She smiled and nodded her encouragement.

"I should probably send some focused energies, but I don't want to wake anyone if something explodes."

"I think you've warmed up enough. Let's work on the stone."

The two of them approached the hewn rock table. He looked down at her. "I don't know where to begin."

"What were you thinking when you brought the table forth?"

"I'm still not convinced it was me."

"What were you thinking about, Nico?"

"I needed to perform. I didn't want to be the weak one again."

"So you were determined?"

"Sure. I guess so."

"Not you guess so. You need conviction. Can you muster up some confidence?"

"Yes?"

"Are you asking me or telling me?"

"Yes. Yes, I can do this." He took her hand.

"Damn right, you can. Sad as I am to see it go, let's put this beautiful rock back where it came from."

Nico held the dagger out in front of him. Donni lifted their joined hands in the air and stretched her free hand out toward the table, mimicking his motions with the dagger. He began chanting something softly under his breath. She couldn't make it out, but he started moving the dagger in small circles in time to his mantra.

Donni moved her hand in a similar manner and focused on drawing energy from the ground and sending it to Nico.

Nothing happened right away, and Nico started to lower their joined hands. She grasped his hand tighter and lifted it higher. He sighed, but then his voice got stronger.

A breeze picked up and brushed her hair against her cheek. It tickled her face, but then she noticed her whole body tingled, thrummed with energy.

The ground vibrated. Trembled. Shook so violently she was almost tossed off her feet. Nico grasped her hand more tightly and raised his voice over the din.

The rock plunged into the ground as though something grabbed it and yanked it under. Earth filled in the hole in an instant, and grass sprouted over it. Then a sapling sprouted, grew into a mature tree, and burst into blossom.

Lemon blossoms.

Nico lowered his hands. His body was slicked with sweat, and his arms had a slight tremor to them.

"Now do you believe me?" she asked.

He shook his head. No words escaped his lips.

"Lemon blossoms. I'd have to ask Toni to be certain, but I think they symbolize discretion."

Nico took a shaky breath and let it out slowly. "Perfect. I'm all for us being discreet. Don't tell anyone. Not until I figure out what this means."

She knew what it meant. But until he was ready to accept his abilities, she couldn't force him to embrace them.

Instead, she embraced *him*.

He returned the hug, then stepped back and searched her face. "Why would you know the meaning of lemon trees?"

"I like lemons. And I learn everything I can about things I like."

"You smell like lemons." He pulled her close again, nuzzled under her ear, and breathed in deeply. "Mmm."

The whispered syllable against her neck vibrated, sent a jolt of delicious sensations through her body. She moaned.

"*Che cazzo,* Nic." Vinnie's voice carried to them in the darkness. "*You* did this?"

She and Nico jumped apart and turned around. His three brothers and her three sisters stood on the patio.

"Fuck," Nico whispered.

"Look on the bright side," she said so only he could hear. "Mike, Scalzotto and his crew, your mentors… none of them came outside to question you."

Vinnie strode across the yard, the others only steps behind him.

"That's small comfort, Don," Nico said, "when the inquisition is here."

NICO STEELED HIMSELF. He knew an explosion was coming.

He wasn't disappointed.

"Start talking, Nico," Vinnie said. "Now."

"I don't know what you want me to say."

Gianni let loose a string of expletives. "Why don't you start with where the stone went? Or where the tree came from. Why your powers don't work one minute and are too advanced the next."

"Or what my sister has to do with any of this," Toni said.

"Kind of hard to answer all those questions at once," Nico said.

"Then start with my sister."

"That's enough," Donni said. "You all complain about the rock popping up, then you complain when it's gone. Make up your minds. And Toni, my involvement with—well, with any of this, is *my* business and not up for group discussion."

"It's not your business." Coz pushed his way forward through the crowd. "Not when it affects the Brotherhood. Then it's all of our business."

"Which this clearly is," Gianni said.

"Can this wait until morning?" Nico said.

"No." They all answered in unison.

So much for a few hours to gather his thoughts. "Well, let's at least go inside. I'm not going to stand around under a tree in the middle of the night like some weird cult or something."

"You're the reason there's a tree here to begin with!" Vinnie said.

"But at least the table's gone."

This time Vinnie cursed a blue streak.

Nico didn't wait for anyone to agree or argue with him. He pushed through everyone and headed into the house. Because they stood there arguing for a moment, he had a decent head start. Instead of going to one of the rooms they tended to meet in, he darted down the hall, entered the garage, and grabbed the first set of keys off the wall.

Vinnie's Diavel Carbon. Awesome.

He straddled the Ducati, gunned the engine, and took off.

Sure, he should have worn a helmet. Actually, he shouldn't have gone at all. But he needed some time, some space. Some clarity.

The wind through his hair gave him a sense of freedom he'd been missing. And he flew down the hill, for the first time in a long time just enjoying the drive instead of dwelling on the problems he ran from.

18

THEY'D BEEN AT it for two hours, and Donni was beat. She sat at the kitchen table sipping on a demitasse cup of espresso—her third of the night—and again wished it was a full-sized mug.

Although, given the buzzing in her head and the tremor in her hands, she'd probably had enough caffeine without super-sizing the dose.

"Okay." Gianni looked at her. "Let's start over. Again."

"No. I've had enough of this interrogation. If there was a single bulb above my head and a one-way mirror in the corner, I'd swear I was at a police station. I've told you everything I know."

"You haven't told us much that we didn't know," Vinnie said.

"I can't help that! Nico's not exactly an open book. That I knew anything you didn't is a miracle."

"So," Toni said, "if he's been working on his powers at night, why aren't they more consistent?"

"I don't know." She caught a sense of movement out of the corner of her eye and turned to look out the doorway. Everything seemed still, but a niggling feeling plagued her.

"How long have you been working with him?" Jo asked.

"Hmm?" Donni turned her attention back to her sister. "This is why people confess to crimes they haven't committed. They're badgered until they'll say anything to make it stop."

"You're not a criminal, Don. Stop being so dramatic."

"Dramatic? Come on, Jo. I've been answering everyone's questions for hours, and I just want to go to bed. Tonight was the first night I practiced with Nico. I suspect he's been working on his powers when everyone is in bed because I hear him sneaking around at night. Other than the times he snuck out looking for Mama, I have to assume he was practicing. That's why his powers have strengthened."

"But none of that accounts for why he couldn't help you when you were shot," Toni said. "Or help Mama when she wouldn't wake."

"And of course I would know why, right?" Again, a shadow of motion in the hallway caught her attention. And again she turned toward it but saw nothing.

"Well, it makes sense," Coz said. "You've been spending more time with him than anyone else."

Donni heard faint notes of sadness and jealousy in his voice. Nico and Coz weren't just brothers. They were best friends. He probably felt like she was replacing him. She softened her tone when she replied. "We have been spending more time together, but only because I've been following him or nagging him about trying something. Nothing's changed between the two of us. Or between him and any of you."

"That's not true," Vinnie said. "Something's changed between the two of you. You're slee—"

Jo elbowed him.

"You've become romantically involved. That changes things."

"How?" she asked.

Vinnie and Gianni glanced at each other.

"You think you're so discreet," Donni said. "Do you honestly think no one noticed that once you guys committed to my sisters, you came fully into your powers? I don't know why you don't talk about it, but it's not a secret. Something about us helps complete you."

"Donni, it's not like that," Franki said. "You don't have to—be with Nico just so his powers grow."

"On the other hand," Gianni said, "it might help him be more consistent if you were in a committed relationship."

"I'm not going to pimp out my sister just so Nico can control his powers."

"It's not like that, Franki," Gianni said. "All I mean is—"

"I know what you mean. And it's not happening. Not with Donni and Nico. Not with Toni and Coz."

"Hey!" Toni's cheeks pinked. "Don't drag me into this."

"Before this gets way out of hand, I have something to say," Donni said. "I know you guys are stuck with us, at least until Italy's revolution plays out. And I'm sorry, because I know we don't always make it easy on you. But you've got to stop meddling in my love life. In *all* of our love lives. First you worried about Franki and Gianni, then you basically forced them together. You were all concerned about Jo and Vinnie. Now you're trying to put me with Nico—all in the name of advancing Brotherhood powers. It has to stop. Stop worrying when a couple gets together, stop worrying if they won't. It's no one's business but that of the two people involved."

"But—" Franki said.

Donni held up her hand. "No. You don't have to protest. I know you and Gianni are in love." She turned toward Jo. "And you and Vinnie. And I couldn't be happier for you. But you can't force me and Nico or Toni and Coz into a relationship. It has to happen organically or not at all. It doesn't matter if the powers are somehow tied to us or tied to love. Love can't be forced or manufactured. And I won't have you trying to manipulate us to get what you want. It's a hard-line limit for me."

"We'll table this for now," Vinnie said. "But we still need to know where Nico might have gone."

She ran trembling fingers through her hair. Definitely had too much caffeine. "I don't know where he is or even where he might be. Your guess is as good as mine. Now, I'm going to bed. And I thank you not to follow me."

Donni left her cup on the kitchen table and hurried out of the room. In the hallway, she started toward the stairs, then stopped mid-stride. Instead of going upstairs, she backtracked and headed toward the den. She paused outside the door for a moment and listened. A quiet click sounded from the darkness beyond. She stepped inside and flipped the wall switch.

Light illuminated the room, revealing Marcus and Enrico pressed against the wall, trying to escape detection in the darkness. Enrico held a laptop behind his back.

"Busted," she said. "I know you were eavesdropping outside the kitchen, and I know you were snooping through Nico's system in here. Tell me what you're up to, or I'm getting the guys."

DESPITE THE WARM weather, the air was brisk and chilled Nico. Didn't help matters that he only wore shorts. Rushing out without at least throwing on a t-shirt suddenly didn't seem like such a great idea, even with the adrenaline rush of freedom.

At the bottom of the cliff, he'd turned away from the orphanage, but after only a kilometer or so, he changed his mind, turned around, and drove to San Crisogono. No one wants to end up in an orphanage, but his time there hadn't been too bad. Certainly wasn't as bad as Vinnie's.

Sometimes a guy just needed to go home, wherever "home" might be, whatever it might mean. In his case, he wanted a walk through the olive groves.

Nico cut the engine early and coasted onto the property so as not to disturb the residents. The kids were staying in the convent until the orphanage proper was rebuilt, but the Ducati was pretty loud, and he didn't want to take the chance of waking anyone. When he reached the circle out front, he parked the bike, climbed off, and made his way around back.

Rows and rows of olive trees stretched as far as he could see, the canopy of silvery leaves shimmering in the moonlight and blocking his view of the Brotherhood's villa at the top of the hill. He walked through the grove, his footsteps silent on the well-trod path.

When he came to his favorite tree, an old gnarled one at the very center of the property, he sat beneath it and rested his back against the trunk. As a young boy, he'd climb the tree and hide there for hours when he was supposed to be picking olives. He'd pretend he was a lookout on a pirate ship or a sniper in a jungle. Miss Teresa never complained when he returned without even one full basket of olives. And Sister Catherine never kept her eye on him—she was much too busy making Vinnie's life hell to bother with Nico or any of the other boys.

Yeah, that old tree provided him with plenty of hours of fun as a child. It let him be whoever or whatever he wanted to be, without judgment.

Too bad he didn't have that same luxury now.

He sat there in the dark for who-knew-how-long, picking at the few blades of grass that bloomed under the trees and ripping them into confetti. He took a deep breath, inhaled the scents of damp earth, loam, and ripening olives. Any day now, little hands would be working the trees as he and his brothers once did. The orphanage relied on the crop as one of their primary sources of income, and harvest season was nearly upon them. Thankfully the explosion that destroyed the building hadn't carried destruction into the grove.

Despite the peace he felt in solitude, he found no answers in the dark. In fact, the time he spent there in reflection had, if anything, only yielded more questions. He stood and stretched. The bark had dug into his back, and on top of everything else, made him itchy. It was time to go. Fleeing had been a nice reprieve, but it hadn't solved anything. And it undoubtedly made everyone angry. Hopefully they'd all be asleep when he returned and he could sneak in without incident.

When he emerged from the grove and walked around to the front of the property, he glanced at the convent. It was too early for the boys to be awake, but there was a light on inside. Curiosity got the better of him, and he walked toward the building to see what was going on, praying it wasn't another problem to deal with.

HE COULDN'T BELIEVE it. Before now, it didn't seem like he'd ever have a chance to redeem himself, but this was just what he needed to get back in Sal's good graces.

Nico hadn't been going out at night since he took Mary from the clinic. Now there he was. Alone. Unprepared.

Had to be fate smiling on him. This was his chance at redemption. His chance to make things right with the organization, to get off the hot seat.

Should he call it in or take matters into his own hands?

What was that saying? Better to ask forgiveness than permission?

Fuck that. The organization didn't give second chances. He pulled his phone out and called Sal, who picked up on the first ring. Sounded completely alert and lucid despite the late hour. *"What do you want?"*

"Micelli left the compound. I'm at his location right now."

"Where?"

"San Crisogono. Came home, just like I said he would."

"I don't have time to get a unit there."

"Want me to follow him when he leaves? I can tail him, get a fix on the location of their operations."

"No need. I already know where they are."

Bastardo.

If he knew, why didn't he report it? Why didn't they raid the place and take the Brotherhood out? "So, we going to make a move on their compound?"

"No. What are you, simple? Do you know how heavily that place will be guarded, fortified? We wouldn't stand a chance."

"Then why am I on stakeout duty? What's the point?"

"Divide and conquer. You said he's by himself, right?"

"Yeah."

"Here's what you're going to do."

He listened to Sal with rapt attention, a smile spreading on his face. Finally, not just a chance to set things right with the organization, but a chance to make a difference.

A chance to turn the tide in their favor.

When he was through, he'd have a place of honor with the group. Maybe even pass Dante and become Sal's number two.

They ended the call, and he sat, struggling for the patience to wait until he could put the plan into action.

"NICO? IS THAT you?" A soft whisper floated to him, feminine but strong, in his native Italian.

It was good to hear his mother tongue, and from a familiar voice, too. He responded in Italian. "Teresa, it's me. Don't be frightened."

She stepped out of the shadows and into the moonlight, and she held her arms out to him.

He crossed the distance quickly and stepped into a hug.

When they parted, she spun him around and wiped off his back. "What are you doing out this late? Or this early?"

"Late," he said. "I needed to clear my head. What are you doing up? It's too early to be making breakfast."

"I heard a motor and came outside to see what it was. When I saw the motorcycle, I thought Vinnie had come down here. Figured I'd enjoy a cup of coffee and wait for him."

"Sorry to disappoint you."

"Nico." She placed her hand on his cheek and looked up into his eyes. "You're not a disappointment. I'm happy to see you."

Miss Teresa was the closest thing to a mother he had growing up, and hearing her say that warmed his heart. He squeezed the bridge of his nose and avoided looking at her. "Thanks. I'm glad to see you, too."

"Come inside. Tell me all about it."

He met her gaze. "There's nothing to tell."

She merely climbed the stairs and held the door open. He followed her and crossed the threshold, then she closed the door behind them. "There's always something to tell. Let's have some coffee, and you can tell me all about it. Or maybe I should give you warm milk so you can sleep when you go back. You cold? Want a blanket? I don't think any shirts the boys have will fit you."

He smiled at her ramblings. "I'm good, thanks. Well, maybe coffee."

"Okay," she said. "Start talking."

While she bustled around the kitchen, making a fresh pot of coffee and putting biscotti on a plate, Nico blurted out everything bothering him—his powers coming and going, his distrust of Marcus and Rico, his concern about them still not having a lead on Paolo, his taking on IT duties for Scalzotto, his abject fear of failing to protect the girls, his brothers riding him about every little thing.

Donni's theory behind his powers.

Even his feelings for her and whether they were real.

Before he knew it, he'd had two cups of coffee and a whole plate of cookies. He'd need to work that off before his gut got soft.

Teresa sat across from him and listened with rapt attention. And despite his caffeine intake, when he finished pouring his heart out, he was exhausted.

"Oh, my sweet boy. They've really put you through the ringer, haven't they?"

Nico dipped his head and closed his eyes. He let her words envelop him like a warm hug.

"It seems to me that almost all your problems are tied up with Donni and your feelings for her."

His head snapped up. "How do you figure that?"

"Oh, sweetie. Your powers fail when you fear you'll fail her. And they work best when you work with her. The stresses you feel with your brothers are because you're worried about how they affect her. Even your new duties are weighing on you because they take time from her."

"But what about the dagger? I think that could be influencing everything, and if it is, then the feelings aren't true."

"Says who?"

"Says the guy with manipulated feelings."

"I don't think the dagger is manipulating you or your feelings in any way. But what if it is? You're the one with the weapon, not her. Her feelings for you, therefore, are genuine."

"But maybe my feelings for her aren't. And if the weapon stops working and my feelings change, I could hurt her."

"The fact that you're worried about hurting her tells me it's not the dagger influencing your feelings. It's just your heart."

"But what if it is?"

"What if it isn't? Are you going to throw away a chance at happiness because of some stupid chunk of rock?"

"I just wish I could be sure."

"Have you talked with her?"

Nico swirled the remnants of coffee in the bottom of his cup. "A little. Probably not enough."

"Well, I think it's time you stop talking to me and start talking to her. If anyone has a say in whether you explore this relationship, it's Donnatella. Not me, not your brothers, not her sisters. Talk to her."

His stomach flopped. "I think that's scarier than Brotherhood work."

She smiled, patted his hand, and rose. "Then it's definitely your heart at play. Now go home."

He sat there, staring at her, his feet not quite willing to move.

"Go on. You have an uncomfortable conversation to have. And I have a bunch of rowdy boys to make breakfast for."

Nico rose, kissed her cheek, and headed for the door. Right before he stepped out, he turned around. "Thanks, Teresa."

She smiled at him. "Anytime. Now go talk to your girl. And drive safely. That thing scares me."

"It's not the machine that's dangerous. It's how it's driven."

"And you boys are all reckless. Be careful."

"Always."

"You're always reckless or you'll be careful? No. Never mind. Don't answer that." She blew him a kiss and turned toward the sink.

He smiled and walked outside. Dawn hadn't quite broken the horizon, but the sky had begun to lighten. The moon was gone, the stars had dimmed, and the black gave way to a milky deep indigo. If he went straight back, he'd arrive when the sun just crested the skyline. Maybe everyone would be asleep and he could catch an hour or two of shut-eye before facing the music.

He straddled the bike, started it, and pulled out slowly so as not to make the engine roar. Only when he reached the end of the long drive did he increase his speed.

Nico whipped around the corner to the main road. At the last second, he saw the black panel van. It came out of the brush on the side of the road and headed right for him.

He hit the brake. The bike skidded, the van rushed toward him. Out of control, he released the brake. The machine found traction right before he collided with the van, and he swerved, yanking the handlebars hard to the left.

His back tire grazed the van's bumper, jolted the bike. Nico tried to course-correct, but he'd run out of room.

The bike plummeted over the embankment, tossing him over the handlebars and down the rocky hillside.

On first impact, pain exploded in his head. That was the last thing he experienced before the blackness overtook him.

DONNI GUARDED THE door so Marcus and Rico couldn't leave. She crossed her arms over her chest, hoping she looked brave and intimidating, praying her fear didn't betray her. "Start talking. Now."

Marcus was the first to peel himself away from the wall. He held his hands up in a gesture of surrender as he took a step toward her.

"Stop right there. I want answers, not a physical altercation. One more step, and I scream."

"Come on, Donni, it's me. Us. We've done nothing but help you. You know you're safe."

She took a deep breath.

"Don't!" Rico stepped away from the wall, put the laptop on a table, and raised his hands, too. "Don't scream. You're not in danger. We'll stay right here."

"Why were you spying on us?"

"Because that's what we do," Marcus said.

"Honestly, I'm impressed that you caught us," Rico added.

"But why were you spying? What are you looking for?"

"Answers," Marcus said.

"Mike invited us here, but no one tells us anything. We can't help anyone if we don't know what's going on."

"All you had to do was ask," she said.

"We've been asking," Rico said. "No one says anything. And we're concerned."

"About what?"

"About Paolo, for starters," Marcus said. "Why hasn't anyone reached out to him yet?"

"Because no one can find him. Even Mike said his leads have dried up."

Marcus and Enrico looked at each other.

"What?" she said.

Marcus dropped his hands. "We know where he is."

"Then why didn't you tell someone?"

"We didn't know you couldn't find him," Rico said. "Remember? No one's letting us in on the loop."

Donni still wasn't sure if she could trust them, but it sounded like the Brotherhood could use their information. She studied them, looking for signs of deception, but she didn't really know how to read micro expressions, and they looked sincere enough to her. Still, she had to be cautious. "What's with the laptop?"

"We heard Nico talking to you about a journal," Marcus said. "We couldn't find where he hid it, but he said he was translating it, so we thought we'd read what he'd done so far."

These guys were good. Which was bad. But the Brotherhood had to know this before they opened the villa to them. These were their mentors. They passed their knowledge down generation to generation. If Nico, Coz, Gianni, and Vinnie were stealthy, they had to know Marcus and Enrico were, too. So they'd taken precautions, right?

She didn't know. She wished Nico was there to advise her. Without him, though, she had no recourse but to go to the other guys. "I think you need to come with me. Tell Coz and the guys about Paolo."

Coz burst into the room, face pale and eyes wide. "What's going on here?"

"I'm okay, Coz," Donni said. "Relax. But we do need to talk. I was—"

"We don't have time for this right now," he said. "Maybe you should sit."

Her scalp tingled, and dread formed a nauseating ball in the pit of her stomach. She clutched the closest thing she could find, which happened to be Coz's arm. Her nails dug into his skin, but she couldn't let go. And when he didn't even flinch, she knew the news was bad. "What is it?"

"Vinnie's mom just called."

"Teresa? Okay, it's a little early in the morning, but—"

"There was an accident."

And the ball in her gut exploded into writhing snakes of doom. She placed her hand over her abdomen and shook her head.

"It's bad, Don. It's really bad. She said Nico wasn't wearing a helmet..."

Donni didn't hear the rest. She just focused on taming the snakes and let Coz lead her out of the room.

19

DONNI COULDN'T PROCESS what she was seeing. Vinnie's bike was a mangled mass of smoldering metal. The smoke provided a screen to what lay beyond, for which Teresa told her to be profoundly grateful.

Nico's body was down there, somewhere behind the wafting smoke, the mutilated motorcycle, and the snapped branches of crash-damaged foliage.

Several times she tried to go down the hill, and each time various strong hands pulled her back.

"Keep her up here," Coz said to Teresa. "Keep all the girls up here. Marcus, come help us. Rico, go down the road and try to ward off the ambulance. We need time to get Nico up here before any emergency personnel show up."

"Shouldn't he go to the hospital?" Donni asked.

"No. We got this."

"But the doctors can treat him. Do x-rays or scans and find out what the damage is. His best chance is—"

"His best chance is us. We can heal him once we get him back to the villa."

"But Teresa said—"

"*Merda!* We don't have time for this!"

Donni recoiled like he slapped her.

Coz sighed. "Look, I have to get down there and help my brothers get Nico up here. Enrico won't be able to hold off the ambulance and cops much longer, and if they get here before we leave, they'll take Nico and hold us for questioning. You have to believe me, Nico is safest with us."

Donni bit her lip. What would Nico want? He'd trust his brothers. She knew that. But they weren't doctors, despite their in-house medical suites and their magical healing powers.

She just wanted him to be healthy. His power healed bone. He couldn't heal himself if he was unconscious, so wasn't his best chance a hospital? She glanced over the hill, hoping to see him climbing up even knowing he wouldn't.

Coz pointed to the far lane of the street Nico had been on when he wrecked.

Donni saw pieces of broken plastic on the ground and black streaks from the tires burning rubber on the pavement when he braked.

"See the skid marks? The flattened brush past the berm?" Coz said. "Nico didn't just wreck. Someone was waiting for him, and he was run off the road. If we let him go to the hospital, we won't be able to protect him from the people who tried to kill him. We have to get him and take him home, where he'll be safe."

She hadn't considered this to be anything more than an accident. Her blood turned frigid as she processed what Coz said. Nico was in danger. They were all in danger. "Go," she whispered.

He dashed down the hill and out of her line of sight.

Toni held her hand. Franki wrapped her arm around her. Jo hovered near the hilltop, looking back and forth between the wreck and her sisters.

What if he was dead? Coz hadn't mastered his power yet. Didn't matter that he was supposed to hold dominion over death. If he didn't have full powers, Nico was—

She couldn't even think the word.

Her stomach roiled. A chill consumed her, started in her core and sucked all warmth from her extremities until she stood, shivering uncontrollably, her fingers and toes freezing and numb.

"They're coming," Jo said.

A few seconds later, Donni heard the rustling of branches and the men's grunts of exertion. She stumbled over to the side of the road, but Jo grabbed her arms and steered her away.

"Let me go!"

"You don't need to see." Jo struggled to keep her turned away from the hill, pushed her across the road and past Vinnie's vehicle. "Let them get him in the car, get him home and—cleaned up."

"If that was Vinnie, you'd be right there. You'd be holding his hand, checking his vitals. Something! You'd be there."

Jo shook her. "It's different with us. Vinnie and I are in love, Donni. The two of you are just—"

Tears fell down Donni's face, and she didn't bother to swipe them away.

"Oh. Oh, Don. I didn't know. I didn't realize you and... go. Go to him."

Jo released Donni's arms, and she nearly crumpled to the ground. When she gained her balance, she rushed to Nico's side.

The guys had cleared the hillside and were hauling his body to the car. And that's the only way she could describe it. That wasn't Nico. That was a body—a lifeless corpse—burned and bloodied almost beyond recognition. There was no way anyone could survive injuries like that.

A strangled sob escaped her lips. The world spun, she wove on her feet, and the ground rushed up to meet her.

DONNI'S EYELIDS FLUTTERED open. Everything was blurry, and she strained to focus. Noises—voices—came to her, like from a far distance or an echo chamber. When they coalesced into sounds that made sense, one word snapped her to full attention.

Nico.

She jumped up from a cot against the far wall and ran toward the commotion. Her sisters and the Brothers were gathered around a gurney on which lay a bloody and battered Nico. His face—his beautiful face—was swollen almost beyond recognition and was crimson with blood. His left leg and arm bent in the wrong places. He had cuts and bruises all over his body.

God help him. None of them could heal bone but Nico, and he wasn't conscious. And maybe, at the moment, that was for the best. Because anyone in that condition who was awake would be in agony.

But what if he never woke? What if he wasn't even alive now?

"Is he…?"

"He's alive," Coz said.

Donni took a trembling breath and pushed her way through the throng to his side. She grabbed his right hand, clutched it to her chest, then realized she might be harming him. If his hand had broken bones in in—and honestly, what part of him didn't look damaged?—her squeezing it couldn't be good for him. Gently, she lowered their joined hands to the gurney and released him.

Then she looked at Gianni. His face was white, and he leaned against Franki, letting her bear some of his substantial weight. "Well? What's the plan?"

He met her gaze and slowly shook his head. "I don't know what else to do. He had some internal bleeding and some swelling."

"Some?"

"I dealt with what I could. Not much I can do for his face. I think he has a shattered cheekbone."

She noticed he didn't say how bad the rest of Nico's body was, but she didn't press for more details. Hopefully Gianni had found all the internal issues and healed them. "What about the bones? He clearly has numerous breaks."

He shrugged. "I don't know, Don. Nico's the bone guy, but he's out cold. And that's probably for the best at the moment, because these breaks are pretty severe. They've got to hurt like hell."

"We can't just leave him like this. The longer you wait to set a bone, the worse the healing is. He could be looking at permanent damage."

"Well, he's not awake, so he can't help."

"Get Mama's doctor in here. Maybe he can set the bigger breaks."

"You think we didn't already do that?" Coz said. "Dr. Russo was already in here and checked on both of you."

"So what'd he say?"

"He said you took one hell of a fall. Whacked your head pretty good. Might have a concussion. Gianni will fix you up after he recharges. We were more worried about him treating Nico than you. Sorry."

Donni raised her hand to her head. She'd barely registered a headache, but when she touched her temple, she felt a large lump, and pain shot through her brain. She winced and dropped her hand. "Thanks, but I'm not worried about me. What did Dr. Russo say about Nico's injuries?"

"He doesn't have the resources here to do the surgery. Surgeries. Wants to take him to the hospital."

"But you guys said the hospital is too dangerous!"

"We didn't say we were letting him go," Vinnie said.

"We sent the doc with Rico to get the supplies he needs," Coz said.

"For reconstructive surgery? Here?"

Vinnie shrugged.

"And in the meantime, we just let Nico suffer?"

"That's why it's best he's unconscious right now," Gianni said. "He's not in pain while he's out."

Donni didn't necessarily agree with their decision, but she didn't have a better alternative. Then she looked at Vinnie. "What about your powers? Any strategy we can use that we haven't already considered?"

He shook his head. "Nothing. I'm still blocked when I try to read him. It's frustrating. I can see possibilities and outcomes with anybody else, but with him, all I see is a stone wall."

"Why can't you read him?"

"I used to think I couldn't because he was too emotionally conflicted. He didn't know what he was going to do, so I couldn't see the ramifications of any of his actions. But this isn't like that. This is just physical treatment, nothing he needs to decide. I should be able to see options for that. Since I can't, my best guess is that he's blocking me."

"He's not even conscious. How the hell would he block you? Why would he want to, if you could help?"

"The 'why' is easy. He's intensely protective of his privacy, and my reading him would violate that. The 'how' is another matter. He's clearly grown more powerful if he can maintain a block when he's not even consciously trying to. I can't break through."

She sighed. Why'd Nico have to be so damn stubborn? Why couldn't he just let them in?

Gently, she leaned over him to embrace him. She needed the contact, needed to feel his lungs rise and fall, feel his breath in her hair. Instead, his breath was weak, rattled a little, came in infrequent, shallow gasps. His skin was cooler than she'd like, clammy. Something poked her in her rib.

Donni stood and looked for what jabbed her. His dagger. Of course. He was never without the damn thing. She grasped it, yanked it from the scabbard at his waist, and cocked her arm back to throw it across the room.

The guys ducked, but she stopped right before releasing it.

It was warm in her hand. Almost hot. Felt like… no, that wasn't right. It wasn't the dagger. It was *her*. She felt the way she did when they buried the rock table and grew the lemon tree. Her body sang with energy. The closer she held the dagger to Nico, the more her body thrummed.

Could it be that simple?

She glanced at Vinnie, who stared at her, wide-eyed and slack-jawed.

"Will it work?" she asked him.

"I—I think so."

Donni closed her eyes, focused on drawing energy from the world around her. Through the floor she stood on, from the very earth itself. The room grew dark, but Nico glowed. She held the dagger to his face, watched the swelling recede. Held it to his arm, and the unnatural bend snapped rigid. She waved it over his chest, waited until his breathing grew stronger, more rhythmic. Then she passed over his pelvis before settling the blade on the broken leg. It snapped into place with an audible pop.

He bolted up and screamed.

NICO BLINKED AND looked around the room while he waited for the wave of pain—and the several waves of nausea—to subside. It took him a moment to process where he was, a moment more to remember what happened.

When it all rushed back to him, he swore, swung his legs over the side of the gurney, and jumped to his feet. His legs gave out, but Coz caught him before he hit the floor. He grabbed his brother's arms. "We have to go!"

"Easy. You're not going anywhere for a while."

"But Teresa. The *kids*—"

"Fine. All fine. Marcus is there keeping an eye on things. And I'm pretty sure Mike is popping in and out."

Nico sighed and sat on the table. "Thank God."

"How you feeling?" Donni asked.

He thought for a second, took a mental inventory. Wiggled his fingers and toes, bent his elbows and knees. Tipped his head forward and back, side to side. "Fine. Great, even."

She smiled and took his hand.

Warmth shot through him. "How did…?" But she didn't have to answer for him to know. Somehow she'd channeled his healing power and helped him.

"Gianni healed your tissue injuries," she said. "Your dagger did the rest."

Coz cleared his throat and stared at Donni even as he answered Nico. "Your dagger had a little help."

Nico grabbed her hand and squeezed it.

"Donni!" Nico reached toward her face. "Your head!"

"I'm okay. Just a little bump."

"Gianni? Can't you—"

"If I hadn't been so busy saving your ass, I'd have done it already." He closed his eyes, and the bump and bruising disappeared. "Of course, if you hadn't gone off on your own, it wouldn't have happened, anyway."

Nico had the sense not to answer him. He met Donni's gaze, instead. "Are you okay?"

"Fine. What about you?"

"No complaints."

"Since you're feeling so fucking good," Vinnie said, "mind telling me why you took my bike? And then totaled it?"

"Wasn't my fault. The guy aimed right for me."

"You were targeted?" Coz said.

"You see him?" Gianni asked.

"No. Windows were tinted, and it was dark. But it wasn't an accident. He aimed for me."

Coz grimaced. "The organization. Had to be."

"Did they stick around to see if I made it?"

"Nobody around when we got there," Coz said. "Thought it was a hit and run."

"It was."

Vinnie scowled. "What were they driving?"

"Black panel van."

"Well, then," Gianni said, "that's something in our favor. They think we're down a guy. Maybe we can use that to our advantage."

"How?" Coz asked.

"Don't know yet. Vin, you think you can put this to good use?"

"Maybe." He frowned. "Not like I've been able to see anything having to do with this moron lately, though."

Nico didn't meet his gaze. Didn't feel like getting into it at the moment.

"While I work on that," Vinnie said, "let's circle back to my bike."

"I grabbed the first set of keys I saw. Just happened to be your bike. I didn't plan to take it."

"*Steal* it."

"And I didn't think I'd be run of the damn road."

"No helmet. No leathers. *Cazzo*, you didn't even have on a shirt or jeans! Do you have any idea what that did to us seeing you torn to shreds? What that did to Donni?"

Guilt washed through him. He hadn't thought of anyone when he ran. He just wanted to get away. Instead of relief, he had more problems. He'd trashed Vinnie's bike. He'd worried everyone. By the looks of things, he'd totally drained Gianni.

And he hurt Donni. Again.

"I'm sorry. About the bike, about running. About everything. I'd make it up to you, to all of you, if I could. But there's nothing I can say or do to fix what I did."

"I'd settle for you being open and honest instead of shutting us out and running all the damn time," Vinnie said.

"I'll replace your bike."

"I have insurance, dickhead. I don't care about the bike. I care about you." And he stormed out of the room. Jo rushed after him.

"Well. Guess I know how he feels about my apology."

"It's not that, and you know it," Coz said.

"I know. It's just—" But he didn't have the words.

Coz clapped him on the shoulder, leaned in, and whispered so only Nico could hear. "Talk it out with your girl. Then the rest will fall into place."

Nico tried to smile, but it felt more like a grimace.

"Come on, guys," Coz said to the room, "let's give them some privacy."

The rest of the group left, muttering versions of, "Glad you're okay," on their way out. Then it was just Nico and Donni.

Talk about an awkward silence.

"Was it rough?" he asked.

She raised her brows and looked at him like he was nuts.

Maybe he was. "I mean, tonight. After I left. Were the guys mad? Did Vinnie bitch you out?"

Donni shrugged. "He was really more angry with you than anything. You have him really frustrated right now."

"Me? Why?"

"He can't read you. Just sees a stone wall when he tries. It's making it hard for him to come up with strategies because he can't figure out what your actions will be, and therefore what the consequences of them will be."

Nico thought about that. "I can see why he'd be pissed."

"Why are you blocking him?"

"I didn't know I was. Not consciously, anyway. Makes sense, though."

"That you're blocking him?"

"No. Sorry. Why he's been so mad lately."

"You don't let anyone in." Her voice was so quiet, he barely heard her.

"Okay. All my cards on the table." He took a deep breath. "Given everything that's gone on between us, you must know I have feelings for you."

She sat silently, waiting.

He figured she wouldn't be patient for much longer, so he just blurted it out. "I'm worried the dagger is influencing how I feel. How we feel about each other."

"Why on earth would you think that?"

"Well, most of the time, when we end up kissing or… or other stuff—"

She smiled.

He never felt so awkward in his life. "—it's when I'm holding the dagger. Or it's in close proximity."

"You carry it twenty-four, seven. Of course it's with you when we're being intimate. That's hardly a surprise. Besides, we've been naked together, and I don't remember you holding the dagger then."

His cheeks burned. God help him, he was blushing. Guys didn't blush. This wasn't going as he'd hoped. At all. "But my powers are increasing. Just like Gianni's and Vinnie's did when they fell for your sisters."

"One, you've been practicing on your own, so it's no surprise your powers are growing. And two—and much more importantly, in my opinion—are you falling for *me*?"

Yep, definitely blushing, because his face felt like it was on fire, and she was grinning at him. He hated to make her feel bad, but he'd said he was going to lay it all on the line. "I don't know how I feel. Because I don't know if my feelings are real or if the dagger is influencing them."

She took his hand, squeezed it, and then placed her hand on his cheek and turned his head until he met her gaze. "I have an idea."

"Yeah?"

"Yeah. Something that will help me with how stir crazy I've felt and will help you make sense of your feelings."

"I'm all for that."

"Let's go somewhere."

"We can't take a trip now. There's too much going on, what with Scalzotto here and the organization ramping up their attacks. They may know where we are now. And besides, that doesn't address the dagger, and—"

"You do babble when you get worked up."

He took a deep breath.

"While I'd like nothing better than a month-long stay with you on a private beach, that's not what I meant. Not a vacation, but a day trip. Let's go explore a nearby town. I'll look for furnishings and art for your new complex and some other things for the orphanage. Leave your dagger here. If we can spend the day together, away from the dagger, and you're still attracted to me, then you'll know for sure."

"And if I'm not? I don't want to hurt you."

"You're an idiot, you know that?"

He leaned back and looked at her.

"Of course I'm hoping you're still interested. In fact, I'm counting on it. But now I want to know for sure, too. I'd be more hurt being with you and finding out in a year that it was a manipulation than knowing right now."

Nico shook his head. "You're amazing, you know that?"

"I do. Let's just hope you feel that way when we try this out."

He sighed. "I don't think I can."

"What's the problem now?"

"I can't leave you unprotected like that."

"So bring a different weapon. Besides, we're only going for an afternoon. We'll go somewhere crowded, where the people will add to our safety. Anyway, the organization thinks you're dead, so no one will be looking for you. With all that in our favor, what could happen?"

20

DONNI SIPPED HER coffee and listened half-heartedly to her sisters as they made plans for the day.

"Maybe after we check on the progress to the changes in the plan," Franki said to Gianni, "we can head over to the proposed site of your new compound."

"I don't know if that's a good idea."

"Why?"

"It's a hundred kilometers away. If anyone needs us, it'll take us a while to get back."

"I really need to see the site before I can finalize the first draft of the design."

"I love what you've done so far." He nuzzled her neck.

She pulled away, but she giggled. "You're not distracting me from my point. I need to see the land."

"Fine." He popped a piece of bacon in his mouth. "If nothing comes up at the construction site, we'll take a drive over. Maybe I'll pack a picnic." This time when he kissed her neck, she allowed him.

"You don't even need to stop by," Jo said. "It's all under control."

"I just want to be sure," Franki said.

"Don't you trust me?" She put her hands on her hips and stared at her sister.

"Of course. I just—"

"You just like to micromanage everything."

Vinnie laughed and slung his arm over Jo's shoulders. "If anything comes up, Red'll call you. Just go."

Jo bumped her hip against his at the nickname referring to her hair, but she grinned.

"Fine." Franki stood up. "Don't have to twist my arm. I'm getting a scenic ride in an exotic sports car and a picnic out of the deal."

Gianni was already headed to the refrigerator.

"Need a ride to the site, Toni?" Jo asked.

"No. Coz and I will go ourselves. I'm going to need a trip into town for more supplies after I check on a few things."

"Truck or van?" Coz asked.

"Truck."

He smiled. "Good. I hate the van."

"You guys all hate vans. But they have their uses."

"I can think of one," Coz said.

Toni flushed, mumbled some kind of excuse, and hurried out of the room.

"Why do you tease her like that?" Jo asked.

"What're you talking about? What'd I say?"

"Like you don't know how she took that," Franki said.

"I was talking about all of us traveling together. Like when we went to Marcus's and Rico's in the States."

Vinnie clapped him on the back on his way out of the room. "I don't know if that's nice or sad."

Coz followed him out of the room.

"So, Donni, what's on your agenda for the day?" Jo asked.

She took another sip of coffee while she smoothed out her lie. "Probably just going to do some textiles shopping on the Internet. Look at a few auction sites for some pottery. Maybe take a swim."

"Must be nice to have all this leisure time. Enjoy the day." Jo walked out of the room, and Franki followed, waving behind her.

Gianni finished packing the picnic basket and looked at Donni. "Nico will be here, if you need anything. He's updating proxy-something-or-others, I think. Marcus and Rico are taking your mother for a ride today, just to get her out for a bit. But then they'll be with Scalzotto the rest of the day, if you need them. You'll be okay here."

Even her mother got out of the house. Figured she was the only one they sequestered. Or tried to. "I'm not worried."

"Well, I worry about you. You're always here alone when we're all gone."

"Never alone. Like you said, Nico's here. He's always here when you guys leave me behind."

"We aren't leaving you behind. It's just that you don't have to be anywhere. And it's safer here."

"But Franki gets a picnic? Nice try, Gianni."

"We aren't taking a picnic. I mean, we are, but that's not why we're going out. I'd never take her on a frivolous trip."

"Never?"

He had the decency to look uncomfortable. "Today, we're going to the MDH site for her to get a lay of the land. Business."

"A picnic is business?"

"Today is mostly business."

"I get it. Just go. Have a nice day. Like I said, I've got plans of my own to keep me busy."

He stared at her for a moment, then he shrugged, grabbed the basket, and left the room.

She sighed in relief. They were all leaving, thank God. Nico was taking her into town and none of them would be around to argue about it.

She was getting away from the compound. Off the hill and into society. She'd walk the streets, shop the little *mercatos* and tiny shopping stalls, wander to little *osterias* and *trattorias* to sample the local cuisine. Maybe, if she was lucky, there would be some hand-holding and cuddling during the day. Perhaps a kiss, lips and tongues cool from the tart lemon ice or decadent chocolate *gelato* they shared.

They had to experiment at least a little, right? That was the whole point of the excursion. To get far from the dagger and see if the feelings were there. Were *real*.

Donni grinned. She and Nico had the whole day together—away from the compound—and they'd be back before anyone was the wiser. The deception just added to her anticipation, and she rushed upstairs to get ready for the day.

VEHICLE AFTER VEHICLE came down the hill from the Brotherhood's private villa. He couldn't believe Sal hadn't told him about its location sooner. They could have been watching the entire time, staking out the facility and making plans to move on any of the Notaro bitches when they were alone with their protectors.

But, no. He had to earn the right to be in the loop.

Well, he was earning it today. He grabbed his phone and called Sal.

"What now?"

"You know how I never see Donnatella at the construction site?"

"What of it?"

"She's the only one at the compound now."

"How do you know?"

"I'm staking it out, and everyone just left. We can raid the villa. Eliminate her and get out of there before anyone gets back."

Sal let loose a string of curses. *"Who the hell told you to sit on the place? We've been staying clear of there because there's nowhere to hide. If even one of them sees you there, we lose our advantage."*

"No one saw me. I'm totally inconspicuous. I could sit here for days and no one would be the wiser."

"You said everyone left?"

"Yeah. Everyone but her."

"Doesn't make sense."

"Why not? They're probably all going to the orphanage again. They do that every day."

"Not that, idiot. Why would they be working when their brother just died?"

He thought about that for a moment. No way Micelli lived through that crash. But if he didn't, the Brotherhood should be in mourning, right? "Maybe they're trying to hide his death from us. They've got to know they're under our surveillance. By them going on like nothing happened, they think they'll convince us they aren't down one."

"Or they aren't down one. You should have confirmed the kill before fleeing. Can't do anything right, can you?"

"I didn't want to get caught there. I had to leave quickly."

Sal sighed. *"Well, not this time."*

"What?"

"You're not going anywhere. You're going to sit where you are and keep watch. Don't move and risk blowing your cover. Call me if anything—and I mean anything—happens. Tell me everything you see."

"But if we hit them now—"

"We're not ready now. We still have no idea if anyone else is there or what their security protocols are."

It pissed him off to sit and do nothing, but Sal might be right. Maybe a little caution is what they needed.

"Let me know who comes, who goes, real time. No detail is too small to mark. Capisce?"

"Capisco." He understood just fine. When they figured out the traffic patterns at the villa, they'd be able to form a plan. And if he happened to see an opportunity in the meantime, he'd take it.

He called for backup. If a situation did present itself, he wanted to be sure observation was covered. But he was going back to stake out the orphanage. Cover all their bases.

Then he started daydreaming about what he'd do if he got the chance he was looking for. A grin spread over his face. Wouldn't be the first time he killed, but it would be the most rewarding.

The grin left his face as fast as it appeared. A car rolled to the stop at the bottom of the hill. That Donni bitch was in the passenger seat. And fucking

Micelli was driving. Bastard lived, after all. More to the point, he seemed perfectly fine.

He'd be sure to rectify that situation. Pronto.

NICO STOPPED AT the bottom of the hill before turning toward town.

"What's wrong?" Donni asked. "Why are we stopped?"

"I thought I saw something out in that field."

She stared into the tall grass. "I don't see anything."

"It looked like sunlight reflecting off… never mind. There's nothing out there. You ready?"

"More than."

He reached into his pocket, grabbed his phone, and switched it to silent-mode.

"What are you doing?"

"I don't want to be interrupted today."

"Me, either. Good idea." She did the same to her phone.

"Let's go." He pulled onto the road and headed away from the orphanage, toward the Apennine Mountains.

"Isn't the town in the other direction closer?"

"It is, but I don't want anyone at the site to see us leaving the compound."

She smiled. "I didn't tell anyone, either."

"The argument wasn't worth it."

"Agreed." She reached across the car and patted his torso.

He squirmed and jerked the wheel of the car. "What are you doing?"

"I was checking to see if you brought your dagger."

"No, I didn't. The whole point of this was to see what things are like without it, right?"

"Right."

"Good. Now, stay on your side of the car until we get there."

"What's the matter?" Donni squeezed his side again, and he jumped. She laughed. "Nico Micelli. Are you ticklish?"

"Keep your hands to yourself, or I'm turning this car around right now and going back."

"You sound like my dad."

"Trust me. The thoughts in my mind right now are anything but fatherly."

She grinned and looked out the window, enjoying the scenery as it flew by. "Do you have a plan for the day?"

"You mean other than leave my weapon at home and take you out in public?"

"That's not what I meant. I'm not asking for an itinerary. I figured we'd play it by ear. What I was concerned about was Franki and Gianni's picnic. It would be best if we avoided them. Or anyone else."

"They won't be anywhere near us. He's headed about an hour and a half in a different direction."

"What about Toni? She said she might run into town."

"Which is why we went in this direction. She'll go the other way. I promise, Donni. We're going to have the day to ourselves. All alone. Trust me."

"I do, Nico. With my life."

He looked at her for a moment, then turned his attention back out the windshield. After everything that had happened, she did trust him. It was a heady feeling, knowing that—and it meant the world to him. He had a funny feeling in his chest, a constriction coinciding with a fullness. Then realization crashed down on him. "Maybe we should go back and get my dagger. I'd feel safer knowing I had it on me."

"That defeats the purpose of this excursion. You wanted to test your feelings, remember?"

"That's the thing, Donni. I don't think I need to."

She took a deep breath and squared her shoulders before she answered. "And why is that?"

"Because I know the answer. I think I've always known and was hiding behind that as an excuse."

"An excuse to screw around with me and keep me on the hook without committing?" Her voice was weak, had a slight tremor.

"No. An excuse to protect my heart from getting hurt. But thinking about going out and leaving you vulnerable because my dagger is at home? The realization that you trust me to care for you?" He looked at her. "Just the thought of you. It all becomes so clear."

"What does?" She barely spoke above a whisper.

It was his turn to take a deep breath. "I love you, Donni."

Her breath left in an audible whoosh, and she leaned over to plant a kiss on his cheek. "I love you, too, Nico."

The pressure in his chest lifted. He was determined to give her the afternoon of her dreams, and that included sharing a secret he hadn't even told his brothers. He didn't share his plan, but he sped down the road, anxious to get to their destination.

21

NICO DROVE INTO the Apennines.

"This is the same way we went the night we rescued Mama."

"I'm surprised you recognized it. On the way there you were hiding, and on the way back…" His voice trailed off, and he frowned.

"None of that. It all worked out. So, I'm guessing we're not going back to the place she was held. Where are we going?"

"I'm assuming you don't mind being in the car for an hour and a half."

"Not if I'm with you."

"Good. No more questions. It's a surprise. Now put on some music and enjoy the ride."

"Yes, sir!" She gave him a mock salute, then she connected her cell to the car sound system and played a smooth jazz track.

"You think this is good travel music?"

"Would you rather hear Beyoncé?"

"No."

"How do you feel about Simon and Garfunkel?"

"You've got eclectic tastes in music."

"I like pretty much anything but rap."

"I like rap."

"I call it crap."

He chuckled. "We'll agree to disagree on that one. Play whatever you want—as long as it's not Beyoncé."

He glanced in his rearview mirror. A black car had been following him for a while. Not that that was unusual, but it still unnerved him. He sped up and lost the car when he rounded a bend.

"I have just the thing."

"Hmm?" He turned his attention back to her. "What are you playing?"

Lynyrd Skynyrd's "Free Bird" blared through the speakers.

"Fair enough." He put the black car out of his mind and continued down the road. They made easy conversation for the next hour and half, and no surprise, Nico made excellent time. When he pulled over on the side of a road near a sign signaling their location, the disappointment on her face was almost laughable.

"Oh. Here?" She looked at the sign. "Dozza?"

"Dozza. A comune in Bologna. Population less than six thousand."

"I see. I mean, I'm sure it's a lovely little town—"

"Comune."

"—Comune. I just thought we were going to a city. Or at least a decent-sized town. You know, to shop and eat and browse and—"

"Trust me. You're going to love it."

"You know I trust you." She reached for his hand. "Okay. Lead the way."

HE FOLLOWED NICO and Donni, and a couple of hours later, he was in Dozza, setting his sights on his target. Then his phone rang.

"Yeah?"

"It's Luca. Gallo and Moretti are back, and the mother is with them. From what I can tell, they're alone. All alone. We can get them."

"Go scout the house and call me back." Could he be so lucky? Two targets in one day?

Fifteen minutes later, his phone rang again. "Talk to me."

"They aren't even inside. They're out back, sitting on the patio."

"Did they see you?"

"No, we were careful."

"Staff?"

"Nowhere in sight."

"Just Marcus and Enrico with her?"

"That's the thing. They're sitting with her, but that guy from the Internet is there, too. And one other guard."

"What guy?"

"That Scalzotto guy."

"Carmen Scalzotto *and* Mary Notaro? In the same place? Virtually unprotected? You're certain?"

"Just three guys. Older guys."

"How many men do you have with you?"

"Me and six others."

"Perfect. Here's what I want you to do."

He outlined the plan and made Luca repeat it to him. When he was satisfied that all the details were in place, he gave the other man the green light to execute it.

Then he continued with his own surveillance.

If everything worked according to plan, he'd have at least one Medici descendant plus two people for leverage. And a Brother would be dead. Then he'd be elevated in the organization and get the recognition he deserved.

"FOOD OR SHOPPING first?" Nico asked her.

"Mmm... let's shop first. I'm not really hungry yet."

"Walk or drive?"

"Doesn't look that big. Let's walk."

Nico found an area he deemed safe to leave his Maserati, parked and locked it, and took her hand. He looked back at a black car that rolled slowly down the road. It sped up when he looked at it.

"What's wrong?"

"Probably nothing." He'd have to keep his eye out for that car, but he wasn't going to let his concerns spoil their day unless he had to. He pulled her into a stroll and headed toward the center of town. "Let's go."

They hadn't walked one hundred yards when she stopped and squealed. "Look at these lovely houses!"

Dozza was known for the painted houses and buildings comprising the municipality. The structures were canvases for various contemporary artists to paint on.

"The frescos are easiest to see on foot," he said, "so most tourists come between May and September."

"I can see why."

"The third week of September kind of closes out the season. There's a big festival, and the artists come and interact with the public. It's something to see."

"That's not too long from now. Maybe we can come back."

"I'd like that." He laced his fingers with hers and led her down the street. "You don't want to miss the Historical Center... that building down there with the spire. And we'll want to see the Fortress. It was completely remodeled by the Malvezzi-Campeggi family and now has a wonderful art collection, a center for the study of the wall paintings, and a renowned wine cellar. And I know you'd enjoy seeing the church. It has an original panel painting by Marco Palmezzano that you won't want to miss."

"I want to see all of it. Let's go!"

They headed down the street. Nico swore he saw the same face in three different places, but the guy kept his distance. Nico hoped it was just coincidence, but he took them in circles just to be sure. He didn't see the dude again, and no one else bothered them. Soon he put both the man and the car out of his mind. They spent the remainder of the morning and the first part of the afternoon exploring the little village. Bright colors adorned the fronts of buildings. Fanciful paintings of people and places adorned façades everywhere they looked.

He'd never seen an expression of such rapt pleasure on Donni's face.

Well, not when they were in public, anyway.

The thought put a grin on his face.

"What are you smiling about?" Donni asked.

"Just enjoying my time with you."

She smiled and hugged his arm as they walked down the stairs at the Fortress toward the wine cellar.

They browsed for a bit, and Nico made a couple of selections. Then they headed back up toward the main level and out to the street. "You hungry?"

"Yes. All that exploring whetted my appetite. I'm famished."

"I know just what to get. We'll have to see the church the next time, if you want to get back before anyone knows we're gone."

"Do we have time to eat here, or should we get the food to go."

"We have time. We could make the time to see the church after lunch, but there was somewhere I wanted to take you."

"Where?"

"It's a surprise."

She smiled. "I'm starting to like surprises. Let's grab lunch and go."

In addition to the frescos, Dozza was famous for its handmade pasta, and despite the carbs, they enjoyed a lunch of tagliatelle ragout and squash-filled tortelli in a brown-butter/sage sauce. Because of the hearty lamb ragout, they chose the local Sangiovese DOC red wine as their accompaniment.

"This was delicious," Donni said. "I'd wanted dessert, but I'm stuffed."

"Maybe after the surprise."

"Which is…?"

"Let's go and see." He led her back to the car and began the long drive.

After about ten minutes, she looked at him. "Aren't we just going back the way we came?"

"We are." He turned the volume down. "We're actually going right back where we started and then about ten kilometers further."

"Why?"

"Because I want to show you something."

"Where?"

"Outside of Scandicci."

"What?"

"Do you know what a surprise is, Donni?"

"Fine." She sat back and looked out the window.

Nico's chest constricted again. Even his brothers didn't know about what he was going to show her. He hoped she loved it as much as he did.

She dozed as he drove, and every now and then a soft little snore passed her lips. He found it adorable, but he'd never tell her, because he knew she'd be mortified. Hopefully one day they'd be comfortable enough to share even those silly little details.

Today, though, he was sharing a big secret instead.

He turned onto an unpaved road outside of Scandicci, and the ruts jostled the car, waking her.

She rubbed her eyes and stretched. "Where are we?"

"Just about there."

"Where?"

He didn't answer, but a few minutes later, he stopped the car. "Here."

She gasped and got out of the car. They were on the top of a hill, and stretched out below them were hectares of grapevines. Beyond were the ruins of a castle, and then kilometers of woodlands. Distant mountains formed the horizon line.

Nico thought everything the eye could see was breathtaking, but Donni only seemed focused on the vineyard.

"It's gorgeous." She looked right and left, following the plants with her eyes. "Why would someone abandon a place like this?"

"No one did."

"I don't understand."

"This is my land. I planted the vineyard."

"This is yours?"

He nodded. "I have a crew who comes every morning and tends the grapes. We sell the majority of the yield to local winemakers, but someday I'd like to have my own label."

"Do you know how to make wine?"

"I do. I took classes, did research. See that little clutch of buildings over there?" He pointed to structures that sat far right of the vines.

She nodded.

"That's kind of like my lab. I keep some of the grapes every year and make a few varieties. The first few batches were dreadful, but I'm pretty good at it now. I want to put a large production facility over on the left." He gestured to the opposite side of the crop.

"Why do you have this in the middle of nowhere? Isn't it going to be a big commute for you?"

"I don't intend to work for MDH forever. Or the Brotherhood. Eventually, I'll need a fallback plan. And this is it."

"Still seems like a long drive from your place in Florence. Or do you plan on living at the compound?"

"Neither. I know an architect, contractor, landscaper, and interior designer that I'd like to hire."

She looked at him. "You want to build here?"

"I can't think of a better view every morning."

"Me, either. Seeing the sun rising over those mountains…"

"That's actually west."

She chuckled. "Like I said, seeing the sun set over the mountains. What a wonderful way to end an evening."

He pulled her into his arms. "So, you like the property?"

She wrapped her arms around his neck. "I love it. It's perfect. What a beautiful place to settle down, raise a fami—" She blushed. "I'm sorry. I didn't mean to make plans for you. I'm too presumptuous."

He shook his head and kissed the tip of her nose. "You aren't. I love that you love it here. That you can see the potential. That you saw what I see." He dipped his head and kissed her.

She tasted faintly of the wine they'd had, yet he still thought he was getting drunk on her. His head spun—the whole world rocked on its axis—and he lowered her to the grass.

Before, he'd taken her fast, taken her hard. Desperately explored every inch of her. But had he ever savored her? Worshipped her?

No. Not like he wanted to. Not like she deserved.

So he set about doing just that.

Nico tangled his fingers in her hair and turned her head so he could reach her jaw and neck. *"Tesoro, sei bellissima."* He nuzzled under her ear and pressed his lips to her collarbone. A deep breath, then he sucked on her soft, tender flesh.

Dear Lord, she smelled like limoncello. Tasted better.

Donni moaned under his affections. She trailed her fingernails down his back and along his sides, sending shivers up his spine. Wasn't ticklish any longer. No, every touch was a lightning bolt of desire straight to his loins.

He wedged his leg between hers, groaned in anticipation when his groin connected with her hip.

She smiled, pressed against him, and whispered in his ear. "I love to hear you groan."

The heat from her breath combined with her gyrating her hips was almost more than he could bear. Moaning, he shifted his weight to avoid the friction.

Donni pouted, but he wasn't going to deny her for long. She wore a stretchy, scoop-neck tank and jean shorts. He pulled the neckline of her shirt down, exposing her barely-there bra. Before her breasts distracted him, he unfastened the button on her waistband, ripped the zipper down, and yanked the shorts off her.

The bright yellow thong was a perfect match to the lace bra. Even her underwear reminded him of lemons.

Her breasts were thrust up, lifted by the tank's neckline. As much as he enjoyed the sight, he wanted more. So he pulled her up, stripped the shirt off her, and lay her back down.

Her tan skin showed off the bright yellow beautifully, and he couldn't keep his hands off her. His finger traced the lace cups, trailed downward to the erect nipple poking through the material, and circled the sensitive flesh.

Donni sucked a breath in through her teeth and thrust her chest higher. He leaned down and took her free nipple into his mouth, sucking through the lace and letting the sensations of the rough material, his hot tongue, and the sharp edges of his teeth drive her wild.

As she writhed under him, he removed her bra, exposing her breasts to him. She reached down and wiggled until she'd divested herself of the thong, too. Her naked body was a glorious sight to behold, but seeing her in the bright sunlight, open to him and all he offered, was more than he could take.

Nico tore off his clothes and stretched out beside her. The grass prickled the most sensitive parts of his body, and he rolled so he was on his back, taking her with him.

She straddled him eagerly, took him inside her in one swift and magnificent thrust. He had to hold her still so he didn't embarrass himself.

"Slow down, *tesoro*. You feel so good."

"Mmm. *You* feel so good." She rolled her hips, and he rolled his eyes. Then she bent down and kissed him.

He lost himself to the sensation of her hot mouth on his, her hot body on top of him. She started to increase her tempo, but he clutched her hips and slowed them down, setting a languorous pace.

"Too much." She panted and sat up, braced her hands on his chest.

But it wasn't nearly enough.

He trailed his hands up her sides and fondled her breasts. She tried to maintain eye contact, but soon her eyelids closed. Her head tipped back. He watched with rapt attention as she gave herself over to the sensations he stoked in her.

Her hips began to thrust harder, faster, and he knew she was ready. He again grabbed her hips but allowed her to set the pace… and it grew harder and faster with each stroke.

Nico reached between them and rubbed his finger on the sensitive bundle of nerves, making her scream and buck on top of him. He continued stroking and thrusting until she started to calm, then he gave a final push and followed her over the edge of sanity.

After several minutes when they both struggled to calm their breathing, Donni lifted herself off him just enough to look him in the eye. "That was amazing."

"You're amazing."

She smiled. "I love you."

"And I love you, *tesoro*." He stifled a yawn.

"I tired you out, huh?"

"You're too much for me."

She giggled. "So I guess a round two is out of the question?"

"After a nap. Just let me hold you."

She snuggled against him, and he started to relax. A thought tickled his brain, a concern skittered up his spine. He sat up and looked around.

"What's wrong?" she asked.

"I don't know. I just got this feeling…"

"What feeling?"

He scanned the horizon, his property, the road leading back to town. Something moved in the brush far down the hill—probably just an animal—but his blood iced over. "I don't think we're alone."

"What?" She scrambled into her clothes and threw his at him. "Who's here?"

"I'm not sure." He hurriedly dressed while he filled her in on the black car and the reappearing man in Dozza. "I think he followed us here."

She slipped into her shoes. "Why do you think that? Do you see someone?"

"No. It's just a feeling. I think it's related to my powers. But something's out of balance. Something's wrong."

"Your dagger power? You don't even have it with you."

"Doesn't matter. I feel it." He reached into his pocket, grabbed his keys, and tossed them to her. "Take the car, follow this road, take a left at the bottom. It'll take you right to the orphanage. You know how to get back from there. I'll walk back when I'm sure no one's here."

"It's got to be ten miles!"

"Don't worry about it."

"Nico," she pleaded, "just come with me and—"

"Donnatella." His voice was soft, his words measured. It silenced her faster than yelling would have, although he would have liked to have screamed as loud as he could. "I need to investigate, and I need to know you're safe. You have to go."

"I don't know how to drive a stick."

"You'll figure it out. Use the clutch when you shift. This whole hill is a private drive. No one will get in your way. By the time you get to the bottom, you should have enough control to make it back to the villa."

Tears now flowed freely down her face, but she didn't wipe them away. "I'm scared for you."

He kissed her forehead. "I'll be fine. But I need you to be safe. Please. You're wasting time. Go. Now."

She looked back a few times, but she finally got in his car, executed the worst turn in the history of driving, and ground the gears before driving down the hill.

Cazzo. He prayed she'd be okay, but he needed her away from there. Away from danger. Something wasn't right. He felt it.

He kicked a rock, watched it dance across the road and into the grass. The day was quiet, the landscape still. What was setting him on edge? The silence? His body thrummed with nervous energy, his mind buzzed with thoughts he couldn't quell.

Maybe he should call for a backup.

Backup for what? He had no proof of any danger. Just a niggling feeling. And if he did call for support, he'd have to explain why he sent Donni off without him. God, he shouldn't have done that.

With any luck, he was overreacting and she'd be back at the compound before anyone else. The guys would think he left her with the mentors while he went somewhere. Fingers crossed that would work out for him.

Hell, he'd cross his damn toes if he thought it would help all this to work out. But he just couldn't shake the idea that something was off.

Scanning the land on both sides of the road, he started jogging down the hill.

22

DONNI FOUGHT WITH the gear shift and clutch for the first couple of minutes, but then she gave up and drove—coasted—in second gear all the way down the hill. She white-knuckled the wheel, terrified she'd wreck Nico's car, which she couldn't begin to pay for.

When she came to a sharp bend, she hit the brakes hard. The car started to shudder, and she stomped on the clutch and tried to downshift. There were one too many pedals for her feet, and she feared letting go of the wheel to grab the gearshift. A quick glance down assured her she'd put the car in the right gear, but when she looked back up, another vehicle was headed right for her—and fast.

A black panel van!

She swerved, skidded. With nowhere to go, she ran off the road and slammed into a tree. The abrupt stop exploded the airbag, and the car was consumed with a cloud of powder.

A fit of coughing overwhelmed her, and she struggled with the door handle. The lock was still engaged, and she fumbled to release it before tumbling out, landing on her hands and knees as she wheezed and fought for clean air.

The impact on the ground hurt her hands, and a searing pain shot through her left wrist, but her eyes stung and watered, and she couldn't see well enough to assess her injuries.

When her breathing normalized and her vision cleared, she saw her forearms and hands had been burned from the airbag explosion. Her wrist was bruised and swollen. Wouldn't surprise her if she'd broken it. She sat back to examine her injuries and heard a distinct click right before cold metal pressed against the back of her head.

She'd forgotten about the van, forgotten about who might be driving it and what he might want.

It was all foremost in her thoughts now, though.

"Stand up." He jabbed the gun against her skull. "Now."

Donni scrambled to her feet. Her whole body had begun to hurt, and she held her left arm tight against her torso to try and support it. When she started to turn around, he poked her head again.

"No looking. Here." He handed her a handkerchief. "Put this over your eyes."

She tried to tie it loosely, but she was hindered with only one working hand. He hit her with the gun, and stars exploded in her vision.

"Tie it tight."

She did the best she could to fasten the cloth tightly around her head, all the while trying to leave a tiny gap at the bottom so she could still see.

When she was blindfolded, he took the gun away. She could make out the ground, but everything hurt too bad to try and run away. Besides, she had no idea if anyone was with him or how closely he was paying attention to her.

She had to assume it was pretty darn close.

He yanked her right arm behind her and held it against her back. When he grabbed her left arm, she screamed in pain.

He only pulled tighter, and he secured both hands behind her with a zip tie.

"Please," she gasped. "My wrist. I think it's broken."

"Then you probably won't want to struggle."

His accent was thick, but his language was flawless. She tried to focus on his voice to see if she could make out his identity, but she didn't recognize him. Concentrating on his voice had another benefit, though—it helped keep her mind off the pain. It might help her not pass out. So she kept her attention on his words.

"Start walking." He poked her back with his gun to get her moving.

Donni stumbled a bit, almost fell on her face, then gained her footing. "Where am I going?"

He clutched her arm and pulled her over the uneven road.

She heard the sounds of the van door opening, and he shoved her inside. She landed on her left arm and passed out.

THE FIRST THING Donni noticed when she came to was immense pain. She gasped and went to cradle her wrist, but pain lanced through her arm. She was still zip-tied.

It was pitch black because of the blindfold, but there was no movement or motor noise. She assumed she was no longer in the van. But where was she?

With her hands bound and vision compromised, she had to rely on her other senses. The bare skin of her legs, arm, and cheek were chilled. She wriggled slightly to get a sense of the texture of the floor. Rough, cold, gritty—definitely not the metal of a van, and not any kind of upholstery or wood. Felt like stone.

She took a deep breath through her nose. Clearly she hadn't recovered fully, as it hurt to expand her lungs. She succumbed to another hacking fit, yet even as she coughed, she noted she'd smelled a dank, mineral-like smell. Once she could breathe again, she listened carefully and made out a faint and constant *drip-drip-drip*.

More disturbingly, she heard footsteps and scuffling.

Soon she heard a familiar voice protesting. "It's me you want. Let her go."

And then a more familiar female voice, sniffling and pleading. "I won't say anything. You have my word."

Mama! They'd taken Mama. And Scalzotto.

Her heart nearly broke for her poor mother, who'd already been through too much at the hands of these monsters.

"Mama?"

There was a beat of quiet, followed by everyone talking at once.

"Donni? Oh, my poor girl!"

"Let her go this instant! You want *me,* not them! They're innocent bystanders!"

"You're not in charge here, so shut up."

But one voice cut through them all. "Silence!"

Donni could only hear the *drip-drip-drip* again, and she struggled to sit. Her arm protested, and she moaned.

"Remove her blindfold and bindings. Now."

"Yes, sir."

Hurried footsteps echoed around her, and she was roughly hauled to her feet and divested of the zip tie and handkerchief. She blinked a few times to get used to the light, dim as it was. For the love of God, she was in a cave! Her worst nightmare—the prophetic vision—was coming to fruition. A few candles placed in the corners of the large "room" cast long shadows up the rough rock walls. Stalactites reached down toward them, menacing cones of danger that could break off and kill any one of them.

Or could be used as a weapon against her captors.

What did it matter? They were who-knew-where. Escape was unlikely, and no one would ever find them.

She looked at the man who released her, probably also the man who abducted her to begin with.

He wasn't much older than Nico and the guys, but he looked a lot more worn. Like life—or likely the organization he worked for—had been rough on him. He sneered and shoved her aside. She stumbled, hit the wall, and winced at the pain that wracked her body.

The man in charge cleared his throat and said, "That's enough, Bruno."

"But I thought—"

"I said that's enough."

Bruno skulked back to where a group of men stood, holding her mother and Carmen Scalzotto in their clutches. She didn't recognize any of them. Not the men holding Mama and Carmen. Not the man who unbound her.

Certainly not the man in charge.

And clearly he was the boss. His henchmen seemed to cower in his presence, and no one met his gaze.

The thing that disturbed her the most, though, was that he held a dagger—a blue marble dagger, identical in size and shape to those the Brotherhood wielded.

"Who are you?" she asked.

He smiled. "You'll be so surprised when you find out. If you live that long."

"What do you want?"

He nodded, and the men dragged her mother and Carmen over to the wall near where she stood. Each of them was shackled with irons Donni hadn't noticed before. Bruno then chained her to the wall not far from Mama.

He was much gentler with her than he had been previously.

The boss spoke again. "We've been more than patient with you and your sisters. We told you we'd prefer you take control of the government and let us direct things from the shadows. But you remain stubborn, like your father."

"Of course we're not going to help you. You're a murderer. You're insane!"

"Is it insane to want to lead your country to greatness? I think not."

"It's insane when you try to take over a revolution and work behind the scenes, killing people who disagree with you or get in your way."

"I'm doing this for my people!"

"No, you're not." Indignation and rage rippled through her. "You're doing it for you, for the power. If you were really concerned for Italy's future, you'd be a reluctant leader. Like Carmen. He didn't want the responsibility. It's been thrust on him. But you? You're trying to seize it. For yourself. If your intentions were truly noble, you'd be out in public, talking to the people and seeking their support of you as a ruler. You'd be voted into power. You wouldn't have to steal it."

"I can't. I think they'd notice when I never aged, never died. I have to work behind the scenes to protect my secret. That's why I need you. A Medici descendant would be easier to seat in government than this fool." He gestured to Scalzotto. "And much easier to control."

Fear took a backseat to fury. "What do you mean, you don't age or die?"

"I think that's self-explanatory."

Her body chilled as the blood drained from her extremities. "Oh, my God. That's how you've been one step ahead of us this whole time. You're a mole. You're working both sides. You're Michelangelo!"

He scoffed. "Hardly. He's a pale imitation of me."

"Then who—? How—?"

"Like I said, eventually I'll reveal my name. But not now. If you're alive, you'll be amazed." He paused, tipped his head. "Maybe I should just tell you now. Perhaps my identity will make you realize who you're up against and how fruitless your lack of cooperation is."

"I don't care who you are. I'll never help you."

"Don't be so certain." He stepped out of the shadows and approached her mother. He held his dagger to her neck, trailed the tip of the blade from one ear to the other. A tiny trickle of blood dripped onto her shoulder, and she turned her head away. He turned from her and pointed the dagger at Donni. "You have a choice to make. A life for a life."

Her blood chilled. This was her vision—unaltered. And she couldn't do anything to change it, to stop it. "What did you say?"

"A life for a life. I'm not going to kill you. Not yet, anyway. Because I still think I can make you join me."

"Don't bet on it. I'll never join you."

"I'm going to make you one of us. I'm going to make you take a life. When you realize how easy it is, how necessary it is, you'll understand. And then you'll join me."

"I'd never kill someone!"

"Ah, Miss Notaro. Not just anyone. Your choice has much more dire consequences than a random murder. You will choose—a life for a life."

"What are you talking about?" Donni's whole body trembled. He stomach lurched, and she feared she'd be sick.

"Someone in this cave will die today. And the choice is yours. The question is, who will it be? Will you kill your mother to save the country? Or will you kill Carmen Scalzotto to save your mother?"

She shook her head. "No. No! I won't be a party to your madness."

"I'd reconsider, if I were you. Because," he looked at his watch, "at midnight tonight, you'll make your decision. Or you'll all die. You have until then to make up your mind. Then I'll be back for your answer." He turned to leave, gestured for his men to precede him.

"You're insane! I'll never choose. You hear me? Never!"

"A life for a life, Miss Notaro. Seven hours."

And he walked down a dark passageway.

RATHER THAN CALMING down, Nico grew more agitated with every step he took. His concern propelled him down the hill, and he made much better time than expected. It should have taken him about two and a half hours to get back to the compound, but after only an hour and half, he was already nearing the bottom of the hill. He'd be back at the villa in another thirty minutes.

Or so he thought. Until he noticed a waft of smoke dissipating in the sky.

He hurried around the bend, his stomach already churning.

His knees buckled when he saw his mangled car, and he almost fell.

"Donni!" Nico quashed the nausea and ran to the Maserati. The door hung open, but she was nowhere to be found.

There was no sign of her having walked toward town, either.

But there was a second set of tire tracks in the dirt. He didn't need to do a thorough investigation to know what happened. On a cellular level, he already knew. She'd been run off the road and abducted. Or worse.

She'd been vulnerable and alone. Because of him.

He'd sensed danger and sent her away to protect her, but instead of securing her safety, he thrust her right into peril.

No time to hike the half hour back to the villa. His brothers could get to him in a couple of minutes. He grabbed his phone and, ignoring the notifications of several missed calls and texts, scrolled to his favorites and dialed Coz.

His brother answered on the first ring. *"Where the hell have you been? We've been calling and texting you for hours."*

Nico was already running toward the road. "I don't have time to explain. Or listen to lectures. I need help."

"So do we, man. You need to get back here. Pronto."

"Coz, shut the fuck up and listen. Donni's been abducted. My car is wrecked. I need you to come get me, and we have to go find her!"

"Donni, too?"

His stomach lurched again, and he slowed down for a moment. "What do you mean, too?"

"Where are you? I'm coming now."

He heard Coz's motor rev, so he yelled into the phone, "What do you mean, too? Who else?"

"Mary and Carmen are gone."

"What happened?"

"Where the fuck are you? I'm already headed down the hill."

"Turn right at the orphanage and head toward Scandicci. I'll meet you on the road. Now tell me about what happened!"

"Marcus called as I was driving home."

Nico reached the road and saw Coz's Ferrari barreling toward him. He crossed the road and waited. His brother must have seen him, too, because the line went dead.

Thirty seconds later, they were headed back to the compound and Coz had resumed his story.

"They were all on the patio."

"Who?"

"Marcus, Rico, Mary, Scalzotto, and his head of security. They got jumped. Never heard anyone approach, then all of a sudden, there was a hail of bullets. Gianni healed Marcus and Rico—their wounds weren't that bad—but the security guy, Stefano? He was DOA. I tried to… Well, I guess my powers still aren't developed enough. There was nothing I could do."

Coz whipped into the garage and they jumped out of the car. Nico grabbed his arm before he went inside. "You sure Marcus and Rico were the victims?"

"They were shot trying to keep Mary and Carmen safe."

"Yeah, but not bad, right? How'd Stefano die and they just got flesh wounds?"

"It was a little worse than flesh wounds, Nic. You weren't here. Trust me, they aren't part of the problem."

The door to the house banged against the wall. Vinnie stood in the doorway. "Where the fuck have you been, and why didn't you answer your phone?"

"Donni's gone."

"What? *Cazzo.*"

"Any leads on Mary and Carmen?" Nico looked back and forth between his brothers. "Maybe the people who took her took them?"

"*Took* her?" Vinnie said. "I thought you said she was gone. Like, she left on her own."

"Not exactly."

"Then what, exactly?"

He didn't want to waste time going over all his mistakes, but he knew the Brotherhood wouldn't jump into action unless they had all the facts.

"I only want to say this once. Let's grab Gianni, and I'll fill you in." They joined Gianni in the kitchen. Unfortunately, the girls and the two mentors were there, too. "Let's go to the office. It'll be more private."

"If this is about my sister," Toni said, "you aren't going anywhere. Spill it."

No point in wasting time arguing. Nico bit the proverbial bullet and launched into his story, covering the important points and glossing over the more private details.

To everyone's credit, no one interrupted him. But when he was done, people started yelling over each other.

"What were you thinking?" Coz said.

"Going off without telling anyone?" Gianni yelled.

"You and Franki went off together. Alone."

"And everyone knew where the fuck we went!"

Nico couldn't argue that point. He rubbed the back of his neck.

"Why'd you send her home alone?" Toni asked.

"I can't even imagine how she must feel!" Franki said.

"Did you process the scene?" Jo asked. "The car? Any leads? Any at all?"

Marcus and Rico sat, silent and still. They both looked disappointed, but more to the point, they looked ready to fall over.

Only Vinnie had a look of determination. He was still, quiet.

It unnerved Nico more than if Vinnie totally lost his temper. He swallowed and faced him. "What are you thinking?"

Vinnie gave him a hard stare, cold and heated at the same time. "You don't want to fucking know what I'm thinking."

That about summed it up. "Your power? Any ideas? Any strategy for getting Donni back? For getting them all back?"

Vinnie's eyes clouded over, and he frowned. His brow furrowed, and he closed his eyes. A soft growl escaped him, and he grabbed his dagger. He held it to his temple, then put the blade across the flat of his forehead. Finally, he pointed it at Nico.

Nico stepped back, but Gianni and Coz grabbed him and walked him forward. Vinnie held his dagger over Nico's head, then against his temple, then pressed it to his chest over his heart.

Nico continued to watch him for any sign of possibilities.

Vinnie threw his dagger across the room. The blade embedded in the wall and the handle vibrated.

"*Merda,*" Coz whispered.

"Nothing," Vinnie said. "Not a damn thing. Because of you." He shoved Nico. "Because I can't fucking see past your block. You need to let me in."

"Come on, Nico," Toni said. "This is my sister. And my mom."

"And Scalzotto," Gianni said. "This isn't about your privacy. This is about their lives."

"You act like I'm blocking on purpose," Nico said. "I'm not. I wouldn't know how if I wanted to."

"You must want to, because I can't see anything!" Vinnie turned and slammed his fist into the wall, leaving a hole in the plaster.

Jo went to him, fussed over his bloody knuckles, and whispered something in a soothing voice.

Nico was just grateful he hit the wall and not his face. For a change.

Gianni flicked his hand in Vinnie's direction, and the cuts healed. "Good?"

Vinnie shrugged.

"I think he broke his hand," Jo said.

Figured. Nico walked over to him and looked at the swollen bones. "I'll fix it. As soon as I get my dagger."

Vinnie lifted his head slowly and pierced him with a look of fierce rage. His voice was low, measured, when he finally spoke. "Where the fuck is your dagger, Nico?"

"I—it's in my room." Nico's voice was quiet, too.

But for a very different reason.

"You took my sister off property and didn't even have your dagger with you?" Toni's voice rose with each word and squeaked at the end.

"Tell me you at least had your piece," Coz said.

But his gun was upstairs with his dagger. He shook his head. "I'll go get them now."

"Don't do it on my account," Vinnie said. "I don't want your help."

"Vinnie, be reasonable," Jo began.

Nico dashed upstairs before he heard the rest of the argument. Or anything else anyone had to say. He didn't need the lectures, the recriminations. No one could possibly feel worse than he did.

Vinnie was their best chance of finding Donni before... before it was too late. And because of his block, whatever the hell was causing it, Vinnie was shut out. Not only was it his fault that Mary and Carmen had been unprotected and abducted today, it was his fault Donni was in danger, too. None of this was on anyone but him.

So it was up to him to make things right.

Nico put on his weapons, then thought about facing everyone and decided against it. He unsheathed his dagger, put it to his head, and concentrated. He felt the power flow from him to his brother, felt the bones in his hand knit.

He had failed at healing Donni when she most needed him, but he knew he'd come through for Vinnie. Maybe he was finally getting the hang of his powers.

Donni. Powers. Connection...

Nico concentrated on Donni, on her health and life essence. He felt the distance between them, but he also felt her strongly—more powerfully than his brother who was just one floor beneath him.

She was injured.

He sensed the broken bone in her wrist and wished it well. A wave of power washed through him, out of him, and crossed the distance.

Even without confirmation, he knew he'd healed her. Thank God his powers finally worked.

Better still, he sensed everything about her. The chains, the cold, the rough wall against her back.

Nico knew where she was. And he would save her.

He grabbed his phone, pulled up a map to confirm his route, then he opened the app that let him monitor the villa.

Everyone was still in the kitchen, gathered around Vinnie and looking at his hand. At least he'd done something right.

Nico crept out of his room and down the hall. He had to sneak past the kitchen and slip into the garage, but once there, he figured he was clear. The gang made too much noise to hear him leave.

And he kept the security monitor feed active on his phone, so he'd know if plans changed. He was going to mount a rescue, and despite the danger and stupidity of doing it himself, every cell in his body said lives would be lost if he didn't go alone. His brothers were just too big for all four of them to go unnoticed, and stealth was of the essence.

Nico could slip in undetected. And after he freed everyone, maybe they'd be less angry.

Didn't really matter to him either way, though. Once he'd saved Donni, he was leaving the group. They could all hate him. It wouldn't impact his life at all.

He didn't deserve to be part of the Brotherhood when he'd failed at his duties so miserably.

He checked the monitor again. As expected, they were too noisy to hear him leave. He got to the bottom of the hill and turned to follow his earlier route, back to the Apennines.

This time he wouldn't go to the medical facility, though. He would explore the caves.

DONNI CLOSED HER eyes and tried to tune out her mother and Carmen. Both of them pleaded with her.

But the decision was hers.

And she simply wasn't going to make it.

"Donnatella, I am your mother, so you listen to me. My life isn't important any more. One life pales in comparison to an entire country."

"I'm not a country," Carmen said. "I'm just one man, too. Save your mother."

"And who will save Italy?"

"It's not even your country. It's not your concern."

"It's my heritage," Mama said. "I have as much right to protect it as you."

"But you aren't protecting it. You're protecting me."

"You are what this country needs to thrive."

"And you are what the House of Medici needs to survive. Your girls will be destroyed if they lose you."

"They survived their father's death, and they'll get over mine."

"No one gets over a parent's death. They just learn to cope and accept."

"Then they'll have to cope with and accept mine. Because Donni is going to save you. And I'm going to be reunited with my husband."

Donni sighed.

"You hear me, young lady? You do what's right."

"Yes," Carmen said. "Do what's right. Choose to let your mother live."

"Would you both stop?" Donni couldn't take it anymore. "Even if I could decide, which I can't, it wouldn't matter. That nut bar is going to kill both of you, anyway. And me, too."

"You don't know that," Mama said. "You could get away."

"Making a decision like that won't just end someone's life. It'll destroy my soul. I can't do it."

"You have to," Carmen said. "Please. I absolve you. Try to save you and your mother."

"Her and you, not me."

"Mary, be reasonable."

"I am."

"I said stop!" Donni banged her head off the cave wall. Suddenly her wrist snapped, a sharp pain shot through it, and then she felt relief.

Nico.

She smiled. She sensed him, knew he was coming for them. "I don't have to choose. We're all going to be okay."

"Donnatella," Mama said. "You aren't thinking clearly."

"Trust me, Mama. All three of us are going to be just fine."

23

NICO SPLIT HIS attention between the road and the monitor on his phone. It had taken about ninety minutes for them to track Mike down, but Vinnie finally got through. And Mike had materialized immediately.

"I know my powers are exceptional," Mike said, *"but I cannot be everywhere at once, observe everyone at once. Nor would you want me to."*

"So you didn't see anything? About Donni or Nic?" Vinnie said.

"You have the power of strategy, Vincenzo. It is immaterial what I have seen. What do you see?"

"Not a damn thing. Nic's blocking me. And the SOB bolted. We don't even know where he is."

"You have not yet learned how he is blocking you? Nothing you do works to break through?"

"No. Best I can tell, he's conflicted, so he doesn't know what he's doing. And because of that, I can't see what results his decisions will lead to."

Mike tapped his chin. *"I feared this. Given the rituals to create the daggers, the powers they imbue... It was always a possibility."*

"You act like you were actually there when Michelangelo made the daggers," Gianni said.

"I am his emissary. He has no secrets from me. I know how the daggers were created. And I know the potential problems."

"So what did you fear would happen?" Coz asked. *"What's the problem?"*

"Dominico's powers are of life, balance, and transformation."

"Yeah, we know," Gianni said. *"So what?"*

"Balance, Giovanni. A yin for a yang. A tit for a tat. For every reaction, there is an equal and opposite reaction."

"Physics was never my favorite subject," Vinnie said.

Mike sighed. *"No, it was not."*

Vinnie scowled.

"Balance, son. The harder you try to see his path, the harder he will block you. Intentionally or not."

Hmm. Nico was surprised by that. He'd never considered the problem was his power and not actually him.

"So just how the hell am I supposed to strategize for him when he's shutting me out?"

"Tell him to try to keep you out. If Dominico actively attempts to block your sight of his decisions, you will see every option available to him. You may even know what decision he will make rather than only what choices he has. If your brother is willing to do this for you, you will read him and the outcomes better than you will with almost anyone else."

Good to know. That could come in handy.

Nico took a deep breath and ignored his ringing phone. Again.

"Well, that's just great," Vinnie said. *"If he'd just answer his damn phone, we could tell him."*

"Tell me again the details of the vision."

"Donni's or Nic's?" Vinnie asked.

"I am sorry. Dominico had a vision?"

"More like a dream, I guess. Seemed prophetic, though."

"Tell me."

"Something about fires and a ritual of some sort," Vinnie said.

"Crazy laughter," Gianni added.

"Did he see who was laughing?"

"No," Coz said. *"But he mentioned a blue dagger."*

Mike paused for a moment. When he spoke, his voice wavered. *"He is in grave danger. We must find him. Now."*

Grave danger? Nico slowed down and considered Mike's words. What did he know that the rest of them didn't? He was just about to call and ask when his phone rang yet again.

"Yeah?"

"Why the fuck did you leave without—"

"Now is not the time for recriminations, Vincenzo."

Vinnie fell silent.

"Dominico, where are you?"

"Why?"

"You are in mortal danger."

"We're *always* in mortal danger."

"Not like this. You must stand down until we can reach you. You will need everyone's help."

"No. If there are too many of us, we'll be seen before we get to them. The best option is a stealth one."

"We can all be stealthy," Coz said. *"It's what we trained for."*

"Listen, Nic," Gianni said. *"We think we know how to get around the block. If it works, V can come up with a plan. You have to—"*

"I know."

"You knew this whole time and let me struggle with it?" Vinnie asked.

"No. I learned when you did. I have the monitor app up on my phone. I've been listening."

"So let's try it. We can see whose way is right."

"I'm almost there. You'd never get here in time."

"We have all the time we need! You can wait for us."

"No, Vin. I sensed her. She's on a clock."

"Then let me in so I can come up with a plan for you!"

Nico thought about it. It might be nice to have some kind of strategy before he barged into the cave. Honestly, he didn't even know what cave he was searching for. "If you swear to tell me everything."

"Why wouldn't I?"

"Because I know the general area but not the specific location. If I let you in, you'll see everything that might happen, so you'll know where she is for sure. You have to give me the precise coordinates."

"I don't even know if it works like that!"

"But he'll try," Coz said. *"Right?"*

Vinnie sighed. *"Right. Yeah. I'll try. Now end the damn block."*

"Nico, please!" Toni yelled. *"Let him in!"*

Her sisters echoed her sentiment.

"Fine. But don't you hold out on me, Vin."

"I said I wouldn't."

"Do you think I need to pull over?"

"How the hell should I know? You've been blocking me and going about your business for how long now? Probably not."

"But perhaps the reverse is different," Mike said. *"It might be best if you stopped, at least until you know how the effort will affect you."*

Nico sighed. He didn't want to waste the time. But he also didn't want to drive off a cliff or into a tree. He pulled over, cleared his thoughts, and took a deep breath.

"Any time, Nic," Vinnie said.

"Shut up and give me a second." He took another deep breath, then he imagined throwing up all kinds of blocks. Doors, walls, boulders. He pictured his brother on the other side of them, struggling to get in and only getting pushed further back. He concentrated so hard, he broke out in a sweat. His whole body trembled.

"Merda!" Vinnie said.

Nico opened his eyes. A boulder lay on the road in front of him, blocking his way. Apparently it wasn't him trembling. It was the ground. He'd done more than wish for a mental block. He'd manifested a tangible one.

"Nico?" Vinnie said.

"Did it work?"

"Too well."

"Where is she?"

"It's bad, Nic. Really bad. You need to wait for us."

"You promised."

"Donni, Mary, and Carmen are being held in a cave."

"I already know that."

"I've seen you go in at least half a dozen ways. And all of you die. Every time."

"What else did you see?"

"I can't help you!"

"What. Did. You. See?" Nico peeled out onto the road, cut into the other lane to pass the boulder, and then floored it up the hill.

Vinnie sighed.

"Dominico. I will go with you."

"No. I need to go alone. Too many people—"

But Mike had already teleported into the passenger seat of his car.

NICO SWERVED INVOLUNTARILY when Mike appeared. "What the hell? You could have killed me."

"If you continue on this fool's errand alone, you will die."

"What do you know about it?"

"Why did you not tell me about your vision?"

"It never came up."

"I have been back to the property. You did not mention it. You send status reports daily. It has never been referred to in any way."

"It was a stupid dream," Nico said. "It doesn't mean anything."

"Take the next left."

"What? Why?"

"Now." Mike grabbed the wheel and turned it.

Nico slammed on the brakes and skidded into the turn. After the car came to a stop, he turned and glared at Mike. "Are you crazy? You could have flipped the car! There's not even a road here!"

"Look carefully, Dominico. This is a path. Old and overgrown, but a path nonetheless. And it has been traveled recently."

Nico stared at the foliage where his headlights illuminated the path. Mike was right. There was a path. And someone had used it recently. "How did you know this was here?"

"Because I know who wields the blue dagger. I know where he would go."

"How?" Nico made his way slowly down the path. His car wasn't made for off-roading, and the bottom scraped often.

"Because we were once friends. And I know that this cave has special meaning to him."

Clearly Mike didn't intend to give him any more information, so he concentrated on the road, such as it was. Occasionally he saw glowing eyes in the brush. Had to be the wolves. Again. And they seemed to be following him.

Mike sent a text and then turned Nico's phone off.

"You text the Brotherhood?" Nico asked. He still believed a large group could ruin everything. He also believed they couldn't get to them before it all hit the fan, so it might not matter. But he was still curious. "What'd you say?"

"I was preparing your brothers. Now I must prepare you. I will project to Donnatella. If I believe it safe, I will then teleport in. The element of surprise is imperative here. Follow this path another two kilometers, then pull into the brush and approach on foot. We may just be lucky enough to save them all."

"Before you teleport—"

"*If* I am clear to teleport."

"Will you just tell me if she's okay?"

Mike closed his eyes and took a deep breath. A few minutes passed, and he didn't say anything. He didn't ghost out, either.

Nico reached the two-kilometer mark and pulled over. He wasn't sure what to do.

Mike turned to him. "She is physically well, Dominico. But she is frightened. As she should be. We do not have much time. Follow the path. When you get to the cave, do not use a flashlight. There should be just enough ambient light for you to make your way to the cavern. There are many paths. Remember—first right, second left, third left. If you miss a turn, you will be lost."

"What if—"

But Mike teleported.

Son of a… Nico sighed. No time to be angry. He checked his weapons, made sure his phone was on silent, and stuffed it in his pocket. Then he exited the car, shutting the door carefully so no sentry, if there was one, would hear him. God only knew how far a sound would travel.

Nico started picking his way down the path when a prickle skittered up his spine and into his scalp. He was being watched.

A glance left showed no one. But a quick peek right had him stopping mid-stride.

Glowing eyes.

Then five wolves left the brush and crept toward him.

DONNI HUNG HER head. Mike said he'd be back—in corporeal form—in a second. But in the few seconds his spirit had been gone, the Blue Dagger Man reappeared.

And she had no way of warning Mike not to come back.

Mike teleported right in front of her, then leaned back, a look of concern on his face. "Donnatella, why are you crying?"

She shook her head and whispered, "I had no way to warn you not to return. We aren't alone anymore."

Mike turned around slowly.

Blue Dagger Man stood mere feet from him, a nasty grin on his face.

"It's been a while, old friend. And I do mean a while."

"Leo. I should have known you were behind all of this. Now it all makes sense."

"Such malice in your tone. Aren't you happy to see me?"

"Under other circumstances, perhaps."

"Ah, but I'm rather happy with this circumstance."

"I knew you had copied my formula and created your own dagger. But I never recorded the recipe for the philosopher's stone. How did you manage it?"

"I'm the greatest mind who ever lived. If you could do it, you must have known I could."

Donni's mind spun. The greatest mind ever? The recipe for the philosopher's stone. Mike was talking like… No. For the love of all that was holy, no. "Oh, my god. You're joking. Please, tell me I'm wrong."

"I can hardly do that when I do not know the conclusion to which you have jumped."

"All these years," Leo said, "and you still talk like a novice. No colloquialisms? No slang? Not even a contraction?"

"There is nothing wrong with proper sentence structure."

"Let me guess. It helps with your pathetic little sonnets."

"Mike!" Donni was tired of their banter. "Or should I say, Michelangelo?"

He sighed and nodded.

"How could I not have seen it? You look younger than your portraits, but now I can see the resemblance. The name should have been a dead giveaway. Mike Buoni. Michelangelo di Lodovico Buonarroti Simoni. It's all so obvious."

"Then you can surely make one more leap," Blue Dagger Man—Leo—said.

The blood drained from her face and settled as an icy pool in her belly. Leo. Leonardo. Dear God. "Da Vinci."

He offered a dramatic bow with a flourish of his hand. "In the flesh."

If her hands were free, she'd rub her temples. A massive headache bloomed behind her eyes. "What is all this about?"

"You said so earlier. Power."

"But you are two of the most famous men in history. You've conquered death, for Pete's sake. What more do you want?"

"I want only to fulfill my vow," Mike said, "to protect the Medici family."

"And I want the recognition I was denied in my own time. Working for rich benefactors… I was the talent. I should have had the money and the clout, not them."

"And centuries later, you haven't amassed enough wealth to satisfy you?" Donni asked.

"I can create gold from simple metals. I don't need more wealth. I grow bored with it. I want to affect change. I hear the chants of 'Medici! Medici! Medici!' from the rabble in the streets. The Medici already had their chance. It's my turn now, as it should have been centuries before."

"You want to be a dictator!"

Leonardo's men came in. The one who abducted Donni spoke. "You okay, sir? We heard an argument."

"Fine, Bruno. We're just having a friendly discussion before Miss Notaro makes her choice."

"Bruno?" Mike said.

"Do I know you?" the thug asked.

"You are responsible for the gruesome murder of Fredo Baroni. You tried to blame Roberto for it."

Bruno looked at Leonardo, who shrugged. "Go ahead, Bruno. Tell him. Tell him what he never managed to work out on his own."

"I didn't want to blame Coz. Not at first. I was supposed to recruit Micelli. But he wanted nothing to do with me. DeSanto and Falco made sure of that."

"Giovanni and Vincenzo? Smart boys, even then."

"Smart? Hardly. They chose you when they could have been on our side. Didn't matter, though. They made sure Micelli blew me off, so I figured I'd get his closest friend. Almost had Cozza over on our side, too. But then we had to accelerate the timetable on the murder, and all of a sudden, the little shit was gone. The other three, too."

"You are talking about my sons." Mike advanced on him.

Leonardo pushed him back. "This history is all very fascinating, but it's also water under the bridge. It's almost midnight, Donnatella. It's time for you to make your decision."

24

NICO COULDN'T BELIEVE it. When the wolves crossed his path, he thought he was done for. He prepared for death even as he wished they were just pups—those he might be able to fend off.

But they didn't attack. They became pups. Tiny little wolflings, smaller than a baby wolf should be.

Instead of frolicking like young wolves or running from the big stranger, they just stood there, looking at him.

"Did I do that to you?"

The one in the front blinked. Nico swore it was a sign for the affirmative.

"Can you understand me?"

The wolflings all blinked.

Life, balance, transformation. Looks like he figured out more about the "life" and "transformation" parts.

"Can you help me?"

Again, the lead wolf blinked.

"There are some bad men in there." Nico pointed toward the cave. "They have my… girlfriend. And her mother. And another man. My associate went in ahead of me, but we're outnumbered."

The wolfling reared onto his hind legs and growled. Well, it was probably a growl. An animal that small couldn't really sound intimidating.

Nico clutched his dagger and wished for them to grow. Grow past their natural size and transform into uberwolves—something even a werewolf would cower in front of.

He wasn't disappointed. He heard snarls, snaps, and deep growls, and he opened his eyes to giant wolves. Nico stood a full six-foot, two-inches, and these animals were taller. On four legs.

He let out a low whistle. "Just what I wanted. Better, even."

The lead wolf lowered his head.

Nico took it to be a bow of agreement. Weird how he understood the animals despite such a communication barrier.

"Are you ready?"

All the wolves stood alert, then the lead wolf bounded into the cave. His pack followed.

"Wait! You don't know where to go!"

But apparently they did. Either they used their sense of smell or they read his thoughts, and they went exactly where Mike had told him to go. They went so fast, Nico struggled to keep up.

They reached a cavern, and the wolves charged. Nico started to go in after them, but he saw movement out of the corner of his eye. Without the wolves for backup, whoever ran would escape unless he did something about it.

He never even entered the cavern. Instead, he turned and gave chase.

A GROWL ECHOED through the cavern.

Donni looked up as everyone turned toward the sound.

Wolves. Giant wolves. Monsters. They leaped into the crowd.

Leo and Bruno ran. Mike chased after them.

The other men weren't so lucky. The wolves cut off their escape routes, then they attacked. Screams echoed through the cavern. The wolves snarled and snapped their jaws, rending clothes and tearing flesh. They were getting closer to the wall as they created all the carnage.

Carmen, Mama, and Donni were all still shackled to the wall. They had no way to protect themselves. A wolf was thrown off one of the men, and it landed in front of her mother. She screamed, and Carmen yelled for help.

Donni cringed against the imminent slaughter and prayed for their lives. And their souls.

NICO DASHED AFTER the men who fled the cavern.

Mike joined him, seemingly out of nowhere. "Be ready."

Nico didn't know exactly what that meant, but he nodded and grasped his dagger tighter.

Mike disappeared. Nico knew he teleported somewhere, he just didn't know where. Still, he prepared for anything.

His boss reappeared in front of the man with the blue dagger. He tackled him, and they both crashed to the ground, knocking the other man off balance.

Nico leaped and landed beside the man. He slammed him face-first into the wall, and then the guy fell to the ground. Nico jumped on top of him, grabbed him by the shirt, and lifted his fist, intending to knock him out.

"Nico Fucking Micelli." The man's mouth was bloody, his grin macabre.

Nico paused and loosened his grip. "Do I know… Bruno?"

"Glad to see me?" He punched Nico in the face, knocking him back. "What about now?" Then he scrambled to his feet while Nico regained his balance.

They squared off against each other. Memories flashed through Nico's mind, clouding his concentration. Bruno had been kind to him. Had taken him under his wing when he felt alone at San Crisogono's. But the guys had said he was bad news. They'd steered him away from Bruno and kept them apart. Then he'd turned his sights on Coz. All right before Fredo's murder and then their adoption. It all made sense.

He hadn't quite been able to see it before. But he could now. The guy was evil. Nuts. Of course he worked with Sal and Dante. He was just the type to be swayed by the lure of money and power.

Mike and the man he battled continued to struggle, working their way up the passage. Nico lost sight of them in the darkness.

Then Bruno charged, wrapped his arms around Nico's waist, and tackled him. They grappled on the gritty floor, their combat too close for either to get in a good shot.

Nico tried to grab his dagger, but Bruno knocked it out of his hand. So much for an energy pulse. He twisted to get more room and elbowed Bruno in the face. The other man howled, rolled aside, and clutched his nose. Blood spurted through his fingers.

Nico turned and scrambled for his dagger, but he froze when he heard a soft click. He spun back around, slowly, hands up, and faced Bruno, who still held his gushing nose with one hand but pointed a gun at Nico with the other.

"I've waited a long time for this."

DONNI'S TEETH CHATTERED.

Since learning of her heritage, she'd pictured her death a thousand ways. Being ripped to shreds by giant wolves while shackled to a cave wall was not one of them.

It was also probably the worst way she could conceive of.

Her legs trembled, gave out. She would have collapsed but for the chains holding her captive. Instead, she dangled at the ends of manacles—too weak to stand, too strong to pass out and avoid the terror about to befall her.

The wolves had run out of struggling prey, and one of them—the biggest of them all—turned its attention on her. It approached her slowly, as though stealth was necessary.

Two other beasts approached Mama and Carmen in a similar manner. Her mother whimpered, begged, but still the wolves came.

The giant wolf was right in front of Donni. She smelled its fetid breath, hot on her clammy skin, when it opened its jaws wide. Its teeth were bloody, its eyes intense with concentration.

Donni closed her eyes and cringed. She had nowhere to go, and no one was coming to her rescue. She could only pray the pain was short lived.

Her chains clinked, tugged at her healed wrist. What?

She opened one eye just a crack and peered to the left. The wolf hadn't attacked. It had bitten through her chains.

Who knew a wolf's bite was that strong? Of course, that was no ordinary wolf.

When it had freed her left hand, it turned to her right. Another bout of gnawing on the chains, and she was released.

Although she feared averting her gaze from the beast, she had to check on Mama. No screams or cries from her, or Carmen, either. The other giant wolves were biting at their chains, but they weren't as powerful as the wolf who had freed her, so they hadn't snapped the chains yet.

Donni looked at the wolf again. It sat patiently, just looking at her.

"Tha… thank you."

The wolf bowed its head.

Did it understand her?

It nodded toward the passageway. Once. Twice. Scraped its paw on the ground and nodded again.

"Do you want me to go?"

Again the wolf bowed its head.

Maybe the wolf had attacked, and this was some weird hallucination to protect her from the pain before she died. She couldn't possibly be communicating with a giant wolf, could she?

For that matter, could a pack of wolves this size even exist?

The wolf huffed and again looked toward the passageway.

"Mama, I'll be back for you. I just need to check something."

"Donni, wait!"

But she couldn't. She slowly stepped around the giant wolf and headed for the passage. It nudged her a couple of times with its snout, and she picked up her pace.

It matched her stride, although it seemed impatient with her, kind of lifting its chin like it wanted her to hurry.

Donni sprinted down the tunnel, but she was lost. More than once, she turned one way only to have the wolf whimper until she went another. A loud, bang echoed through the passage. The wolf whined and nudged her again.

When she rounded the next corner, she stopped dead in her tracks.

Nico had come for her.

But Bruno had stopped him… by shooting him. Nico lay motionless, blood blooming all over his chest.

PAIN EXPLODED IN Nico's chest, in his back. Radiated down his arm and up his neck. Was it his shoulder? His clavicle? Didn't know, but it hurt like hell. He took a deep breath. Didn't seem to have nicked a lung, so that was good news.

He lay still for a moment, hoping to delude Bruno into thinking he'd killed him. As soon as Bruno turned to leave, Nico would grab his dagger and try the energy pulse. It could work, provided Bruno didn't plug him in the head before leaving, just to be sure he was dead.

It was Nico's only move, and he ignored the pain as he waited patiently for his chance.

Then he heard a scream.

God, no. Donni!

"You?" Bruno said. "How'd you get out?"

A low growl echoed through the tunnel.

Three more gunshots, and a yelp.

Nico rolled, grabbed his dagger, and pointed it at Bruno.

Bruno watched him and grinned. "You dumb enough to bring a knife to a gunfight?"

Nico shot the energy pulse before Bruno fired.

He lasted just long enough to look surprised before he crumpled to the ground in a heap.

Donni ran over to Nico and threw herself into his arms. He hissed with the pain, but when she tried to pull away, he only held her tighter.

Sobs distorted her voice, her head buried against his chest muffled it. "I thought you were dead."

"You're not getting rid of me that easily." But he closed his eyes and lay back down, drained of energy.

"Nico? Nico! Are you okay? Talk to me."

"Just tired."

"You can't sleep."

He heard a commotion and opened his eyes a crack. Mary and Carmen had emerged from the cavern, followed by the other four wolves, who licked at their alpha and whined.

Mike teleported in, and his brothers ran down the tunnel, stopping and pointing weapons toward the wolves.

"Stop," Nico said. "They're friendly."

"What the fuck is going on here?" Vinnie asked.

"Mike?" Nico managed.

"He is gone," Mike said. "For tonight. But I did not defeat him. He will continue to try and convert the House of Medici, or he will attempt to kill them."

"Who?" Coz said.

"Later, Roberto."

"Nic, do you have bone injuries?" Gianni said. "I can heal the tissue, but—"

"Help the alpha wolf first."

"What?"

"Bruno shot it. I don't know how bad. I'm okay. Heal the wolf."

Gianni shook his head and muttered something, but he turned his attention to the wolf.

"Did you say *Bruno*?" Coz asked.

"Long story," Nico said. "After I'm healed."

"Don, you better call your sisters. We had to move heaven and earth to keep them from coming."

"I don't want to leave Nico."

"Then don't. Just call them."

She took her phone out of her pocket, looked at it, then waved it at Coz. "No service."

"You really should call them," Nico said. "Just step outside."

"Not alone," Coz said. "I'll go with you."

"But—"

"Please, go," Nico said. "So they don't worry."

She hesitated, then she kissed his forehead. "I'm coming right back."

He managed a weak smile and watched her run out, Coz right on her heels. He didn't want her to go, but he didn't want her to see him while he healed. The pain would be excruciating, and he didn't want her to see him like that.

Gianni came over to him. "The wolf's going to be fine. I think. Bullet passed right through the shoulder."

"I know the feeling."

"You're both damn lucky. Could have been a lot worse. You might want to check it for bone damage. After you heal, of course. Ready?"

No. "Yeah."

Gianni closed his eyes and rocked a little.

Nico felt warmth where the gunshot wound was, felt a little more fortified.

His brother's eyes snapped open. "I can't do any more until you fix the bone. Then we'll see if you need another dose of treatment."

This was what Nico dreaded. He closed his eyes, went inside himself. Mentally inventoried his injuries. Damn collarbone was shattered. Knitting it back together would hurt like a—

He screamed, the tiny shards of bone slicing through tissue before fusing together into a whole clavicle again.

"I got 'cha." Gianni healed those micro cuts, too, and soon Nico could breathe easily again.

"Better check on your wolf."

Nico was wiped, but he wasn't done yet. He approached the wolf and looked up into its eyes.

It hurts still.

"I know, buddy." Nico rubbed his fingers through the thick fur until he found and scratched its good shoulder. "I'm going to take care of it."

The wolf whimpered.

Nico closed his eyes, sensed the injuries to his giant friend. Another shattered bone, not unlike his own had been. "This is going to hurt a bit, but then you'll be okay."

Just do it.

Nico took a deep breath, pulled energies from the mineral-rich earth he stood on, and sent healing power to the beast.

The wolf howled, but soon it could put its paw down.

Nico looked into his eyes and smiled.

Thank you.

"You saved my life. And many others. It's me who owes you gratitude."

The wolf bowed its head.

"Let me make one more pass over the tissue," Gianni said.

I'd appreciate that. Something still doesn't feel right.

"Thanks, Gianni. He needs it."

Gianni closed his eyes for a moment, then opened them. "That should do it."

Nico looked at the wolf, who smiled. Never thought he'd see a giant wolf smile. It was kind of cute, in a weird sort of way.

"I should probably put you back now."

The wolf nodded.

Nico summoned his gratitude for the gift of size and protection, and his profound sorrow at having injured his new friend. Then he wished the pack returned to normal.

A little snarling, a bit more snapping sounds, and the wolves were once again their regular size.

Nico scratched the alpha behind its ear. *"Grazie, amico mio."*

The wolves bounded toward the cave's entrance as Donni and Coz returned.

"Was that...?" Donni's voice trailed off.

"Yes," Nico said. "Another long story."

"We'll cover all of the details back at the compound," Mike said.

"Wait, what?" Vinnie said. "Did you say 'we'll' and not 'we will'?"

"I'm nothing if not flexible."

Vinnie scoffed.

"At the compound." And Mike teleported away.

Donni frowned.

"What is it?" Nico asked. Although he was afraid of the answer. Now that she was safe, everything that had happened came rushing back to him.

"We'll see what Mike has to say before I discuss it."

Mike? What did he have to do with anything?

"Let's get the hell out of here before more bad guys show up," Gianni said.

Nico walked over to Bruno, bent down, and checked his pulse. Nothing. He took a deep breath. His power was life. He always thought that meant he'd protect the living. Never thought that meant he'd take a life.

Vinnie clapped him on the back and nodded toward the entrance to the cave. "Let's go. I'll ride with you. Donni can ride with the guys."

Donni raised her eyebrows but followed Gianni and Coz up the tunnel.

Nico handed Vinnie his keys. He suddenly felt nauseated and didn't think he was up to driving.

25

NICO REALLY BENEFITTED from the ride alone with Vinnie. His brother didn't provide him with any methods to get over the soul-shattering pain of taking a life—there probably weren't any, or Vinnie would have used them by now—but he listened. He understood. And that was all Nico really needed at that moment.

There would be time for recriminations later. And Nico knew they'd be coming from everyone as soon as they reached the compound.

So he sat in silence and accepted the new—and dark—bond he and Vinnie shared.

When they pulled into the garage two hours later, Vinnie returned the keys. "You ready for this?"

Nico shook his head. "I don't really know. I feel kind of... you know, *detached* from everything."

"Get used to that. It's your mind's way of coping with what happened. Eventually you'll feel again."

"I look forward to that."

"No," Vinnie said. "No, you don't."

Nico took a deep breath and tried not to think about that dire warning.

"Tonight, though, we have a different situation to get through. And want to know who's on the hot seat this time?"

Like he had to guess.

"Time to pay the piper, Nic."

That's what he was afraid of. He followed Vinnie into the house.

NICO LOOKED AROUND the dining room table. They were all gathered there—his brothers, Donni and her sisters, Mike, the mentors. Between all of them, they would probably get answers to most of their questions.

But of all of them, he had the most to answer for.

He had no idea what time it was—what *day* it was. All he knew was he was exhausted. And there was no end in sight.

Someone—probably Gianni—had put snacks on the table. The antipasto platter looked exceptionally tempting, and he put a scoop of wrinkled, oil-cured olives on his plate along with some cubes of cheese and a few multi-grain crackers.

"Clock's ticking," Vinnie said. "Let's get this meeting started."

"Why don't we begin with why Nico left my sister alone in the wilderness?" Toni said. She and her other sisters glared in his direction.

"Now, wait a minute," Donni said. "I was hardly in the wilderness. It was a private road a few miles from here."

"Well, clearly the distance doesn't matter," Toni said. "Jo was nearly blown to bits at the orphanage, and you were abducted just down the road."

"That brings up safety concerns," Coz said. "I think it's safe to say that our location has clearly been compromised."

"We can relocate," Mike said. "That will not be an issue."

Donni leaned back in her chair, crossed her arms, and glared at Mike. "I think the fact that we now know who's behind this is an issue we should address."

"We do?" Gianni said. "What'd I miss?"

"What'd we all miss?" Vinnie asked.

No one said anything.

Mike returned Donni's stare with a level gaze of his own.

"Are you going to tell them, or am I?" she asked.

Mike clenched his jaw, then he looked at Vinnie. "I have only one request before I begin."

"Of me?" Vinnie asked.

Mike nodded.

"What?"

"No matter what you hear, you do not run out. This is a long and complicated story, and even once all the details are out in the open, there are other issues to cover before we all go our separate ways."

"Fine."

"Your word, Vincenzo."

"You have my word."

"I will stop you if you try to leave."

"I said I promise. What more do you want?"

"I want you to keep your word. You will not like what I am about to reveal."

"When do I?"

Mike stared at him.

"Okay." Vinnie's tone was more subdued this time. "I promise I won't bolt. No matter what."

"Very well." Mike took a deep breath, looked around the room, and then settled his gaze on his son. "For centuries, it has been the policy of the Protectorate to use an intermediary between Michelangelo and the Brothers. A roll I currently fill."

"Yeah," Coz said. "We know. So?"

Mike didn't look at him, but continued to make eye contact with Vinnie. "That policy has been... disingenuous."

"What do you mean?" Vinnie's voice was low, his words measured.

"No one is ever allowed to meet Michelangelo because his secret would be revealed."

"What secret?" Nico asked. "That he's still alive? We already know. And we aren't telling anyone."

"No. Not that."

"Then what?"

Again Mike was silent.

"That—" Donni began.

"I said I would tell them," Mike interrupted.

"Then stop stalling."

"Would one of you please just tell us what the big deal is?" Gianni asked.

"I am Michelangelo."

No one spoke.

Mike looked at Vinnie again. "My son—"

Vinnie held up his hand. "No. Don't. Don't say it. Not another word to me personally." He took a deep breath. "I promised I wouldn't storm out, and I won't, as long as you give me time to process…" he waved his hands around "… all of this. So skip over the fatherly concern and explain yourself to the group."

"I didn't want anyone to know my true identity, because it made me, and the Brotherhood—the whole Protectorate—vulnerable. By creating a buffer, false as it was, I assured a level of safety. For all of us. No one could go after Michelangelo if no one knew where he was."

"Why bother?" Nico said. "Other than the Brotherhood, no one even knew Michel—*you*—existed."

"One man did."

"Who?" Vinnie asked.

"I didn't know for certain, not until tonight."

"Who?" he repeated.

"An old enemy. A former friend."

"Who?" Vinnie yelled.

Mike lowered his head. When he spoke, his words were barely audible. "Leo. Leonardo da Vinci."

"Are you fucking *kidding* me?" Vinnie jumped up. "Our enemy is your old adversary? The smartest man who ever lived?"

"That title is debatable," Mike said. "And you promised not to leave until we are done here."

"I can't believe you and your secrets." Vinnie stomped around the room. "You're lucky I gave my word, or otherwise, I'd be *so* out of here."

Jo reached for his hand as he walked by, but he just squeezed her shoulder and kept pacing.

"Leo is behind Legatus," Mike continued. "He has a dagger with powers similar to ours, and he has money and reach that rival mine. We are facing a truly formidable foe."

Nico squeezed the bridge of his nose. So far that day he'd declared his love, been terrorized, had a painful separation, learned his decisions caused Donni's abduction, chased her half way across the country, found out he could manipulate and communicate with animals, been shot, killed a man, and discovered they were embroiled in battle with one of the smartest and most powerful men ever to have lived. That was more upheaval than most people contended with in a lifetime.

He'd experienced it all since the morning.

And he couldn't take much more.

DONNI BREATHED A shallow sigh of relief. Keeping Mike's secret was too big a burden to bear, and she'd held onto that nugget of knowledge the whole way from the cave to the compound. Just those two hours had nearly driven her mad.

Gianni and Coz had questioned her silence, but she led them to believe she was just in shock.

Maybe she was. It wasn't every day a girl in the twenty-first century interacted with two masters from the Renaissance era—one of whom wanted her dead, the other sworn to protect her and her family through the generations.

Yes, she was relieved to have it out in the open. But she dreaded everything that was to follow.

"Marcus, Enrico," Mike said, "you have been here under false pretenses. We let you believe we needed the extra support, but in reality, we have been monitoring you. It was not until you were shot today that we knew where you had truly placed your loyalties."

"Kind of figured that," Marcus said.

"Didn't mind waiting it out," Rico added. "We knew you'd eventually trust us, and we had too much at stake to tap out this late in the game."

"You were released, relieved of duty," Mike said. "What stakes do you have?"

Marcus scoffed. "We raised these boys."

"And we watched these girls grow up," Rico said.

"You didn't honestly think we'd walk away when things were critical?"

"At least someone knows the meaning of family," Vinnie said.

"Vincenzo—"

Vinnie whirled around and glared at him. "Does Teresa know?"

"I hardly think that is relevant."

"Does. My. Mother. Know?"

Mike's jaw ticked. "Yes."

"Did she always know, or did you tell her recently?"

This time he spoke through clenched teeth. "In between."

"What the fuck does that mean?"

He sighed and ran his hand through his hair. "She did not know when we met, nor even when you were young. I told her just before I took all of you to America."

"So she's known for years and didn't bother mentioning it."

"It was not her secret to tell!"

"I don't know why any of this surprises me. You've been lying for more years than anyone can even count, and she was all too willing to hand me off and never see me again. Neither of you gives a good goddamn about me." Vinnie stormed out of the room.

Jo followed.

"Vincenzo, you promised!" Mike called after him.

But Vinnie didn't come back.

"My apologies, but I must talk to him." And he hurried out of the room without another word.

Donni was speechless. Apparently so was everyone else, because they all sat in stunned silence.

This wasn't what she had wanted. They all needed to talk, but her heart ached for Vinnie. She knew what it was like to have parents keep family secrets. Her own hadn't told them about their Medici heritage, or the Protectorate, or the fact that they could at some point face danger. Learning all that hurt, especially coming from strangers. But she knew her parents loved her. Knew they only tried to protect their children with their secrets.

Vinnie didn't have that luxury, because he believed his mother abandoned him and his father didn't care. True or not, that was his perception. And now, just as they were starting to make progress as a family, he had the rug pulled out from under him.

It truly broke Donni's heart.

DONNI'S HEAD HURT. She wanted to go to bed.

But more, she wanted answers.

"While Mike's not here," Marcus said, "is there anything we can do to help fill in the blanks?"

"How well did you know Carla?" Gianni asked.

"Pretty well," Rico said. "It kills me that she's dead."

"Kills me that it was at Sal's hand," Marcus said. "She was a good lady. And he loved her."

"But why?" Gianni asked. "Why did he kill her? She was no threat."

"If he thought she knew anything about his extracurricular activities," Rico said, "he wouldn't have had a choice. Not with da Vinci in charge. It wouldn't have been an option. Her life, or both of their lives."

"Mike said we have more than just her letter. That there was a secret compartment in the box."

"What letter?" Marcus asked. "What box?"

"When her body was pulled from the river, I went back to her house,"

Gianni said. "She'd said something to me one night years ago, and thinking about her triggered the memory. I found a box there, and she'd left me a letter. It implicated Sal and his associates in Legatus. But we can't find much on them, other than the business information posted online."

"But Mike said the box had a secret compartment," Franki said. "We still haven't gotten around to looking at it, though. And of course he hasn't told us what was in it."

"Go get the box," Rico said. "Let's have a look."

"Mike has it," Gianni said.

"What do you know about Legatus?" Nico asked.

"Not too much," Marcus said. "Yet. Other than da Vinci is behind it."

"It's a lead," Nico said. "More than we had earlier today. It's something to dig into. I'll get on it tomorrow."

DONNI TRIED TO look at things objectively and put her emotions aside. It had been one hell of a night, and there were so many things she didn't understand. But it was late, and she was tired.

And Mike was gone, so what was the likelihood that anyone had the answers she wanted?

"I don't know if we should continue this discussion without Mike and Vinnie," Coz said.

"And Jo," Franki added.

"And Jo. But there are still a few things we need answers to."

If they weren't going to bed, Donni had more questions she wanted answers to. "For starters, did you know Nico found a journal? And he hasn't shared its contents yet."

Everyone turned to look at him.

"Nic?" Coz said.

"I didn't find anything. Mike gave it to me. It's his. Michelangelo's. The entries are only sporadic, but they date back to the Renaissance."

"He clearly wanted you to know something," Gianni said. "What'd you find?"

"Not much, yet. I've been transcribing it so the girls can read it, too. I haven't gotten very far."

"I can help with the translation," Coz said. "And Gianni. We don't type as fast as you, but sometimes we're free when you're busy. It'll get done faster."

"Great. I'll keep it in the office and show you where the file is on the server."

"But don't think this show of good will lets you off the hook for not telling us about it," Gianni said.

"Or for abandoning my sister," Toni said.

"I know. And I'm sorry. You'll never know how sorry."

Donni had a twinge of guilt. He was bearing all the blame, but he'd done it for her safety. And she'd agreed. It wasn't fair that Nico took all the responsibility.

"She almost died, Nico," Toni said. "Do you really think 'sorry' is enough?"

"Toni, stop." Donni shot her sister a look. "The decision for me to leave without him was a mutual one. It's not entirely Nico's fault. I'm to blame, too. And it all worked out okay in the end."

"Okay?" she said. "You nearly died. Mama and Carmen, too. The compound is compromised. More people were killed!"

"*Enough*, Ton." Donni slammed her hand on the table. "Do you honestly think you're telling us anything we don't already know? Do you think you're the only one who had a bad night? This was hard on all of us, but it was hardest on Nico. Cut him some slack."

"But it was all his fault!"

"Was it?" Donni said. "Were you there to see what happened?"

"No. But that's the point. I want to know what happened so I can be certain it won't happen again."

"This isn't your business," Donni said.

"And it won't happen again," Nico said.

"How can you be so sure?" Toni asked.

"Because I'm leaving the Brotherhood."

NICO WINCED AT the noise. Everyone screamed at him at once, but his mind was made up.

"Stop," he said. "Just stop. It's for the best."

"Don't be ridiculous," Gianni said.

"Nic, come on. What are you thinking?" Coz asked.

"I'm not discussing it now. The subject is closed."

"But—" Coz began.

"No. I mean it. The topic's off limits. At least until tomorrow."

"Nico, why?" Donni asked.

He looked at her. She, more than anyone, should know why he was leaving. His unbalanced decision-making had nearly gotten her killed.

"Can we have the room?" Donni asked.

"It's late," Gianni said. "Mike, Vinnie, and Jo have already gone. We shouldn't cover any more ground until we're all together. But we're talking about this tomorrow, Nic."

"Let's go to bed." Franki gave Donni a wide-eyed stare.

Very discreet. About as subtle as a train wreck.

"Goodnight, sweetie." Franki blew her a kiss.

"Wait!" Donni jumped to her feet.

"What?" Franki asked.

She ran over to her sister and grabbed her left hand. "Something you want to tell us?"

A smile bloomed on her face. "It's not the right time."

"You're engaged!" Donni threw her arms around her sister and squeezed. Soon she was in a group hug with all her sisters, and she cringed at the squealing. When they broke apart, she saw the guys clapping Gianni on the back and shaking his hand. She gave him a hug, too. And then Toni did.

"The ring is beautiful." Donni held Franks's hand. "Tell us the story. We want details. Don't leave anything out."

Franki looked at Nico. "Tomorrow."

"Tonight," Toni said. "Now."

Nico nodded at his brother.

Gianni grinned. "I proposed at our picnic today."

Franki smiled up at him, then looked around the room. "I'll give you the long version tomorrow. It's late. And Jo's not even here."

"But this is good news, for a change," Donni said. "We should celebrate. Mark the occasion somehow."

"And we will." Franki hugged her. "Tomorrow. Let's go, everyone."

The group said their "goodnights" and left the room, leaving Nico alone with Donni.

"What do you mean, you're quitting the Brotherhood?" she asked. "Why are you trying to abandon me? And by the way, I won't allow it."

"You don't have a say in where I work, Donni."

"You swore to protect me," she whispered.

"This is the best way I know to protect you."

"We're stronger together."

"We were together tonight, and look what happened. My decision almost got you killed. You need someone who will do better for you."

"You're crazy, you know that?"

"You think this isn't killing me? I want to be the one to keep you safe. It terrifies me to think the decisions will be under someone else's control."

"Then why let it?"

"Because I can't think straight around you!"

Donni sighed. "Nico, we're better together. You aren't responsible for what da Vinci and his goons did. But if we'd been together, it might not have happened."

"That's exactly my point."

"No, that's my point."

He cocked an eyebrow.

"We shouldn't have separated, Nic. You shouldn't have suggested it, and I shouldn't have agreed. From now on, we stay together. *That's* how I'll be safe."

He was quiet a long time. The thought of trusting someone else with her made him sick. Maybe she had a point—they were stronger together. "I probably overreacted."

She squeezed his fingers. "You think?"

"Can you forgive me?"

"There's nothing to forgive."

Relief washed through him. He leaned over and kissed her. She smelled of lemons and tasted both tart and sweet.

She smiled, and it lit up the room. Lit up his heart.

"So you're going to stay with the Brotherhood?"

"Where you go, I go. Promise."

She sighed, and her shoulders relaxed.

"*Tesoro*. I love you."

"And I love you." She kissed him again, and the room faded away.

"Ah-hem." A throat-clearing interrupted them.

Nico looked up to see Mike standing there. SOB ghosted in again, and in a private moment, too. He pulled away from Donni.

"You find Vinnie and make things right?"

Mike sighed. "It is going to take more than a quick conversation in the middle of the night to get through to him."

"So, that's a no."

"What do you want, Mike?" Donni asked. "Or should we call you Michelangelo?"

"Mike is fine." He sighed. "Dominico, if you would not mind humoring me, would you please try something?"

"What?"

"Hand me your dagger."

Nico arched an eyebrow, but he passed the weapon over.

"Go look out the window. Tell me what you see."

"I know what I'll see. Darkness. It's the middle of the damn night."

"Watch your language."

Nico huffed.

"The lights are on outside. Tell me what you see."

Nico crossed the room and looked out the large picture window. A small rose garden was planted there, a small replica of Michelangelo's *David* in the center.

Well, it probably wasn't an imitation. It might have been a practice sculpture, or a duplicate, but it was done by the man himself.

The thought was too much for Nico to wrap his head around.

"A rose garden. A statue. Pretty enough, but fairly standard for a dining room view, I'd guess."

"Now join me at the table, keeping your back to the window."

Nico rolled his eyes but did as he was asked.

"I want you to think about the flowers."

"All right."

"Donnatella, do you have a favorite flower?"

"Not really. They're all so pretty."

"Choose one. Not a rose."

She shrugged. "Freesia. I like red freesia."

"Dominico, close your eyes. Think about red freesia."

"I don't know what that is."

"Then think the words."

"Fine."

"Call them forth. Replace the roses with them."

Nico opened his eyes and stared at Mike. "I already know I can make plants grow. The earth move. Animals transform."

"You are not now in possession of your dagger."

"Oh. I get it. You're trying to show me that I'm not the force, but the weapon is. I've already come to terms with that."

"Dominico!" Mike raised his voice, then took a deep breath and continued in a calmer tone. "Would you please just do as I ask?"

"Fine." Nico closed his eyes and half-heartedly thought about red freesia. Well, the words, anyway. He had no idea what they looked like. He just wanted to get this over with. It was late, he and Donni had some make-up sex to get to, and Mike was just trying to embarrass him, probably as a punishment for getting Donni abducted and then running off alone.

"Donnatella, please look at the garden."

Donni got up and walked to the window. "Oh, my—Nico! Come see!"

Nico rose and crossed the room to stand beside her. The garden had tripled in volume and was overflowing with stalks of red flowers. They looked like the bloom he'd given her on her food tray after they'd spent the night together.

"It's gorgeous!" Donni smiled and clapped her hands.

"It is as I assumed," Mike said.

"What the hell just happened?" Nico asked.

"You have come fully into your powers." He handed back the dagger.

"Because of the battle tonight? Because of the wolves?"

"No. Because you have finally opened your heart. Donnatella is the other half of your power."

Nico's blood turned to ice. "So it's what I feared all along. The dagger needed Donni to fully work. Our feelings aren't real."

"Of course they are!" Donni reached for his hand, but he recoiled.

"Dominico, you are mistaken. There are few immutable truths in the world. One is that light trumps darkness. Another is that love is light. Donnatella is your light. Your love. But it did not have to be her. As long as you have love in your heart, you will have full control of your dagger and its powers."

"See," she said. "You worried for nothing."

"So my powers aren't connected to Donni?"

"They are, but they are not forcing you to connect to her. Do you understand the difference?"

He thought about it. For the first time, it made sense. His brothers only received their full powers when they embraced love. And now it was his turn. It was only coincidence that they all loved the same family, right?

For the first time, he didn't care. He loved Donni, she loved him, and his powers were complete. No more practicing in the middle of the night. No more power failure from uncertainty. He was complete.

"All the daggers have light and dark properties. Male and female. Yin and yang. I am delighted you chose the light path. That puts us one step closer to winning the war."

"Life, balance, transformation. Those are all positive things, right? Light things? What dark path could I have chosen?"

"What is the dark side of life? Of balance? Of transformation?"

He couldn't put his thoughts to words. He felt sick.

Donni spoke up. "Balance would be inequality. Transformation would be lack of change. Life would be—"

"Death," Nico whispered.

"And you passed the test."

"Passed? I killed someone tonight!"

"Dominico, your power is over life. You can give it, you can take it away. But it's your intent that counts."

"I thought Coz had dominion over death," Donni said.

"A technicality. Roberto has dominion over the dead. Not over death itself."

"So I'm life or death?" Nico's voice was small. He'd never felt a larger burden.

"Yes. And every time, you choose life."

"No. Remember? I killed a man tonight."

"No, Dominico. You saved a life tonight. More than one, actually."

"Semantics, I think."

Donni clutched his arm. "Would you have killed him, or even battled him, if lives weren't at stake?"

"Of course not. Why would I?"

"Exactly. You are not predisposed to death, Dominico. You choose life."

He was going to have to sit with these new details for a while. Taking a life was hard enough. Knowing he had the power to choose?

It was too much.

"Mike, if I wanted, could I... could I kill da Vinci and all his followers and end this all?"

"Is that what you want?" His voice was cold, flat.

"I didn't say that. I'm just trying to understand the full scope of my powers."

Mike sighed. "Yes, Dominico, I believe you could. But you of all people must be careful, because you are balance. If you do good in the world, the scales tip toward good. But if you do evil, well... as they say, karma is a bitch."

Nico sat there, chills skittering up his spine.

"It's funny to hear you talk like that," Donni said. "I like it."

He spoke slowly, as if choosing his words carefully. "If I'm still welcome in the Brotherhood, you'll hear more of it."

"It's your group," she said. "How could you not be welcome?"

He smiled sadly and disappeared.

Donni put her head on Nico's shoulder. "So, are we okay?"

"Hmm? Yeah. Fine."

She shifted so she was facing him and took his hands in hers. "I know what you're thinking."

"Oh?"

"You didn't kill Bruno on purpose."

"Donni, it's not just him. I could kill *anyone*. At any time."

"But you won't."

"I could end this now. Save all of you."

"But you won't."

"What does it matter? My soul is damned now, anyway. I could at least make sure everyone is safe."

"Nico! Your soul isn't damned. You don't really believe that, do you?"

He couldn't reassure her, so he said nothing.

She placed her hands on each side of his face and tipped it so he met her gaze. "Do you think Vinnie is damned, too?"

"What? No. That's different."

"How?"

"How? Because he had no choice. And because this is war."

She dropped her hands. "And how is your case different? Same lack of choice. Same war."

Logically, it made sense. But his heart didn't operate on logic. He shrugged.

"Nico, you're not really considering it, right?"

He saw the concern in her eyes and did what he could to alleviate it. "No. Not really."

"You sure?"

"I'm sure. It's kind of tempting, but I know it's not right. Still, when I think of you in danger…"

"That's why I have a warrior to protect me." She leaned back in her seat and lifted her feet onto his lap.

He rubbed her toes, and she moaned. He smiled and traced her tattoo.

She wiggled her foot. "That tickles."

"Why didn't you finish the tat? Did it hurt too much?"

Donni snorted. "It is finished. Toni has the other part."

"Hmm. I thought it was sexy, but now that I know she completes you instead of me…"

She put her feet down and snuggled against him. "She completes the tattoo. You complete me."

Nicer words had never reached his ears. He pressed his lips to the top of her head and took a deep breath. Lemons. "Mmm."

"What?"

"You smell delicious."

"Are you hungry? I thought we could go on up to bed, but if you'd rather eat something—"

"Bed," he said. "Definitely bed."

She smiled, grabbed his hand, and pulled him to his feet.

As she led them upstairs, he thanked all the saints in heaven he'd been able to save her. He knew he'd do whatever it took to keep her safe.

Then he prayed they'd find another solution to da Vinci's quest for power. Because if they didn't, he'd succumb to the darkness to protect her.

HI! I HOPE you enjoyed *Body Armor*. This story is near and dear to my heart, and it's not done yet. The next installment, *Tortured Soul*, is already in the works and will be released in 2018.

If you wouldn't mind investing a few more minutes in this work, I'd really appreciate it. Please let me know what you thought of this story by leaving a review online (Amazon, Barnes and Noble, Goodreads—wherever you got the book and wherever you share your opinions with other readers). It doesn't take long, but it really helps me craft stories you enjoy, as well as reach other readers. I value your comments and am grateful for whatever your share.

The other way we can connect is through social media. You can find my contact information with my bio. I'm really looking forward to hearing from you.

After you leave a review, please check out my other published titles and my soon-to-be-released works. You can read more about them on my website or my Amazon author page.

Until next time…

Staci Troilo
—September, 2017

STACI TROILO grew up knowing family is paramount. She spent time with extended family daily, not just on holidays or weekends. Because of those close knit familial bonds, every day was full of love and laughter, food and fun. Life has taken her a thousand miles away from that extended family, but those ties remain. And so do the traditions, which she now shares with her husband, son, and daughter... even her two dogs. And through her fiction, she shares the importance of relationships with you. Mystery or suspense, romance or mainstream—in her stories, family is paramount.

Facebook: Author Staci Troilo
Twitter: @stacitroilo
Amazon: http://amazon.com/author/stacitroilo

www.stacitroilo.com

www.ingramcontent.com/pod-product-compliance
Lightning Source LLC
Chambersburg PA
CBHW030635020726
47493CB00006B/1727